Items should be returned on or before the last date shown below. Items not already requested by other borrowers may be renewed in person, in writing or by telephone. To renew, please quote the number on the barcode label. To renew on line a PIN is required. This can be requested at your local library.
Renew online @ **www.dublincitypubliclibraries.ie**
Fines charged for overdue items will include postage incurred in recovery. Damage to or loss of items will be charged to the borrower.

Leabharlanna Poiblí Chathair Bhaile Átha Cliath
Dublin City Public Libraries

Dublin City
Baile Átha Cliath

PEARSE STREET BRANCH
BRAINSE SRÁID PIARSACH
TEL: 6744888

Date Due	Date Due	Date Due
1 6 MAY 2018	0 9 MAR 2020	
0 9 JUL 2018		

Dublin City Libraries
Withdrawn From Stock

Dublin City Libraries
Withdrawn From Stock

D0318286

This novel is entirely a work of fiction. The names, characters and incidents portrayed in it are the work of the author's imagination. Any resemblance to actual persons, living or dead, events or localities is entirely coincidental.

Published 2018
by Poolbeg Press Ltd.
123 Grange Hill, Baldoyle,
Dublin 13, Ireland
Email: poolbeg@poolbeg.com

© Gemma Jackson 2018

The moral right of the author has been asserted.

1

Copyright for editing, typesetting, layout, design, ebook
© Poolbeg Press Ltd.

A catalogue record for this book is available from the British Library.

ISBN 978178199-8298

All rights reserved. No part of this publication may be reproduced or transmitted in any form or by any means, electronic or mechanical, including photography, recording, or any information storage or retrieval system, without permission in writing from the publisher. The book is sold subject to the condition that it shall not, by way of trade or otherwise, be lent, resold or otherwise circulated without the publisher's prior consent in any form of binding or cover other than that in which it is published and without a similar condition, including this condition, being imposed on the subsequent purchaser.

Printed and bound by CPI Group (UK) Ltd, Croydon, CR0 4YY

www.poolbeg.com

About the Author

Gemma Jackson is the fifth of seven children born to Rose and Paddy Jackson. The family had very little money, but big dreams were encouraged. Gemma grew up in inner-city Dublin, being told to reach for the stars – never believe you can't succeed – the world is your oyster – and at the same time having her ears boxed and being reminded to know her place. Is it any wonder she is still confused?

Gemma loves to tell stories and has vivid memories of sitting on the stairs with gangs of children while stories were told. The storytellers seemed to have magic on their lips to the children. They could see the world being painted by the storyteller's words.

At age seventeen Gemma set out to see the world. The only countries she has not visited are Australia and New Zealand. She has travelled in style some of the time but on a shoestring most of the time. The memories of her adventures are a treasure chest – and she is not finished yet!

Acknowledgements

Thank you to the many incredible people I've met on my travels. The dreamers and doers who refuse to accept the box society has tried to fashion for them. They not only think outside the box – they've smashed it!

To the many wonderful authors who have inspired and educated me – a book can take you into a world of the imagination – my favourite place to visit.

The people of Dublin that I grew up with – true characters every one – they refuse to meet the day with a frown – if a smile and a joke doesn't cheer you, a swift kick up the backside can be delivered.

To the people of Poolbeg Press who allow me to tell my stories and live my dream. Gaye Shortland, thank you for polishing my manuscripts until they shine. Paula Campbell, you have given me the chance to share my stories – thank you.

Also by Gemma Jackson

Through Streets Broad and Narrow
Ha'penny Chance
The Ha'penny Place
Ha'penny Schemes

Published by Poolbeg

Dedication

My daughter Astrid – thank you for the constant supply of hot tea. I couldn't function without it or you.

Chapter 1

March 1898

"Did yez hear what that girl said?" Bridget O'Brien whispered softly.

It wouldn't do to attract the attention of the nuns. The beds were so close together that a whisper of sound carried to the next bed. She didn't wait for her friends to respond.

"She said when it was cold her mam wrapped a hot stone in an old sheet and put it into the bed with her. Can yez imagine? What would it be like to be warm and snug when you lay down to sleep?"

"Did you see her hair?" Sarah Black hissed. She lay in a bed to one side of Bridget. The orphans had shaven heads. Sarah planned to have the longest hair in the world after she left here. She often lay in her bed dreaming of combing out her long hair.

"You two are going to get us into trouble!" Ruth Brown hissed from the other side of Bridget.

The orphanage dormitory had twenty iron beds, with

Leabharlanna Poibli Chathair Baile Átha Cliath

Dublin City Public Libraries

thin pallets over wire springs, placed along the two longest walls of the room.

"That girl, she says her da is going to come for her." Bridget wanted to tell all she knew. The arrival of a stranger was a point of interest in their ordered life. "That girl, she says she's only in here for a few days – just until her mam is better. Then . . ." she had to pause because she couldn't imagine the magic of being able to even say it, "then, she says, she's going home."

"You'll be going into the cupboard if you don't shut up and go to sleep," Ruth Brown warned.

"Bridget O'Brien, do I hear you speaking?" a disembodied voice called. The sound of leather shoes marching along the bare boards of the dormitory had little girls pulling the hairy grey blankets over their heads.

"I'm just saying my prayers, Mother!" Bridget called piously.

"You have need of them, Bridget O'Brien."

Bridget didn't know which nun had caught her. It didn't make much difference. They were all the same to her – black-clad visions that followed her into her nightmares.

"Peggy and Hannah are leaving in the morning," Sarah Black whispered when the nun had left. "We had to sew their going-away outfits for them." Sarah worked in the attic sewing room. She helped prepare the orphans leaving this place.

"It will be our turn soon." Ruth Brown didn't know how to feel about escaping the orphanage. Ruth worked in the kitchens of the nuns' home. She'd learned a lot in the nine years she'd worked there – she'd be placed in the kitchen of a great house somewhere when she left. Sarah

2

was the same age as she but Bridget, the youngest of the trio at eleven, was a full year younger than them. What would she do when they had to leave her?

"Most of the twelve-year-olds will be leaving in June." Bridget was dreading losing her two friends. "I wish you could wait until December. I'll be twelve then."

"We have to do what's most convenient for our new employers. The families move to their country houses at the end of May. Some even take foreign holidays." Sarah was repeating what she had heard. "Then the staff in the town houses can train up new servants without fear of offending the family."

The orphans were early to bed and early to rise. The ringing of chapel bells woke them at five in the morning. They washed in cold water, made beds, washed and polished the floors of the dormitory building and restored pristine order before leaving for their assigned work. They ate a bowl of porridge at eight thirty. Then, from nine, those still young enough attended school. A midday bowl of soup was followed by more work in the orphanage. They never left the orphanage grounds.

"Do not breathe on the glass, Bridget O'Brien." A bony knuckle to the back of her head snapped Bridget's attention back to the work at hand. She'd been watching Peggy and Hannah, two girls she grew up with, leave this place.

"Yes, Mother Consolata." Bridget wanted to ask the nun how she was supposed to clean the tall windows of the nuns' home without breathing. She knew better than to open her mouth though. She'd be on her knees praying for the rest of her life if she did that.

Why was she always the one to be sent to work in the nuns' home attached to the orphanage? You had no chance of escaping the eagle eye of the nuns there. She scrubbed at the fog left on the glass from the deep sigh that almost rattled her skinny ribcage. It did no good to look out on the green lawn that ran from under this window to the tall iron fence that surrounded the convent and orphanage. She sometimes thought of running screaming into the streets of Dublin. It would do her no good – where would she go?

"Idle hands are the devil's workshop, Bridget O'Brien." A slap from the metal cross hanging from the huge rosary beads across the back of her head drove the words home.

"Yes, Mother Consolata." She'd only leaned back for a moment to relax the pinching in her back. Scrubbing the black-and-white tiles of the entryway to the nuns' house was a long backbreaking chore – especially when she'd been ordered to do it alone. She bit her tongue when the dark robes appeared in front of her.

"Do not turn those cat's eyes on me, Bridget O'Brien."

The nun, who seemed to take a personal delight in tormenting Bridget, strolled onto the freshly washed floor.

Bridget knew she was never going to get to heaven. She had bad thoughts she couldn't repress. She allowed a lovely mental image of Mother Consolata slipping and falling onto the hard tile floor to form in her mind's eye. She offered up a quick prayer asking for forgiveness and waited. She wasn't going to scrub that floor again until the nun had walked back across from wherever she was going.

"Reverend Mother is expecting visitors." Mother

4

Consolata's voice echoed around the vestibule. "Clean this floor up immediately." The nun danced across the floor, deliberately leaving black marks across the white tiles. She snapped her fingers and tutted in disgust at the young girl kneeling on a piece of sacking.

Reverend Mother Aloysius stood at the bend of the wide oak staircase, watching one of her nuns torment an innocent girl. It wasn't the first time she'd observed a scene like this with this particular pair. She swore to her Maker it would be her last. Could the nun not see the white-knuckled grip the child had on the scrubbing brush? She well knew that child's temper. The shaking of the young back clearly revealed to her old eyes the effort it was taking for the child not to throw that brush. The nun might deserve the punishment – but it would be the child who suffered.

"*Mother Consolata, your arm!*" the Reverend Mother called sharply.

The effect of that shout on the tall looming figure almost made Bridget laugh aloud.

"Reverend Mother," Mother Consolata simpered. "I didn't see you there." She ran up the stairs to offer her bent arm.

"I thought not." Aloysius glared at the younger nun. How many times had she taken this woman to task over her treatment of the orphans in their care? She put her arm through the proffered one and, with one age-twisted fist on the banister, slowly made her way down the carpeted stairs. She bent her head to hide her smile as the young girl below them scrubbed the entrance tiles with more speed than precision.

"Bridget!" Reverend Mother called when she was

5

standing on the vestibule floor. "Tidy up here quickly, child. You may join Sister Immaculata in the kitchen."

"Reverend Mother –" Mother Consolata started to object.

"You have classes you must supervise, Mother Consolata."

Aloysius wanted to sink down to the floor – her old bones ached. She could not do that however. She had one important chore to complete before she could take to her bed. She could feel her Maker calling her home. She prayed she would not answer the call until she had completed one last task.

Aloysius watched Bridget pick up her bucket of dirty water. The long grey woollen uniform dress the child wore had been refashioned from blankets donated to the orphanage. The string tied at the waist prevented the garment from dragging along the ground.

Bridget turned and set out in the direction of the kitchen at the back of the nuns' home.

"Biddy, what are you doing here?" Molly Grey cast a nervous look over her shoulder at the three nuns working away in the large kitchen. "You'll be in trouble if they see you." Molly was one of five orphans assigned to the big kitchen which prepared meals for the nuns' home.

"Reverend Mother told me to come in here." Bridget didn't dare look at her friend Ruth Brown.

She wanted to close her eyes and groan at the smells in this room. The heat in the kitchen was delightful. She thought Ruth was lucky to work in this big bright room. She didn't know what they were cooking but it smelled better than anything she'd ever smelt before. At night, when they should be asleep, Ruth would tell Bridget and Sarah all about the wonders created in this kitchen.

"*Bridget O'Brien!*" The tall, heavily built, red-faced nun glared at the young girl invading her domain. "You're making the place look untidy. What are you doing here?"

"Reverend Mother told her to come in here, Sister Immaculata." Molly ran over to the sink. There was a mountain of pots to be scrubbed clean.

"Bridget O'Brien is well known for having a tongue in her head." Sister Immaculata wiped her flour-dusted hands on the white pinafore protecting her habit. "Let her answer for herself, Molly Grey."

"It is as the youngster said." The Reverend Mother entered the kitchen, causing everyone to stiffen and stand by their stations. "I want you to give the child something to eat and a mug of tea. She will remain in the kitchen with you until I send for her."

"Yes, Reverend Mother."

"I am expecting visitors, as you know." She glanced around the kitchen. There were no secrets in this house. "I will call for her when I am ready but feed young Bridget well, mind." She walked out of the kitchen, leaving a buzz of conjecture at her back.

"I wonder what that's about – the child can't be leaving," one of the nuns said as she scooped soup into a bowl. "She's not yet twelve – is she?"

"Molly Grey, how old is Bridget O'Brien?" Sister Immaculata called over her shoulder.

"Eleven, Sister," Molly answered.

"There, what did I tell you!"

The kitchen gossip gathered momentum over the bowed head of young Bridget O'Brien. She didn't care.

She was sitting down for the first time that day.

Bridget had been excused from school. She had learned everything they wanted to teach her. If she had known her fate she'd have hidden how quickly she learned her lessons. Still, here she sat with a bowl of soup, the likes of which she had never tasted before, in front of her. The fresh white bread roll was spread thickly with butter. She'd enjoy what was in front of her and wait to see what the rest of the day would bring.

"Ruth Brown, pour Bridget a mug of tea and give her a slice of that fruit cake you made!" Sister Immaculata called. The child had eaten that bowl of soup so quickly it was a wonder to her she wasn't ill. "Molly, take that bowl from her and wash it – hurry now, both of you!"

The two young girls jumped to obey.

"What have you been up to now, Biddy?" Ruth Brown placed a white enamel mug of tea in front of her friend.

"Sure, I get blamed for which way the wind blows," Bridget whispered. "How do I know what I'm in trouble for now?"

"I'll have no whispering in my kitchen, Bridget O'Brien," Sister Immaculata said. "If you have something to say you may say it loud enough for all to hear."

"I was praying over the good food, Sister." Bridget dipped her shaven head to hide her smile.

"I'm sure you were, Bridget O'Brien – I'm sure you were."

Chapter 2

That same day, in a town house on Percy Place, Georgina Corrigan Whitmore glanced at the butler and footmen standing ready to serve. She didn't feel like eating.

Her two eldest stepsons were in the habit of using the town house as a resting place between their sea voyages. She had never been consulted on the matter. She hated sharing a meal with her husband and his two eldest sons. Her nerves were frayed – was everything as it should be? – her husband made his displeasure at any failings on her part painfully clear.

Without glancing at the faded creature at the other end of the long mahogany table, Captain Charles Whitmore clicked his fingers to indicate he was ready to be served.

There was silence while breakfast was served. The men ignored the only female in the room, allowing their plates to be filled to overflowing.

"Charles Junior, David –" Charles Whitmore said eventually, wiping his full-lipped mouth with his linen napkin. Everyone at table knew to wait until he signalled it was permitted to speak. "I have sent word for William and Henry to come and to stay here. Edward will remain at his grandfather's. The estate needs someone to oversee the running of the place." He should never have agreed to allow his three sons by his second wife to be raised by their grandfather. Still, the stipend he received for a father's pain in being separated from his sons was generous. He met the eyes of each of his sons. "Edward will join us whenever he can get away. I want all of my sons around me." He had plans to amass a fortune. It would be cheaper to have his sons – all strong healthy men – to serve as his crew on his next adventure.

"Are you now ready to tell us of your plans?" Charles Junior – Charlie to his friends – asked. His father hadn't sailed out of Dublin at all this past winter. That was unusual enough to have attracted attention. "You appear to be spending a great deal of money refitting your ship."

"That has everything to do with my plans for the future of this family."

"So what are these plans?" David too pushed his plate from him. "If you are gathering us around you, it obviously concerns us. We do have lives of our own to live, Father." He glanced at Charlie to see if he would say something but as usual the firstborn son remained silent in the presence of their overbearing parent. Charlie was too afraid of risking his inheritance by displeasing their father. "A little notice of any sudden changes in our circumstances would be appreciated."

"I will tell you when I feel you need to know." A wave of Charles' hand signalled silence. There were servants present.

David bit back a curse, wondering when his father would realise they were men grown. Charlie was almost forty, for God's sake! Time and past he married and had a family of his own. The old man had warned them well in advance that he would pocket any funds his sons might expect from an advantageous marriage. It was a disgrace. Would the old man ever release the strings on the family purse? He'd hoped to learn something of what he might inherit before he returned to sea. He had no intention of being under his father's fists ever again.

Georgina had watched from under lowered lashes while the three men tucked into Cook's excellent fare. The tension between them was very obvious to her. She couldn't understand how they could calmly shovel food into their mouths. Her own stomach was knotted. She had something she needed to say and was thinking of the best time to mention the subject. The presence of his sons would not stop her husband from physically showing his displeasure.

While the men, three seafarers, spoke of tides and cargo and the changes to the trade all three depended upon, Georgina allowed herself to become lost in thought. If all five of her husband's sons were to be living in this house, changes must be made. Thankfully the two orphans she'd taken from the convent to train had recently left this house. The girls were sixteen and too much of a temptation to put before virile men raised with Charles Whitmore as their example of manhood.

She would have to contact the Reverend Mother about a new batch of orphans. They would be of no interest to her stepsons. The girls arrived at her home practically bald and skinny – no sign of any promise of feminine beauty about them – they should offer no temptation.

A loud click of fingers drew her attention. While she'd been mentally planning, the servants had withdrawn.

"Leave us." Charles Whitmore pointed a thick finger at her.

Georgina pushed to her feet without objection. She had not touched the food on her plate. She looked down the table at her husband and decided now was the time. The man came and went as he willed. She never knew when he might next be available. The matter could not be delayed.

"There is something I have to say. The tradesmen are refusing to supply more goods until their invoices have been settled." She almost groaned at the weak ineffective sound of her own voice. "If you wish to house your five sons comfortably, the increase in household expenses will have to be taken into consideration." She had said what needed saying. She could leave now.

"*Georgina!*"

The sibilant hiss froze her in her tracks.

She'd been so close to escape – her hand upon the doorknob.

"Come here."

She had to force her feet to obey. Longing to run instead, she slowly made her way to where her husband waited. She watched his seated figure carefully. What would he use – his feet in their heavy boots would hurt – her ribs ached in memory of other injuries – his fists too could cause damage. She hated walking to him like a whipped cur.

"Closer." He waved his fingers, a smirk on his face.

"Really, Father!" David hated to see his father abuse a woman. His own mother had died at his birth. He had watched and been powerless to stop his father from destroying his second wife with his constant verbal abuse. If he had physically abused his second wife that was

12

hidden by the concealing garments the poor woman had taken to wearing. He well knew how painful his father's fists could be and the woman was skin and bone. He wished to God he had never answered the call to present himself in Dublin. But there was little he could do to stop the man from abusing this, his third wife. "Could you continue your marital discussion later?" He didn't look at the poor woman. "I have matters to attend to. I am interested in learning what you have planned for the future but I do not have a great deal of free time." He would judge if the matter was of interest to him. He was a merchant seaman, master class, and had not yet signed on to a ship after his last voyage.

"Oh, very well!" Charles used the flat of his hand to push his wife from his sight. "I will speak with you later, woman." He had used enough force to knock her off her feet. He turned his attention back to his sons. "The matters I have been working on," he didn't look in the direction of the woman – he'd already forgotten her presence, "are the culmination of my lifelong ambitions."

Georgina dragged herself to her feet, being careful to remove her body out of his reach before she stood erect. While the men entered into conversation, she opened the dining-room door and stepped out into the hallway.

"Madam!" Lily Chambers, the housekeeper, had been waiting in the hallway in case she might be needed. She hurried to her mistress and carefully put her arm around the trembling shoulders, afraid of causing injury. Who knew what that man might have done to the poor woman?

"My private sitting room." Georgina allowed the woman who had worked for her family since before her birth to assist her. She waited until the housekeeper had closed the door before saying, "This cannot continue." She collapsed back into a nearby easy chair and closed her eyes.

She thought back over the miserable existence she'd lived with this man and the many injuries she had suffered. She was not willing to continue living in this fashion. One day he would kill her. She had to get away. There was a secret society in place to help women like her. She would contact them. It was time to take to her heels.

"Are you hurt?"

Georgina had forgotten the housekeeper was still with her. She'd been too lost in her own thoughts. She had to be more alert.

"I'm shaken but not injured, thank you." Georgina looked at the faithful woman, wondering why she stayed in this hateful situation. Lily, at least, had options. She was an excellent housekeeper. "I have just learned that the Captain has sent for his second family to stay here. Edward, it seems, will come and go from the estate." She held up her hand when Lily looked ready to question her. "That is all I am allowed to know."

"I'll set staff to preparing rooms," Lily contented herself with remarking. What was the point of cursing the day her young mistress's father had introduced that man to the household. The deed was done and had been for some time. They were married. There was nothing anyone could do about the situation – short of murder – and she'd been tempted many a time. "Will you be safe with all of those young men underfoot?" Surely the man would keep his fists to himself while his sons were in residence?

"There are no secrets between us, Lily. I don't enjoy the

thought of all of my husband's sons here. This is a very unhappy house. The male servants offer me no respect. My husband's sons ignore my very existence." Three of the five sons were older than Georgina yet none had entered into matrimony. "Changes must be made. That man has buried two wives. I don't intend to be the third."

"What can you do?" Lily had prayed for the man's ship to sink on one of his many trading trips. It would appear God didn't answer that sort of prayer. "What can any woman do when she has entered into matrimony?" She herself had chosen never to put that noose around her own neck. You saw too much of the personal details of marriage when you were in service.

Georgina leaned forward and whispered, "There is a way for me to escape." She looked towards the door fearfully.

"Don't tell me!" Lily begged. What she didn't know she couldn't tell.

"Very well. In any case I need to think some more on the matter."

Chapter 3

Aloysius heard the sound of carriage wheels coming up the long lane towards the convent. The man and his wife had for many years taken and trained the young girls under her care. She had accepted a request for an unscheduled meeting. It was unusual, but she believed it was an answer to her fervent prayers. That it should be *this* woman showed God Himself was on her side. The month of March was not the usual time of year to take new servants – but the request had come at a time when Aloysius felt almost at the end of her strength.

How would she manage to speak to the woman without the man being present? She had planned to set up this meeting on her own terms. It seemed fate had other plans. She gripped the long string of wooden rosary beads that hung from the waist of her black habit.

Loud sounds from the entrance to the convent broke the cloistered silence. She imagined the young nun on duty in the foyer greeting their guests.

The door to her office was flung open without the usual polite knock and request for entrance.

"Mr Whitmore?"

"Reverend Mother." Charles Whitmore bullied his way past the young nun trying to prevent his entrance into the inner sanctum. He was a tall, broad-shouldered, red-faced man – a ship's captain. He carried his years well and seemed to dominate the room.

"Is your good lady wife unwell?" Aloysius looked behind the man. This would never do. She needed to speak with the man's wife.

"I have come alone." Charles threw his body into a chair without waiting for an invitation to sit. He wanted this matter concluded with speed and efficiency – not with the tea and dithering his wife and this woman indulged in. His plans were well under way. He had matters in hand. This visit to the nuns was the last of the details that needed tending.

"It is not the custom of this convent to deal with males. If your lady wife is unable to attend then I would be willing to speak with your housekeeper – Mrs Chambers." Aloysius got to her feet.

"Look here, woman!" Charles was not willing to be pushed aside. He had a list of his requirements. What more could the bloody woman want? "The two girls you placed with my wife turned sixteen. The wife found them both good positions with families of impeccable breeding."

The girls had already left his home. Why had she not been informed? This was all very irregular, Aloysius thought, while the red-faced man continued to bark his orders.

"We need three more of your little sinners. You will receive the earnings of this new batch until they reach their sixteenth birthday. What more do you need to know?"

"I do not place my young girls into male custody. Surely you can understand my position." Aloysius could not believe the man dared to sit in her presence while she stood.

"This is most annoying. I can't be running back and forth. I'll send the wife to see you." Charles got to his feet. He removed a written request on headed notepaper from his inside pocket. He opened the paper and with a heavy hand slammed it onto the desk. "I want three girls – one chambermaid, another for helping the cook and the third as a general help." He glanced at the loudly ticking clock on the mantelpiece. "You choose the girls. It's gone eleven now. I will make sure my wife is here about four to see you. That should give you plenty of time to have the girls ready."

He turned away without waiting for her response. With ground-eating strides he crossed the office and jerked open the door. He erupted into the vestibule shouting for his hat and coat.

In the kitchen the nuns stood frozen, listening to the unusual sound of a male voice shouting and door banging. Who dared to disrupt their safe haven? Was Reverend Mother being attacked? Sister Immaculata picked up her rolling pin and with great daring ran out of the kitchen.

Sister Concepta grabbed a heavy iron pan from the draining board and followed.

The orphans didn't stop working but they exchanged glances, wondering what was going on. They would have to wait until lights out tonight before they could discuss this change in the stifling routine of the convent.

Bridget tried to make herself invisible, praying the nuns would forget she was there.

Charles Whitmore pulled the door of his waiting carriage

open himself, shouting up to the man on the driver's seat. He collapsed back into the well-padded leather seat, his mind already occupied with things yet to be achieved. His plans were finally coming to fruition.

When the horses came to a stop before the four-storey town house on Percy Place, Charles waited impatiently for a servant to open the carriage door. He glanced briefly in the direction of the Grand Canal, his eyes seeing not those waters but a blue sunlit ocean.

He jumped down from the carriage before the steps could be lowered and ran up the granite steps leading to the open front door. The carriage moved off towards the mews to the rear of the house.

"*Where is everybody?*" Charles roared while throwing his hat and coat at the waiting servant.

In the drawing room Georgina Whitmore closed her eyes while taking a long deep breath. Her master's voice, she thought to herself. She checked her image in the mirror over the fireplace. She looked grey and faded – just as he liked her to appear.

She stiffened her shoulders and walked slowly towards the door of her private sitting room. The sound of many footsteps pounding down the stairs caused her to pause. The sudden appearance of her husband's second family had come as a surprise – she had thought she would have more time to prepare. All five of her stepsons would be joining them for lunch, it would appear. Would she now discover what was going on? She imagined biting her own tongue, fixed a blank expression on her face and exited the room.

"Good, you are all here!" Charles barked out as all five of his tall muscular sons appeared in the hallway. He had expected nothing less than immediate obedience to his summons.

He strode to the end of the hall.

"*Chambers, have the meal served!*" he shouted down the stairs leading to the basement kitchen. He clapped his eldest son on his shoulder. "We need to talk. We may as well eat while we're about it. I'm sure you boys are hungry and I'm starving."

He led the way into the dining room, ignoring his wife completely.

Georgina took her place at one end of the long dining table. The mahogany table sat eight comfortably – it could seat as many as twenty when extended. She kept her eyes lowered as her tall stepsons took their places along the length of the table. She busied herself fixing her linen napkin on her knees, refusing to raise her eyes to the commanding figure seated at the other end of the table.

"My wife will serve the soup," Charles stated.

He waited until the servants had placed the dishes for the soup course and withdrawn before continuing.

"I have a great deal to say." He held up his hands as his sons opened their mouths. "I will accept no questioning of my decisions. You are to listen only at this time."

Georgina pressed her napkin to her trembling lips. Were they finally going to learn the details of matters that had kept her husband busy and under her feet over the last year? She gathered her nerves and stood to begin serving soup from the large tureen placed near to her hand.

"I have accepted a very lucrative three-year contract for the use of my ship and its company."

All movement froze in the room for an instant before the men continued passing their soup bowls down the table to be filled.

"The contract is primarily with the French government. We will be on the high seas and exploring the globe for science and profit."

"Why?" Henry, the youngest son at twenty-one, seven years younger than his stepmother, asked.

Georgina wondered if it would be unseemly to dance and laugh with joy at this news. Could she dare dream that running away would no longer be necessary?

"Do you believe I am unaware of my sons' activities?" Charles glared around the table, waiting to see if any would be brave enough to answer him. When all seemed to be concentrating on spooning soup into their mouths, he continued. "I ordered you all to my side for a reason. This contract is the culmination of my life plans. I want my sons at my side."

"You might have asked our opinion, Father." William, the middle son of Charles's second family, accepted his bowl of soup. "We are all of us grown men – we have matters we will need to attend to, after all."

"Matters to attend to? Indeed. You think I don't know what you have become involved in? You young fools could be hanged for your actions. They won't waste a bullet on you. The balance of power in this country has always been unstable – we are all aware of how delicate matters are at the moment. I will not see my sons shed blood for the fool notion of Ireland's freedom. *I will not have it!*" He slapped the table top with his open palm. "You will all be under my command aboard my ship. I am removing you all from the troubles of this land."

There was very little sound in the dining room while all consumed the soup. The five sons of Charles Whitmore knew it would serve no purpose to question their father's commands – here or aboard ship.

Georgina was trying not to shout in joy at the very thought of being free from the demands of her husband and his sons.

When the soup had been consumed, she stood and walked over to the tapestry bell pull – the signal the waiting servants knew meant they were ready for the next course.

Charles waited while servants removed the remains of the soup course before placing dishes piled with food onto the low mahogany dining-room sideboard. "Leave us," he ordered when everything stood ready. "You may serve us." He clicked his fingers at Georgina, not even looking in her direction.

She went to the sideboard and began to fill a plate.

"I have sold all of my rental properties," he informed his sons.

Georgina stiffened momentarily before she regained control of her nerves. They were not his rental properties. The money received in rents from those properties supported this household financially. The houses were hers – part of her dowry.

"I have need of every penny to outfit the ship." He leaned back to allow Georgina to place a brimming plate on the table before him. "I couldn't sell this town house unfortunately." He began shovelling food into his mouth, not waiting until the others at the table were served. "The bloody house is tied to your stepmother's female line."

He held up his glass and waited until his eldest son

22

Charlie jumped to fetch one of the bottles of red wine sitting open on the sideboard. Charlie filled the glass to the brim. His father grunted to acknowledge the deed, and Charlie proceeded to serve his brothers.

Charles swung his glass around the table to give silent permission for all to indulge. "I've ordered my man of affairs to sell all of my stocks and shares." He was enjoying himself. He knew how much his wife hated hearing this and being unable to react. It would amuse him to think of her struggling to survive while he sailed merrily away. He'd soon taught her what her place in this house was – under his fist. Serve that stuck-up bitch right – did she think he didn't know she'd been looking down her nose at him ever since they married? She hadn't even seen fit to give him a child. There was nothing wrong with him as the five sons his first two wives gave him could attest. In ten years this woman hadn't even given him a daughter – someone to inherit this house. He could have taken out a large mortgage on the property in the name of any child of her body but oh no – the selfish barren bitch couldn't even do that.

Chapter 4

"Mary Margaret?" Aloysius looked down the long dining table, noting absently the changes that had taken place in the long years she had served at this convent – so many new faces – so many old friends gone to the Lord.

Sister Mary Margaret almost dropped her spoon into her soup at the honour of being singled out by the Reverend Mother.

Aloysius sipped at the potato soup, trying not to grimace – why could they not use more salt? She sighed silently. She was getting old and bad-tempered. The years seemed to pass so swiftly now. It felt to her like only yesterday she'd arrived at this convent as a fresh-faced girl. "It will be June before we know it. Have you the supplies on hand to equip the new batch of twelve-year-olds?"

"I have a plentiful supply of second-hand maids' uniforms, Reverend Mother." Mary Margaret was afraid to bring her spoon to her mouth. Her hands were trembling – she feared spilling the soup onto her habit. She was very conscious of the eyes of every nun present moving silently from her own face to that of their beloved

Reverend Mother and she disliked being the centre of attention. "The gentry of Dublin have been generous in sending unwanted staff uniforms to us." It was an easy matter to adjust them to fit the girls. The girls were so small and thin when they left the orphanage that one uniform could sometimes be turned into two. She always left enough room for the seams to be let out as needed. The uniforms had to do the girls for years.

"I will need three complete undermaid uniforms and outdoor clothing for girls leaving this afternoon," said Aloysius. "I appreciate this is short notice but you know well what is needed." She pushed her bowl away from her. "I put my trust in you to tend to this matter."

"Which of our girls are leaving, Reverend Mother?" Mother Columbanus, head teacher of the orphanage, asked. It was unusual for girls to leave before June but not unheard of.

"That has yet to be decided." Aloysius waited while Sister Immaculata directed the orphans in the removal of the dishes and the serving of the next course. "Ruth Brown!" she then said, breaking the heavy silence of the room. She examined the young girl serving the table from a tureen of vegetables. "You turned twelve recently, did you not?"

"Yes, Reverend Mother." Ruth didn't stop serving to look at the nun at the head of the long table. She was proud to note her hands didn't even tremble. Well, she'd been serving at this table for years.

The young girls continued to serve the meal under the sharp eyes of the nuns. They would discover what was left for them to eat when the dishes were returned to the kitchen.

Only when the girls had left the room and closed the door did conversation resume.

"Ruth Brown is one of the best I've ever trained," Sister Immaculata sighed. "The girl has a feel for cooking. It has been a pleasure to teach her – such pleasure is rare, I can tell you. I have been dreading losing her." It took years to train the girls in kitchen duties only to lose them out into the big world. She blessed herself and offered up her suffering to the Good Lord before pulling her heaped plate closer to her.

"That one!" Mother Consolata sniffed. "If Bridget O'Brien told her to run under a tram, the young fool would."

"Sister Mary Margaret, come to my office after you have eaten." Aloysius pushed her plate away from her and rose slowly to her feet. "I'll give you the names of the three girls then."

"Reverend Mother, you haven't eaten enough to keep a bird singing," Mother Columbanus remarked.

"I have consumed all that I need, thank you." Aloysius turned to leave the room. "Pray continue with your meal," she said over her shoulder. She wanted time alone to offer up prayers for the girls who would be leaving with Mrs Whitmore this afternoon.

She stood for a moment outside the dining-room door, listening to the buzz of conversation that rose and fell as the names of each twelve-year-old was mentioned and dissected. Well, the decision was hers alone. She knew Mrs Whitmore well – the Good Lord had provided one more time for his servant.

"Come in!" Aloysius called in response to the rap of knuckles on her office door. "Sister Mary Margaret," she smiled when the nun popped her head around the door. "Come and sit down a moment. I wish to discuss the matter of the three who will leave us."

Mary Margaret sat down on the opposite side of the desk.

Then the Reverend Mother pushed a piece of paper across to her.

The sight of the Reverend Mother's beautiful calligraphy was a joy to behold for any teaching nun but as Mary Margaret glanced at it she gasped in shock.

"Bridget is not yet twelve," she said. She refused to voice her own sorrow at losing Sarah Black, one of the girls named on the list.

"I am aware of that, but we will not reveal that fact to outsiders." Aloysius stared at her underling.

"But," Mary Margaret dared to protest, "Bridget O'Brien and these other two – they are a force to be reckoned with when they get together." She gulped before asking, "Is this wise?"

"Bridget O'Brien has been treated as an Imp of Satan ever since she first began to toddle. Such treatment of an innocent child cannot be allowed to continue."

It had broken Aloysius's heart over the years to see the poor child tormented by those into whose care she had been entrusted. She could not be seen to protect the child. That would have caused more problems for the girl. But before she went to meet her Maker she would remove the child from her tormentors.

"I ask your assistance in this, Mary Margaret," she said softly. "I want you to remain silent on the matter of Bridget O'Brien leaving the convent at this time. You will take her and Ruth Brown up to your sewing room. Sarah

27

Black will be at her work there. You will inform all three of this matter. They will need to be scrubbed and polished before meeting their employers this afternoon. Can you do this without alerting the entire convent to our plans?"

"I can but try, Reverend Mother." Mary Margaret's mind was in a whirl. How was she to keep such a big secret from the rest of the convent? She took a deep breath, pulled back her shoulders and determined to do everything in her power to earn the trust the Reverend Mother had placed in her.

"What I suggest you do . . ." Aloysius almost crossed her fingers, praying her scheme would work. "I made it my business to insure Bridget be fed her noon meal in the kitchen here. I had not thought the decision would be so fortuitous. You may tell Ruth Brown that she has been found a place in service. It would not appear strange if you were to invite Bridget to accompany her good friend to your workroom in order to say goodbye." She paused a moment to stare at Mary Margaret. The nuns were not known for their kindness. Mary Margaret was an exception to this rule. "Do you think my suggestion has merit?"

"As long as Mother Consolata is not in the vicinity of the kitchen." Mary Margaret could not perform miracles. Consolata would make it her business to object to anything that might bring joy to young Bridget's life. Why, she might even contact the Bishop and report Reverend Mother. It could not be allowed.

"Yes, she does appear to hover around Bridget, does she not? If you should happen to see Consolata on your journey to the kitchen, inform her I need to see her on a matter of urgency." She would remove the nun from the convent for the rest of the day. She would send her to one of their sister convents with a message. The Good Lord would understand and forgive any lies she might need to tell.

Bridget O'Brien wished she could put her head down on the table and sleep in the comforting warmth. After she had finished her meal and drunk her tea earlier, she had sat on quiet as a mouse, waiting for the Reverend Mother to call for her and hoping the nuns would forget she was there. They didn't, however. The longer she sat there, the more the nuns threw exasperated glances over at her and muttered among themselves, wondering whether they should remind the Reverend Mother that she was still there. Time passed and Bridget began to nod off.

"*Bridget O'Brien!*"

The barking cry of her name made her jump.

"Mother Consolata!" Mary Margaret rushed into the kitchen, her long black veil flying in the wind of her passage. "Reverend Mother has sent me to find you." She had seen the nun approaching the kitchen. "It is, I believe, a matter of urgency."

The tall harsh-featured nun almost pushed Mary Margaret out of her way, fuming at her failure to remove that disgrace to the convent from the kitchen. She would spend time thinking on the punishment she could inflict on the brazen child for laziness.

"Sister Immaculata!" Mary Margaret tried not to pant. She spent too much time bent over her sewing. She needed more exercise. "You are to lose Ruth Brown, I'm afraid."

Bridget tried not to cry out. They were taking her friend away. What would she do without Ruth to listen to

29

her dreams and complaints? She said a quick silent prayer that her friend would be going to a house where she would be treated with kindness.

Ruth fought the tears rushing to her eyes. She couldn't look in Bridget's direction. If she made any move towards her friend it would be Bridget who would suffer.

"Bridget, perhaps you would care to accompany your friend to my workroom," Mary Margaret shocked the kitchen staff almost rigid by saying. "I know you would like to say goodbye."

The sound of frantic whispering echoed around the kitchen as Mary Margaret, a child on each side of her, left the kitchen.

Chapter 5

Mary Margaret stood before the attic window that framed a clear view of the main entrance to the convent. She ignored the whispers going on behind her back. She didn't have to look to see the line of girls hunched over the long work tables placed to catch the natural light, the girls ironing and folding the finished work, those putting items on shelves. They would all wonder about the presence of Ruth and Bridget.

She heard a great deal about the workings of the orphanage up here in her eerie. She allowed the children to whisper and gossip while they worked. It was little enough. The work the children performed in shifts from early morning to dark was backbreaking and blinding. They deserved to be allowed some leeway as long as the speed of their little fingers didn't suffer.

She briefly turned her head at the sound of the sewing machine. Sarah Black was hunched over one of their two machines, a train of white cotton running under the needle. Mary Margaret blessed the benefactor who had gifted the convent with three of the new-fangled sewing machines. She had immediately been granted two of the wonders for her workroom. Sister Veronica, who worked on the nun's habits in her basement workshop, had received the third.

Mary Margaret's patience was rewarded. Mother Consolata – impossible to mistake that tall bony figure – marched along the pathway to the open iron gates of the convent. Mary Margaret didn't move until she'd seen the figure being picked up in the street by the convent's horse and cart. Only then did she feel as if she was breathing freely. She watched a moment, to be sure the other nun was well away, before turning from the window and slapping her hands loudly to draw attention.

"Sarah Black, Ruth Brown and Bridget O'Brien!" She hurried across to the stacks of cleaning cloths sitting on one of the long work tables and picked up three. "Take these cloths and hurry down to the baths." She ignored the shocked gasps of the girls bent over their tasks. "I want all three of you to tell Mother Dominic that you have my permission to indulge in a long warm scrubbing. Do not forget your hair, ladies." If it could be called hair, only spikes of new growth appearing on their heads – no matter – what little there was of it needed to be clean, she thought. "I want each of you to run the fine comb through your hair with vigour. Do not let me down." She clapped her hands again. "Come along, ladies! We do not have all day."

"Mother?" Sarah Black had seen many others leave the convent in the years she had worked in the sewing room – she held out her shiny thread-pulled grey skirt, "We have no clean clothing."

"What am I thinking of?" Mary Margaret slapped her hand to her forehead. The employer of these three would pay dearly for the items they took away with them.

"Ladies, we need three white petticoats for these three girls who are soon to leave us." She spun around in place, not wanting to meet the desperate hope that was shining in three pairs of eyes. "We also need three pair of girls' unmentionables and three liberty bodices – as quickly as may be." She clapped her hands sharply.

"Sister Mary Margaret?" Bridget was almost afraid to ask the question, but she had to know. Was it possible that her prayers had been answered? "I am to leave at the same time as Ruth and Sarah?"

"Yes, yes. Hannah Silver, we need three pairs of inside shoes." She could not allow Bridget to mention the fact that she would only turn twelve in December. "Patricia White, please lower three of our carpet bags down." The convent constructed their own carpet bags from the discards of others. "We can start assembling the items needed while these three laggards clean themselves."

She watched the children under her command run around the room fetching the items she'd listed from neatly folded piles in the cupboards that lined the walls.

She then had the three girls line up with their arms out. Into each pair of arms she lowered a white cotton petticoat, a pair of unmentionables, a liberty bodice, stockings and indoor shoes and finally a grey shawl cut down from the blankets donated to the convent. "Get rid of your work clothes, dress in these, then cover yourselves with these shawls and return to me after your bath. Do not tarry."

She pushed the three young girls in the direction of the servants' staircase that went from the attic to the basement – only the orphans used that stairway so no nuns would be aware of their comings and goings, she

33

prayed. In spite of Reverend Mother's wishes it was impossible to keep anything truly secret in this building.

The baths in the basement of the orphanage were a copy of the public bath houses that dotted the city. Reverend Mother insisted on this – cleanliness was next to godliness after all.

"Where are you going?" Angela White hung over the half-door of one of the bath cubicles to ask. The long-tiled room had individual cubicles marching along two walls of the bath house. "Do you know?" She hadn't heard anything about these three leaving. She sighed – that wasn't unusual – stuck as she was down here in the bowels of the home.

There was silence for a moment as all waited for Bridget to respond. She was always the spokesperson. Bridget however was up to her chin in hot water, desperately trying to keep silent. She wanted no one and nothing to stop her escape. Finally it was Sarah who answered their curious classmate.

"We don't know where we're going, Angela." She was enjoying her first ever clean hot bath. On Saturdays the water in the bathtub was used by several, the older girls bathing the youngest first. A bath full of clean hot water was a treat she wanted to enjoy.

"Do I hear whispering and gossiping in my baths?" a disembodied voice demanded.

"*We were praying, Mother Dominic!*" Angela shouted, her voice echoing off the tiled walls and floor.

"*No need to shout, child! I'm not deaf!*"

"Yes, she is," Angela muttered.

She picked up the ragged work clothes that had been

thrown over the door into the hallway. A quick glance assured her the items were only fit for the rag bin. She walked back to her work station and dumped all of the items in a large bin. She'd sort them out later.

"When are you leaving?" she returned to ask, not caring who answered. It was lonely down here in the bowels of the orphanage with only a deaf old nun to pinch and scold her all day long. The girls working in the laundry room that shared the basement had no time to gossip.

"We don't know that either," Ruth whispered. "We were told to use a fine-tooth comb."

"Don't know why they bother." Angela went to fetch the requested item. "They don't let us have much hair."

Bridget listened to all that went on around her, afraid to open her mouth. Birthdays were not celebrated at the orphanage – indeed they were never mentioned. She was mortally afraid someone in power would realise she was not yet twelve years old.

Chapter 6

Georgina was seated before the window in her private sitting room trying to control the rage that shook her body. She had left the men in the dining room, talking over their cigars and port. Her eyes were fixed unseeingly on the horse-drawn barge that travelled along the Grand Canal. How dare he? She punched her clenched fists onto her knees, unaware of the pain she was inflicting on herself. How dare that man who had stolen her dignity, her joy in life, her very way of life! How dare he steal her dowry and plan to leave her in virtual penury!

She turned from the window and quickly crossed the room to turn the key in the door. She wanted no one to disturb her.

"Thank you, Grandmamma," she whispered, picking up the ear trumpet the old woman had used in her declining years.

She put the trumpet against the wall that separated her sitting room from the dining room. The sounds from that room were carried through the trumpet into the earpiece. She needed to know more of her husband's plans.

"Right, Father dear," Charlie said when all had lit their

36

cigars and each held a glass of port. "It's about time you told us more of your plans."

"We are well into the year 1898. Before we are aware of it we will be in a new century. Think of it, lads – 1900! What will that new century bring?" He bit the tip of his cigar. "It's damned exciting."

"That is not exactly ground-breaking news," David said.

"This country is going to explode." Charles puffed on his cigar and stared at his sons. They were men a man could be proud of – not a weakling among them. "It might not be this year or next but it is coming. We all here know that." He leaned forward to stare into the eyes of each of his sons.

"We were hoping to be part of that fight." Henry didn't meet his father's staring eyes. Being the youngest of five boys was no great blessing in his eyes. He had learned to be fast and use his fists at an early age. Now he was ready to step out of the shadow of his brothers.

"I will hear no more of this nonsense! I will not have you give your life for something that can never succeed!" Charles barked. "We are here to discuss your futures. I want you all at my side when we sail out to seek our fortunes."

"I rather thought you had already amassed a fortune." David knew his father had received healthy dowries from each of his three wives. He had turned everything he could from the two who had died into hard cash. His own mother had been a wealthy woman. What had happened to the monies that should have come to him and his brother? "Have you squandered our inheritance, Father?"

"No, I damn well haven't, you impudent article!"

Charles glanced around before continuing. "I'm removing my monies from Ireland. I want all the cash I can lay my hands on to invest. Jean Claude," he named his long-time first mate, "is of the opinion that we will make our fortunes on this voyage. He knows something of the men who have retained our services and believes that with careful planning we will all return from this voyage as rich as nabobs."

"Jean Claude has always had a good nose for making money." Charlie looked at his brothers. Were they finally going to receive some of his father's wealth? He was tired of being at the man's beck and call.

"When do you plan to sail?" Henry asked.

"We will up anchor no later than three months' time. The work on my ship is almost complete. There is only a question of last-minute changes."

"Nice of you to give us some time to attend to our own affairs," David said sarcastically. He didn't want to be under his father's command ever again – yet what could he do? He'd never forgive himself if he missed the chance to make his fortune and win his freedom from parental tyranny.

Georgina, her ear pressed to the trumpet, felt the strength go from her knees. Three months. Dear Lord, they would all be under her feet for three more months! What was she going to do? How would she bear it?

Chapter 7

"Mrs Whitmore, Reverend Mother," the nun's soft voice preceded Georgina into the nun's office.

"I had not expected to come here today," Georgina was saying as she stepped into the room. She was embarrassed by her shabby appearance. The gleaming surrounds of the nuns' home seemed to point out the worn-out state of her garments. "I am happy to see you looking so well." She crossed to where her great-aunt sat behind her desk.

Aloysius waited until the door had been closed at her guest's back. Her prayers had been answered once more. She stood to kiss the pale cheeks of her great-niece.

"I was praying you would attend this meeting alone, Georgina." She made no mention of the sad state of the younger woman's appearance. Poor Georgina, she knew, was married to a man who offered her no care or consideration. She thought briefly of the well-tended and wealthy appearance the husband presented to the world. She sighed deeply – ours not to reason why, she thought.

She gestured towards the two visitor chairs pulled close to the desk behind which she sat.

"Pull those chairs closer together, please." She walked around her large desk. "I am feeling my years, my dear." She watched as the chair was positioned.

They sat down.

"You are up to something, Aunt Allie!" Georgina did not feel capable of dealing with this relative of hers. She had been ordered to attend this meeting. What was her husband up to now? He had never interested himself in the hiring of staff before. He was not known for kind gestures. Everything that man did hid a barb – where was the barb in this?

"Your husband came to see me demanding three of our girls – immediately. Are you aware?"

"That is why I am here." Georgina could well imagine the reception he'd received if he had barged into this office demanding his way.

"It was your place to inform me of the departure of two of our girls from your home – why did you not?" She liked to know where her girls were and how they were handling life in the world.

"I had to move quickly." Georgina offered no apology. It had been her decision to make. "I had not the time to inform you of the changes being made. The two girls were sixteen years old. I didn't like the way my stepsons were regarding them. I removed them from my home for their own safety. I found both good positions in homes that are well regarded." She had not been able to place the two girls together. That saddened her, but the situation had been urgent, she felt. "I could not let them be endangered."

"That was well done of you." Aloysius let the matter drop.

Georgina changed the subject. "I did not know my husband was coming to meet with you." She wondered if he had mentioned anything of his intentions to her great-aunt.

"Your husband sent a note demanding an immediate meeting with me. I thought at the time that you would be present. I decided to agree to his demands – as they matched my own needs." Aloysius reached slowly and painfully to pick up one of the three brown cardboard folders sitting on her desk top. She put the folder in Georgina's hands.

"Bridget O'Brien," Georgina's whisper was a hiss when she read the name on top of the file. "Surely not?" She glanced from the pages to her relative. "The child cannot be old enough?" She was glad she was sitting. She felt quite faint.

"Once upon a time you begged me to aid your friend Eugenie." The two women leaned in close to each other and glanced around the room as if the very walls had ears. "I did all that I could for her. We have a convent in the vicinity of her husband's family estate. I nursed her back to health there. It was too dangerous to move her. She was injured so badly. She extracted a promise from me. I am endeavouring to fulfil that promise."

"At the time I could not help her." Georgina's tears flowed freely while she clasped the folder to her breast. "I have long regretted my failure to assist such a dear friend." They had both been so young with no knowledge of the world. She had wanted so much to help and turned to the one woman she felt could offer the best care to her friend. She had not been wrong.

"I have always felt I was guided by the Good Lord in this matter," Aloysius said.

"My goodness, of course it has been more than ten years!" Georgina was shocked to think so much time had passed. "I had so many problems of my own at that time – I was deeply involved in discussions about my marriage." She had fought her parents – without success – to avoid marrying the man they had chosen for her.

"Eugenie's husband has never stopped looking for her," Aloysius sighed. "The man is obsessed."

"But it's been years! Surely he has moved on?"

"No." Aloysius shook her head. "And what I have heard of the man fills me with fear and disgust."

"I planned to take the child into my own home," Georgina remembered. "The nature of the man I married forced me to see how great an error that would be." She bowed her head for a moment, forcing the memories of the first days of her marriage from her mind. "But to take the child into my home as a servant – how can I?"

"It is the only way to protect her." Aloysius had given the matter long thought over the past year. "I have not long for this world."

"Aunt Allie!" Georgina touched the twisted hands with one of her own.

"I am more than ready to meet my Maker, child." Aloysius didn't allow sentiment to intrude. "You and your staff treat the girls we place with you with kindness. I have heard only good of your household staff." She waved a hand dismissively. "We do not have time for this discussion – you must take the child. If anything should happen to me before her service with you is completed, as I fear it will …" she leaned forward to stare intently into the eyes of her grandniece, "you must not allow the nuns of this convent to remove her from your care. This is vital

– she must remain with you until you feel she is ready to face the world."

Georgina nodded. "What is she like?" She had wanted to get to know the child but she'd been afraid her interest would bring danger to the little one. She had long dreamed of taking the child into her home. She would have loved her as a true daughter of her heart.

"She has her father's beauty."

"Beauty? Surely not? He is handsome, I will grant you."

"I made it my business to see the man. I have never seen such a beautiful male in my life. He was breath-taking with that leonine mane of golden hair – green eyes that sparkle with the promise of pleasure – the body of a young pagan god. Even to an old woman such as myself he appeared truly a thing of beauty – but then I have always thought the devil too would have to be beautiful to attract so many sinners."

Georgina was put to the blush by the old woman's recounting of the beauty of a male. "Has the child any of his nature?" she asked.

"No – the Good Lord has blessed the child with her mother's loving heart and nature." Aloysius had watched carefully through the years. The child showed no sign of the evil that resided inside her father's soul. "She is extremely clever – quick to learn new things – hungry for knowledge."

"But for me to treat her as a servant," Georgina said. "The daughter of my dearest friend – it does not sit easy with me."

"I have protected her to the best of my abilities for ten long years." Aloysius had to make her see that this was the only way to keep the child safe – give her the belief in herself to fight her own parent. "I am entrusting her to your care now. When the child is sixteen – keep her with you. Prepare her as best you can to stand on her own two feet and face the world. She must be protected from him. Besides, if he should place his hands on the child," she felt tears in her eyes, "he will control the mother and this we cannot allow. I have nightmares still about the injuries that man inflicted on Eugenie. I thought she would die in my care. It was love for her unborn child that kept her on this earth. He must never know the whereabouts of his wife and child."

In all of her years as a nun she had never seen such cruelty. The abuse carved with care into the trembling flesh of such a young woman! It had horrified her and given her the strength to break the law of the land. She could not return that young woman to a man who delighted in harming her.

The old nun pushed herself to her feet. Georgina watched as she pulled a key chain from the folds of her habit and unlocked a deep drawer in her desk. She removed a beautiful golden-haired rag doll from the depths of the drawer.

"Keep this safe." She pushed the doll into Georgina's hands. "Eugenie made it for her child. I could not allow her to have it in the orphanage. I have sewn instructions inside the doll. You but have to unpick the back seam to find my letter and instructions. You must wait until the child is eighteen before revealing this secret." She almost collapsed into the chair behind her desk. The secrecy might appear ridiculous to an outsider, but she had seen true evil at first hand. She could not leave this earth without doing everything in her power to keep the child put into her care safe. "I have done all that I could." She would pray with her last breath for the safety of the mother and child she had helped escape the clutches of evil.

The sound of young voices and hurried instruction drifted into the room.

"That will be the terrible threesome." Aloysius smiled. "You will enjoy having them in your home. Ruth and Sarah believe they protect Bridget. They are mistaken. Bridget has tried to protect every child in the home. She has a loving nature."

Georgina felt as if her head would explode with all of the problems placed in her hands. How would she keep a house running with so little money available to her? She had to try and keep some of her family's long-term servants. She could not throw people who had served her well onto the street. Now she had the safety, care and education of three new girls under her command. One of whom formed part of a sacred trust. How would she cope?

"You should see your new servants." Aloysius stood and crossed the room to a heavy wooden cross that hung beside the door. She gestured with her hand.

Georgina joined the nun. She had used the peephole hidden by the cross before. It offered unobstructed views into the vestibule. She put her eye to the hole. Three young girls sat on a wooden bench pushed against the far wall. They were dressed alike in black clothing. The black woollen skirts they wore reached the top of their laced-up black boots. Their ill-fitting jackets were also of black wool. Each had a carpet bag at their feet. They appeared

45

to be waiting patiently until one observed the tight grip the figure in the middle had on the hand of each of the girls at her sides.

"Bridget is the one in the middle," Aloysius whispered.

Georgina tried to get a clear picture of the child but they were all three staring at the floor. The straw bonnets covering their heads hid their faces.

"Time to meet them." Georgina pulled open the door.

The three girls jumped to their feet. In synchronisation they each offered a quick curtsey to the woman who would control their destiny for the next four years.

Chapter 8

"What do we think?" Bridget asked when they were once more seated on the wooden bench.

"What does it matter what we think?" Ruth leaned in closer to say. "We have to go where we are sent. When did what we think ever make a difference?"

Sarah too leaned closer. "If you two don't hush up you're going to get us into trouble."

The three girls sat for a moment in silence. They had been examined by their new employer. They had each been given a gift of wooden rosary beads by the Reverend Mother. They were to spend time in prayer thanking the Lord for their good fortune, she had told them. They were to wait here while she and their mistress took care of the paperwork relating to their new positions.

Bridget couldn't sit still. She was terrified someone would realise she was too young to accept employment. If they sent her back to the orphanage on her own, what would she do?

"We are allowed to think, Ruth Brown," she said. "I want to know what we think of our new mistress."

She leaned back against the wooden bench. Her two

friends leaned over without conscious thought. Bridget was almost completed hidden by their bodies.

"Her clothes are very shabby." Sarah had been disappointed by the lady's appearance. She didn't look as she had imagined the lady of a great house would.

"What do we know about fashion?" Ruth rolled her eyes.

"I'll have you know I've spent years learning to refashion garments!" Sarah said. "You should have seen the lovely fabric and beading we worked on up in the attic." She was going to miss that part of her life. She so loved making something beautiful out of the garments sent to the orphanage.

"I thought she looked hungry," Ruth said. "She doesn't look like someone who enjoys her food."

"I thought she had the saddest eyes," Bridget gave her opinion. "They were a funny colour – a browny yellow."

"My stomach feels funny." Ruth ignored Bridget's words. They had no right to pass comment on their mistress.

"That's because we're scared," Bridget said.

"Maybe it's because we're excited." Sarah too had a sick stomach.

"I wonder what they're doing in there?" Bridget wanted to pick up her feet and examine her boots. She'd never worn anything so hard before and they were pinching her feet. "I want to run along this hall and make the floor dirty." She wanted to dance over the hated black-and-white tiles. She seemed to have spent half her life on her knees washing and polishing those things. "I wonder if we spun around would these white petticoats fly out around us?" She didn't feel like herself in these clothes.

"Would you hold your whisht, Bridget O'Brien!" Ruth wanted to run back to the kitchen. At least she knew what she was doing in there. She felt smothered in all of these clothes.

"You sounded just like Sister Immaculata when you said that," Bridget laughed.

"When I have time I'm going to adjust this jacket to fit." Sarah pulled at the ill-fitting jacket. "It's hitting me in all the wrong places."

"Pity about yeh!" Bridget said. "It's keeping me lovely and warm." She hated to be cold.

"I'll do your jackets too when I have the time." Sarah was saying anything to pass the time. What were they doing in there? "You'll see what I'm talking about then."

"I'm going to miss the young ones." Bridget was sad at the thought of leaving the babies in the nursery. "I wonder what part of the house we'll be working in?" She sighed deeply. "I think I'd like to work in the nursery. I wonder if that woman has any children. The nursery nurses take their young charges out into parks, I'm told. I'd like that. I think I'd like being outdoors. Maybe I could be a gardener."

"Maybe you could fly to the moon!" Ruth said with another roll of her eyes. "Honest to goodness, Biddy – where does your mind fly away to?"

"Would you want to keep working in the kitchens, Ruth?"

"Sister Immaculata told me I have a real feel for cooking," Ruth said. "That's very important, to hear her tell it." She shrugged her shoulders in the uncomfortable jacket. "I never gave a thought to any other work. I've been in the kitchen since I was six years old. I know what

I'm about there."

"Do you think we'll get any say in where they put us?" Bridget didn't want to spend the rest of her life scrubbing floors. There had to be more to life than that – hadn't there?

"No!" the others said in unison.

In the Reverend Mother's office, the elderly nun sat behind the desk while Georgina filled out the paperwork necessary for the convent's files. The Connemara marble inkstand – a gift from a wealthy patron – sat in pride of place on the desk. Georgina dipped the nib of one of the pens kept ready in the indentation on the stand into the black ink. The three brown paper files were open and ready for the completed forms. Georgina only skimmed over the form. It was a standard document she had seen many times before.

"These papers are for Ruth and Sarah only." Georgina signed her name to the contracts. It was agreed that the convent would receive the girl's wages every quarter until they turned sixteen – as was standard practice. If the wages of a young worker were not sent to the nuns, the parents received the money. In addition, the cost of the supplies – such as shoes and clothes – that the orphans took away with them was charged to the employers.

"The papers in Bridget's file will state that she has been returned to her family." Aloysius stared into Georgina's rich whiskey-brown eyes. The old nun's blue eyes were faded and sad.

"What address have you given for the parents?" Georgina couldn't dispute the old nun's actions.

"A cottage in Cavan," Aloysius said. "I may be worrying unnecessarily – but I know if any enquiries are made about the child at that home I will be informed. It is the best I could think of."

"Cavan is closer to Belfast than Dublin as the crow flies." Georgina thought the idea was a good one but anyone making enquiries could travel easily to Belfast from Cavan. She had heard her husband and stepsons discuss Clive Henderson, Earl of Castlewellan and Bridget's sire, at table. It seemed the man had one of those horseless carriages, the speed of which was promised to shorten any journey.

Aloysius frowned. "I must confess I hadn't given the proximity to Belfast and that man's estates a thought." She stood with difficulty, while doing a mental review of all the women in her care.

She walked to the three tall filing cabinets pushed against one wall of her office. She pulled open a deep drawer. Her crippled fingers moved slowly over the files inside. She had several nuns from County Cork, the furthest place from Belfast on the island of Ireland.

"May I help?" Georgina hated to see the old woman struggle. She was very fond of her great-aunt.

"I am attempting to perform a mental inventory of my nuns and novices," Aloysius said without stopping her fingers moving. Everyone she thought of was too old. Their families might not be living. She needed someone who would contact the convent at the first suggestion of any enquiries.

A soft knock on the door of the office interrupted her thinking. "Come in," she almost sighed. What new problems had arisen that she must be disturbed?

"Reverend Mother –" A young woman dressed all in white held the office door open. She did not step into the room. "I'm sorry to disturb you but those young girls have been sitting on that bench for some time. Sister Immaculata is saying they are making the place look untidy. Should we move them to the kitchen?"

"That won't be necessary, Mary." Aloysius knew Sister Immaculata wanted the chance to pump the girls for information. "We have almost concluded our business. Now run along."

"Yes, Reverend Mother." The young novice's cheeks filled with colour as she stepped hastily back, closing the door softly.

"The Good Lord will provide." Aloysius pushed the file drawer closed and pulled open another one. "I should never have doubted Him." She pulled a file from the drawer with a satisfied grunt. She opened the file on her desk and raised her eyes to Georgina. "Young Mary comes from Glengarriff – that is in County Cork."

"It is fortunate you became a nun, Aunt." Georgina smiled at the old woman's pleasure. "The world would not have been safe from your shenanigans otherwise."

"I gave my word to that poor woman. I promised to keep her child safe." Aloysius wrote a note to remind herself to have a talk with Mary. She would fill out the paperwork later. "I would not like to meet my Maker having failed in my duty."

"Do you really think Henderson will look here for his wife and child?"

"Do not mention that man's name in my presence." Aloysius fingered her rosary beads. "He is evil. I want no part of him in my domain."

When the paperwork was completed for Ruth and Sarah, the two women stepped into the hallway. The nervously waiting girls jumped to their feet. At a word from their new mistress they picked up their carpetbags and walked towards the door of the convent which was being held open by the young novice on hall duty. The three young girls – faces white as sheets – eyes opened to their widest extent – stepped out and into their new lives.

Chapter 9

"I hear the carriage." Lily Chambers moved to the window in the basement kitchen that overlooked the back courtyard and mews. "I don't know what we are going to do with these young girls. We received such short notice – I don't like to be found unprepared like this." She resisted passing any comment on the master's sudden decision to involve himself in the area of household staff. "Cook, a pot of tea and some of your delicious scones in my sitting room, I think." She needed to interview all three – find out which areas of housework they had been trained in.

She shook her head when the cook, Betty Powell, opened her mouth. A quick jerk of her head in the direction of the stairs leading up into the main body of the house signified her wish for silence. The five young men of the house were presently shouting in one of the drawing rooms. It was a disgrace. And the three sons of the master's second wife had brought their own male servants with them. Those men would be standing in the hallway listening to everything that took place, she had no doubt. They were not the usual cut of servants in her opinion but nobody asked her.

"I'll be in my sitting room." Lily was not going to be waiting at the back door to greet new servants. It was beneath her dignity. No doubt the mistress had been dropped off at the front entrance.

"Cora, go show them young girls where to put their coats and hats," Cook ordered the kitchen maid. The young woman had been with her for years and was shaping up to be a good cook – if she did say so herself – after all, she'd trained her. "Make sure they put their indoor shoes on as well, mind."

"I'll give you a hand getting the tea tray ready for the housekeeper, Cook." Violet Boyle, head housemaid, wanted a good look at this new crop of orphans. The last two girls sent from the orphanage had been good little workers. She missed their help around the place.

Georgina herself led the three new members of staff into the kitchen through the back door. The attitude of the coach driver, Lewis, left a great deal to be desired, she thought. The man had been less than helpful with her young charges. Thank goodness the girls knew no better. The group stepped from the short rear hallway into the main body of the kitchen. Georgina sighed in relief at the warmth of the kitchen. It was bitterly cold outdoors.

"I've ordered tea and scones for my sitting room, madam." The housekeeper stood in the open door of her private room. "I thought to interview the new girls before setting them to their duties."

"Tea for two only, please, Cook." Georgina smiled as she removed her hat and coat. She dropped the items on a nearby chair. "I believe the youngsters are hungry – if you would serve them a little something here while I instruct Mrs Chambers?"

"Certainly, madam." Mrs Powell pointed the three young girls towards a table set into an alcove. The heavy table sitting proudly in the middle of the room was her work station. She preferred that it was not used for taking meals. "I'll take care of your tray first."

"I don't want them housed in the servants' quarters in the attic," Georgina said when the two women were behind the closed door of the small room off the kitchen, set aside for the housekeeper's use.

"Why?" Lily Chambers was familiar enough with her mistress to ask.

"My stepsons have never bothered the help so far." Georgina almost collapsed onto one of the two wooden chairs placed by a small round table. "I am aware that is a mercy with young men running around the place." She had taken steps to insure that would remain so. Violet and Cora didn't live in, so they had never been a worry.

"I have kept a close eye on staff." Lily was insulted.

"I am aware, Lily." Georgina patted one of the hands clenched on the small table. "But I believe my stepsons are not overjoyed by their father's plans for their future." There had been so many changes in the household already. It seemed every day brought a new challenge lately. How much did her old friend know already? It was hard to keep secrets from servants. "Who knows what might happen with blood running hot and tempers fraying?"

"I believe you worry unnecessarily but I will be guided by your feelings in the matter."

"There is a vacant room off the kitchen," Georgina had been thinking about the matter on the silent carriage

56

ride home. "We have never found a use for it. We can put three beds in there easily. It will have the heat from the kitchen range to keep it snug."

"Liam sleeps on a mat before the range at night."

"I doubt the girls have much to fear from a ten-year-old boot boy."

"If you think it's necessary." Lily stood to answer a knock on her sitting-room door. She held the door open for Violet to carry a well-stocked tray into the room and over to the table.

The two women waited until the maid had returned to the kitchen before resuming their talk.

"I will order Brian and Pat to bring three beds from the attic." Georgina was referring to two of the male servants who had accompanied her stepsons to the house. "They will complain bitterly at the indignity, I know, but they will do it if they want to continue under my roof." She watched Lily pour tea into two small china cups. "The young men will be under our feet all day every day." She smiled at the look of horror on the housekeeper's face. "Those employed have been ordered to give notice at their places of employment. My husband wants his sons close to hand during the final fitting out of his ship."

"That's asking for mischief." They had never had all of the master's sons present at one time. It would make a great deal of extra work for the already overextended staff.

"Indeed," Georgina accepted a cup of tea and sat silently for a while. "I forget – every time I take young girls such as these I forget how sheltered they are from the real world. The three of them sat in the carriage apparently struck dumb at their first sight of the outside world. They, all three, had eyes open wide in wonder as they stared around the Dublin streets."

The three girls sat in the alcove drinking tea and eating from a plate of delicious sandwiches. All three were watching the strange world around them.

"I keep expecting someone to knuckle my head and order me to move," Bridget whispered.

"I could stay here all day," Ruth leaned forward to say. "This kitchen is wonderful." She sniffed in delight. "I hope I'm allowed to work in here."

"*Shh!*" Sarah tapped the table top gently. When she caught the eyes of the other two she jerked her head in the direction of the cook. The woman was ordering a young boy to serve them fresh tea. They watched the lad carry the big metal pot over to the table.

"Serve yourself a mug of tea, Liam, and sit down with the girls out of the way," Mrs Chambers, coming from her room, ordered.

"Are you hungry?" Bridget asked when the boy had joined them at the table. She pushed a plate of roast beef sandwiches across the pitted table top.

"Nah." Liam nonetheless took one of the sandwiches. "I get well fed here. Cook says I've hollow legs. I eat everything in front of me and never put on weight." He grinned widely. "My name's Liam by the way and I'm a growing boy, you know."

"My name is Sarah."

"Right, the one with the blue eyes – that one is Sarah," he noted. "What about you two?"

"My name is Bridget."

"Bridget with the green eyes." Liam knew he'd be

58

questioned about these three by the other staff members –
always good to be in the know.

"And I'm Ruth."

"Ruth, you have beautiful silver eyes. I've never seen
eyes like those before." He was smitten.

"What's it like to work here?" Ruth felt brave enough
to ask.

"It's been alright so far," Liam said. "But there are
changes in the wind." He tapped the side of his nose to
indicate he knew things they didn't.

"What changes?" said Ruth.

Liam ignored that. "How come they cut your hair so
short?" he asked while the area around them suddenly
became a hive of activity.

"The nuns say it's less fuss." Bridget watched open-
mouthed as two tall young men travelled back and forth,
burdened with items she couldn't take the time to identify.

"Looks funny," Liam shrugged. "Still, it will soon
grow. It's hard to figure out what colour hair you have
when it's that short." He leaned forward, trying to
examine the stubble on each head.

The fuss continued unabated while the four youngsters
learned about each other. The housekeeper and cook
shouted orders to the maids. The two men grunted,
banged and moaned. It was strange and wonderful to the
girls so newly released from the strict confines of an
orphanage. Shouldn't they be doing something?

"This will be your room." Violet led the three girls into
the room that had been prepared for them. Strange
goings-on if you asked her – but then nobody ever did.
"I'll fetch you sheets and pillows. Yez can make up yer

own beds." She hurried out to fetch the linen.

"A room for us three alone," Bridget said blissfully.

"Which bed do you want?" Sarah stood by one of the three metal bed frames that had been carried into the room and hurriedly constructed. The three bed-heads were pushed against the wall furthest from the door. Three small bedside cabinets stood to the side of each bed.

"We have a table and chairs all of our very own!" Ruth took a seat at the small round table pushed into one corner of the big room, a smile of sheer joy on her face. "Do you think we'll be allowed have tea parties in here – wouldn't that be wonderful?

Before anyone could answer they were interrupted.

"Here yez go!" Violet hurried into the room, the bed linen almost spilling from her arms. She was followed by Liam carrying an armful of pillows. "Get these beds made and your things put away." She dumped the linen onto one of the beds and sent Liam on his way before standing with her hands on her hips to check the room out. "The house is all at sixes and sevens at the minute so I can't tell yez much." She didn't know what was going on but something was. "I don't live in nor does the kitchen maid Cora. You three will be down here with Cook and the boot boy." She began to leave the room. "We'll see how you go. Better get busy. Mrs Chambers will be sending for you soon I shouldn't wonder . . ." Her words trailed behind her as she left the room.

The three girls moved as one well-trained group. They soon had the beds made and then they began to unpack their bags.

Ruth and Bridget exclaimed in delight at the wonders they pulled from their individual carpet bags. The stocked bags had been handed to them and they had not been able to examine them before. Only Sarah had been aware of the items that were normally provided for girls leaving the convent.

Chapter 10

"The three new girls are good little workers." Lily Chambers was taking tea in the mistress's private sitting room. She was awaiting her instructions for the day. "One thing you can say for the nuns, they train them well." She'd been keeping a close eye on the new servants in the two weeks they had been in the house.

"Yes, I suppose they do." Georgina pushed her cup away from her with a sigh.

"The men left the house early which was a blessing," said Lily. "It was possible for the staff to get the house cleaned down." It had amused her to hear the comments of the three young girls when they observed the untidiness of the men of the house. The girls under Violet's tutelage had been unaware of the housekeeper's presence on the stairway.

"The routine of the house has been so disrupted, Lily." Georgina stood to walk to the window. The sharp icy light of the sun glistened on the flowing water of the Grand Canal, almost blinding her. "I can give no instructions this morning. I have no idea of the needs of this household at the moment, I'm afraid."

She had been awakened at an early hour by her husband demanding his rights. She'd suffered through his embrace and blessed the fact that he was in too much of a hurry to linger.

"The master and his sons will be dining at their club." Lily watched her mistress with great sadness. All of the joy had been beaten out of her. "They'll be late back to the house."

"Will they really?" Georgina spun from the window. That was more information than she had been given.

"So I was informed." Lily Chambers was glad not to have that crowd under her feet. They were very demanding.

"I need Liam to take a note for me." Georgina was hurrying over to her desk while she spoke. This was her chance. She might never get another. "It doesn't matter what else you might have planned for the lad to do. I need him. Let him quickly get ready and send him to me here, please, Lily." Her mind was in a whirl. She needed to plan this swiftly and carefully. She turned to ask frantically, "You're positive the men will not return till evening?"

"The master," the word tasted bitter on Lily's tongue, "informed me that he and his sons will be away from home all day – Cook was not to plan meals for them."

"Send Liam to me." Georgina was at her desk now, rapidly writing a note for the young boy to carry. "In the meantime have the three orphans washed, fed and changed into outdoor clothing. You and I, Lily, are going to show them around the streets of Dublin."

"You and I, madam?" That was highly irregular. What was bringing that flush of excitement to her mistress's cheeks, she wondered? She had an air about her that Lily had not seen in years.

"Yes, yes, now go!" She waved one hand without looking. "Send Liam to me at once."

"You sent for me, madam." Liam's face was shining from the scrubbing cook had administered before sending him upstairs. He'd been brushed and polished to within an inch of his life.

Georgina, the sealed envelope in her fist, stared at the young boy. "Liam – I want you to deliver this note to this address –" She almost whispered the nearby Stephen's Street address. She thrust the envelope into his hand. Such a young person to put her trust in but she was desperate. "There will be a response – please wait for it." She bent to stare into the young boy's eyes. "Liam, you must tell no one of this." She clenched his shoulders tight enough to hurt. "Do you understand – *no one must know of this message*."

"But they are sure to ask where I've been." He didn't want to let his mistress down but he was sure the servants would try to pinch it out of him. And those men who had come with the master's sons always wanted to know what was going on. They were hard men to say no to. Old Lewis the coachman was another who always dipped his nose into everything going on at the house.

"Of course." Georgina should have known better. "Let me think." She marched back and forth across the polished wooden floor under the boy's fascinated gaze. "Do you know where the wise woman in The Lane lives?" she swung around to ask. The Lane was a hidden warren of poverty across the canal from the posh houses on Percy Place. It was where Liam's family lived.

"I do and all," Liam was proud to say.

"Then go to her after you have delivered my note." Georgina hurried to her desk. She took a threepenny piece from the change she kept in the desk. "Ask her for a tonic for my nerves." She was pleased with her own solution. "Then you may tell the other servants where you have been. But you must make no mention of the note you carried. Can you do that?"

"Yes, madam," Liam had never seen the mistress like this. "Wild horses wouldn't drag it out of me!" he promised fervently.

"Good lad," Georgina said. "I'll let you out by the front door. When you return go through the kitchen and give the tonic to Mrs Chambers in full view of any staff that linger. She will know what to do."

"Yes, madam."

"Right, come along. I'll let you out." She checked the hallway was free of staff before hurrying the boy away. She opened the inside door that led into the tiny vestibule, then pulled open the heavy outer door.

She stood for a moment watching the lad run down the granite steps. He was such a young boy to carry her hopes but what else could she do? She had to grab this opportunity.

In the room set aside for their use the young girls were almost sick with excitement. They had been told they were going into town with the housekeeper. Their working day began at five o'clock in the morning – with so many people in the house the daily chores seemed never ending. They were learning and becoming quicker at cleaning and lighting the many fireplaces throughout the house – their first chore of the day. They had not expected to be allowed leave their duties. Mrs Chambers had promised they could each have one afternoon a week free when they had completed their three months training. Today's outing was a delightful shock. It had taken all of their time to keep from screaming with excitement when told of the treat in store for them.

"Sarah, what are we supposed to wear?" Bridget, like her friends, had never had a choice of outfit before. She stared at her two friends, her beautiful face a ghostly white.

"Take off your mob cap, silly!" Sarah pulled the white elasticised cap from her friend's head. "We don't need to change our clothes – remove your aprons and hang them up." She pointed to a row of nails hammered into the bare brick walls. "That should be sufficient – I think."

"Cook said we were to wash our face and hands." Ruth too was pale and shaking. "Mrs Chambers said we should wrap up warmly because it is cold outside."

"We are going out!"

The three girls clutched each other and danced wildly on the spot.

"I wish we had long hair to protect our heads," Sarah said sadly when the first moments of high spirits had passed. "Those straw bonnets won't offer much protection from a chilly wind."

"You can grow your hair now," Bridget knew how much it upset her friend to have her hair shorn. Well, none of them liked it.

"I hope and pray that we can do many things now that we couldn't do before," Ruth said.

It was a scary and exciting time for all of them.

"*We are going out.*" Bridget repeated the words in

wonder. "I can't wait. I wonder where we're going. What will we see? It's all so exciting."

Violet, on Mrs Chambers' order, took control of the three young girls. It was a wonder to her how excited they were to be offered the chance to walk in this cold weather. She'd stay in the warm house, thank you very much. Look at the carry-on of them – daft articles – you would think they'd been offered diamonds.

"Let me see you." She had the three girls stand before her. They were in the small hallway off the kitchen where staff left their outdoor clothes. She carefully examined the trio to insure they would bring no shame to the house. "You will need to wrap these scarves tight around your neck." She had found scarves left by long-ago servants in the cupboard. They weren't ideal but they would keep the youngsters warm at least. She pulled at Bridget's scarf and watched the other two repeat her movements. The knitted gloves held inside the sleeves of their black woollen coats by a string would keep their hands warm.

"Take those hats off again." She sighed at the sight of their shorn heads. They would freeze out in this weather. She thought for a moment before hurrying into the kitchen to consult with Cook.

"Mrs Powell," she said as soon as she opened the door that led off the back hallway into the kitchen, "them straw hats on the girls are worse than useless for this weather. I saw some of those woollen hats the men wear at sea in the clean laundry. Should I take three of them to put under those straw bonnets, do you think? We'll have to do something to keep their poor heads warm."

"I don't know why them nuns have to shave them girls

like convicts." Cook was at a loss with no meals to prepare for the family. She had a pot of stew on the go for the staff. "You need your hair to protect you from these cold winds. Everybody knows that. You better take three of them hats. There are so many of them three won't be missed. Tell the girls to keep them by them. That will have to do until they grow hair on their heads, poor little mites."

"Thank you, Cook," Violet hurried into the laundry room to seek three of the men's knitted skull caps, the smaller the better.

"That feels ever so much better." Bridget smiled at Violet. "Thank you."

"Never mind all that." Violet examined her charges one last time. "Come along now. You'll be leaving by the front door with the mistress." She didn't know what the world was coming to – servants leaving by the front door! Still, nobody asked her opinion. She ushered her three charges ahead of her towards the stairs leading up into the main body of the house. She'd be able to have a good old chinwag with Cora and Cook when this lot left.

Mrs Chambers too was wondering what was going on. It had never been known for the housekeeper and the mistress to lead the maids around Dublin. That was left to an underservant should the need arise.

Liam had returned to the kitchen clutching a familiar bottle of tonic in his cold little hand. He had passed on a very confusing verbal message to the housekeeper. Lily had passed this on to the mistress who seemed almost overcome. She'd thought for a moment they might need the smelling salts.

Lily stood adjusting her hat in the hall mirror. She felt almost guilty and looked over her shoulder to see if anyone had seen her. She dusted imagined smuts off her best black coat and waited for the three young maids. When all were ready, Lily, her mistress by her side, led the three girls out into the big wide world for the first time. The three girls, holding each other's woollen gloved hands tightly, followed the adults, breathless with excitement.

"This, girls, is the Grand Canal!" Georgina gestured widely.

She was fighting the urge to pick up her skirts and dance in the street. Richard, her dear friend Richard – the recipient of her note – had assured her he was available to her at any time. She had hope at last.

"You will, of course, have noticed the horse-drawn barges." She waited while the three young girls looked at the strange traffic that travelled the waters of the canal. "So much passes along this waterway – coal, grain, fodder, foodstuffs. The bargemen move it all." She pointed to a tall wooden structure standing high in the water. "That is the lock, it is used to regulate the depth of the water. Under no circumstances are you ever to attempt to cross it. Many people have lost their footing and indeed their lives on this canal."

Ruth and Sarah stepped away from the lock as if they were in immediate danger.

Bridget determined to cross it as soon as she was able.

Lily looked at her mistress, wondering what on earth was going on.

"This is the Mount Street Bridge," Georgina continued. "Remember that – if you are ever lost anyone can direct you to this bridge. I want you to stand here and look back at the house you will call home for some years. You all need to familiarise yourselves with the Dublin streets."

They continued in this fashion – Georgina instructing, the girls gasping at the wonders they beheld, Lily taking it all in and wondering – until they reached Grafton Street. Then Georgina demanded the three girls lead the way back to the Percy Place house. She planned to use this outing and others like it to organise her own freedom. If the girls were asked about these outings – well, they could answer honestly: they were being taught their way around the streets of Dublin.

Chapter 11

"Georgina Corrigan!" The smiling man stood when Georgina was shown into his office. "I cannot begin to express my delight on receipt of your note." He crossed the room, a tall beautifully groomed slim figure with a full head of dark hair, his hands held out to her. "How wonderful it is to see you, my old friend!" He had left his card with her butler so many times through the years, all to no avail.

Richard Wilson had to fight hard to hide his shock at his friend's careworn appearance. It had been years since he'd seen her. He wanted to pick her up and run away with her. What had happened to turn a fun-loving girl into this faded tired creature?

"It has been far too long, Richard." Georgina clasped the offered hands. She had forgotten how handsome he was. The smiling blue eyes gleaming down at her put a pain in her heart she didn't recognise. "Thank you for agreeing to see me at a moment's notice." It had been ten days since she sent that note and so much had happened in that time.

"My family have been advisors to the female members

of your own family for generations," Richard said simply.

He led his childhood friend to one of the leather chairs that sat close to a blazing fire. He'd had his man of affairs cancel his next two appointments when told Georgina was finally at his door.

"My father was upset when your husband removed your affairs from our care." The man had done this after the death of her parents in a train accident while on holiday in Switzerland.

"My husband –" Georgina bit back the words she almost said. She took a deep breath before speaking, "I don't know if you have heard." She didn't know how to continue. Richard and his family were well connected throughout Dublin and the surrounding area. He had probably been aware of her husband's plans long before she had been informed.

"It is the talk of the town, my dear," Richard didn't want her to have to force out her words. He knew what was going on. He too was biting back the words of scorn he longed to spit out. "Your husband has refused all requests for investment in his new venture. It is very rare to find the captain and owner of a ship willing to take all of the financial risks involved in a long sea journey. Dublin is positively agog with rumour and speculation." He deliberately kept his tone light.

"Richard, I need help and advice." Georgina stared into the fire, unable to meet the friendly blue eyes staring so intently at her. She had never before realised just how isolated she'd become. When she'd tried to think of anyone who might be of help to her this man's name had been top of the list.

"Anything, Georgie, you know that."

"I will not be able to pay your fees at this time." She needed to get that shaming fact across.

"There can be no mention of fees between us." Richard longed to take her in his arms. If ever anyone needed a hug it was his friend at this moment.

"That man, Charles Whitmore," she refused to call him her husband, "he left it to the last minute to inform me of his decision to undertake a long sea voyage. I had no idea of his plans." She was ashamed of the position she found herself in. "He delighted in telling me he plans to leave me penniless, Richard." She would not cry. She had little time and much to discuss. Tears were a luxury she could not afford. "He has liquidated all of the assets I brought to the marriage."

"All of them?" he was shocked into saying. He was aware of the goods Georgina brought to her marriage because his family had handled the Corrigan family assets. Georgina Corrigan had been a very wealthy plum on the marriage market. Why her father had chosen Whitmore for her was a mystery. The man had already buried two wives and was much older than Georgie. The rental properties in Georgina's portfolio would have been worth a small fortune. His man of business would never have advised selling those properties.

"It is my understanding he has sold everything he can put his hands on – I wait only for him to begin selling off my family's silver."

"Surely it can't have come to that!" Richard didn't know what he could say

"The man has dismissed all of the male servants." Georgina looked into the fire, fighting tears. That had been a shock. He had kept only Lewis, his coachman and

73

lackey – an unsavoury type she would dismiss immediately if it were possible. "He plans to remove all of my long-serving household staff. If it had been at all possible I believe he would have sold the very roof over my head." She could not hold information back. If she wanted his help she had to tell him all.

"My dear Georgie, I am so very sorry." He had seen Whitmore about town escorting a woman who was not his wife. He presented the woman to polite society, for goodness' sake! It had been so long since anyone had caught sight of Georgina Corrigan at social venues that many believed her locked in an asylum or dead and buried. He'd tried to keep interest in her alive in society but it was difficult when the woman herself seemed to have disappeared. He'd worried about her safety. He wouldn't trust Whitmore as far as he could throw him.

"I need help and advice, as I've said." Georgina straightened in her chair. "I want to know my legal position as far as my home is concerned. It is the only item of value left to me. My husband is not a young man. His first-born son is more than ten years older than me. Whitmore wasn't a very young man when he married for the first time." She took a deep breath. "If something were to happen to him on this long journey he plans – am I obliged to offer a home to his adult children?"

"My dear!" Richard almost laughed aloud. Georgie might look as if she were beaten down but her very sharp business brain was ticking over just fine. The man was a fool to underestimate her. "The house belongs to the female line of your family. You have no obligation to house Whitmore's male issue by other wives."

"I need to know what my position is. And I need to

plan how to survive on very little income. The house – at my husband's orders – is to be practically closed up." A broken-hearted sob escaped her. "I am to be a caretaker-in-waiting apparently." She knew without being told that the thought of her struggling to survive amused Whitmore. He had demanded three orphans – not out of kindness – but to embarrass her in front of her relative when she was forced to return the girls to the convent through lack of funds.

"How long do we have to plan?" Richard didn't offer any sympathy. It would serve no purpose at this time.

"He plans to sail – if nothing prevents it – in less than three months' time." She glanced at him. "That is all I am allowed to know." She'd only learned that much by pressing her ear to the walls. No need to share that with her old friend.

"I believe we need to begin a whispering campaign," Richard said after thinking for a few moments. He slapped the arms of his chair. "The situation you find yourself in is disgraceful."

"A whispering campaign?" she questioned.

"You cannot be involved, my dear Georgina. It would not be at all the thing. If, however . . ." he smiled at her, his blue eyes twinkling with all of their old mischief, "your housekeeper should happen to mention to others of her ilk the disgraceful way her mistress is being treated . . . if your maids should happen to mention the matter while tending their daily chores … that would be different."

"A whispering campaign – I see." Georgina almost smiled. He always did have a cunning mind.

"You have friends in society who would be only too willing to add their efforts to the campaign. If, that is, you will give me permission to discuss the matter with them." He waited to see her reaction. She had been absent from the usual round of society since her marriage. Did she know Whitmore was cordially despised?

"I owe my husband no loyalty," Georgina contented herself with saying. She had lost touch with her own friends. She never saw her parents' old acquaintances. She had been so shamed by her situation she had allowed herself to disappear from all of her old haunts.

"I must speak to my father about this matter," Richard said. "I have not handled the financial affairs concerning your family's holdings. He will be far more knowledgeable. If there is a way of helping you, Georgie, I will do everything in my power to find it."

"That is all anyone can ask." Georgina stood. "I have arranged to meet my housekeeper. I must not tarry here. I could only arrange this meeting on the spur of the moment." She knew if her husband found out she'd visited these rooms he would make her pay in pain.

"I will endeavour to find someone to carry messages to you." Richard had long wanted to be in contact with Georgina. He'd held back, not out of fear of her husband, but out of respect for Georgina herself. "The young lad you sent with your note is I fear too young to be entrusted with your wellbeing."

"I have not had a great deal of time to plan my efforts." Georgina had not realised – until she'd tried to think of a contact – how much her husband had separated her from all of her old acquaintances.

"You know how my father loves to be thought a modern man," said Richard. "He has had one of those darn telephones installed in his office. The service is patchy and only available in Dublin at the moment. He has invested in the company and claims it will make him rich in years to come."

"Really?" Georgina had read about the wonders of telephones but she had never seen one.

"I wondered if that darn machine might be a way of you contacting me." Richard thought it was ridiculous that they lived but moments away from each other yet had to play hide and seek to contact each other. "The post office has telephones available to the public, I am told."

"I have never even seen a telephone much less used one." She wouldn't have a clue how to use the machine to contact someone. But surely someone at the post office could show her?

"I will think long and hard on the matter. We must be in contact. The time left to you is very short. We must begin our whisper campaign at once. You must be aware of everything we are doing in your service." He knew society loved a whisper of scandal. People loved to think they were the first with any information going around town.

"I have to leave you now." Georgina stood. She was nervous of being seen leaving this house. She did not believe she could hold her secrets under the power of her husband's fists. The man was relentless when he wanted to know something. "I have three young maidservants newly arrived at my home. I intend to be active in showing them around Dublin over the next few weeks. I will do everything in my power to let you know where we might bump into each other. My husband would never lower himself to question servants."

"I will seek advice from my father. He is a wise old

owl, as you know." Richard stood to accompany her out. He hated to see her leave. "He will want to do everything in his power to help in any way he legally can." His father was very fond of Georgina Corrigan and detested the man she'd been forced by her parents to marry.

"In my free time over the next days I will give all of my attention to devising a way of keeping in touch with you, Richard." She could feel her old joy in life returning to her – it was a heat in her blood. The promise of freedom from her husband was heady stuff. She needed to be careful her husband was not made aware of her rise in spirits.

Chapter 12

"Mrs Chambers, if I might have a private word." Violet Boyle was shaking in her sensible shoes. She'd had enough. This house had never been her idea of a happy home but the last month had put the tin hat on it as far as she was concerned.

"Of course, Violet." The housekeeper tried not to sag where she stood. She was exhausted from trying to run a house understaffed. "Come into my sitting room." She turned to the cook. "Any chance of a pot of tea, Cook, for two?"

"I'll have Ruth serve you." Betty Powell too was feeling the pressure. Thank goodness that young girl Ruth Brown knew what she was about in the kitchen. Say what you would about the nuns, they trained the youngsters well.

When Ruth had served the two women she withdrew from the sitting room, returning to her duties. Only then did Violet speak.

"Mrs Chambers, I want to talk to you as one woman to another." Violet's hands were shaking so much the cup was dancing in the saucer.

"When have you ever done anything else, Violet Boyle?" Lily waited to see what other headaches were to be delivered.

"I have to tell yeh first off that I'm looking for other work." Violet had been working in this house for years. She felt it only right that she give the poor housekeeper some warning. "Me and Cora both – we don't want to leave – this place is very convenient for the two of us, being only a short walk away from our own doors."

"I will be very sorry to lose you both." Lily wasn't surprised. The work load with extra people constantly underfoot and no male servants was backbreaking.

"It's not only that ..." Violet leaned forward to refill her cup. She hadn't even noticed drinking the first one. "This morning while cleaning the grate in the second drawing room Liam heard something he didn't understand . . ." She took a deep breath, still unable to believe her own thinking. The lad had asked her to explain the matter to him. "Liam was on his knees in front of the fireplace with the door open. The young men were in the hallway, getting ready to go out." Violet felt she should explain. "Liam said the men were talking of turning the room into a gentlemen's club – they were planning where to put furniture. They discussed the best place to order large quantities of spirits – the Lord knows that room is a disgrace every morning."

"Spit it out, Violet." Lily knew there was more to be said. She needed to know what was going on in the house.

"There's talk around the town." Violet said. "I've heard it and so has Cora. Truth be told, we've tittered about it on our walks home of an evening."

"Violet . . ."

"They're saying as how a house of pleasure is opening up in Percy Place." She'd heard a lot more than that. "I couldn't imagine such a thing happening – this has always been a respectable place – well-thought-of, like – Mrs Chambers – I'm sorry for even thinking it – but I have to say it – what if everyone is talking about this house?"

"In the name of God, Violet Boyle!" Lily was shocked to her toenails. Surely such a thing wasn't possible. Could that man be that evil? Oh, the shame of it – at that thought she froze. It would be just like him to spread those rumours while he sailed away, leaving her poor mistress to deal with the disaster he had created.

"I'm only telling what I've heard." Violet and Cora had talked long and hard before deciding to tell the housekeeper what they thought they knew. Violet was afraid. Those three young maids had been here a month now. In spite of the hard work, the good food they were eating showed. They were becoming three little beauties with softly glowing skin, bright eyes and a smile always on their lips. The way the master looked at those young girls whenever he passed them made her skin crawl.

The two women sat in silence for a while, neither knowing what to say.

"I wanted to ask your permission to remove those silk Chinese rugs from the second drawing room." Violet had said what needed to be said. Now she had work to do. "Those men haven't gone into the first drawing room, thank heavens." The best room in the house was kept perfect at all times in case of visiting dignitaries. "I can't clean in a way I'd like with only two young girls to help me. Cook needs Ruth's help in the kitchen. The tables and floors in this house are scuffed and burned from those smelly cigars. The entire house is a mess and I'm ashamed of it!"

"Show me." Lily pushed to her feet – her stomach had been knotted for weeks. The house felt like a powder keg.

The two women hurried up the stairs. As soon as they stepped into the main part of the house the mistress appeared from her sitting room.

"I want the three maids to accompany me around town today," she said as soon as the two women reached her side.

"If you would come with us first, madam," said Lily. If what Violet believed could possibly be true, the mistress needed to be made aware.

Georgina followed without question.

"Before I open this door," Violet stood with her hand on the doorknob of the second drawing room, "I want to say I have only two hands." She pushed open the door, allowing a waft of stale cigar smoke to escape into the hallway.

"Dear Lord!" Georgina stood in the open doorway, staring in shock. The room was a disaster with overflowing ashtrays on every surface. The floor seemed to be covered in overturned dirty glasses.

"The maids and me have removed the worst of it," Violet said.

"I've been retiring early," Georgina said, almost to herself. She been escaping the all-male household in the only way she knew.

"Those poor little maids haven't," Violet offered. She was leaving this place but not before she'd had her say. "They don't get to their beds till all hours of the morning. They run up and down them stairs all hours of the night, carrying sandwiches and fresh glasses and whatnot. Cook and me have tried to let them sleep in of a morning but the work in this house is never-ending."

Georgina walked around the room and examined the damage done to the furniture. "I am going up to the attic. There is furniture there that has been ignored for years. I intend to remove the best pieces from this room." She hurried from the room, fighting tears. "Send the young girls up to help me move items."

"The bedrooms haven't been cleaned yet!" Violet protested as she lost the only help she had.

Georgina turned at her words. "My husband's sons brought their own servants with them. What exactly have those men been doing?"

"Not making beds and washing linen, that's for sure," Violet said.

Georgina stood for a moment, sucking in great gulps of air. It would do no good to start screaming – she feared she'd never stop.

"Violet, return to the kitchen," she said. "I want the three maids sent up to help me. Mrs Chambers, come with me if you would." She started to walk towards the stairs. "Violet, have Cook make a large pot of tea. Tell her I said that she, Cora and you should sit down and drink it." Picking up her skirts, she hurried up the stairs.

"Heavens above!" Georgina, with Lily and the three maids at her back, stood in one section of the attic used for storage and stared around. "How on earth are we supposed to find anything?" She spun slowly on her heels, staring at the small mountain of travelling trunks stacked against the walls and spilling over the floor.

The three maids stood with their eyes wide open, hands behind their backs, longing to open the boxes and discover what they were sure was hidden treasure.

Lily looked at the three maids. There were far more urgent matters to take care of and she needed to let Georgina know Violet's news. She gave her mistress a look, with a tilt of the head towards the door, hoping she would interpret it, and took charge.

"I'm afraid this will have to be tackled and sorted before we know what we have." Lily wanted to shove everyone from the attic. She forced herself to think. "Madam, if you would give Sarah paper and pencil. Ruth can fetch cleaning cloths and a bucket of water."

"Come with me, Ruth, Sarah." Georgina felt a sinking in her stomach. She had noticed the worry in Lily's eyes. What more could happen?

When the others had left, Lily turned to Bridget. "I want these travel chests opened – make a list of what each contains." She almost pushed her hands through her hair in frustration. This was not how she had planned to spend the day. "I need to know what we have on hand."

She hurried from the attic, leaving a delighted Bridget behind her.

"Dear God above," Georgina stared at Lily, unable to believe what she had just been told. Violet must be mistaken. "Surely even that man could not be so vile?" She had withstood physical and mental abuse for years. But this – this had the power to defeat her – such evil intent was beyond her understanding. "His sons would surely object." She stared at her housekeeper, longing for the woman to reassure her.

"What young man would sneer at having his own brothel?" Lily wasn't going to put a fine hat on it. That was what they were talking about.

"I can't think." Georgina could feel the tears running down her face. She didn't fight them. She had thought her life with her husband to date had been a nightmare existence – but this – what was she to do? She literally shook herself. She could not afford to sit here, waiting for events to happen. She had to do something. "Send Liam to me. I want him to run over to The Lane and fetch the wise woman. If there is any truth in what Violet suspects that woman will know. Granny hears everything, it seems." The woman was not that old but had long ago earned the title of Granny Grunt as a sign of respect for her knowledge. She was happy to answer to it.

"Is that wise?" Lily asked. "Do we really want to wash our dirty linen in public?"

"It would appear we are the last to know what is being said and done." Georgina felt her energy drain away. She had to fight the longing to take to her bed and pull the covers over her aching head. She was so tired of fighting. "I need to talk to Granny. We cannot act on Violet's suspicions alone. If Granny knows anything of this matter, then I'll meet with Richard Wilson." She'd had several chance meetings with her friend over the last month. The whisper campaign had been put into effect. She had thought to wait but that was now impossible. The man she had foolishly married must be stopped.

The girls in the attic were forgotten while Liam was sent for the wise woman. The Lane, an area across the Grand Canal, was hidden from its wealthier neighbours. The tenement block in The Lane housed a great number of people. The wise woman lived and worked in the tenements and surrounding areas.

"It's true enough, I'm afraid, petal," Granny said as she sat in a comfortable chair pulled close to the fireplace. "I wasn't sure what house they were talking about." She'd wondered who would be foolish enough to do something that would have their neighbours up in arms. This was a respectable terrace.

"I can't allow the rumours to continue." Georgina had been hoping against hope that Violet had been mistaken.

"That husband of yours is a bad bastard." Granny stated what she felt to be truth. "I didn't believe men raised by the Earl of Camlough would behave in such a fashion." She tried to nudge Georgina in the direction she wanted her to go.

"The grandfather?" Georgina had rarely met the man. The three stepsons he raised came to visit during the holiday periods only.

"He's in Dublin, you know," Granny informed her. "The man has a house on Merrion Square for when he comes to visit."

She wanted to shout aloud at the woman's dazed expression. She had a man of standing and wealth close to hand. She needed all the help she could get to fight this battle. If she didn't come to that conclusion herself soon Granny was going to shake her.

86

Chapter 13

Betty Powell looked at the letters in her hand with a shiver of distaste.

"The tradesmen said I was to put the messages into your hand," Liam said importantly. He'd waited until Cora had stepped out to the wash house to pass on the letters. He'd been told to be sure Cook was alone. Well, he'd done what they said. "They paid me an all." Money he'd passed to his ma with his chest puffed out. "They said as how they have sent their boys with letters that aul' Lewis took." Liam, with Betty's permission, had been to see his family in The Lane. His mother had just had another baby. "There was a message waiting for me with me ma when I got home so I went to see what they wanted."

"Good lad," Betty said. "Go find Violet. She'll have little jobs for you." Poor Cora would be up to her elbows in hot water. There was so much linen to be washed these days. The work went on forever.

Betty opened the first of the letters addressed to her when the lad ran off. She skimmed the typed message – the contents gave her such a shock she stood with her hand on her heart for a long moment. She tore open the second envelope. The message inside was almost a copy of the first. She sat on one of the stools pulled up to her kitchen work table.

"What is the world coming to?" she whispered, staring at the letters she'd dropped onto the work surface. "I never ordered this lot – I never received it either – and just look at what's on order for next week." The third envelope was addressed to the housekeeper. "Lily is up with the mistress," she said to herself. She had sent Cora up earlier with a tray of tea. They would be still together. "I'm not fit to handle this."

With a deep sigh Betty got to her feet and walked towards the stairs leading out of her little kingdom. She didn't often visit the main part of the house.

Upstairs, she knocked and received permission to enter.

"I'm sorry to disturb yez," she said as she pushed open the door of the mistress's sitting room. The envelopes were clutched in her fist. "I didn't think this could wait."

Georgina and Lily were trying to make a list of chores that the lack of staff prevented from being carried out. The two women looked at the cook in surprise.

"I gave Liam permission to run home and see his ma." Betty accepted the seat at the table that Lily indicated. "His ma – God love her – had another baby." She held up her hand when the others looked like commenting on the matter. "The local tradesmen had left messages with Liam's family." She held up the letters in her hand. "Two for me and one for you, Lily." She passed the closed envelope to the housekeeper. "You need to see these, madam." She passed the other letters across the table to Georgina.

"What on earth?" Georgina looked from the letter to Betty. "Did you order all of this food from the greengrocer and butcher, Cook?"

"No, I did not!" Betty snapped. "I didn't receive any of it either."

"This is from the wine merchant." Lily held up the papers she'd taken from the envelope. "The orders he has received from this household would do a public house credit." She passed the two pages to her mistress.

"Liam told me," Betty tapped the table top, "that the tradesmen told him Lewis has received copies of these invoices and letters. He never passed them along to me." The house was beginning to feel like an armed camp to her. It was them and us now. Lewis the coachman had always been a disagreeable sort but she had never taken him for a thief.

"Cook," Georgina was at a loss, "you and Lily perform wonders with the pitiful sum my husband allows for household expenses. These luxuries," she shook the papers she held, "have never been available in this household."

The three women stared at each other, each hoping the other would offer a solution to this conundrum.

A knock on the door solved that problem – for the moment.

"Sorry to bother you . . ." Violet pushed her head around the door at the brisk "Come in!" from her mistress. "Have you sent those three girls out – only I could do with a hand?"

"I asked them to work in the attic until you had need of them." Lily said. "They are enjoying clearing that space." She'd been using the attic to keep the three girls out from underfoot while the work in the house was so uncertain.

"They didn't come to the table for lunch," Betty said.

"What on earth are they doing?" Lily stood, glad of the break.

"Them little lambs are too used to the nuns – you stay where they put you – until they tell you to move. Those girls don't take a piss without asking for permission." Betty didn't consider she was being vulgar. They were all women after all and understood bodily functions.

"I should check what they've been doing." Lily went towards the door still being held open by Violet.

"I'll come with you." Georgina needed to move – her body ached from the latest series of blows, even if they were not physical in nature.

"I'd like to see what they've been up to." Betty had lost all pride in her kitchen – she didn't know if she was coming or going down there these days. She welcomed the prospect of a break. The letters from the tradesmen had upset her. Surely, if there were to be functions that needed so many supplies, she should have been the first to know. But obviously the mistress hadn't been informed either. She'd be glad to have something to take her mind off the problems that never seemed to stop coming these days.

Violet went about her business. The house was looking neglected. It hurt her pride to see the place she had tended for years looking as if no one cared. She had only two hands. She could only do so much.

The three women stood panting in the open doorway of the attic room – it was a long climb up there.

The three young maids crawling around the floor were

unaware of their audience, intent on their discovery of the wonders the open chests contained.

"What in the world have you been up to?" Lily asked. "You three are dirty as chimney sweeps!"

The three girls jumped to their feet. They stood almost swaying, the window they had opened blowing a gentle breeze at their backs.

"We've been making a list of the contents as you asked." Bridget held up pages filled with her fine writing. "We open the trunks – make a list – put a number on the side – then we dust the outsides. We push the ones we finish over there." She pointed to a nearby wall with satisfaction. Tall stacks of polished leather trunks and boxes stood almost to attention. The three girls were covered in dust and cobwebs.

"Why didn't yez come down for something to eat?" Cook looked around the packed room. "Yez must be starving."

Lily looked around, surprised by the amount of work the three youngsters had completed. "You need to clean yourselves now and get something to eat." She turned to walk away. "Come, madam," she said to a staring Georgina. "We need to complete our own list."

"Please, Mrs?" Bridget's voice stopped the women from leaving.

They turned back.

"Tell them!" Bridget nudged Sarah.

Sarah lowered her head till her chin rested on her chest.

"Tell them!" Bridget insisted.

"Tell us what?" Lily said when Sarah remained silent.

"For goodness' sake, Sarah Black," Bridget said, "will

you tell them what you told us?"

"*Biddy!*" Ruth hissed in warning.

"Sarah?" Lily prompted.

"I found the most gorgeous crinolines I've ever seen." Sarah raised her head to say. She dropped her chin back on her chest.

"Bridget, why don't you tell us?" Georgina said gently. They would be here all day if they waited for Sarah to gather her courage – poor child.

"Please, madam," Bridget stepped forward, "Sister Mary Margaret said Sarah had," she had to stop and think for a moment, "the most talent for sewing that she had ever come across." She waited for the adults to nod. "Sarah can turn a crinoline into a fashionable dress for you, madam." She tried not to allow her eyes to examine the shabby outdated garment the mistress of the house wore. It was so faded it was difficult to know its original colour. "Sarah is 'a genius with fabric' – Sister Mary Margaret said so." She took a deep breath. "We found a sewing machine –" She pointed to one of the polished crates.

Lily looked at the three girls carefully. Why had they been sent to this house ahead of the normal season for staff changeover? She had wondered this before. Ruth, to hear Cook tell it, was a natural cook. Now they were being told Sarah was an exceptional seamstress. Bridget was organised, intelligent and a self-starter – something rare in orphans. Such orphans were sought after by the big houses with large staff numbers. The nuns could charge a premium for them. Why had they been sent to a modest town house? It didn't make sense.

"Can you truly do this?" Georgina took Sarah by the

chin and gently raised her head. "There will be no shame in it if you can't." She smiled down at the blushing maid.

"Oh yes, madam!" Sarah would be thrilled if she was allowed handle the dresses they had found in many of the trunks. "It's very easy to change crinolines into fashionable garments. There's so much fabric in the crinolines – you just pull the excess in the skirt back into a bustle – I've done it before. It works."

"Just a moment," Cook said when it looked like they were going to attack the matter immediately. "Before we get lost in a fashion parade," she smiled at Ruth who was looking lost, "I think these three young maids need to be washed and fed. These aul' boxes are going nowhere."

"Very sensible, Cook," Georgina smiled. "I was lost in the thought of having something I'm not ashamed to wear." She pulled at her faded skirt. She did not consider it foolish to speak so in front of staff. They had eyes in their heads after all and her appearance was a disgrace.

"Come along!" Lily held out her arm. "We will let these youngsters go downstairs with Cook. We can discuss the matter of what has been found here when they have been washed and fed."

"Yes, Mrs Chambers," the three maids said almost as one.

Now that they had stopped working they realised they were hungry and thirsty. They hadn't noticed the passage of time.

With Cook leading the way, the group walked down the attic steps and then to the servants' stairs, while Georgina and the housekeeper made for the main staircase. "Yez can wash yer faces and hands first." She stood at the top of the stairs while the three maids started down the stairs, then gave a nod to her employer and the housekeeper before following.

Georgina turned to her housekeeper when her cook had taken the youngsters away. "Do you think it's possible that child can do what she says?"

"Sarah is not one to boast," Lily said.

"She doesn't need to," Georgina laughed. "Bridget will do it for her."

Chapter 14

"What a strange day!" Bridget was rubbing her short hair with a drying cloth. They had all three had long hot baths this evening. The work in the attic had been particularly dirty – but, oh, what fun!

"The dinner was wonderful." Ruth kicked her indoor shoes off and collapsed onto her bed. "We made a cold collation for the dining room. I'm learning so much from Cook."

"Mrs Chambers said she would find me a room to turn into my very own sewing room." Sarah spun around the room – thrilled. She had not enjoyed scrubbing and cleaning up after those very untidy and ungrateful men. "She is going to have one of the men carry the sewing machine down for me to use."

"Do you think we could have a pot of tea in here? I'd love to have our own little tea party – just like the grown-ups." Bridget hugged herself. "We could set the table and all."

"You should ask Cook if it's alright, Ruth," Sarah suggested. "You know her best."

"I couldn't," Ruth objected. "It would sound too rude

– don't you think?"

"I'll come with you." Bridget wanted to hold their very first tea party. "We can ask her together. She can only say no. Oh Ruth, come on! We'll go ask her right now." She waited impatiently while Ruth put her shoes back on.

The big kitchen was empty.

"I don't think anyone would mind us making a pot of tea." Bridget wasn't willing to let go of the idea.

"You most certainly can make a pot of tea – use some of the pretty china." Lily Chambers had returned to the kitchen unseen. "Let me help you choose a pattern."

"May we truly use the good china?" Bridget asked breathlessly.

"Of course – you three have worked extremely hard." Lily was touched by how excited the two girls were – it took so little to give them pleasure. "You may each have a slice of cook's excellent cake. I'll leave you to organise that – be sure to leave the kitchen tidy." She disappeared into her own sitting room. The mistress and Cook were going to join her shortly for a glass or two of sherry.

Bridget ran off to share the exciting news with Sarah.

Ruth began to fill the kettle.

"Well, hello, who have we here?"

Ruth let the kettle down with a clatter and spun around at the unfamiliar voice.

"I say, you *are* a pretty young thing! What is your name, my dear?" The man opened his arms as he approached.

Ruth was frozen with fear. She was all alone here. Where had this man come from?

She opened her mouth, trying to force words past her trembling lips as he came close.

96

"*Bridget, Sarah, help!*" The sound she forced past her lips was a scream of sheer terror.

"Mr Richardson!" Lily almost exploded out of her sitting room.

Bridget and Sarah were now at Ruth's side, glaring at the man breathing alcohol-scented fumes all over their shaking friend.

"How may we help you, sir?" Lily Chambers took the aging roué by the elbow and practically pulled him away from the young girls. The dirty old man had grandchildren older than Ruth.

"I was feeling a mite peckish, thought I'd ask Cook for a bite to eat." Cyril Richardson turned to look again at the three little beauties he'd discovered in his old friend's kitchen – very tasty morsels all three of them.

"Ladies," Lily commanded the three frightened girls, "go to your room."

Cook strolled into the kitchen just as the girls took to their heels. It was the work of seconds to understand the situation.

"There she is!" Richardson was weaving on his feet now, the alcohol in his system showing clearly. "Wonderful woman Cook – felt a mite peckish – came to beg sustenance from your clever hands."

"Indeed," Cook contented herself with saying. She took his other elbow and between the cook and the housekeeper they began to tow the man towards the stairs.

"What on earth is going on here?" Georgina was standing at the open doorway leading to the stairs down to the kitchen. "Brian!" she snapped at her stepson's servant who was standing in the hallway. "Assist Mr

Richardson up the stairs if you would." She stepped back to allow the young man to enter the stairwell.

"Just a little peckish, my dear ..."

The man's breath was enough to intoxicate an ox, Georgina thought as he passed.

"I say, found a bouquet of beautiful young blooms just ripe for the plucking in your kitchen!" He chortled with great good humour.

"There is a selection of cold foodstuffs in the dining room!" Georgina snapped. "Brian, please serve Mr Richardson." She stepped through the door and with enormous satisfaction shoved the bolt on the inside into place.

"He badly frightened the young maids," Lily said softly. "Such a shame! They were so excited about having a tea party."

"They must still do so." Georgina worried that the drunken men upstairs might try to storm the basement to search out the beauties that Richardson would no doubt boast about discovering. She was ashamed. She knew her husband would be amused by his friend's disgusting actions and offensive comments.

"I've waited to speak to you both until I had something to report." Georgina was sitting sipping sherry in the housekeeper's room with her two old family retainers. "While I've been out and about with our young maids these last weeks I've made it my business to speak with people I pray may help me deal with the situation I find myself in."

Violet and Cora had left for the day. The three young maids were asleep in their beds. Liam had been granted permission to sleep with his family in The Lane.

"I've met with Mr Simpson, my husband's man of business." In the guise of chaperoning the new maids around Dublin's streets she had managed to arrange several quick meetings with her friend Richard Wilson.

The two women exchanged horrified glances as they Georgina reported what Simpson had told her.

"He really said Whitmore means to dismiss all of the staff before he sails?" Lily asked.

"He'll have a hard time dismissing me and Lily. We were here before that man came and I for one plan to be here when he's gone," Cook declared bravely. "I'll hide down here until he has sailed away if I have to." She held out her glass for a refill.

"I'll hide with you," Lily said.

"I'd be lost without you both." Georgina was touched by their words.

"Those poor girls can't be returned to the orphanage." Lily stood to fetch the sherry decanter from its place on her sideboard. "I believe they sent us the pick of the crop. We want to keep them – in the weeks they've been with us it's been like watching birds released from a cage."

"That's true." Cook accepted the refilled glass. "They are a joy to have around – nothing is too much to ask. And laughing – I've never heard the like."

"No, according to Simpson I am to be allowed keep the three youngsters and the boot boy," Georgina said. "Simpson was embarrassed. My husband informed him that he would pay me a sum equivalent to a housekeeper's yearly salary." She didn't know what she had done to earn such contempt.

"Did he know anything about the actual date of their departure?" Lily didn't know what to say for the best so she ignored what she couldn't change. She had some savings and a handsome bequest from Georgina's parents and grandparents – as did Cook.

"No, he didn't say."

"What are you going to do?" Lily actually thought the troubles in the house were bringing her young mistress back to life. She was showing signs of the young girl who had met life with her chin up and her fists clenched. Since the tragic deaths of her parents in the Swiss train accident five years before the old Georgina had disappeared into a grey shadow of her former self.

"I plan to release the dogs of war," Georgina said dramatically with a smile at her friends.

"You better wait until you have something decent to wear before you let these dogs loose." Cook hit the small table with a clenched fist. "If you are going to stand up to that miserable excuse of a man you need to feel your best." She turned to Lily with a scowl. "You and me, Lily, are better dressed than the mistress of the house. That man –" She stopped to take a deep breath before she said something she regretted.

"Well, you were never backward in coming forward, Betty Powell!" Lily said.

"We will have to wait and see if Sarah is capable of the things Bridget promised." Georgina liked the idea of appearing before her husband in a brilliantly coloured gown – she prayed it was not a pipe dream.

"Well," Cook tipped her glass to her lips, "listening in to our three little birds as they plotted and planned . . ." she giggled – she'd better stop drinking, "that girl Sarah was the talk of the orphanage. The nuns used her to adjust all kinds of garments they sold on – she may well be able to surprise us all with what she can craft from that old clothing."

"From your lips to God's ears, Cook." Lily well remembered the wonderful gowns the ladies of the house used to wear in times past. "I remember your mother – God rest her, madam – buying that sewing machine."

Georgina looked at her two friends with hope in her heart. She was terrified of facing her husband and his sons. How much it would hearten her to appear in a fashionable gown! That was perhaps a frivolous thought in the circumstances, but she was so tired of looking like something the cat dragged in. That too she'd come to realise was part of her husband's scheme to demoralise her. It had been a slow systematic scheme to destroy the woman she had been – and she'd let him.

"So, ladies," Georgina straightened up – she hadn't realised she was slumping in her chair, "your instruction for the coming weeks – leave the housework. But the staff remaining to us must be fed of course, Cook. We will act as a team and tear apart the basement and attic looking for hidden treasure."

"But the bedrooms!" Lily gasped. "The drawing rooms – hallways!"

"If my stepsons want to live like pigs," Georgina gulped, determined not to weaken, "they can live in a sty." She winced at the loud noises coming from upstairs. This was not the first time that her stepsons had abused her hospitality. The gossip about her home frightened her. She had confirmed the rumours with Richard.

"The neighbours will complain." Cook looked up at the ceiling in disgust. "But it won't be *him* has to face them."

"If there are to be more drunken gatherings," Georgina looked around at the cosy sitting room, "I will be making my bed down here."

"I am tired and, unlike that crowd," Lily sniffed, "I have to rise early in the morning."

"I, at least, have my bed down here to go to." Though Cook didn't think she'd be getting much sleep with that noise going on over her head. Lily's small private apartment was in the attic. She would have to fight her way up to her eerie.

"I am being forced out of my own home."

Georgina wanted to storm up those stairs and throw everyone out. It was time to take a stand. But she could not act this evening. She had not enough strength to wrestle drunken men around. Tomorrow, however – well, tomorrow was another day.

"I am going to bed." Georgina stood suddenly. "I will not cower down here. I will, however," she beamed a smile, "carry a big stick upstairs with me."

It delighted her two friends to see shades of the old Georgina emerging.

"I'll come upstairs with you." Lily too planned to carry something to protect herself even if she was forced to borrow Cook's rolling pin.

The kitchen was spotless. The girls had left everything in order. There was not a sound from their room.

"I want you to lock the door leading down into the basement after we've left, Cook." Georgina had a heavy wooden mallet she'd pulled from its hook in her hand.

"It's coming to something when we have to arm ourselves to go to bed." Lily took a meat-tenderiser from its hook near the stone sink.

Georgina put her ear to the door leading into the main hallway. "We will step through quickly – Cook, you get ready to slam the door behind us."

A loud baying sound echoed when they pushed open the door. They stepped through, their weapons at the ready. A crowd of drunken young men faced them. The door was slammed shut and locked at their backs.

"No little bouquet of beauties here," one wag shouted. "We bagged two old birds."

To jeers from the crowd the two women pushed and shoved their way upstairs.

"That," Georgina gasped. "Is more than enough!"

Chapter 15

"I hate to wake yez!" Cora's voice followed swiftly on her rap on the door. She'd heard all about the goings-on in this house from next-door's maid on her way to work this morning. Well, she'd been given permission to speak her mind by the mistress – she'd let next door know all about what was going on in here. "I hope yez got a kip with all the noise I hear went on last night. It's gone five o'clock, ladies – wake up now!" She left the door open at her back, allowing the light from the main kitchen area to seep into the bedroom.

"*Ruth! Sarah!*" Bridget, always the first to wake, almost fell out of her bed. She shook her friends by the shoulders. "*We have to get up! Ruth, Sarah, rise and shine!*"

"We only just went to sleep!" Ruth groaned.

"It can't be morning already." Sarah felt as if her eyes were glued closed. The noise from the party last night had been the worst yet.

"It is morning, I'm afraid." Cora appeared in the door she'd left open. She carried a tray with three mugs of tea – an unheard-of luxury for the three maids. "That catering crowd they got in for last night's party have left the place in a right old mess. Violet is fit to be tied. She needs you three at once if not sooner." She put the three mugs of tea on the table. "Get yourselves outside of them and get dressed. You can wash and what-not later." She hurried away, closing the door behind her this time.

"Tea served in our own room!" Bridget sipped at one of the mugs. "Can you believe it? Come on, get up!" She hardened her heart and pulled the covers from over her friends. She ignored their moans, pulling her nightdress over her head. "You have to get up and dressed."

"I hope we can finish work early this evening!" Sarah yawned. She had spent hours bent over the sewing machine yesterday. Then had to change into her dress uniform and run back and forth at the beck and call of those caterers. The noise from that party last night had been frightening.

"I don't think my legs will work," Ruth tried to stand. "We ran up and down them stairs so many times yesterday."

"Come on!" Bridget didn't want to start the day in trouble. "Cora brought us tea – drink it and you'll feel better."

The three girls hurried to dress. They gulped down the tea and, with Bridget carrying the empty mugs, left the room. They didn't stop to clean their own room. They could attend to that when the house was put back in order.

"Bridget, you stay in here with Cora and give her a hand with the washing-up," Violet ordered as soon as the girls appeared in the kitchen. "Cook would have a canary if she saw her kitchen in this state."

She thought there might be a late guest or two sleeping around the place. She'd had a look at some of the guests before she left last night. She hadn't cared for the way some of those young gents had stared at the young maids. Why, one old goat had tried to pull Bridget onto his knees. It was disgraceful. She'd told Cook who sent the maids to their room and locked the door.

"Sarah, I know you need to work on your sewing but I'll need your hands for a few hours. I'll let you go as soon as I can. Come with me now." Violet made for the stairs. "Be as quiet as you can – the house is asleep. I hate to think what the rooms upstairs are like after seeing this kitchen."

Reaching the hall, Violet hurried over to the dining room.

"Dear Lord!" She stood in the open doorway, staring into the long room that had been created by folding back the doors that separated the dining room from one of the drawing rooms. It was a blessing that the lady of the house had refused to allow the party to enter her private sitting room. "It's worse than I thought." She turned to share a horrified glance with the two girls. "Ruth, you'll have to wake Liam, I'm afraid. I'd hoped to let at least one of you sleep on this morning but this . . ." She shook her head and pushed up her sleeves. "These fires will have to be cleared out. Liam can do that. Give the lad a mug of tea, please, Ruth. Me and Sarah will get started here. We'll carry away all of the empty bottles first. It's a wonder to me anyone was able to walk out of here after drinking all of this . . ." Still, it wasn't her place to pass comment on her betters.

Working as quickly and silently as possible, they set to

106

and restored order to the main public rooms of the house. There was food walked into the carpets – spilled drinks made the floor sticky underfoot.

In the kitchen Cora and Bridget washed a seeming mountain of dirty dishes with more appearing all the time as the three maids carried trays of dirty glasses and crockery from the dining room downstairs.

"There is not a surface in the place left untouched!" Violet groaned on one of her many trips to the kitchen.

When the sweating servants at last collapsed at the kitchen table with groans, they had been working steadily for three hours. They were not finished by any means.

"I'll put the kettle on." Cora wiped sweat from her brow. "It's time to make up trays for Cook and Mrs Chambers."

The underservants served the upper servants their breakfast in bed. At one time the footmen would have carried tea trays and hot water to the men of the house. This custom had been cancelled through lack of staff.

"What time did that lot leave last night?" Violet rested her aching head on the table.

"Cook sent us to bed early. She told the caterers if they didn't have enough staff that was their problem," Bridget answered. "The noise seemed to go on for a very long time."

"Well for them," Violet said. "They don't have to get up and work."

"Can you manage to cook a full breakfast for all of us?" Cora asked Ruth. The girl was a wonder in the kitchen for someone of her age.

"Won't we get into trouble?" Ruth worried.

"We have all worked like Trojans and so I'll tell

Cook." Cora said.

The rules of the house had gone out the window with these latest shenanigans.

"How on earth did you manage this, child?" Georgina stared at the stranger in her dressing-room mirror.

She had spent two nights sleeping in one of the servants' rooms in the attic and they were the most restful nights she'd passed since her marriage. The drunken revelries could not continue. She had a plan in place. This gown played an important role in that plan.

"I cannot believe you completed such a stylish gown in such a small amount of time!"

Lily too stared. "The gown was originally one of your grandmother's old crinolines. It's fortunate that paisley is once more in fashion." The contrasting blues of the summer-weight fabric flattered her mistress and lent colour to her cheeks.

"I have enough material to make matching full sleeves," Sarah said from her position on her knees behind her mistress. She stroked the fabric of the small bustle with pleasure. Such lovely soft material – she'd never felt anything like it. The rich colours hadn't faded with time.

"You have done a very professional job, Sarah." Lily had kept the meat-tenderiser close to hand during two wakeful nights. She had been ready to rush to her employer's side if needed.

"Thank you." Sarah now had a workroom in the basement with windows that opened out on the mews garden. She'd been waited on hand and foot while she worked frantically to adjust the bodice and skirt of the old crinoline.

Sarah pushed to her feet and stepped back to examine her work. She kept her eyes well away from her mistress's bare arms and shoulders. Madam had requested the dress be made with bared shoulders with only a puff of fabric across the upper arm. She walked around to study the fall of the skirt. It looked wonderful. A far cry from the rags her mistress had been wearing. The separate boned bodice now fit her mistress like a glove.

"Thank you, Sarah – you can go. You've done a splendid job."

Georgina waited until Sarah had picked up her supplies and left the room, then she turned to Lily.

"It's almost time for the noon meal." She felt sick to her stomach. She'd never felt less like eating in her life. "My husband informed Violet that he's invited Simpson, his man of business, to join us. I don't know what his plans are. I have made no mention to him of the Earl of Camlough who will also be present."

She felt faint at her own daring. She had taken the time to visit the grandfather of her stepsons in his Merrion Square home. The man had been shocked by what she had to tell him. He too was aware of the rumours of a new pleasure palace. That had helped – but would he support her in her efforts? Only time would tell.

"Lily, can you do something with my hair, please?" She had dragged her hair back into an unattractive knot at the back of her neck for years. "I need a style that suits my sudden glamour." She walked over and gingerly took a seat in front of the dressing-table mirror.

"With pleasure, madam!" Lily couldn't wait to dismantle that ugly bun. She positively loathed it. She removed the pins holding the hair in place. "If you would lean forward and shake your head." She had often thought her mistress had hair like a deer hide – streaked with so many shades of gold and brown. It was a shame to hide her crowning glory.

"I'm afraid to move," Georgina said. "I'm afraid the dress will fall apart. How did that child achieve this wonder in so few hours?" She did however lean forward and shake her long hair vigorously.

When Lily had fashioned her mistress's hair into the latest full flattering Gibson Girl style, piled up on her head, she stepped back. The eyes of the two women met in the dressing-table mirror.

"Are you sure about this," Lily asked. "You are trembling." She was shaking with fear herself – so much depended on the outcome of this day's meeting.

"I refuse to cower from bullies in my own home anymore." Georgina stood away from the chair. She picked up a soft cobweb-fine lace shawl and spent some time before the mirror fashioning it into place. The shawl was vital to her plans.

"Cook and I are armed and dangerous," said Lily. She had kept the meat-tenderiser close to hand during two wakeful nights, ready to rush to her employer's side if needed. "We will not let any harm come to you. At the first sign of trouble we'll be there." She feared the master's temper. Would they be quick enough to assist should the need arise?

Georgina watched her bosom rise over the low bodice. She was terrified, but she was determined. Today was the day she took back her life.

"I'm ready." She raised her chin, secured the shawl and with careful steps, conscious of the delicate stitches holding her armour in place, walked from the room and down the stairs.

Lily watched her go with tears in her eyes and a prayer on her lips.

"I did not believe you," Alfred, Earl of Camlough, said when she led him into her sitting room.

He had stood with his hostess in the hallway, listening, while the servants attempted to rouse the young men. The swearing and abuse shouted from the rooms had been shocking – not what he'd expected in the home of a lady. He'd had reports from the servants he'd sent with the lads. But this – this was beyond all reasoning. How dare they behave in such a fashion? That was not how he had raised them.

"I have been quite at the end of my wits, my lord."

"I am sorry you were subjected to such horrors as you have told me of." Alfred stood cringing while listening to his grandsons insult the people employed to assist them. He would have to increase the monies he paid to the three males he had sent to accompany them.

Chapter 16

"*Woman!*" Charles Whitmore roared almost before the door had been fully opened to him.

Brian stood ready to receive the gentlemen's hats, coats, gloves and canes.

"*Where is that bitch?*" the bellow continued.

Elias Simpson passed his outer clothing to the waiting servant, wishing himself anywhere but here.

Brian kept his mouth closed. His eyes, however, expressed his disgust for the man before him.

"Father, please!" Charles Junior strolled rather gingerly down the stairs. "Some of us are feeling rather delicate this morning."

"You will feel worse by the time I've finished with you!" Charles glared around at the smudged furniture and floor of the entrance hallway. "If you are going to drink and carouse all night you'd better learn to jump out of bed with a clear head. I'll have no weaklings on my ship." He stood with his hands on his hips. "What the hell have the servants been doing? This place is a mess. Where is that barren bitch I married? *Woman! Where are you – get the hell out here!*"

Mr Simpson cringed at the vulgarity of one of his most important clients. What had he become a part of? This was not the behaviour of a gentleman.

"You bellowed." Georgina stood in the open door of her sitting room. She held one arm across her body, her shawl pulled across her torso. "Good day, Mr Simpson. How nice to see you again! I believe you are to join us for the noon meal. Have you met the Earl of Camlough?"

Alfred stepped from the room at her back.

"I haven't had that pleasure." Simpson was embarrassed for his client. What must the Earl think of this behaviour?

"What have you been up to, woman?" Charles would not be ignored. He had things to say to this bitch. He didn't care who heard him. What the hell was that man doing here anyway? He had interfered enough in his life. This was none of his business.

"Perhaps I have come at an inconvenient time?" Simpson looked ready to run.

"*You stay where you are!*" Charles roared. "Well, woman, explain yourself!"

"Father," Charlie put his hand on his father's shoulder and squeezed hard, "I am sure we are all hungry." His brothers appeared on the staircase. "We can discuss whatever has upset you while dining surely?"

The three youngest men looked positively ashen. It was Edward who found the poise to ask. "Grandfather – what are you doing here, sir?"

"We will speak later." Alfred wanted to see and hear more. He wanted his grandson's sire to forget his presence as the man seemed wont to do.

"Well, come on, all of you!" Charles growled. "I'm

hungry if you are not. I've been aboard ship since the early hours of the morning." He led the way towards the dining room, stopping only for a moment to roar, "*Chambers, see the meal served!*" Without a hitch in his stride and no vestige of embarrassment he entered the dining room.

"Allow me, madam." Alfred offered his arm to Georgina.

With only a moment's pause to consider, she accepted the offer.

Simpson silently followed after them, heartily wishing he had not come.

"Sit there, Simpson!" Charles waved his arm towards the chair to his left.

Charlie took his place at his father's right-hand side.

Georgina was seated at one end of the table. The Earl of Camlough sat in the chair his grandson indicated. He did not expect to enjoy this meal

Ruth placed bread rolls and butter curls on the table. Cora ladled a light soup into soup dishes from the tureen on the sideboard and Ruth carried them one by one to the table, placing each before a diner. When the soup had been served Cora, Ruth at her heels, withdrew.

"Now, woman," Charles glared down the table, ignoring everyone else, "Simpson tells me you have been spending my money like water flowing from a tap." He beat the table, upsetting his soup bowl. "Explain yourself!"

"Mr Simpson is mistaken." Georgina leaned forward for a bread roll, deliberately allowing the shawl to fall away from her body. She ignored the shocked intakes of breath and continued. "I have been unable to touch any monies without your express permission since the day of our wedding." She took the bread roll and continued with her meal. They couldn't see the trembling in her limbs.

"Madam . . ." Elias Simpson stared at the bruised, scratched and cut skin and heavens above – he sucked in a breath of horror – were there actually marks from teeth on the bruised woman's bosom? He found himself unable to utter another word.

"I deny spending any of your monies, sir." She raised her chin in a fashion that allowed all to see the bruising left by her husband's fingers around her long graceful neck.

"How do you account for the monies Simpson informs me he has paid out over recent weeks?" Charles was aware of the horrified expressions directed at him. He refused to lower his eyes. The bitch deserved everything he meted out to her. She annoyed him on an hourly basis. "He has told me he undertook these excessive payments upon your express instruction. Are you calling the man a liar?"

"Not at all – my apologies if it should appear so, Mr Simpson." Georgina forced soup past her numb lips. "You men have invited scores of rowdy friends to my house. You have delighted in ordering every delicacy available. The outstanding tradesmen bills were of an amount I could not pay. I merely informed the tradesmen of that fact." She shrugged her white shoulders – shoulders marked by her husband's teeth, hands and nails. "You gentlemen must pay for your entertainment."

"I have accounts at all of these stores." Charles pushed his empty soup bowl away. They could all stare as much as they liked. They didn't have to live with the woman. "I do not pay on demand like some peasant."

"I merely informed your creditors that you planned to leave the country for an extended period of time." Georgina felt incapable of forcing another bite down. "You hardly expected me to meet the bills you and your sons have been running up." She glared at the man at the end of the table.

It had been Richard who had pointed out to her that she would be responsible for any outstanding balances her husband left behind. It had obviously been his plan to mortify her. She'd visited each and every tradesman – her three devoted maids at her heels – and warned them to supply cash on delivery only. She had passed out a printed leaflet – prepared by Richard's office assistant – stating that she would not be responsible for any amounts outstanding.

"You have boasted to all willing to hear of your intention to leave me almost penniless while you and your sons sail gaily away, have you not?" Georgina stood, allowing the shawl to remain on her chair. She walked across to the tapestry bell pull giving everyone there a clear view of the injuries that decorated her back and arms. "Have you informed Mr Simpson that you have no intention of doing business in Ireland from the moment you sail?"

She took her seat again. She waited for the servants to respond to the bell. She had no doubt that Sarah had already told them of the marks she carried on her body. The poor child had almost cried when she'd seen them.

"Is this true?" Elias Simpson felt as if he were in a nightmare. He was to lose his most valuable client and the man hadn't told him? How could any man sit there calmly while the damage he had inflicted on his own wife was

116

shown clearly to all? "You are to withdraw all of your business concerns from Ireland? I really believe this is something you could have discussed with me. It would have been the decent thing to do." Elias stood abruptly, shoving his chair away from the table. "But then," he said icily, "from my own observations decency appears to be something you are devoid of, sir. I will offer you no salutations – you deserve none. Madam, Lord Camlough, I bid you good day." He almost ran over the servants carrying the next course in as he exited.

Alfred, Lord Camlough, remained a silent observer – forgotten for the moment by the two people glaring hate at each other.

"You will pay for that, woman," Charles growled.

"I pay for breathing," Georgina answered. "What is one more small matter?"

"Where are the silver chargers?" Charles demanded when he finally took note of the porcelain dishes the servants were holding. "Do not tell me they have not been cleaned." He beat the table. "*I am to be served my meals from solid silver, damn it!*"

The servants ignored him. They served the meal before departing with almost indecent haste.

"I have lodged all of my family's silver with a pawnbroker," Georgina said when the door closed behind the servants. "I am awaiting their valuation. I will need to borrow money, will I not?"

"*That silver belongs to me!*" Another bump of the table.

"No, it does not." Georgina had been well informed of her rights by Richard Wilson. "In fact, there exists a list of contents that are to be held in trust by the female owner

117

of this house. The list is lodged with my parents' man of business – Mr Wilson."

"Wilson, *pshaw!*" Charles tucked into his meal, appetite apparently unaffected. "I dismissed him – useless individual."

"However," Georgina delighted in informing him, "I never dismissed him therefore he holds the documents concerning all matters to do with this house."

"Well," Charles glared at his sons, "have you all lost your tongues – nothing to say to all of this? What about you, Charlie boy? And you are usually quick to put your oar in, Camlough."

"I have been rendered speechless." Camlough wondered what his own child had suffered at this bully's hands. Dear Lord, had his own daughter been physically abused under his very eyes?

"I believe my brothers and I are beyond speech," Charlie almost whispered. Had his own mother been forced to suffer as this poor woman had? He had been so young when his mother died – he would not have noticed. He did recall the decline of his father's second wife however. Had she too been abused? A slap or push when a woman was being disobedient could be forgiven – but this? What on earth had his father done to her? She had so many shades of horror running over the parts of her body on view she looked like a tattooed lady he'd seen at the fair as a youngster.

Georgina made a point of meeting the eyes of every young man there. "This house and its contents belong solely to me. Your father – because of our marriage – is allowed to live here in his lifetime. This house will never pass out of the female line of my own family." She waited while they adjusted to that knowledge. "You have all abused my hospitality beyond the bounds of decency."

"Hear, hear!" Camlough glared at his grandsons.

"The servants and I will conduct a detailed stocktaking of the items listed with the Wilsons to ensure no articles of value have been removed from the premises." Georgina took a deep breath. "While we are tending to this matter, I wish all of you to leave my home. I am forced to allow your father to live here – you lot, however, can go to hell. I have had quite enough of all of you. You are not welcome to return until you have learned manners."

"They are my sons!" Charles laughed at her feeble attempt to take control. "They live where I say."

"I want you all out of my home." Georgina ignored her husband. She knew she'd pay later in pain but things could not continue as they were. "You young men have come and gone for years. You have abused my home, living rent free for all that time. You have all treated me not as a stepmother or even a distant relation but as a rather dim-witted servant. It has not been a pleasant experience."

She waited to see if any would be brave enough to offer excuse. When they remained silent, she continued.

"I am obliged to house your father under the laws of the land." She pushed her untouched meal away from her. "However, I am under no obligation to house his adult children. You are all off on your big adventure – all men together out to conquer the world. I am to sit here quietly with no servants and not enough money even to heat this house. I think not. I wish you bon voyage."

Alfred waited for his grandsons to apologise for their abhorrent behaviour. The silence in the room was almost painful. He too remained silent, not wanting to be asked to leave.

"At this very table you have all heard your father gloat about his ability to leave me in penury. I have never heard you object to his plans. This house will be my only source of income and my greatest expense. I will need to rent out the rooms you have used up to this point at no cost to yourselves."

Not even the sound of cutlery being used broke the silence that fell after these comments.

"What are we to do with all of our goods?" Charlie looked to his father who now remained silent. Only his eyes moved, promising deadly retribution to Georgina.

"My God!" Alfred jumped to his feet. He had had enough. What kind of men were these? They should hang their head in shame. "I will remove my three grandsons and their servants from your home, madam." He bowed from the waist to Georgina. "I cannot express my horror at the behaviour of my relations."

"The fault is not yours, my lord. They are all old enough to be independent and responsible for their own actions." Georgina stood and, with a look of disgust at the men who remained seated, turned to walk from the room. "I bid you good day, m'lord. You will excuse me, I pray. I have matters to attend to."

She walked out of the room and into the open arms of her housekeeper and cook. It was only their combined efforts that succeeded in getting her down the stairs and into the kitchen.

Chapter 17

"Yer white as a sheet." Betty Powell helped the housekeeper lower Georgina into a chair at the kitchen table in the alcove. They had no soft seats to offer. She wanted to cry at the marks of long-term abuse decorating her poor mistress. The man was a monster. "Did yeh manage to get a bite of that good food I sent up there down yeh?"

"I had some soup." Georgina knew Betty equated food with love. "I'm deathly afraid it's going to make a reappearance." She clamped one hand over her mouth, the other pressed against her stomach.

"Biddy, put the kettle on!" Cook shouted towards the three maids standing at the stone sinks scrubbing pots and pans. "Never mind, I'll do it meself." She thought better with something to do.

"He'll kill you for what you said up there." Lily collapsed into a chair across the table from Georgina. "I heard it all – I was in the hall."

"Richard Wilson believes killing me formed part of his original plans."

"Dear Lord!" Lily gasped. It made a horrible kind of sense.

In the dining room the five sons of Charles Whitmore stared at their father, each of them feeling as if they were seeing him for the first time. Edward shuffled his feet under the glare of his grandfather's eyes.

"You three will pack your bags and move to my house," Alfred said. "It seems you are still too young to be allowed out in polite society. I will take my leave of you now. I have never been more ashamed." He left the room, unable to remain a moment longer.

"We need to discuss the plans being made for all of us." Edward cringed as his grandfather stormed from the room. He had things to say. He had been putting off this discussion. The events that had taken place in this room had released him in a way he didn't yet understand.

"*There will be no discussion!*" Charles beat his fist on the table. "*You are all coming with me. You are all my sons.*"

"You behave as if we have no choice in the matter." Edward looked around at the others who avoided his glance. "I can't accompany you. I have the running of my grandparent's estate to attend to."

"Landlubber!" Charles dismissed the people who tended the land. "You are my son. The sea is in your blood. I want all of my sons to accompany me. It will be a great adventure – perhaps my last great adventure."

"I don't know how the others feel – but this last month together as a family has been a revelation, Father dear." Edward felt released from chains.

"You will speak to me in a respectful tone." Charles stood abruptly. His enjoyment of his meal had been ruined. It was that woman's fault. He jerked the tapestry bell pull. "I have never beaten you younger boys as your grandfather was too lily-livered to allow it, but it is not too late to start!"

"It would appear you now reserve your beatings for females much smaller and softer than yourself." Edward stood away from the table. "That is not something to be proud of, Father." He had known this day was coming. He'd seen it often enough in the animal world. There could be only one stud.

"We will have no fisticuffs in the dining room!" Charlie stood. He bravely held steady when his father tried to push him aside. "Edward, sit down. We will discuss this matter calmly."

"There is nothing to discuss." Charles glared around the room. "You will all be sailing with me – if I have to pressgang you!"

He pushed past his eldest son and stormed through the opening dining-room door. He used the flat of his hands to push Violet and Cora, who were bringing dessert in response to the bell, off their feet. He ignored the clatter of the falling trays and ran up the stairs, roaring for his wife. The bitch was hiding somewhere. He'd find her. This was her fault. How dare she come between him and his sons! The bitch had to die.

Brian and Pat, who had been waiting in the hall, hurried forward and helped the two maids to their feet. Cora bobbed a curtsey and took to her heels while Violet, with Luke's help, began to pile the remains of the dessert and coffee course scattered over the floor onto a tray.

Angry bellows echoed through the house.

Violet was back on her feet, the remains of the dessert course on her tray, when the master ran back down the stairs – still shouting. Without stopping for a moment he used his forward motion to push poor Violet back onto the floor. The food and tray went flying again.

"*Father!*" Charlie stood glaring at his parent. "*Pull yourself together!*"

Charles ignored him. He put his boot on the shaking maid's chest. "*Where is she – your bloody mistress?*" He applied pressure, leaning down to glare into Violet's terrified face. "*Where is she?*"

"*For God's sake, man!*" Edward pushed at his father's chest, almost knocking him off his feet.

"I want to know where she is!" Charles's voice was a soft whisper which was more frightening than his roars.

"She took the young maids into Dublin!" Trembling, Violet sat up. She buried her head in her knees and began to sob.

"Running away, is she?" Charles pulled his coat and hat from the hall cupboard, not waiting for a servant. "I'll soon find the bitch. I'll teach her to interfere in my affairs!"

He pulled open the door to the vestibule and still pulling on his coat opened the front door. He ran from the house, leaving the two doors open at his back.

"The man has run mad." David shook his head. "I don't know about you lot but I need a drink."

"Leave that stuff," Edward said to Violet, pulling her to her feet. "Go get cleaned up. We'll call if we need anything."

Violet took to her heels.

"Should we go after him?" William stared down at the mess on the floor. It would have been delicious, he thought, before shrugging. He too could do with a drink.

"What are we going to do?" Charlie looked at Edward.

124

"We have been given our marching orders – but we need to talk."

Charlie closed the entrance doors after staring down the street. Lord knows where the man had gone. He was seriously worried. If his father committed murder on a Dublin street they would hang him.

He turned to face his brothers. "We have to stop him finding Georgina."

"You don't really believe she ran away – do you?" David asked.

"The maid said she had," said Henry.

"She was protecting her mistress." Edward sighed and walked towards the drawing room. "Anyone seeing that poor woman's scars would protect her from the monster that fathered us." He paused at the doorway. "Brian – Pat – Luke!" He jerked his head at the three servants. "We are perfectly capable of pouring our own drinks. You three start packing up the rooms Henry, William and I occupied in this house. We are leaving as soon as our affairs are in order. Go!"

The astounded men obeyed.

"Wait a minute, big brother," William objected. "It is all right for you to walk away. You have the promise of the estate to return to – what do the rest of us have?"

"Do you really want to be on the high seas with a lunatic as captain?"

Edward took Charlie by the shoulder and gently pushed him into the drawing room. He waited till all five brothers were inside then closed the door.

"Who made you the man in charge?" William objected.

"No one." Edward poured a whiskey before falling

125

into one of the easy chairs. He winced when he noticed the mess in the room. "Could you not have asked the men to tidy up this room? I pay them to serve us, not join in our carousing."

"That's your job, big brother." Henry held up the whiskey decanter in silent question to the others.

Charlie took a glass of whiskey from Henry. "Edward is right – we do need to talk. I have to say this house has been a handy berth for years. I'll be sorry to lose it – never really gave any thought to the matter of a home before." He and David had been dragged behind their father all of their lives.

The brothers had just settled down to discuss their futures when a loud bell echoed around the house. Someone was pulling at the front-door bell. Charlie walked over to look out the window. Two soldiers, their red coats shining, stood on the top step. He closed his eyes tiredly – what now?

"It's two soldiers." He turned to the room, remembering his father's words about his sons' activities. "Is there anyone here who needs to disappear before the maid brings them in?" Four heads shook in response. He relaxed slightly. He'd wait to see what brought them here.

Cora made her way slowly to the front door. The hall was a mess with food, coffee and broken dishes spilled across the floor. She pulled the door open and almost swallowed her tongue.

"Is this the home of Charles Whitmore?" the older of the two soldiers asked.

"Yes, sir."

"I need to speak with a member of the family. There

126

has been an accident." He stepped forward as if to enter the house.

"Wait here," said Cora, raising a hand. "I'll inform the family."

She went to knock on the drawing-room door.

"It's two redcoats," Liam almost fell down the stairs in his hurry to report. "They said as how there has been an accident." He'd been hiding in the stairwell that led down to the basement.

"I'll go up." Georgina got to her feet.

"You'll need your shawl." Lily held up the lace shawl.

"Thank you." Georgina pulled her shoulders back. "I won't." She walked through the kitchen and up the basement stairs.

A heavy silence fell at her back for a moment. Then Cook came to her senses and pushed Liam in the direction of the stairs.

"You get up there and listen," she ordered. "Let us know the minute you hear anything useful."

Georgina stepped through the door from the basement just as Charlie was pulling open the door of the drawing room. He reached the soldiers first – Georgina was transfixed for a moment by the mess spilling over the carpet.

"What has happened?" Charlie demanded of the soldiers. "Why are you here?"

"The matter concerns a Mr Charles Whitmore." Cedric Barrett, the older of the two soldiers, would be damned if he'd give this news standing on the doorstep. "May we come in?"

"Gentlemen," Georgina stepped forward, "I'm the

lady of the house – Mrs Whitmore. You find us all at sixes and sevens, I'm afraid, but do please step inside." She sent Cora back to the kitchen and turned to lead the men into her sitting room.

The two soldiers stared at the marks on the woman's body. Shameless hussy, Barrett thought – exposing the damage to her flesh in that fashion. He caught the younger man's horrified expression.

"Domestic," he whispered. "None of our business."

Georgina heard the words and wanted to curse. She turned and smiled at the men instead.

"Charlie," she gestured to her stepson, closing the doors at their back, "is Mr Whitmore's eldest son – he will join us."

Barrett cleared his throat. "I regret to report, madam, that your husband Charles Whitmore was involved in an accident on Mount Street Bridge." The man had been only steps from his own home. "He was run over by a carriage."

"How badly hurt is he?" Charlie demanded. "Good God, man, he isn't dead?"

Georgina lowered his eyes in case her expression gave away her feelings. She had been sick with fear at the promise of violence in her husband's eyes. Had God just granted her a reprieve?

"Mr Whitmore was alive when the ambulance arrived." Barrett had never heard some of the curses the man painted the air with while they waited for the ambulance to arrive. "He has been taken to Doctor Steevens' hospital. I have no further information on the nature of his injuries."

"I'll go there straight away." Charlie ran from the room. He dashed across the hallway, shouting for his brothers.

"Your husband's injuries are quite severe," Barrett informed Georgina. The man wouldn't keep those legs if he was any judge of anything. "It might be best to leave this matter to the men."

"Thank you for coming. I'll see you out." She walked ahead of the soldiers through the pandemonium that seemed to be taking place in the hallway. The sons of Charles Whitmore were demanding answers from their brother, seeking information he didn't possess.

"What is happening?" Lily joined her mistress as the soldiers left.

"There has been an accident involving Captain Whitmore," Georgina said. "I have no details. The men are going to Doctor Steevens' hospital to seek further information."

Chapter 18

Georgina and Lily stood out of the way as the men prepared to leave. Liam was sent to order Lewis the coachman to prepare the carriage. They shouted for their hats and coats. They gave no thought to her nor had she expected them to. She stood for what felt a long time, staring at the mess in her hallway.

"There is no need to clean the carpet in this hall." Georgina watched while the men ran from the house and jumped into the waiting carriage. "I have every intention of removing the carpet. It covers the most wonderful tiles. Time they were displayed again." She couldn't seem to move. Was this shock?

The sound of the horses' hooves faded in the distance. The silence in the house was a welcome relief.

"Lily, if you would accompany me to Mr Wilson Senior's office?" Georgina said then. "We should not be gone long."

She was going to ask Richard's father to telephone the hospital on her behalf. It would never occur to her stepsons to keep her informed. No one had a greater need to know about that man's injuries than she. Would he be in hospital overnight or even longer?

Lily hurried away to prepare. She left the care of the house in Cook's capable hands. A pelisse was fetched for Georgina and when they were ready they stepped out of the house. The two women walked briskly to Mount Street Bridge. It was only minutes away from the house. They stood for a moment looking at the activity around what was obviously the accident site – then without comment walked on.

Georgina was greeted with great courtesy when she reached Mr Wilson's rooms. She was asked to wait and refused an offer of tea. In a matter of moments Richard's father appeared.

"Mr Wilson," Georgina stood, "I hope you will forgive this unscheduled visit."

"I am always delighted to see you, my dear." Walter Wilson smiled. He had known Georgina Corrigan since she was a child. "Do come in." He waved towards his private office.

Georgina stepped into the room. Lily would await her return in reception. Walter indicated a small leather sofa and she sat down.

"Mr Wilson, your son Richard has told me of your telephone," she said then. "I wondered if it would be possible for you to telephone Doctor Steevens' hospital for information. Mr Whitmore has been involved in an accident. The hospital must surely be on the telephone exchange, don't you think?"

"I've heard about the accident. One of my clerks was passing the scene and was a witness to the event."

Walter remained standing as he picked up the ebony candlestick-shaped device from his desk. Even in these circumstances he enjoyed being able to show off the wonder of this machine.

"This will take a moment," he said.

He turned away in reaction to something he'd heard in the device cupped to his ear. "Doctor Steevens' hospital, please, operator," he said clearly and loudly into the mouthpiece.

Turning back, he held the mouthpiece to his chest and looked at Georgina. "Richard has been very busy on your behalf lately." He stared for a moment. The whispers running around Dublin society disgusted him. Surely the situation could not be as dire as it was portrayed. Surely it was idle gossip exaggerated for the titillation of the masses. "Is it really that bad, my dear?"

Without a word Georgina unbuttoned her short pelisse. She allowed the garment to drop until it was caught on one hand. Still without speaking, she held out her arms and turned slowly. "Those are only the sites acceptable for public viewing." She kept her eyes lowered.

"Yes!" Walter said into the phone. "Doctor Steevens' Hospital?" He was grateful for the distraction. What could he say when viewing the horrors inflicted on an innocent woman by one of his own sex?

Georgina replaced her pelisse. There was no need for words. What could one say?

"I am enquiring after Mr Charles Whitmore," said Walter. "The man was injured in an accident on Mount Street Bridge and brought to your hospital by ambulance." He waited. "What . . . repeat please . . . I'm calling on behalf of his wife Mrs Georgina Whitmore," He listened intently for what felt like an eternity to Georgina. "Thank you." He replaced the earpiece and with care put the device back on the polished surface of his desk. "He is in surgery."

Walter walked to his office door and invited Lily to join them. Poor Georgina would need a female with her, he thought.

He waited until Lily was seated beside Georgina on a small leather sofa. Then, standing before them, he said. "There is no easy way to tell you. They are removing both of his legs."

The women gasped in shock.

"Will he live?" Lily took Georgina's hand in hers.

"It rests in the laps of the gods." Walter thought it would perhaps be better if the man died. A legless captain could not go to sea and the sea was Whitmore's life.

"Thank you so much for your assistance." Georgina stood up abruptly.

"Please! Allow me to order tea," Walter objected.

"Not at this time, thank you." Georgina waited for Lily to stand. "I appreciate your efforts on my behalf but now . . . I need to go home."

She was shown from the office with a tiring amount of fanfare.

"This day has felt as long as a week," Georgina remarked while the two women walked back home. She felt numb – unable to process the information she'd just received.

"And it's not over yet," Lily replied.

"Shame about this costume – Sarah worked so hard on it." Georgina passed her hand over the beautiful material. "I don't think I will ever be able to wear it again." She had been terrified that she'd pushed her husband past the limit of his rage. The very thought of meeting up with him again after her defiance of him at lunch had driven fear for her very existence deep into her bones.

"The design of the fabric is young and gay." Lily was willing to follow this inane conversation. She was dealing with the vast relief and enormous guilt she felt at her reaction to the news. She was glad the man would be unable to hurt her mistress further. "Sarah might be able to make three skirts from it for our three little maids."

"A wonderful idea."

They walked in silence until they reached the house. They turned into the gated garden and onto the walk that led to the front steps. Lily ignored the tall granite steps, making instead for the entrance into the basement hidden behind and underneath the steps. Georgina followed without conscious thought. She didn't want to think about or discuss the accident and its outcome. She would never have wished such horrific injuries on anyone. How should she feel when she'd feared the man planned to end her life? Was there a correct way to react to a situation like this?

When they entered the kitchen the girls were busy there with the cook.

Cook studied her mistress's pale face. She looked at Lily who shook her head, warning her not to ask for details. There was an uncomfortable silence as everyone seemed frozen in place.

"A lad came with a message from Edward." Cook turned to put the kettle on.

"For me?" Georgina stood with no idea what to do next. Surely she should be doing something?

"No, it was for his servants." Cook wanted to spit. They didn't even have the decency to keep her poor mistress informed. Georgina had entered the house by the front. The servants had a flatbed wagon and horses waiting at the back. She wouldn't have seen that. Should she mention it?

"Madam?" Sarah couldn't bear to see the poor woman standing there like a broken statue. She approached her mistress shyly. "I found this." She held up a lace garment in a beautiful jade colour that matched the jade in the pattern of Georgina's costume.

"What is it?"

"An indoor cover." Sarah began to remove Georgina's outdoor pelisse. Her mistress was in shock – she allowed her to remove the heavy woollen pelisse, turning like an automaton. Sarah pulled the jade long-sleeved lace garment over her arms and fastened the buttons that closed from waist to neck.

Lily gave Sarah a nod of approval. The jacket concealed the damage done to her poor mistress.

Then she said, "I regret to tell you the master has been badly injured. The nature of his injuries are such that it is believed he will be in hospital for some time. The mistress will need our support."

"Brandy," Cook said. "I'll put some in the tea – it's good for shock."

"I'll have some in my sitting room." Georgina turned towards the stairs like a sleepwalker. "Mrs Chambers, if you would ask Mr Edward's servants to share any information they might possess."

"It's a disgrace!" Cook slammed the black kettle onto the hob.

"Not now, Cook!" Georgina kept walking. "And there is no need to prepare a family meal – something warm and filling for the staff only, if you please." She picked up her skirts and climbed the stairs.

Georgina stood before the window in her sitting room sipping at a very small amount of brandy. She didn't know what she was feeling. For all her brave words she had truly believed this might be her last day on earth. She had left detailed instructions for her friend Richard as to the handling of her affairs. She had thought herself prepared – but nothing could have prepared her for this sequence of events.

The sound of a heavy item falling on the stairs distracted her. She opened her sitting-room door.

"Sorry, Missus," Brian said. "The thing got away from us." He couldn't wait to get out of this house. He had seen this woman's injuries and it shamed him. He'd wanted to take the man who had injured her out back and teach him a thing or two.

"You three are not quite what you appear." Georgina stood looking up at the three men who served Edward, William and Henry. "Are you?"

"You men carry on," Brian said to his two companions. "We need all that stuff on the cart and ready to go." He looked at the mistress of the house. He was glad she'd covered those scars. "If we could speak in private, madam?"

"Come into my parlour." Georgina stepped back into the room. She filled a brandy snifter while he closed the door at his back. "Brandy," she offered the glass.

"I could do with something." He knocked the brandy back and returned the glass to her.

"Will you tell me what you may?" She stood and

136

stared up into the eyes of a very intelligent man. She'd been watching these three – they were not ordinary servants.

"I serve the Earl of Camlough, madam – he hates your husband with a burning passion." Brian reported to the man he thought of as his commanding officer. "My men and I were sent here to protect the Earl's only grandchildren."

"I believe you received a note?" Georgina needed allies. "Was any mention made of informing me of my husband's injuries or the movements of his sons?"

"To their shame, madam – no." Brian could feel his face redden. He'd be sure to have a word with the young gents over their treatment of this woman.

"I had my man of affairs telephone," Georgina said. "I know he has lost both legs."

"Yes, madam." Couldn't happen to a better man in Brian's opinion.

"Even in these circumstances I will not have his sons under my roof ever again."

"I can't say as I blame you, madam," Brian said. "I have a flatbed wagon and a carriage waiting in your mews. My orders were to remove my charges."

"Thank you for taking the time to speak with me." She offered her hand to this man who was no one's servant.

Brian took the offered hand and held it in both of his. "You need to protect yourself. The man is vicious and he isn't dead after all. He still has that golden tongue in his head that can talk sane men into stupidity. Who knows what he might plan as he lies in that hospital bed?"

"That thought had occurred to me."

A knock on the door interrupted their conversation.

Without waiting for permission to enter, Pat's head appeared in the partially open doorway. "We're ready to roll, Sergeant."

"I'll take my leave of you, madam." Brian had much to do. "Stay safe."

"I intend to."

She walked over and stood in the open doorway as the men saluted her and left.

Chapter 19

Georgina stood at the window of her small sitting room, watching the river flow. The evenings were getting longer. The gas street lamps had not yet been lit. There had been no news from the Whitmore men. Violet and Cora had been allowed to leave for home early. They had worked hard this day. She had ordered the belongings of Charles and David to be packed up and delivered by rented wagon to their father's ship on the nearby docks.

The sudden noise of the doorbell caused her to jump.

She pushed up the sash window and stuck the top half of her body out. It might be hoydenish, but she didn't intend to open that door without knowing who was waiting outside.

"*Who is there?*"

"Is that any way to greet guests?" Richard Wilson stepped away from the doorway to allow her to see him clearly. "I have brought Mr Simpson to see you."

She picked up her skirts and ran into the hallway. She pulled the wooden step stool over to the door. She needed it to unlock the top two bolts. She opened the door, waited for the men to enter, then locked the door again.

"Is that really necessary, madam?" Simpson waited in the hallway.

"I think so." Georgina wasn't going to share her fears with Simpson.

"I asked Mr Simpson to accompany me here, Georgina," Richard said. "My father told me of the injuries to your husband."

"I would have appreciated being notified by a member of the family." Elias Simpson was disgusted that no one had thought to inform him of the accident to his client. The man might well be a bounder and a cad but nonetheless Elias handled his financial matters. He should have been informed immediately.

"I have nothing to apologise for, my good man," Georgina said. "I too have not been apprised of the situation at this time."

Georgina took their summer-weight hats and placed them in the hall cupboard. It would appear both men preferred to keep their briefcases with them. She led the way into the fresh-smelling drawing room.

"Please, help yourselves to a drink." She waved a hand towards the decanters on the sideboard. She took a seat in front of the fire and waited for the men to join her.

"What will you have, Simpson?" Richard asked.

"This is most irregular," Elias objected. "Where are the servants?" Why were none on hand to welcome guests?"

"Mr Simpson," Georgina was not going to conceal the situation from this man, "two red coats came to inform me of my husband's accident. Before the soldiers had left, Charles Junior gathered his brothers and practically ran from this house. I was not invited to accompany them. I have not heard nor seen anything of them from that moment to this. I was forced to ask my family's man of business to telephone the hospital for any news he might be able to gather on my behalf."

"Disgraceful!" Elias sat and accepted a brandy balloon. He sipped and looked from one to the other of his companions.

"I grew up with Georgina as I've explained to you, Simpson." Richard didn't want any scandal to touch his friend. "My family have handled the affairs of the females of Georgina's line for generations. I want to offer my help to her at this difficult time. She needs to know her rights and obligations. That is why I asked you to accompany me here tonight." He sat back and waited. The man had shared with him the horrors he'd seen over the lunch table.

"I have been placed in a very difficult position," Elias Simpson said. He had been shocked out of his mind to think he was doing business with a man who was no gentleman. Still, business was business. He was going to have to burn the midnight oil it would appear. He needed to study how the loss of income would affect his own revenue.

"As have I, Mr Simpson," Georgina said. "I have been left to guess and wonder about my husband's condition. I have received no information – indeed no courtesy from my husband's sons. Without the help of Mr Wilson Senior I should have been unaware of the injuries my husband has suffered. I have been left alone to ponder my position. What am I supposed to do? How do I manage the affairs of this house? Those are but two of the problems that beset me."

Elias put down his glass on a side table and removed a

folder from the depths of the briefcase he'd placed close to his chair. He took a moment to put his spectacles on the end of his nose before opening the folder. "Your husband, madam, has been liquidating his assets for some time." He glanced over his glasses. "He is a very wealthy man."

"Is he?" Georgina didn't know nor did she care. She had never seen any signs of his vast fortune – if such existed. "I myself have been penniless since the first day of my marriage. I have had to beg to cover the costs of running this house."

"Come, come, Mrs Whitmore, the cheques I cut monthly for household expenses I consider very generous." Elias stared at the woman. Did she truly believe he was unaware of her husband's generosity in these matters?

"I beg your pardon?" Georgina glanced at Richard before sitting forward in her chair to stare at her husband's man of business. Was it possible this man could answer some of the questions that had been keeping her awake at night?

"Yes," Elias consulted his notes. He named a figure that made Georgina gasp aloud and clap her hands to her mouth.

"Mr Simpson – I will ask my long-time friend Mr Wilson to bear witness that I am not a liar." She sat back for a moment, truly shaken by these events. My Lord, she wondered. How much more will I have to face? "I can state without hesitation that I have never received funds from your office. I have no knowledge of the cheques you mention. I would have been delirious to receive even a quarter of that amount per month from my husband."

"My dear madam, I personally lodge a cheque every

month in your bank account." He shook the documents he held in his hands. He had proof of all he said.

"Bank account? I have no knowledge of any account at any bank in my name," Georgina insisted.

"There is obviously a problem here," Richard leaned in to say. "Georgina is not nor has she ever been a liar. If she tells you she has seen no funds from her husband – you can believe her."

"But . . . but," Elias looked from his notes to the woman across the fire from him. "You say your husband keeps you short of funds?" He waved at the very fashionable and obviously expensive outfit she wore. "Looking at your attire, I beg leave to question your understanding of the matter."

"The gown I wear was my grandmother's." Georgina had no place for pride in this. She wanted to know what on earth was going on. "I have not received funding for new garments in years. I consider myself fortunate that a new maid of mine had the skill to refashion this garment for me. Today was my first day of wearing it."

"I hadn't seen my friend for some years." Richard sat forward to add his voice. Simpson needed to understand what had been going on here. "Her husband objected to our friendship. When we recently renewed our acquaintance, I was shocked at her threadbare appearance. I beg your pardon, Georgina – but you have looked a fright."

"You speak only the truth, Richard." She had been ashamed to be seen in public dressed in outdated and shabby clothing but what choice did she have?

"But what of the accounts you hold in . . ." Elias named some of the most expensive shops in Dublin. "I have paid their bills, madam."

Georgina stared at the two men for a moment. It was as she had long thought. "It would appear, gentlemen," she took a deep breath before admitting her suspicions aloud, "that there is more than one wife of Captain Charles Whitmore living in Dublin." She ignored their gasps of shock. "I have suspected my husband of having a second address in the city." The letters delivered from tradesmen to the Cook and housekeeper recently had been for purchases that never reached this house. She could swear to that. "I recently received notice of purchases that I had no knowledge of," she shrugged. "I began then to question some of my husband's activities."

Richard couldn't meet her gaze. He had seen Whitmore around town with another woman on his arm. He hadn't mentioned the matter to Georgie.

"Bigamy!" Mr Simpson gasped.

"It may not be that my husband has entered into a marriage with another. He is, however – I have no doubt – living as man and wife with another woman. There can be no other explanation."

The entry bell sounded, causing them to jump. The sound of frantic banging against the wood of the door followed.

"Why is this door locked?" The words in a familiar voice were accompanied by baying sounds.

"That sounds like Mr Charles Whitmore Junior," Elias said. "He sounds inebriated."

"*Let us in, bitch!*" The words were echoed by several loud male voices.

"This is the sort of outrageous conduct I have been forced to deal with in recent days." Georgina had no intention of opening the door.

"Is that why you had the door bolted against us?" Richard asked.

"Yes, I can take no more." Georgina was glad these men were here to witness the disgraceful behaviour she had been subjected to. They would be witnesses she could call upon should it prove necessary.

"What on earth is going on, Georgie?" Richard had been kept informed of some of the goings-on in this house – but obviously not all.

"This is outrageous!" Elias said as the noise of the crowd outside was joined by neighbours shouting complaints and abuse at the drunken men.

"What are you men doing here?" a stern voice demanded over the shouts of the crowd. "This is a private residence."

"No, it is not," a drunken sneer answered. "It has been turned into a gentlemen's club. I've been promised ripe little beauties for my entertainment. I'm not moving until I've been satisfied." The banging of knuckles on the door and frantic yanking on the bell sounded loudly.

"Oh dear God!" Georgina fell against the chair back, the colour draining from her face. She pressed a hand to her stomach, feeling sick.

Richard jumped to his feet. He crossed to the long window overlooking the entryway. "There are two redcoats trying to move the drunken fools along," he said over his shoulder.

"Mr Simpson," Georgina said, "you have been my husband's man of business for some time." She couldn't afford to hang her head in shame. This meeting was too important to her future. "Richard, you have been out of my life for years." She took a deep breath. "My husband, gentlemen – well, I can only say that the man despises me. I have no knowledge why. He laid careful plans to embarrass and bedevil me. It would have amused him greatly as he sailed around the world to think of me struggling to function in the mire he has created around me."

The two men stared at her with almost identical expressions of shock on their faces. They listened to the unruly crowd being forced from the front of the building, unable to doubt her words.

Chapter 20

"Aunt Allie!" Georgina gasped in surprise as she peered through the new view-hole in the front door. After the events of the past weeks she had hired a carpenter to cut it. It resembled – what she imagined from her reading – something that the doors of prison cells might contain. The carpenter had called the small door a 'face plate'. It was kept locked in place until needed.

The very last thing she had expected today was a visit from two nuns. That would give the neighbours yet more to talk about.

"Reverend Mother! What are you doing here? Come in, do!" Georgina opened the door wide, a beaming smile on her face. That didn't stop her examining the area behind the two nuns. It was thanks to Mr Simpson, Richard's warnings, and her timely precautions that she did not have tradesmen picketing her home as her husband no doubt intended.

Aloysius didn't immediately step in. "I don't believe you have met Sister Mary Margaret," she said, indicating the nun by her side. She turned her back to the main door and stood there admiring the view of the Grand Canal from the top of the granite steps. She was aware her very presence at this door would lend support to her beleaguered great-niece. "It can be very difficult to draw Mary Margaret away from her duties in the attic. But on a day such as this we should all take the time to appreciate God's blessings." She turned to enter the house.

"Delighted to meet you, Sister Mary Margaret." Georgina smiled into the kind face of the nun glancing nervously around the vestibule. "I believe I have heard a great deal about you from Sarah Black." She then bolted the door behind her guests' back. "We are living under siege conditions, I'm afraid."

"We have read of your problems in the daily newspapers," Aloysius said.

"Sister Mary Margaret – Reverend Mother." Sarah stepped into the hall and curtsied. It had been her turn to be on guard duty in the stairwell when the doorbell rang. It was all very exciting. She was delighted to see her old teacher but the Reverend Mother intimidated her.

"Mary Margaret, why don't you go with young Sarah and assure yourself of her safety. I will stay here and chat to my great-niece." Aloysius stood admiring the attractive tiling on the hall floor.

"Sarah, ask Cook to prepare a pot of tea and some of her delicious scones and cakes, please." Georgina watched the maid lead her teacher towards the stairs to the basement. With a wave of her hand towards the open door of the second drawing room, she invited her relative inside. She closed the door of the room gently.

"You appear to be looking well for all your recent troubles." Aloysius had been worried about Georgina. "I have not seen you looking so well for years."

"My improved appearance is thanks in great part to young Sarah. The girl has such skill at her fingertips." Georgina helped her great-aunt sit in one of the low comfortable chairs pulled close to the hearth. "I didn't know nuns read the newspapers, Aunt."

"While we are alone," Aloysius grabbed onto Georgina's hand before she could step away, "I want to remind you of how matters stand. I was afraid with all that has occurred you might forget. I have applied to your husband's man of business for the wage of two orphans only – there can be no note taken of Bridget's presence in your home – officially I have placed two girls only in your employ."

"But Sister Mary Margaret will see Bridget downstairs. Those three are always together."

"I trust Mary Margaret – sadly I cannot say that of all of my nuns."

"I don't understand. What is it you fear?" Surely no one would ever think to look for the legitimate daughter of a titled family in an orphanage?

"You joke about nuns reading the newspaper. Sadly, your problems have made front page news. Your name is known at the convent. There has been talk of taking the girls from your care. Bridget must never be allowed return to the convent. She is not safe there." Aloysius closed her eyes for a moment. "I'm sorry to tell you, my dear, that Bridget's father is in Dublin."

"No!" Georgina gasped. "How do you know this? The man has made no secret of his disdain for Dublin society. What on earth is he doing here? Do you know?"

Aloysius almost smirked. It was unusual for a nun to be more informed of society movements than a member of the public. "According to the newspapers, the man is courting a young woman from a very wealthy family." The name of the family she mentioned was unknown to Georgina. "New money but a lot of it."

"As if I don't have enough problems!" Georgina moved as soon as the nun released her grip on her arm. She almost fell into the chair across the cold hearth from the nun. "I pity the poor woman that man is pursuing. I pray she will not fall into his clutches. He is known to be charming. All I can do is promise to keep his daughter and her friends as safe as humanly possible."

"Sarah and Ruth are officially in your home," Aloysius said. "Bridget O'Brien – officially – has been returned to her family."

There was silence for a moment as the two women thought about the situation.

"Tell me about your problems," Aloysius said when she felt the silence had lasted long enough. Mary Margaret would be curious if she returned to a room draped in silence.

"Where to begin?" Georgina passed her hand over the navy-blue skirt she wore. Yet another of Sarah's creations – the girl was a wonder. "Well," a deep sigh escaped her, "Charles' accident was only the beginning. The man's affairs were so convoluted that we are still trying to sort them out. His man of business Elias Simpson has been kindness itself in allowing me to continue to draw on that man's funds. In fact, I am now in receipt of far more money than at any time since my wedding."

"That can only be a good thing."

"It is the only good thing to come out of this mess." Georgina turned to look towards the door as after a brief rap of her knuckles Mary Margaret entered the room.

"Come in, Sister." She jumped to her feet and pulled another chair close. "Are you satisfied with your student's living conditions?" She took the time to move a small table over close to her hand.

"Sarah is full of praise for her mistress," Mary Margaret said. "The girls appear to feel that life in this house is one big adventure. Ruth informed me with delight that tea will be served at any moment."

"I had just begun to tell my aunt of the situation I find myself in," Georgina said. "I appear to have had one problem after another in my personal life since the girls came to work here. My husband's accident has revealed a veritable nest of intrigue around the man. There are people who refuse to believe I am innocent of all knowledge of his actions. I telephone the hospital regularly for updates on his welfare. The man is fortunate that the doctors have kept him in a drugged sleep. He is able to avoid providing answers."

How could she explain the changes in her life to these two women? They had spent all of their adult life cloistered. She was only now beginning to understand the life she had lived with that man. She had never before had a long period to think about the changes he had forced upon her. The weeks since his accident had seemed to her to be a time of constant self-discovery. She had without being conscious of it allowed him to separate her from everyone she had known before he entered her life. The years of physical and emotional abuse she had been subjected to were being revealed in all of their ugliness. She was so angry at herself – what had she been thinking of to allow another to almost destroy the person she had

151

GEMMA JACKSON

been? She didn't understand the position she found herself in – how could she explain it to others?

"The newspapers have certainly taken a great interest in your husband's affairs," Aloysius said.

"What is being revealed has all the elements of a stage drama if not farce," Georgina said. "It had been that man's intention to leave Ireland long before his dealings could be uncovered. He appears to have taken a fiendish delight in creating a great many problems that I would be forced to deal with after his departure. I am sure he would have laughed himself sick thinking of the situation he had left me in." She no longer tried to hide behind a polite smile. If someone questioned her about her husband's dealings – well, she was going to answer – to the devil with the man!

"The Good Lord saw fit to take a hand," Aloysius said. "It is not often one sees God's hand at work but surely that man being laid low is an answer to someone's prayers."

"Reverend Mother," Mary Margaret gasped, "that is surely close to blasphemy!"

"Nonsense!" Aloysius smiled. She so enjoyed shocking her nuns. They needed to be shaken up once in a while. "Has the existence of a second wife been verified? The papers have been full of that possibility."

"I cannot answer that question. As matters stand there appear to be far more questions than answers. I am as much in the dark as everyone else. I too read the newspapers with bated breath to discover the latest scandal that man has created. The 'Second Mrs Whitmore' as the papers are calling the woman appears to be in receipt of a far superior lifestyle to my own. And she

152

appears to be enjoying her taste of notoriety." She was frequently mentioned in the newspapers, usually attending some social event.

"She is helping to keep the attention off you," Aloysius said. "That is a good thing surely."

"When I first heard of my husband's planned departure – he planned to be away for years, you know – I was delighted. I promised myself to take the time to organise my own life. I have been forced by circumstances to keep my word to myself, if that does not sound too strange."

The appearance of the young maid with the tea trolley gave Georgina some relief from the curiosity of the nuns. She had not expected them to visit her in her home. The facts and fictions printed daily in the newspapers were causing a great deal of problems in the running of her home.

She had found a good position in a local doctor's home for Cora. She had thought it dangerous for Cora to walk to and from work in this house. Who knew what those disreputable friends of her husband's might do to her innocent kitchen maid? Violet too would be leaving soon. A position as head maid had opened in a nearby hotel. Violet was excited about the change. Charles' plan to leave Georgina with only children as staff in her home was being put into place without him having to do anything about the situation. She needed to employ more staff but at this moment in time did not care to introduce any strangers into her home.

Chapter 21

"The doctors have reduced the amount of laudanum they prescribe for your husband." Elias Simpson put his briefcase by his chair, avoiding the eyes of the woman sitting across from him.

He had been paying regular visits to Doctor Steevens' Hospital to enquire about his client. The danger of infection had been averted. The doctors were hopeful their patient would make a full recovery. Elias stifled a sigh – it seemed it was true that only the good died young. How much better it would have been for everyone if that man had had the decency to cock up his toes.

"Yes." Georgina had offered and he had refused refreshment. She had no idea why he had asked for this meeting. The walls of her sitting room seemed to be closing in around her.

"The man has lost his legs from the knees down as you are aware. But it is the doctor's stated opinion that there is nothing wrong with Charles Whitmore's mind." Elias begged leave to differ. The man was as mad as a hatter in his own opinion. "You have not been to visit him?"

"I sent his coachman down with his affairs." She had

154

packed a valise with the items an invalid might need and sent it with Lewis to the hospital. No further service had been requested of her. Lewis was at her husband's beck and call. The taciturn man had removed his effects from the coach-house without a word to her. The horse and carriage had been returned. Georgina believed the man to be keeping vigil at the hospital. Bridget and Liam were cock-a-hoop at being allowed to tend the old horse.

"That, my dear lady, is not quite the same as a visit from his wife." Elias could understand why the woman scorned to visit her husband. For appearances' sake, however, it might be better if she were to be seen weeping at his bedside.

"I am assured when I telephone that his two eldest sons are with him as much as they are allowed." Georgina offered no apology.

"It doesn't look good, my dear." Elias had listened to the doctor bemoaning the fact that this woman never showed her face at his patient's bedside. The man was amassing a great deal of sympathy from the medical profession.

"Have you come to chastise me, Mr Simpson?" Georgina asked.

"It is not my place to do so." Elias would not visit the man himself if it were not a matter of business pride.

"Why have you come?"

"Your husband, my dear woman, is insisting that his sons undertake the journey he himself was planning to take." The man – even when drugged – was roaring instructions at his sons.

"He has a great deal of money invested, I believe." She wished he'd get on with it.

155

"With the aid of the doctors and an architect, your husband has designed the changes that need to be made to the structure of this house." He ignored her gasp. "He wishes to be nursed at home, you see, and it is obvious that it would be impossible to nurse him here as the house now stands." He reached into the briefcase he'd left by the side of his chair and passed papers across the table.

Georgina pulled the papers towards her. Her mind was reeling. What was she to do? She had thought herself free from that man at last. She studied the designs, her stomach roiling. She would not accept him back into her home – but if she didn't what was she going to do for money – she needed to survive.

"My dear?" Elias had clients he needed to see. He could not sit here while the poor woman stared at the papers without speaking.

"I cannot allow this, Mr Simpson." She pointed to the papers. She raised tear-drenched golden eyes from the pages. "I will not nurse that man." The very thought of touching him rendered her physically ill.

"My client," he gulped, never thinking to say these words to a member of the gentler sex, "Captain Whitmore requires me to inform you that if you do not carry out his wishes in this matter – he will divorce you."

"Let him," Georgina said without thought.

"He has ordered me to withdraw all financial services." Elias could not believe his client needed the paltry sum he advanced weekly to his wife. It was a disgrace but what could he do? The money belonged to his client.

"I will have to find a way to survive, will I not?" Georgina had feared this very thing. She had not been

156

reared to earn her living. It was unthinkable that a woman of her class should ever have to worry about money. She had been giving a great deal of thought to the matter. Surely the items in this house would fetch her a goodly sum if sold?

"My dear – think of the scandal – you would be unwelcome in polite society."

"Mr Simpson," Georgina pushed the papers across the table in his direction, "I have been out of society since I married your client." She had been a prisoner of her own fears for years. Whenever her husband sailed away, instead of enjoying her freedom she'd sat and worried about his return. She was so angry at her own cowardice. How had she allowed herself to come to such a pass? "He terrified me – I will admit it freely – I sat in this house fearing his comings and goings. I lost touch with any I might have called friend. I have been a prisoner in all but name for years. The thought of society's scorn does not concern me." She was almost breathless at speaking her thoughts aloud for the first time.

"My dear," Elias was at a loss, "the man is bedridden. Would it not serve your purpose better to have him under your roof? You would be financially secure."

"The man is bedridden, you say, yet he continues to issue his orders and commands from his hospital bed, does he not?" She didn't miss the sound of his voice barking out demands.

"I do not know what to advise you."

"There is no need to concern your good self. You may inform your client that I refuse to allow any changes to the structure of – what is, after all, *my* house. He may make other plans."

"He has ordered me to discontinue your financial support." Elias felt sick at the words he was being forced to utter. "He will without a shadow of a doubt blacken your good name." His client seemed to take a perverse delight in inventing ways to punish the woman sitting so calmly before him. How had it come to this? He had to try and make her see reason. "Please, I beg you, think about this matter carefully. You are a woman alone. What will you do? What can you do without a man to support you? My dear woman, you could end up in the workhouse." He had to make her see the gravity of the situation. Her husband might not be any woman's ideal but surely she could see that she could not exist without him?

"Mr Simpson," Georgina stood, "I appreciate your concern. However, I need time to think about the situation I find myself in. I will never agree to the structure of this house being altered." A fact which she knew her husband was aware of. This was another of the games he liked to play. He had sent this man here on a fool's errand. He was no doubt highly amused at the situation.

"What is there to think about?" Elias too stood. "The man will divorce you. There is no question in my mind of that fact. My dear woman, you will be shunned and penniless." Why could he not make her see the jeopardy of her plight? "How will you pay your staff? How can you afford to run this big house?"

"I have no answers to your questions at this time."

Georgina watched him pack his briefcase. She did appreciate his concern. She too was worried about the future that awaited her. However, she would never willingly step back into a situation that gave Charles

Whitmore control over her thoughts and actions. She needed to be alone. She had a great deal of thinking to do. She led the way from the room into the hallway.

"I beg you to consider your options very carefully," Elias said while taking his hat from her hands. He was frustrated by her refusal to see the gravity of the situation she found herself in.

"I will give the matter all of my attention," Georgina promised, opening the door. She stood for a moment watching him walk to his carriage waiting in the street. She stepped back into her home, careful to shoot the bolts on the door.

"What now?" Lily had come to stand behind her mistress.

"Lily!" Georgina said with a start. "It is as we thought." She walked into her sitting room, the housekeeper at her heels. "The man is lucid, it would appear. He has begun issuing orders from his bed." She walked to the window and admired the flowing water of the Grand Canal. "He wishes to be returned to this house to be nursed under my hands." She ignored the other woman's gasp. "If I do not agree he will divorce me."

"What will you do?" Lily thought a divorce would be the best thing to ever happen to her mistress. Society would not agree. There was the matter of living costs however. All of Georgina's funds had been passed into her husband's hands for safekeeping upon their marriage. What could her mistress do?

"I have no intention of nursing that man." Georgina turned to look over her shoulder at her friend and housekeeper. "I have told Mr Simpson this." She shrugged and turned back to the view. "There is the matter of keeping this house running. Lord knows I've learned to live without funds for my own upkeep." She turned from the window and walked across to the housekeeper. "I will not be able to pay your salary, Lily."

"That is of little matter." Lily was comfortably placed thanks to her inheritance from Georgina's parents and grandparents. "Cook and I will manage on what we have. Perhaps we could pay you rent?" She felt inspired at the thought. It would give her mistress some income.

"Out of the question, my friend." Georgina was touched to her core at this generosity. "I will not take your life savings from you." She touched a hand to Lily's shoulder. "I appreciate the gesture more than I can tell you. I will not allow you to work for me and pay for the pleasure." She found a smile from somewhere. "There are items in this house that can be sold. I spoke once of tearing the house apart looking for treasure. It would appear that time has come. I must be able to pay the nuns for our young maids after all." There was no need to mention she only had to find the funds for two maids – that was a slight blessing. There was so much to think about.

"What about young Liam?" The poor lad was the only male in the house now.

"We can't return him to his home," Georgina said. "I know his family have no place for him and cannot afford to feed him – he is a growing lad. We need him."

"This is all very sudden," Lily said, although in fact they had been waiting to see what the master would do. Now they knew – that had to be better surely.

Chapter 22

"I have heard from Richard that the ship is equipped and ready to sail," Georgina said. "Richard has not been able to visit this house, of course – thanks in large part to the Captain's machinations. It would be nice to have visitors." A single man knocking on her door would be suspect. "They are ready to sail with the tide, to hear it told."

The three women – cook, housekeeper, and mistress – were sitting in Georgina's drawing room enjoying a glass of sherry. It had been a week since Mr Simpson's visit and in that time Georgina had tried to form a plan of action for the household. She had finally decided to take the two women into her confidence and ask their advice. The four youngsters – all of the staff left to her – were abed.

"Betty, Lily, you are both highly skilled women." Georgina sipped her sherry. "You could both walk into new positions any time you desired. We all know this. I am asking you both what you want to do. I am unable to pay your salaries at this time. I cannot ask you to continue to work without remuneration."

"Your parents – God rest them – left us well provided

for." Betty Powell often wondered what had happened to the family money. Corrigan had been a wealthy man and he'd married into money with Georgina's mother. Where had all the money gone? She and Lily often discussed the matter and wondered. "I'm too old a dog to learn new tricks. I'll stay where I'm at – thank you very much." It would break her heart to leave this house and the woman trying to grant her leave.

"I too would prefer to stay." Lily and the cook had discussed this matter at length. Both women felt this house was their home. They had lived here since both were young girls. "We will have to discover a different way of living – if handled correctly it could be an adventure for all of us."

"I don't know –" Georgina began when her words were interrupted by a loud banging.

"Dear Lord above," Betty Powell put a hand to her well-developed chest, "what now?" It seemed there was never to be a moment of peace in this house. If that man had died she'd have said he was haunting them.

"There's someone banging on the back door." Liam appeared in the doorway, his hair standing on end. "I'm going to try to see who it is." Without waiting for a response he took off.

The noise of banging was joined by male voices shouting. Georgina jumped to her feet. She grabbed a fire iron and marched towards the door. She refused to cower in fear.

"*Wait for us!*" Betty and Lily said at the same time.

"That noise is coming from the back of the house. How did they get through the mews gate?"

The three women hurried from the room. In the

kitchen Lily and Betty armed themselves with kitchen implements.

"It's the master's two youngest sons." Liam stood white-faced. He'd slipped out of the house through a window to see who was banging at this time of night. "There's trouble, Missus. Master Henry's carrying someone in his arms."

"Do you need us?" came Bridget's voice.

The three young maids stood in the open door of their room.

"You girls get back in your room and bolt the door." Georgina had ordered bolts placed on the inside of the bedroom doors.

She waited now until her order had been obeyed.

"*What do you want?*" she then shouted.

"Please, please, it's Henry!" His voice shook. "I need your help."

Almost before the bolt was released Georgina was pushed back from the door. She gripped her weapon as the two men forced their way inside. One slammed the door at their back.

Liam ran around the kitchen. lighting the gas globes.

"Please!" Henry's voice was shaking. "Please, you have to help her!"

When the kitchen was illuminated Georgina saw the figure Henry was holding in his arms. It was difficult to make out who it was as the figure was wrapped in what must be Henry's greatcoat but it seemed to be a woman.

"In the name of God!" Georgina clapped one hand to her mouth.

"I didn't know where else to go – where to take her." Henry's face was chalk-white in the light. "Please, she's

163

my friend and she's hurt so badly. She needs help."

"I'll send for a doctor," Georgina said.

"*No!*" Henry shouted. "Please, I'll explain everything. No doctor! She needs a woman."

"Carry her upstairs." Georgina took charge. "Liam, I'll need you to be ready to run across to The Lane and wake the wise woman. Betty, boil water. Lily, come with me."

Henry with the unconscious figure in his arms followed Georgina and the housekeeper out of the kitchen.

Cook had Liam rake up the fire. It had been allowed die down to a gentle glow. Before the fire was ready she began to put pots of water on the range. She shouted for the three young maids. She'd need their help.

Liam soon had the fire burning bright and began to pull on his outdoor clothes.

William stood in the kitchen, at a loss as to what he should do.

Upstairs, Georgina ran into one of the guest bedrooms on the first floor of the house, the others following.

"I didn't know where else to take her." Henry was afraid the figure in his arms had stopped breathing. His body was shaking with unmanly sobs. He'd never been so frightened in his life.

"Who is she?" Georgina pulled back the sheets of the bed which was kept fresh in case of unexpected guests, while Lily began to assist Henry in removing his coat from around the figure.

"Her name is Clementine." Henry lowered his burden down gently on the bed. "She is a gentlewoman and a friend from my childhood."

164

The two women stared down at the battered and bruised figure on the bed. The torn clothes and marks of a man's brutal possession were obvious. There was no need of explanation.

"Can you help her?" Henry begged.

"I need to send a note to the wise woman." Georgina knew Granny Grunt would be the best person to help this poor woman. "Lily, I'll send Betty up with hot water. She can assist you in undressing the poor girl." She stepped away from the bed and had to almost pull Henry from the room.

"Now. Explain please." Georgina stood in the cold drawing room staring at the two young men. She had sent Liam across to wake Granny Grunt in The Lane. Lily had stayed with the patient. The young girl showed no sign of waking.

"We are leaving on our father's ship," William said when Henry just stared vacantly about. "The journey he planned is going ahead. Henry wanted to say goodbye to his good friends Christopher and Clementine – twins – he has shared a friendship with the pair all of his life." He waited to see if Henry would say something. When he remained silent William continued. "I went along for the carriage ride and to add my goodbyes even though I am not as close to the pair as my brother." He closed his eyes briefly. "We found her on the private road leading to her home. She was as you see her now. We don't know the details of what occurred."

"Why bring her to me?" Georgina had known these two for years but would never have claimed a close relationship. They had visited with their father – she had been outside of that circle.

"Henry!" William nudged his brother. It had been his decision to bring the girl here. They had little time if they wanted to catch the tide.

"We saw the marks on your body," Henry sobbed. "I'm sorry. I couldn't think what to do. Clemmy is such a great girl. I couldn't think when I saw her lying in the road. I remembered you too would know what it was to be so abused. That is all I was thinking. I thought you of all women would be willing to help my friend." He had held Clemmy close during the carriage ride from her home in Blackrock to Dublin, fearing any moment could be her last.

"Should you not contact her family?" Georgina was at a loss. She could not refuse to help a woman in such circumstances but surely the girl had family.

"I'll let her brother know where she is," Henry said. "I think he should be the one to make any decisions about the matter." He knew it would destroy Clemmy's reputation if word of this got out. She was a young prize on the marriage market. How would she live with the shame?

There was silence in the room as they looked at each other, wondering what to do now.

"Granny is here!" Liam put his head around the drawing-room door after first knocking but not waiting for permission to enter. "She's gone up."

"Thank you, Liam." Georgina walked towards the door. "You two wait here."

"Perhaps you would have the servants light the fire?" William suggested. It was cold in the drawing room. The shock had leached the warmth from their bodies.

"There is no coal to spare," Georgina said. "If you are cold wait in the kitchen. That is the only fire I can afford to run. I'm sure someone will make you a hot drink."

She left two young men gaping at her back.

"Poor girl!" Granny stood back from the bed after making her examination. "There are men in this world who should be gelded," she muttered under her breath. "I don't like the fact that she's not reacted since she was found." She pulled up the girls' eyelids. "Seems to me the young one is choosing to remain unaware." She'd seen it before – people willing themselves not to wake up. "It's a blessing anyway. I've matters to take care of before she wakes." She wanted to make sure there would be no permanent reminder of this night for the young girl. She knew a way of insuring no baby would result from this night's work. "Leave me alone with her now." She opened the door for the housekeeper and her young mistress. "I'd take a cup of tea if there is one going – but give me a bit of time before you bring it." What she had to do was best done in privacy.

While Granny was tending her patient William paced the kitchen. At another time he would have been curious at the goings-on around him. Now, however, he was troubled. They were sailing on the first tide. He did not think Charlie – finally out from under his father's fists – would wait for them to arrive. He wouldn't want to miss the tide. If Henry wanted to find his friend Christopher and inform him of this night's happenings they needed to leave here now.

The three maids, feeling greatly daring, were bustling

around the kitchen in their night attire. They each wore a red plaid dressing gown over their floor-length nightgowns. Sarah had fashioned the dressing gowns from an old travelling blanket that had been found in the carriage house. Sarah's straight white hair – the bane of her existence – was tightly curled in pin grips under her nightcap. They were taking everything in to discuss after they were alone in their room.

"Henry, perhaps it would be best to write a note to Christopher here and now." William's voice was harsh in the peace of the kitchen. He wanted to shake his brother. "If we should fail to find him before we need to board the ship you can leave a message with his servant."

Chapter 23

"How is she?" Henry almost jumped to Georgina's side when the two women entered the kitchen.

"She is in good hands with the wise woman," Georgina said. She looked at the three young maids, wondering what they understood of what was going on here.

"Do you have paper and ink?" William stepped up to join them. "My brother needs to write a message." He looked around the kitchen. Where were the male servants? He'd been forced to climb over the mews doors to open them for the carriage to pass through.

"I have what's needed for letter writing in my sitting room," Lily said as she passed them. "I'll get it."

"Cook, Granny wants a cup of tea sent up – wait a while though, she says, to give her time to make her patient comfortable." Georgina took each male by the elbow and almost pulled them towards the table in the alcove. They were in the way.

"Here we are." Lily, with paper and inkstand in hand, carried the items over to the alcove. She put the items she held on the table and stepped back. "Should we send the youngsters to bed?"

"I might have need of them." Cook wasn't going to run around the house waiting on people. She had enough to do. "Ruth, you may make hot chocolate for all four of you if you so wish." She pulled the kettle over to the hottest part of the range. "You can serve it on the little table in your room." She ignored the men in the alcove – they did not belong in her kitchen.

"I left the girl who brought up me tea sitting with the patient." Granny appeared in the kitchen as if by magic. That young maid Bridget seemed to have a good head on her shoulders. She'd let her know if she was needed. She shouldn't be. The injured girl was young. She'd heal clean – in her body – the mind, that was a different matter. She looked at the two young girls washing dishes at the sink. "I could do with another cup of tea if there's one going."

She frowned fiercely in the direction of the two men sitting at the table in the alcove.

Henry, pen, paper and ink to hand, didn't raise his head from the message he was composing. William ignored the disturbance, impatiently waiting for his brother to complete his task.

Granny wasn't having that.

"So," she marched over to the table, "you two fine gents have brought more trouble to this poor woman's door." She beat the rough table top with a closed fist, making the inkwell dance dangerously. "What do you plan to do about it?"

"Georgina, my brother needs sealing wax," William said as his stepmother appeared from the housekeeper's room in reaction to the noise. Really this house was run far too laxly in his opinion. He got to his feet, dismissing

170

the impudent old woman. "We must be leaving."

Under the fascinated gaze of Lily and Betty who had come to stand at their mistress's side, Granny pushed on William's shoulder, forcing him back into his seat.

"*Woman!*" William was furious. He could not believe the woman had dared lay hands on him.

"Don't you 'woman' me, me fine lad!" Granny stood, hands on her hips, glaring down at the two men. "I asked a question and I want an answer." She turned to see that she had the attention of everyone in the kitchen, just as she wanted.

Georgina passed a block of wax and a candle to Henry. She'd had the items to hand, knowing he would need them.

"If we do not leave now we may miss the tide." William prepared to stand.

"There will be a tide tomorrow and the day after." Granny glared him back into his seat – cheeky young upstart!

"Granny, what seems to be the problem?" Georgina was tired. She wanted to let her staff return to their beds and take to her own. She would be glad when her stepsons took their leave. Why was Granny detaining them – surely she didn't believe one of them had damaged that poor girl upstairs?

"That young woman up there," Granny gestured towards the ceiling, "you may not know who she is, but I do." She beat her fist against her chest. "There will be wigs on the green when her family come looking for her. These two fine gentlemen brought trouble to your door, Georgina, and now they plan to dance away on the tide, leaving you to face the music." She beat the table again while glaring from brother to brother. "*I'm not having it!*"

"The matter is no concern of yours, my good woman." William had had enough. He had matters to attend to before they sailed.

"Oh, isn't it?" Granny's voice was ice. "Who is going to pay my fees for running back and forth to tend the young woman?" She waited to see if they would answer, aware of Georgina fretting at her elbow. The few servants present seemed frozen in place, watching and listening to everything that was happening.

"Never even gave the matter a thought, did you?" Granny shook her head in disgust. "The Whitmore men have brought nothing but trouble to this door and now you fine lads think you can dump your latest problem on your stepmother. Take a good look around!" She waved at the kitchen. There was no smell of stock pots boiling, no game hanging and no bread rising as there would have been in the past. "There is no money coming into this house – as a blind man would notice – so how were you expecting your stepmother to pay for the care that woman needs? The medicines – not to mention that a fire will need to be kept alight in that room. A servant will have to be by her side at all times for the first few days. Who is paying for all of that?" Granny knew about Georgina's money problems. The streets of Dublin were full of whispers about the goings-on in this house. She was sorry for it – Georgina deserved better.

"I never thought." Henry looked up at the woman glaring down at him. There were unshed tears in his eyes. "I thought only of bringing Clemmy somewhere I knew she'd find help." He looked around the kitchen like someone waking from a dream.

"Liam!" he called over to the young lad. "Run out to our waiting carriage. Ask the coachman for my cashbox." They had the service of their grandfather's coachman and carriage until their departure from Dublin. He pushed ink-stained hands through his hair. "I'll send a message to my grandfather with the coachman." He looked at Georgina, ashamed of his thoughtless actions with regard to her. "I will ask him to finance your care of Clemmy. He knows the family and will not object."

"It must be lovely to pass your problems off to other people," said Granny. "You can sail away without a care in the world – sure that someone else will handle the mess you leave behind you!" She turned away in disgust. She'd done what she could for Georgina. The woman needed to stand up for herself.

"He wouldn't give me the box." Liam arrived panting at the table. "That coachman – said he couldn't leave his horses – if you want the box go out and get it yourself." He shrugged. "That's what the coachman said."

"William?" Henry looked at his brother – he didn't feel his legs would support him. "Please."

"At least someone around here has sense," William said. He left the kitchen.

Shortly after, he returned and handed the cashbox to his brother.

"There's nothing more I can do here tonight," said Granny. "I'll away to me own bed. I'll be back in the morning – not too early." She paused, frowning. "Is that young maid to stay with the patient? A young one like that is likely to fall asleep, you know."

"No, we will relieve her," Georgina said as Granny rose to her feet. "Liam, you'd better escort Granny home.

Stay with your family tonight but be back here early in the morning – we'll need you."

"Yes, ma'am," Liam answered willingly. "Come on, Granny!" He led the wise woman to the door and they left.

"Sarah and Ruth, go light a fire in the guest bedroom," Lily ordered. "Then you can go to bed." She turned to Georgina. "Or is there something else to be done?"

"I think it would be wise to have a fire ready to light in the second drawing room too," Georgina said. "I have a feeling we'll be greeting guests. I would like somewhere to welcome them."

"Girls, did you hear the mistress?" Lily asked. "Set a fire in the second drawing room too but do not light it."

"Yes, Mrs Chambers!" the girls chorused.

Cook took one of the steaming kettles from the range and began to fill the stone hot-water bottles she had sitting ready there.

Lily yawned. "I'll go up to sit with the young woman now." She took two of the hot-water bottles from Cook. She'd put one in her own bed in the hope she'd eventually get to it, and the other in the patient's. "I'll send young Bridget down to her bed." With that, she left.

As Cook continued to fill hot-water bottles, Henry approached Georgina. William had left without a word to anyone.

"I'm sorry for bringing my problems to you," he said. He pressed a heavy leather drawstring purse into her hand. "I was so horrified to see Clemmy in such a state." He shook his head, fighting the unmanly tears that filled his eyes. "I could not think what to do – where to go – who to ask for help." He took the hand that held the purse, closing her fist around it. "The money in this purse

174

should cover your expenses for a while." He paused. "I hope you will contact my grandfather. He is a wonderful man. There could be no one better to have at your side if trouble knocks on your door because of my actions."

"I'll take care of your friend." Georgina couldn't send the poor girl away now. "Will you write to me?" she was surprised to hear herself ask.

"I don't know where I will be," Henry said, "but I'm sure arrangements have been made for us to receive communications." He could not imagine his father allowing the journey to take place without him being able to remain in contact with them. "I will write and tell you of our travels." He found the promise easy to make. "And I would appreciate news of Clemmy."

"*Henry, we need to leave!*" William put his head into the kitchen doorway to shout. He popped back out again without waiting for a response.

"Again, I'm so sorry for leaving you my problem." Henry felt torn in two. He longed to set off on the adventure that had been so carefully planned – at the same time, how could he leave Clemmy without knowing if she would recover? It was all such a muddle.

"You need to leave." Georgina gently pushed him in the direction of the door. She was ready for him to be gone. "I'll take care of your friend."

She stood in the doorway watching the luxurious carriage pull away from her stable yard. With a deep sigh she realised there was only her left to lock the mews gates after the departing vehicle. She walked slowly out into the yard, enjoying the fading stars in the early morning sky.

What would tomorrow bring, she wondered as she closed and locked the gates across the rear of her property.

Chapter 24

"Come in, Granny!" It was eleven o'clock the following morning when Georgina opened the front door to Granny Grunt. "Your patient is still asleep. Bridget is sitting with her. She shows no sign of awakening. I became concerned. That is why I sent Liam back to fetch you."

"Stubborn." Granny walked in the front door, Liam holding her bags at her heels. "She doesn't want to wake and face reality. She'll have to, I'm afraid, and no time like the present." She looked around. "No visitors?" She'd expected members of the young woman's family to be waiting.

"I have heard from no one." Georgina too had expected visitors. Surely the young woman's absence had been noted?

"I'll go up," Granny shrugged. There were none so strange as folk.

"*Send Bridget down if you would, Granny!*" Georgina called up from the hallway. "The child has been sitting there for hours."

Bridget heard them. She'd been sitting in a comfortable chair day-dreaming. She jumped to her feet, not wanting to be found idling the time away. She checked the glowing coals of the fire before crossing to the bed. She stood for a moment, looking down on the young woman. It was impossible to tell what she looked like – her face was scratched, bruised and swollen.

Granny entered without knocking. "I'll take over now."

She gestured to the floor. Liam, understanding, left the bags down.

"Now remember what I told yeh to do, Liam." She'd given the lad his instructions.

"Yes, Granny."

Liam and Bridget left the room. The door closed softly at their backs.

"Don't want to wake up, do you?" Granny stood over her patient. She didn't believe in sedating someone until they were senseless. The injured had to listen to the pain in their own bodies and tell her where it hurt. She wasn't a mind reader. She turned away to fetch smelling salts from one of her bags. When she turned back the patient's eyes were open, but only a brief glimpse of blue showed. The poor mite's eyes were swollen almost closed.

"Decided to join us?" She stood for a moment, the small jar of salts in her hand.

"Where am I?" Clemmy tried to croak. Her throat was sore, her mouth so dry she couldn't force words out easily.

"You're safe." Granny poured water from a ewer standing on the bedside cabinet into a glass. She put her hand under the girl's head and lifted her up slightly. "Slowly," she instructed when the girl tried to gulp the water.

"Where am I?" Her voice was just a whisper of sound.

She didn't know this woman. She didn't know this place. There was something hammering at the back of her mind that she didn't want to allow entrance. "Who are you?"

"What do you remember?" Granny put the glass back on the bedside cabinet.

"I ..." Clemmy tried to push herself into a sitting position but failed – everything hurt. "Was I in an accident – is that how I came to be here?"

"What do you remember?" Granny asked again. She would not allow this young woman to suppress the memory of her attack. It needed to be taken out when it was fresh. She needed to scream and curse – punch something – but she could not be allowed to suppress the memory. Such things had a way of coming back and biting you in the arse.

"I was in my room ..." Clemmy winced when the woman began to gently assist her into a sitting position. She groaned as she lay over the woman's bent arm while she adjusted the pillows at her back. With a sigh of relief she settled back into the cool linen of the pillowcase. "I was being punished. I had once again refused to marry a man of my father's choosing." She tried to grimace but the pain in her face stopped her.

"What happened then?" Granny nudged the memory.

"I was hungry and thirsty . . ." Clemmy felt strangely reluctant to bring forth the memory. "I called for a servant but no one answered." She remembered pulling on the bell pull several times. She was angry when no one responded. The servants in her parents' house were well trained. "I became angry and left my room." Her voice slowed down. "It was strange – the lights were burning yet there was no one around. The servants were not in

178

their usual place. The family were not there. It was most uncanny to be walking through the empty rooms of my own home." A shiver shook her body. She didn't want to continue with this. She turned her head to the woman sitting so silently by the side of the bed.

"What happened next?"

Clemmy found it almost impossible to refuse the demand in those deep brown eyes. That soft gentle voice insisted she answer. It was mesmerising.

"Someone laughed." She began to shake. It was not a pleasant laugh. "I tried to run –"

"Why?"

No response.

"Why?" and a gentle shake of her arm. "Why did you feel the need to run?"

"I knew that laugh." Clemmy put her arm in front of her eyes. She wanted to scream. She could feel her stomach heave. She groaned and jerked, unable to keep the contents of her stomach still.

"Go ahead, love." Granny had jumped to her feet. She now held a ceramic bowl under the poor girl's chin. "Get it all out."

Clemmy heaved until she thought sure her intestines would pass through her mouth.

Granny took the bowl away, returning with the glass of water. "Here, rinse your mouth. Then I'll give you a spoonful of honey – that should soothe your poor throat."

"You know what happened to me?"

"Yes." Granny held the spoon of honey to the cracked lips of her patient. She waited until the girl had accepted the spoon.

"He laughed!" Clemmy sobbed, almost gagging on the

honey. "The more I fought and screamed the more he laughed. He was enjoying himself inflicting pain and terror on me. He laughed."

She screamed, an unearthly sound that echoed around the room and hurt the ears. She continued to scream and sob while the details of the attack played through her mind. The devil-green eyes that laughed silently at her struggles. She remembered the flash of pearly white teeth between full red lips – so beautiful – so deadly – so destructive. The pain of the injuries he inflicted with such smiling pleasure on her body were as nothing to the scars he had left on her spirit. She hadn't wanted to remember. Why had they made her remember? Clemmy screamed long and loud, abusing the lining of her throat further – her clenched fists beat the bed, wishing it was his face. She screamed until she exhausted her abused body. She fell back against the bed linen, emotionally drained.

No one came to check. Granny had asked Liam to warn the household that something of this nature might happen. The bile had to be burned from the system. Someone entering the room might cut off the poor girl's screams. She needed to expel the poison in her mind and body.

"Do you want to escape into sleep again?" Granny could offer the girl something to help her sleep but would prefer not to – these things had to be faced sooner or later.

The question was put in such a way that Clemmy knew she would be considered a coward if she agreed.

"Or do you want to face the day and what it might bring?"

"I don't want to get up," Clemmy whimpered.

"I wouldn't ask you to." Granny was pleased with the strength she saw in the young girl. No shrinking violet this one – with time and a lot of loving care she'd face the world with her chin up and dare anyone to comment. The injuries to her body were vile but they would heal. It was her mind and spirit that concerned Granny most.

"Dear Lord, I dread this." Georgina stood in the hallway outside the bedroom. She was holding a well-stocked tray that Sarah had carried upstairs and placed into her hands.

"Cook and Granny's orders." Sarah was glad she wasn't the one stepping into that room. That poor woman's screams. If those screams hadn't curled her hair – well, nothing ever would.

Liam had passed along Granny's instructions. The wise woman had ordered everyone to stay away even after the screaming started. Liam said they were to wait and when things had calmed down they should carry up a tray and try to behave as normally as possible.

"Knock on the door, please, Sarah." Georgina took a deep breath for courage. She stepped through the door Sarah opened on Granny's invitation to come in.

"I thought a pot of tea and some lightly buttered toast might be welcome." Georgina thought her forced cheer sounded demented. "Cook has put a jar of honey on the tray, my dear. It will soothe your throat."

"Who are you?" Clemmy looked from one woman to the other. Where was she?

"My name is Georgina." She put the tray on the dressing table and turned to smile at the battered waif sitting upright in her best guest-room bed. "You are in my home. Henry Whitmore brought you here."

"Henry?" Clemmy shook her head – nothing was making sense.

"You do know Henry Whitmore?" Georgina wondered if her memory had been jostled.

"Yes, of course I know Henry." Clemmy accepted the spoonful of honey being pressed against her lips by the older of the two women. She was forced to take a sip of tea to remove the honey from her palate before she could speak. "Henry is one of my best friends." She didn't feel like saying more. Had he seen what had been done to her? Dear Lord, would she have to face him with that knowledge between them?

"Henry went to your home to take his leave of you and your brother. He informed me you had been friends since childhood." Georgina filled the awkward silence. "He planned to sail on the tide and didn't wish to leave without saying goodbye to you both. He found you injured and brought you to me. He asked me to care for you."

"Where is my brother?" Clemmy looked around as if expecting to find her twin near to hand. Why would Henry bring her to the home of a woman who was a stranger to her? "Why is my mother not here? Have my family been informed of my plight? I need my maid and my belongings. I have need of my own things about me."

"Henry planned to leave a message for your brother if he was not at home." Georgina passed the girl a cup of tea. "I have had no news of him since he left in the early morning hours." She had expected to find some of Clementine's family on her doorstep first thing.

"My father took my mother and brother into the country to visit friends." Clemmy didn't want to give thought to what she believed. Surely even her father could not be so hard-hearted?

182

"I've matters to take care of." Granny picked up the soiled bowl she'd covered with a cloth. "There is not much I can do here. It will take time to heal the injuries to the body. You may send young Liam for me if there is need." She walked towards the door Sarah was still holding open. "Soft foodstuffs and warm liquids until that throat has healed a little should be enough for the moment." She pushed Sarah gently out into the hallway. "I'll be back." She pulled the door closed with a sigh. She wanted something to eat and a pot of tea. That young lady had a long road ahead of her.

Chapter 25

Granny sat to one side of Cook's work table in the kitchen. She hid her smile behind her teacup while listening to Lily Chambers give detailed instructions to the three bright-eyed young maids. You would think the three were off on a trek around the world the way the woman carried on – they were only going shopping on Stephen's Green, for goodness' sake!

"Now, you remember what I've told you." Lily was worried. It was the first time the youngsters would venture out without either herself or the mistress.

"Yes, Mrs Chambers!" they chorused in unison.

"We won't talk to strangers." Bridget was almost hopping in place as she repeated the oft-given warning.

"We'll check that the items we buy are of the best quality." Ruth too was almost beside herself with excitement.

"We won't lose the list and we'll keep a tight hold on the money," Sarah put in. Imagine, the three of them walking around Dublin without adult supervision! It was too thrilling for words.

"Let me look at you." Lily Chambers stood all three

youngsters in front of her and checked them from top to bottom. "I don't want you to be a disgrace to the mistress." What could she do? You couldn't put old heads on young shoulders. They had to be trusted to venture out on their own at some point.

The squeals of giddy excitement the girls gave as they almost ran from the kitchen hand in hand were not reassuring.

"Sit down, Lily," Granny patted the stool alongside her own.

Lily joined Granny at the table. The duties of the house could wait. She had no servants on hand to command. It was a very strange feeling for a woman who had never known what it was to be lazy.

The three women had the kitchen to themselves. Liam was tending the horse and Georgina was still upstairs talking to the patient.

"Make more tea there, Betty, and sit down with us," Granny said.

"Make yourself at home, why don't yeh?" Cook snapped. Her nerves were fragile this morning.

"Do you two know who that girl upstairs is?" Granny asked.

"She's a poor lamb in trouble," Lily said. "That's enough for the mistress."

"She's one of them Winstanleys," Granny informed them. The family were not old money but they behaved in a fashion that would not shame someone born with blue blood. "It's said in the street that they shit gold."

"There is no need for vulgarity," Lily murmured, knowing no one could knock this woman back. She did as she liked.

"Is all of that supposed to mean something to us?" Cook, tending to the kettle, asked.

"The Winstanleys are new money – very new and very, very, rich." Granny was welcomed in almost every house around Dublin. She heard and saw a lot more than she ever said. "That man takes insult if the wind blows under his hat. I wouldn't want to get on the wrong side of him. That girl up there is nothing but trouble." She was surprised her old man hadn't sent the soldiers to rip this house apart. Something she didn't understand was going on here. She prayed to God it didn't mean more harm for a woman like Georgina who harmed none.

"The mistress couldn't turn her away," said Lily.

"Those lads left their headaches behind, you know. They sailed on the tide as they wanted. There was many a one there to watch. It's said they will sail back with gold in their hold. There is many who would have liked to sail with them." She shrugged. "That's neither here nor there. Things in this house can't go on like this."

"Do you think we don't know that, Granny?" Lily dropped her head into her hands. She hadn't been able to sleep for worrying. "The two of us," she waved towards Cook, "are rattling around this house not knowing what to do with ourselves."

"You might have warned me I was missing a performance of *Macbeth*," said Georgina, stepping into the kitchen. She carried the tray over to the work table. "Our guest is sleeping."

"The cheek of you!" Cook stood to fetch another cup and saucer. "Calling us three witches!"

"Did that fella give you any money?" Granny wanted to bang their heads together. They needed to take control

186

of the situation they found themselves in instead of sitting drinking tea and worrying. It was time for action.

"He did as a matter of fact." Georgina didn't resent Granny's interference. She knew the woman had her best interests at heart. "Henry was generous." She sighed and looked at the three women. "I will be able to pay my way for a time on the money he left with me." It was not ideal but it did give her a little breathing space.

"More than that husband of yours has done," Granny grunted. "You need men around the place, Georgina. Anyone could walk into the place from that mews entrance. You can't keep this house running and your people safe without a man around the place."

"I can't pay a man's wages." Georgina wasn't willing to waste the money she had in hand. She had to count every penny.

"That husband of yours is lying in his hospital bed spinning his web of lies and intrigue. You can't afford to sit here waiting to see what he'll do next." Granny knew far more about the matter than she was willing to tell at this time. These women needed to be prepared.

"What can I do?" Georgina refused to be ashamed of the situation she found herself in. She was doing the best she could. "Richard Wilson and Elias Simpson," she raised an enquiring eyebrow and waited for Granny to nod her knowledge of the two men, "have been kindness itself. They have offered me their advice free of charge but . . ."

"Those two are gentlemen." Granny shoved her cup across the table for a refill. "Captain bloody Whitmore was never one of those for all his fine feathers."

"If you have something to say, Granny, for god's sake say it!" Betty beat the table top with an open hand. "We'll be putting down roots if we sit here much longer."

"I hear that that mews house is empty," Granny said as if thinking aloud. "That aul' Lewis has practically crawled up your husband's arse."

"What has that to do with the price of fish?" Lily snapped.

"I know a lad who might be interested in offering protection for the use of that mews." Granny hadn't asked him yet but she was sure Billy Flint would see the advantage of having a big private place like that for his own use. If she hadn't bumped into the man this morning on her way over she'd never have thought of it. God moves in mysterious ways.

"Granny, I simply can't afford to pay a man," Georgina insisted.

Granny waved her objection away. "If it's alright with you, Georgina, I'll send this lad I know over to talk with you. Billy Flint is a good sort. A bit rough about the edges but he's a man you can turn to in trouble. You need a man like that at your side."

"But –" Georgina started to object.

"Now, just listen to me a minute." Granny pushed her fingers into her eyes. "I'm trying to help you. I think Billy could be just what you are looking for. I'll send him over to talk to you and if you'll take my advice you'll treat him like a gent. The lad has a good head on his shoulders. He will deal with you honestly if you take him into your confidence. I can set this up but it's up to you and Billy to make it work." It might be the best thing that ever happened to either of them. She crossed her fingers mentally.

"Make what work, for goodness' sake?" Lily was lost.

"Never you mind." Granny tipped the side of her nose

with her finger. She pushed herself to her feet. She'd better start looking for Billy – heaven knew where the lad would be at this time of day. The sound of the front-door bell stopped her in her tracks.

"I'll go." Georgina said. "I've been expecting someone to come enquiring about our guest before this." She hurried from the room.

Granny sat back down. Lily walked over to listen at the bottom of the stairs. The three women remained silent, listening unashamedly to the sounds from upstairs. The long staircase carried sound down to the kitchen.

"It's the twin," Lily, closest to the door opening off the staircase, whispered.

The other two women stood and moving almost as one they crept up the stairs to the stairwell off the main hall. They listened as Georgina led her guest upstairs to see his sister.

"Should we go up?" Lily asked.

"We can't," Cook objected.

"We'd look a fine lot listening at keyholes!" Granny wished there was some way she could go up there. She'd have to wait to see if they sent for her.

The women returned to the kitchen.

Upstairs Georgina stood back, watching her guest and her twin.

Christopher Winstanley looked at his twin. She looked so frail, her poor face battered and bruised. He was afraid to touch her. He dropped into the chair pulled close to the bed and took his twin's hand in his. He pressed a kiss onto her little hand, fighting tears. He had behaved like a madman when he received Henry's letter.

He looked at the woman standing with her back to the door. "I'm sorry I wasn't here sooner. I only received Henry's note a short while ago." He turned to his sister. "I am so sorry. Tell me what happened." Henry had informed him of his sister's injuries but seeing her so hurt broke something inside his own body.

"Would you like me to leave?" Georgina asked.

"It was Clive Henderson!" Clemmy's moaned words almost exploded out of her mouth. She had needed her twin by her side.

Georgina stiffened. She bit back a gasp.

"No!" Christopher was horrified and incredulous.

The twins talked and cried but Georgina was aware of none of it. She was finding it difficult to catch her breath. It couldn't be. She knew, the Reverend Mother had told her, that the man was in Dublin. Was the poor girl in the bed the one the Reverend Mother had spoken of – his latest victim – the girl he was supposedly courting? Dear Lord! That she should end up in this house! Why was that man staying in and around Dublin? She simply couldn't understand it. His estates and business interests were in Belfast. And he was more often in London or Paris, finding Dublin too provincial for his tastes. Dear God, what would she do now? Where was Bridget? Her father must never see her – there could be no denying whose child she was. She was glad of the support of the wall at her back. She needed to hear more of this. She needed information.

"Father planned it!" Clemmy's words broke into Georgina's frantic thoughts.

"No!" Christopher couldn't believe his father capable of something like this.

"*Yes,*" Clemmy insisted. "I've had time to think about it while lying here. Who else could have sent the servants away? Who else would give that man free run of his house?" She never wanted to see her father again. The man had sent his only daughter into the hands of a monster.

"Father insisted Mother and I join him in his visit to his friends." Christopher dropped his head into his hands, thinking of all of the things that had delayed their return to Dublin. They had been forced to spend the night. "He couldn't have planned something like this!" He almost begged his sister to agree with him. "Not this!"

"He wants me to marry the man." This was the only thing that made sense. Her father had invited that man to rape his own daughter. "You know Father has always wanted his blood mixed with what he considers blue blood! But I wouldn't marry that man if you threatened to hang me."

Chapter 26

Georgina stood statue still, one hand pressed to her mouth, the other to her roiling stomach. She had to think. She couldn't remain standing here like a frozen ninny. She had no time for an attack of the vapours. She had to act. But she was silently screaming.

"I'm terribly sorry." She stepped to the foot of the bed. The look of surprise the twins turned on her demonstrated clearly that they had forgotten her presence. "We are not acquainted, I know, but the situation we find ourselves in forces me to take command." She stood with her hands on her hips, her fingers tapping out a frantic rhythm on the whale bones of her corset. "Clementine, you may cry an ocean – curse – kick – wail – as much as you like – but later. At this moment in time I must question Christopher. You two may be unknown to me but Lord Henderson, I'm sorry to say, is not. The man is dangerous – we are not safe."

"Madam." Christopher pushed to his feet, a look of haughty disdain on his handsome face.

"We have no time to stand on ceremony." Georgina would no longer tend to the male of the species. This was her home. "This is not the time for injured dignity or observing the stupid rules of society. You, sir – have brought danger to my door – I demand you answer the questions I'm about to put to you."

"Demand?"

Oh, he had male superiority down to a fine art, this young man. Georgina ignored him. "I do not know where the Winstanley home is located. I do, however, need to know how you travelled to my home. Answer my question, please. We have no time to waste – not if that man is on your heels."

"Topper," Clemmy nudged her twin, "I will kill myself before allowing that man to lay hands on me again. Answer the lady. She took me into her home without question. If we have brought her to that man's attention we must help her."

"Our home is in Blackrock," Christopher said, very much on his dignity. The area named was a salubrious seaside village a short carriage ride from Dublin city centre.

"There has to be more involved than a pretty young girl." Georgina spoke her thoughts aloud. "I am sorry if that insults you, my dear," she said as Clementine gasped in shock. "The man's god is money, as far as I know. Is there a great deal of money attached to you?" He did have another obsession but she would not mention her friend Eugenie in this room.

"Really, madam, you go too far!" Christopher wondered if the woman was unhinged. Imagine speaking to someone in his poor twin's condition in such a fashion!

"Yes," Clemmy spoke over her twin. She needed this woman's help in escaping the trap her father and her

193

intended groom had set for her. "In three months when we turn twenty-one we both receive a generous sum under the terms of our grandparents' will. In my own case, however, there is a great deal more money," she named a sum that brought a gasp to Georgina's lips, "set aside for when I marry or, should I remain unwed, reach the age of thirty."

"This is ridiculous," Christopher objected. "Lord Henderson has no need of your money, Clemmy." Why were they speaking of his sister's fortune? The man had behaved like an animal – he needed to be brought to book.

"Some people are never satisfied." Georgina wasn't here to give this pair an education. There were matters to attend to. "Did you have your coachman drive directly to my door?"

"No." Christopher looked from one woman to the other. They were truly frightened. "I went first to visit Henry's grandfather, the Earl. Henry neglected to give me your details in his note to me."

"Thank goodness he had that much discretion at least." Georgina thought Dublin must be bursting with all these titled gentlemen running around the place. She knew the Earl kept a house on Merrion Square.

"The Earl's man sent my coachman to a livery he knew of." He hadn't wanted to leave his horses standing in their traces. There was too much traffic on Merrion Square to expect his coachman to walk the horses while he spent time with his sister. "My coachman is awaiting me at a nearby public house." He gave the information he assumed this rather demanding woman wanted. "I walked here from there – it is no great distance." He had needed to cool his temper before he saw his sister.

"So," Georgina kept a tight rein on her feelings, "you walked here from Merrion Square without ever checking to see if there was someone following?" She knew that Henderson would have left someone to keep an eye on his golden goose. He would know her twin would rush to her side. "Then you allowed your coachman to sit for hours in a public house filling the ears of anyone willing to listen. The news of your sister's disgrace is galloping around Dublin even as we speak."

"*Nonsense!*" Christopher barked. "I suggest, madam, that you read too many penny dreadful novels. I was not followed – the very idea! My servant, I assure you, would never discuss the affairs of his betters."

"Topper," Clemmy had been looking and listening, "climb down off your high horse before you take a crippling fall."

"This woman –" he began but a look from his twin stopped him.

"You have a decision to make, Clementine," Georgina said while her mind frantically compiled a list of matters she needed to attend to with all urgency. She rattled the gleaming brass footboard of the bed to demand attention. "Do you wish to marry Henderson? I must know the answer."

"*Never! What?*" the two spoke as one.

"I have no plan in place at this moment." Georgina heard them but her mind was racing in circles. "I will hide you, Clementine. I would not wish that man on my worst enemy. You must remain in hiding but I am uncertain how this is to be achieved. We have a little time. Henderson likes to do his dirty work under cover of darkness. I have no doubt but that the man will present himself at my home – in all of his glory – this evening."

"Madam – you are insane." Christopher felt like one taking part in a drama on stage. None of this could really be happening.

"Take a look at your twin, young man!" Georgina gestured to the battered figure in the bed. "If he would attack a Bride of Breeding in this fashion, then you may tell me to my face, if you would, who is the insane person in this situation?" She watched carefully for any reaction from the figure in the bed. Yes, surely she had blinked at the code words 'Bride of Breeding'. It was the only hope she could see in this matter.

"Can you help me?" Clemmy would not put herself within that man's reach again.

"Are you Catholic, by any chance?" Georgina asked.

"No," Clemmy answered in surprise. What had that to do with anything?

"Shame, we could have put it about that you had entered a convent to become a nun." She shrugged at their looks of incredulity. "Even Lord Henderson would hesitate at storming the gates of a convent." Although with that much money at stake perhaps he would dare even that.

A knock on the bedroom door broke into the silence that had fallen at her words. She hurried over to open the door. Sarah stood outside. Granny wished to leave but wanted a word with the mistress first.

"I'll be right down." She closed the door and turned back to the twins. "You have matters to discuss." She had to allow them time. This would forever change both their lives. "If you decide to hide from Henderson, Clementine, you will most probably lose all contact with your twin for the foreseeable future." It almost broke her heart to see how the pair reached to grasp each other.

She left them whispering and weeping.

"Granny, you were right. I do need men around the place. We have no time to waste!" Georgina almost shouted as she ran into the kitchen. "If you could have the young man you spoke of visit me as soon as possible I would appreciate it."

"I'll send Billy over as soon as I see him," Granny said. "Now I'll be off."

She left the house by the rear door. Liam followed to open and close the gates.

"Ladies, gather around!" Georgina looked at the three pretty young faces of her maids and her heart sank. She had to protect them. "Lily, Cook, we have a problem brewing over our heads. I will need you both to be on hand at a moment's notice. I will keep Liam with me as much as possible. I fear we will have a very unpleasant visitor this evening. Should this happen it will be imperative to remove these young ladies from all eyes." What kind of world was she inviting these three innocents into?

"I'll keep my eye on them," Cook promised.

"You three understand that you may not step into the main house without express permission as of this moment?" Lily Chambers demanded.

Bridget took a hand of each of her friends and lifted her chin. "We are not children. We don't understand what is happening." She exchanged a glance with her friends. Ruth and Sarah tightened their grip on her hands. "But we do understand that you seek to protect us. We will be careful and obey your instructions."

"That is all we can ask of you," Lily Chambers said.

"What's going on?" Liam, his hair windswept, came through the door and looked around the kitchen.

"A great deal we can't explain." Lily ruffled his hair still further. He was the only male in the house – the poor mite. "I'm getting too old for all this drama." She almost fell onto a stool at the kitchen work table.

"I'm half your age and I still feel battered by all of this." Georgina fell onto the nearest stool. "That pair upstairs haven't the sense they were born with." She dropped her aching head into her hands. These two women knew nothing about Bridget or the secrets the girl carried all unknown. Should she tell them? What should she do? She had to protect Eugenie's daughter. She would fight to keep the child out of the father's hands to her last breath. She prayed it wouldn't come to that.

"I need some of that money the young man passed to you." Cook hoped to turn her mistress's mind to other things. "We need supplies. The tradesmen won't send goods on credit to this house." She forced a laugh. "You did too good a job of it telling them to insist on cash on delivery only."

"Sometimes we can outsmart ourselves," Georgina sighed.

Chapter 27

"Please take a seat, Mr Flint," Georgina felt as if she were standing outside of her body watching. She stood in her second drawing room, politely greeting a young man, while her mind was screaming the name Clive Henderson incessantly. She felt she'd go mad.

"I won't if you don't mind, Missus." Billy Flint could almost feel his chest swell. Imagine him, bastard son of the gentry, being invited into a place like this. The mistress herself had opened the front door and invited him in – he was going up in the world. He felt out of place in this fancy room. He'd given himself a brush and a wash but his clothes didn't fit in here.

"I've ordered a tray of tea to be served." Georgina knew the young man felt uneasy standing in his shabby clothing in her drawing room. He was an extremely handsome young man – tall and well-muscled with what they called black Irish colouring – raven-black hair and brilliantly blue eyes. Those eyes burned with a fierce intelligence and pride. She did not feel in any way superior to this young man. If it were not for Sarah's skill with a needle she too would have been wearing tattered garments. "Please take a seat. We can speak in comfort here." This Billy Flint must live close by to come so soon after Granny left, she thought. "Granny surprised me with her suggestion we should meet. I'm rather at a loss."

"Granny believes we could be of assistance to each other." Billy knew a great deal more about this woman than he was revealing.

"Granny made her suggestion and left it to the two of us to work out the details. I have only a vague idea of how we might be of service to each other."

"That's just like Granny!" Billy took a seat. One day, he promised himself, he'd sit at his ease in rooms like this with a brandy and cigar in hand. "She informed me this was a house of women and children – would that be right?" He leaned forward suddenly, deciding to put his cards on the table. "Let's be frank – we can dance around each other and spit polite words but that will get us nowhere – I need somewhere to conduct my business – somewhere with a decent address. To hear Granny tell it you may be able to help me there."

"What is your business, Mr Flint?" He couldn't be much older than the pair upstairs. They had not reached their majority.

"I'll turn my hand to just about anything that needs doing," Billy said. "I have men answering to me. I also have young lads that do a bit of running for me."

"Gambling?" Georgina didn't want to become involved in crime. She had enough problems.

"That's a mug's game," Billy didn't feel she needed to know all of his business. "I gather information and sell it to the highest bidder," he said simply. "I also have a team of ex-soldiers who provide protection and assistance of a personal nature." He thought that sounded just fine – he'd have to remember it.

"Come in!" Georgina called in response to a knock on the door. She watched as Ruth placed the tea trolley close to her hand. Lily stood in the hallway watching. While examining the items on the trolley she asked her guest, "If I understand correctly, Mr Flint," she dismissed Ruth with a nod, "you may be interested in using the carriage house as a business centre?"

"I would wish to live on the premises." Billy had watched fascinated as the little drama – tea with madam in the drawing room – played out in front of him. "There would be at least one man on hand at the coach house twenty-four hours a day." He could promise that. He knew many men who would be glad of a roof over their heads.

"I have three pretty young servant girls – you have seen one – I would not want them to be subjected to –"

"No one will touch them." Billy took the cup and saucer from her hand. They looked like toys in his large rough hands.

"Lewis left the carriage house in a rather untidy state. If we're being honest with each other, the man left it like a pigsty, I'm ashamed to say."

"Look." Billy put his tea on the trolley. Time to prove his worth – he wanted that carriage house and everything he could see came with it. This was his first step up the ladder of success if he wasn't mistaken. He wouldn't let it slip from his grasp. "The state of the place doesn't matter to me. I've women who can clean it till it shines. Let us not beat about the bush speaking of insignificant matters. We need to talk about the young girl you have upstairs."

"How do you know about that?" Georgina's cup trembled.

"In certain areas there are no secrets that can be hidden. I have my ear to the ground. That Winstanley has been boasting for weeks of the fine match he caught for his only daughter. The fool of a man gave all of his staff the night off with full pay. They might live out in Blackrock but such news travels. Does he think the staff won't talk about something like that? The streets are buzzing. It wasn't hard to put two and two together when Granny told me of your guest." He tried to think of a way to delicately tell her the rest. Well, she was a married woman – she must know what's what. "The brothels are full of talk about the fine gent Henderson as well – nothing to his credit. It doesn't take a genius to figure out what happened."

"Dear Lord!" Georgina almost collapsed against the chair back. "Does the man not realise the damage he is doing to his own child's reputation? She will never be able to show her face in polite society again."

"Why?" Billy could learn a lot from this woman. "She did nothing wrong."

"I'm afraid something like this is always the woman's fault." Georgina didn't make the rules nor did she agree but sadly it was a fact that Clemmy would be blamed and punished far more than her attacker. She felt like running into the streets screaming madly with blood in her eyes. She'd like to administer a small portion of the pain on that man that he had inflicted on others. Oh, if only she could!

"The man is strutting around his club, not a worry in the world." Billy knew that for a fact. He had a paper lad keeping an eye on the gentlemen's club. He liked to know what was going on in his city.

202

"Let me show you around the carriage house." Georgina felt as if her brain were going to explode. She jumped to her feet. The feeling of impending doom was almost bending her down. "You need to be made aware of my part in any bargain we might make between us."

They made their way through the house to the stairs down to the kitchen. Billy's eyes were everywhere. He walked through the kitchen, giving a nod to the servants working there, and followed the lady out the back door into a long stretch of green garden. He had no idea these terraced houses had such long-walled gardens at their backs. He'd like a house of his own like this – someday. At the bottom of the garden sat the carriage house and two high wide doors set into the wall.

"Madam," Ruth ran down the garden after them, "Mrs Chambers asked that you come back, please."

"Mr Flint," Georgina passed a long iron key to the man. "please show yourself around. I will join you as soon as I can. I appear to be needed elsewhere." She turned to follow the maid.

Billy wandered off whistling. He couldn't have planned it better himself. He had the key to his own place in his hand. It didn't stop him wondering what had called the woman back to her house.

"I didn't know what else to do. I had to send for you. Perhaps you can talk sense into the young fool." Lily was almost wringing her hands. "That young man wants to take his sister home with him. He is insisting they are leaving. He asked for his carriage to be called."

"I wish I could allow him to do just that." Georgina was torn. She had matters to attend to with Mr Flint. "I'll talk to him." She hurried from the kitchen and up the stairs.

She rapped on the bedroom door, pushing the portal open without waiting for permission to enter. It was her house after all.

"I believe you wish to leave." She was speaking as she stepped into the room. She was trying not to shout and curse. "Is that your wish too, Clementine?"

"I don't know what to do!" Clemmy felt torn in two. She hated that man Henderson but how could she break all ties with her twin?

"What do you think will happen to your sister if you take her home, Mr Winstanley?" Georgina folded her arms across her chest and stood tapping one foot. Surely he was old enough to understand just what would happen to his innocent sister should she step outside this house now.

"My sister will be protected. There is now no question of her marrying that man. I will never allow such a thing to take place. My sister needs the comforts of her own home. She needs the support of her family and those who love her at this time." Christopher just wanted to remove the terrible pain from his twin's eyes. His heart was breaking. He wanted her somewhere he could protect her.

"You have a great many servants on hand, do you not?" Georgina wondered if she could box the lad's ears. He seemed so much younger than she at this moment.

"Yes, of course. Clemmy will be waited on hand and foot. She will be safe."

"Think a minute." Georgina's voice was trapped behind her teeth as she fought the urge to scream. "You know what happened to your sister. You can see her cuts and bruises for yourself. What do you think will happen if you return her as she is to your home?" She hoped to goodness she didn't need to draw him a picture. He was old enough to understand how society worked.

"Oh dear God, Clemmy!" Christopher sank back down into the chair he'd left when Georgina entered the room. He'd been grasping at straws. He stared at his twin with eyes that had aged noticeably since he'd arrived. "The lady is right – I can't take you home." The two stared at each other in frozen silence, the changes in their circumstances that had been forced on both of them becoming a terrifying reality.

"I can never return home!" Clemmy wailed. Her hand shot out, seeking her twin's.

"Nonsense!" Georgina had no time for this. "If the matter is handled carefully – with discretion," she glared at Christopher, "there is no reason for anyone to know what has been done to you."

"But I can't stay here!"

"You have no choice in the matter, I'm afraid. Unless you know of somewhere you can go to hide while your injuries heal?" Perhaps they had some relation that would offer them shelter. She would be glad to pass the problem to someone else.

"There is no one," Christopher sighed, staring at his twin as he spoke. "The members of our family depend upon my father's largesse. They would not be willing to risk their living."

Chapter 28

"This room is chilly through lack of use. I am cold. I want a fire. Why has this fire not been lit?"

The whining voice broke Georgina's concentration on her household accounts.

"Those flowers are too tall. The scent is too strong. It is all beyond bearing – someone ring for a servant!"

Since they were the only two in the room Georgina had to assume that she was the 'someone' in question.

"No." Georgina didn't look up. She was heartily sick of her complaining house guest.

"I beg your pardon!" Clemmy gasped. Who did this woman think she was speaking to?

Since her arrival a week ago Clementine Winstanley's demands had everyone on edge. She needed attention, entertainment, service at the flick of a finger it seemed. Until Georgina had put her foot down Clementine had the three young maids dancing to her every whim. Finding Sarah sobbing in the hallway, the clear mark of a hand across her face, had been the breaking point for Georgina. She had insisted the girl leave her room. They did not have the staff to wait on her hand and foot.

The household was once again living under siege conditions. The females had been advised not to leave the house until this guest had departed. The staff under the direction of Lily Chambers and with the help of Billy Flint's men had totally refashioned the basement. The room they were sitting in had previously been filled with junk. That junk had been removed to reveal a very pleasant sitting room with long French windows looking out over the mews garden. They framed an ever-changing view of nature's wonders. A beautiful black marble fireplace had been polished and the chimney swept. Lily had arranged an attractive floral display in the cold grate.

"You have been staring at those flowers for hours." Georgina put her pen down with care on the blotter. "If you truly want a fire in the grate – though I can't imagine why you would – stand up and take care of it yourself. I have told you repeatedly, Clementine, I do not employ staff to jump to your every whim." It was ridiculous to ask this spoiled darling to even attempt to build a fire but she was at the end of her patience.

"I am accustomed to a higher standard of living." Clementine sniffed. "How can you function without servants? I want to go home. I want my brother."

Georgina tried to find sympathy in her heart for the young girl drooping in one of the fireside chairs but it was difficult. Clementine's bruises had faded to an unsightly yellow. Granny had advised the girl to walk slowly around the garden. They had struggled to find something that would please her, for her to wear. The pink glazed cotton gown she wore was yet another of Sarah's refashioned wonders. Georgina didn't know what to do. The girl simply refused to follow advice. She was sinking into a depression before their eyes. It was difficult to know if this whining, complaining figure was the girl's normal character – but surely not – someone would have smothered her before now.

"Clementine, this cannot continue." Georgina walked over to take the chair across from her at the hearth.

The matter of visitors to the house had been solved in the simplest of fashions by Billy Flint. The man had removed the doorknocker and disconnected the bell. The daytime activities of the household had been moved to the basement. All callers to the front of the house were ignored. This reduced the work for the understaffed household. The situation could not stay as it was – something needed to be done.

"I'm sorry." Clemmy stood up. "I can hear myself complain constantly but you can't understand. I am a twin – half of a pair – I need my brother." She marched back and forth in the room, sobbing. "I need my lady's maid. I must have my own belongings. I simply cannot live like this," she threw her arms wide, "in such straightened circumstances. It is a nightmare." She dropped back into her chair.

Georgina wondered if she was indeed a hard-hearted harpy as her husband had referred to her. She listened and watched Clementine sob and it struck her that the girl cried very prettily, her eyes checking from time to time the effect her sorrow was having on her audience. It was just a little too staged.

The introduction of Billy Flint and his men to the household had been a wondrous change. The men used the carriage for their own purposes and were happy to run household errands. But Liam and the women of the house had been housebound for a week. It was unhealthy and could not continue.

"Come in!" Georgina called in reaction to a knock on the door – glad of the distraction.

"Cook wondered if you ladies would like a glass of lemonade?" Bridget, her growing mane of caramel-striped hair hidden under a mob cab, bobbed a curtsey.

"Oh, Bridget dear!" Clementine moaned and waved a limp hand towards the bookshelf built into the chimney breast. "Come read to me – you have such a pleasant speaking voice."

"Bridget has no time to read to you." Georgina watched carefully. Was it only to her eyes that Bridget's parentage was so apparent? Her guest did not seem to notice the strong family resemblance that she herself noticed more with each passing day. "Thank Cook for us, Bridget, but I know she has a great deal to do. We are both fine."

"I may have cared for some lemonade!" Clemmy moaned when, with a bob, Bridget left.

"You have the same number of legs and hands as Cook," Georgina remarked mildly. "Get up and serve yourself lemonade if that is your desire."

"*Why can no one* understand *my pain?*" Clementine screamed.

"I need you to sit up and listen to me, Clementine." Georgina had had enough of this drama. "I have been giving the matter of your situation a great deal of thought." She'd thought of little else. She wanted this girl removed from the premises. She had her own problems. She could not be consistently at this young girl's beck and call. She was finding it difficult to remain calm when faced with the young girl's lassitude. "I only saw them in the

same place once." She had found that stating something aloud without explanation caught the girl's attention. She walked back to her desk as if to return to her accounts and waited. It was a matter of moments only.

"What are you talking about?" Clemmy rubbed at her cheeks and eyes like a tired child.

"Your brother and Billy Flint. You are more familiar than I with your brother's physique – would you say they appear to be of the same physical shape?" The idea she had was daring and could indeed be a plot in a penny dreadful novel. She was desperate. Clementine needed to leave. The house must be returned to some form of normal – she'd take to her bed with an attack of the vapours if matters continued as they were.

"How on earth would I know?" Clemmy groaned. "I am not accustomed to examining the male figure. And Flint is a servant." She waved a hand dismissively. "I've paid him no attention."

"I'd like you to give it some thought – please." You cannot shake the young chit till her teeth rattle, Georgina told herself.

"I can't imagine why you would want to know such a thing." The sigh this time almost made the flowers dance in their vase. "I suppose they might be – I hadn't really noticed." She waited to see if any more information would be forthcoming. With another lusty sigh, she offered, "If Flint and I should happen to stand side by side I would have a better chance of judging the matter."

"The post has arrived!" Jones, one of Billy's men, entered the room without knocking. He held a bouquet of envelopes in one large fist.

"It is customary to knock and wait for permission to

enter a lady's presence!" Clementine snapped – really, she would be glad to leave this place – it was not the home of a lady. "Since you are already here – you may make yourself useful – I want a fire in this grate – see to it."

Jones looked as if he were going to curse the young madam. The pleading look on the face of the lady of the house stilled his tongue. He passed over the post and walked out. He was no one's servant.

"Anything for me?" Clemmy looked at the post expectantly.

"I sincerely hope not," Georgina snapped. "You are in hiding, my dear – remember?"

"I believe I'll take a nap." Clemmy walked to the sofa that didn't even match the chairs, she noticed in disgust. The furnishings in this room had only recently been removed from the attic for goodness' sake. What kind of a house did this woman run? "Tell the servants I am not to be disturbed."

Georgina bit her lip. Granny had advised gentle exercise. The girl was escaping into sleep far too often. She was at her wits' end as to how to handle this situation. She stood to leave the room, taking the unopened post with her. She'd had more than enough of Miss Clementine Winstanley.

"Liam," Georgina took a seat at the table in the kitchen alcove, "run down the garden to the carriage house – see if Billy Flint is at home. If he is, ask him to join me here." She watched the lad run from the kitchen. Liam had developed an admiration for Mr Flint. "Cook, could I have a pot of tea, please, and no matter how I beg do not allow me to put alcohol in my cup."

"The young madam's driving you to drink, is she?" Cook pulled the big black kettle over the hottest part of the range while giving Ruth instructions on setting the table for their mistress. Lily was upstairs with two of the maids, instructing them in the care of a lady's bedchamber. The world as Cook knew it might be changing but that was no reason to drop standards.

"I confess I am at my wits' end with the chit." Georgina did not consider the people in this kitchen her servants. They were her helpers and at times the only thing standing between her and madness.

"Billy is out and about," Liam returned and reported with a cheeky grin. "The men will send him over as soon as he turns up." He loved having all of these men about the place. "Jones said I was to tell you as how one of them letters was delivered by hand. He recognised the servant who pushed the letter into the box. He said if you want to talk to him – give him a shout."

"Thank you, Liam." Georgina applied herself to opening the post. Two of the envelopes she held aroused her curiosity. She examined the family crests on the envelopes. Why would an Earl and a Duchess be writing to her?

"Anything wrong, madam?" Cook asked in reaction to the gasp from her mistress.

"No." Georgina pushed the letter that caused her unguarded reaction back into the envelope. "I am to have visitors it would seem." It was more important than ever that she discuss her ideas with Billy Flint. Would the man be willing to enter into the deception?

Chapter 29

Billy Flint examined his image in the wall of mirrors housed in the dressing room. When he'd agreed to Georgina Whitmore's mad scheme he'd thought only of the advantage to be found in the scheme for himself. He wanted and needed to know how the blue bloods lived. He had need of such knowledge.

The man in the dressing-room mirror was a stranger. A room for dressing in – he'd never known of such a thing. He was having difficulty hiding his emotions. The man reflected in the mirror was the man he was born to be.

"How does that feel, sir?" The question from the tailor kneeling at his feet drew him from his thoughts.

Billy looked down at the Grafton Street tailor who had been ordered to attend him. They had recognised each other but neither had made mention of the fact.

"You certainly clean up well," the Earl of Camlough, sitting in an easy chair in the dressing room of his Merrion Square house, was enjoying himself. When he sent off a note offering his assistance to Mrs Whitmore, he had not expected an outcome like this. He'd have to leave his estates more frequently. This little drama and his part in it

213

had the old blood flowing.

The young man said nothing, but his shoulders straightened further and his chest swelled visibly.

"What do you think of this scheme?" the Earl asked. He knew the lad's father – the man was a near Dublin neighbour – and a stiff-necked fool. This young man was a son to be proud of unlike the weak-chinned whiner who was his only legitimate issue. I'd have made this lad my heir, he thought.

"I couldn't say." Billy looked around at the servants – did the man think they had no ears? He had been given to understand that secrecy was everything.

"Do you really think it will work?" the Earl insisted. He had thought the notion straight out of a penny dreadful novel when he'd first been approached. He'd agreed to add his expertise only out of curiosity.

"I'll make it work." Billy turned back to his examination of his own image. He'd been polished up like a female. He'd never known men were powdered and puffed. His hair had been barbered, he'd had a hot-towel shave and massage, his nails filed, his skin polished. He wore glove-soft shoes polished to a high gleam on his feet. He almost didn't recognise himself in the elegant gent shown in the mirror. Imagine that Winstanley fellow being able to discard all of these suits! They were being tailored to his figure. The owner could never reclaim them. It must be nice to have that kind of money.

"I doubt young Winstanley will be able to keep his mouth shut about all of this," Alfred said. "It will make entertaining dinner conversation." He would share this adventure with a few close companions. It was too delicious to keep to himself. He intended to take an interest in this young man. He would enjoy mentioning him in front of the man that had fathered him – the young man was a force to be reckoned with if he wasn't mistaken.

"Sir!" Billy glared at the man, hoping he'd get the message. They were surrounded by servants. The Grafton Street tailor was on his knees pulling at the legs of the suit he was wearing. The Earl's valet was pulling and pushing at Billy in a way that would normally have Billy putting his fists up. There was a maid in the bedroom through the open door, packing travel chests – another bustled in and out of the room picking up silver-headed brushes. They all had ears and tongues for God's sake.

"My servants don't talk." Alfred dismissed the man's obvious concerns.

"They are human!" Billy barked. No one with a story this tasty would be able to resist sharing it. He'd objected vigorously to the presence of so many servants. He'd been wrong. He would never have been able to polish himself up in the way they knew how. They were needed but that didn't make him worry less.

"You are almost finished here." Alfred pushed to his feet reluctantly. He'd been enjoying himself. "It appears to me that my staff have succeeded in doing the impossible," he said with a charming smile around the room. "They have created a 'silk purse from a sow's ear'." He laughed aloud. "No insult intended."

"None taken," Billy said. "It is simply fact."

"Join me in my study for a brandy when you are finished here." He left the room with his man Timmons on his heels after thanking the staff for their stellar work.

"An interesting young man," Timmons, the Earl's man,

said, handing him a balloon glass of brandy.

"A bloody handsome brute," Alfred, sitting in a leather chair pulled close to the low burning fire in his study, said softly. He warmed the brandy in his hand. "I know his sire, you know."

"Yes." Timmons helped himself to a brandy without waiting for permission. He'd been the Earl's man for many years. "The man has a family home across the square, I believe." He took the chair opposite. "He houses his mistress of many years close by in Baggot Street. The woman has given him two sons and a daughter. The young man upstairs is the eldest of the three." It was a delight to him to see his friend so excited by the happenings around him. He'd been drifting along for too long.

"Been listening to servants' gossip?" Alfred smiled into his brandy. Timmons always knew what was going on.

"How else would I keep up to date on the world around us?" Timmons sipped the fine brandy. "The servants see more and hear more than your lot give them credit for. That young man upstairs was right to be worried."

Alfred ignored the insult. "Do you think this mad plan can work? I was intrigued when the scheme was suggested. Two young men changing places – I did not think it would work. Flint has changed my mind – if left to him the scheme will be successful."

"It helps that Flint will only be travelling under the *name* of Christopher Winstanley. He is not trying to fool anyone into believing he is that man. If I understand the scheme correctly Flint has only to provide a trail for anyone who may be checking up on Winstanley's movements." He exchanged glances with his master. "If young Winstanley can play his part there should be no problem." Timmons swirled his brandy. "I too have no doubt that young Flint can carry it off."

"Switching places." Alfred smiled in a way that belied his white hair. "I didn't think it was feasible."

"Flint will make it work," Timmons said. "Did you notice his reaction to everything about him? You could practically see him filing everything away for future reference."

"He interests me." Alfred sipped his brandy with obvious pleasure. "I'm going to keep an eye on that young man."

"Have you not enough to occupy your time? You have vast estates and three grandsons to oversee. That should be enough for any man."

"I need to stay away from my estates for the moment." Alfred stared into the fire. "Edward needs to find his own feet without me looking over his shoulder. I have good men in place – men I trained." He would be kept informed – of that he had no doubt. His grandson needed to take up the reins of his inheritance – it was time. While he was still here to help.

"What of the other two?" Timmons had known all three men since birth. "Have you heard anything of them?"

"I wouldn't expect to hear anything yet," Alfred said. "I don't worry so much about Henry. He is always up for a lark. William, however," he sighed, "he concerns me."

"Being the middle child is never easy," Timmons contented himself with saying. He would personally kick young master William up the arse – but then, he wasn't gentry.

"Well, I can do nothing about my grandsons now. I have given them the best I could – now we must see what they do with it."

A comfortable silence fell between the two old friends. They had been raised together and as the years passed the distinction between master and servant had disappeared to a large extent.

"I want you to meet this young woman."

When his master's voice broke the silence Timmons didn't express surprise at the unexpected statement. He waited, knowing it would be explained. His master often spoke his thoughts aloud.

"Look her over and give me your opinion. This Georgina Corrigan as she now names herself – she intrigues me – I've never had anyone request the use of my house and servants before." Perhaps he should have bestirred himself through the years and visited the house on Percy Place instead of relying on the reports from servants – or at least sent Timmons.

"She must be a strong woman. She certainly has a lively imagination if this latest drama we are involved in is anything to go by." He paused for a moment. "What Whitmore is doing to her is worrying." Timmons had never liked the man and had argued against allowing him to marry Miss Regina. Sadly his master had been seduced by the two fine sons following on the man's heels. They had all learned to regret that union.

"Whitmore has a slew of men willing to swear they have had biblical knowledge of the woman, I am told." Alfred had made it his business to find out as much as he could about the intrigue surrounding Whitmore.

"Cronies and liars." Timmons crossed his legs and

relaxed. It looked like his master wanted to chat.

"I have failed to remember any occasion when my grandsons made mention of their father's wife. That is strange – is it not?" His grandsons had visited the woman's home for years. True, only for short holidays – nonetheless, he should have heard more of her.

"Whitmore seduces men," Timmons stood to fetch the brandy decanter. If they were going to rake up old memories he wanted another drink.

"I beg your pardon?"

"Oh, not in that sense!" Timmons brought the decanter over and refilled the Earl's glass. "I watched him with Miss Regina – he made her disappear whenever he was around – I don't know how else to put it."

"I was horrified by the lady's injuries." Alfred had told Timmons of the luncheon he had shared with Georgina and his grandsons. He couldn't bear to think his own daughter might have been subjected to some of the same.

"It was bloody brave of her to expose her injuries in the way she did," Timmons said. "The thought of Miss Regina suffering in the same way has caused me many sleepless hours." Ever since he'd been told of the poor woman's injuries memories of Miss Regina ran through his head. When he lay down to sleep dark thoughts visited him. Had they allowed Miss Regina to be tortured under their very noses? It was not a thought conducive to a good night's sleep.

"We need to set up a meeting with Georgina Corrigan, Timmons." Alfred thought he might stay in Dublin for longer than planned. "We may be able to offer our assistance."

"They have removed the door knocker," Timmons reminded him. An absent door knocker discouraged visitors.

"See what you can do."

The conversation was interrupted by a knock on the study door. Timmons jumped to his feet before Alfred shouted permission to enter.

"Mr Flint, sir." The maid held the door open while making the announcement. The door was pulled closed at Flint's back as soon as he'd stepped through.

"Brandy, sir," Timmons enquired of the figure standing as if frozen. He presented the appearance of a fine upstanding gentleman. Bastard born he might be but he looked a proper gent.

"They are still talking." Georgina returned from standing with her ear pressed to the door of the basement sitting room.

She had never seen anything to equal the way Clementine and Christopher fell upon each other. They had hugged each other fervently and each started speaking in a way that others couldn't understand. The change in the girl was remarkable. Christopher, wearing Billy Flint's rough tweeds and hand-knitted sweater had arrived at the mews gate almost panting. He had run all the way from Merrion Square. The fool could have brought unwelcome attention to this endeavour. Thankfully Billy had thought of this and he too had run through the streets on his way to Merrion Square wearing the same outfit. That lad thought of everything.

"Now we'll have two of them under our feet!" Cook sighed.

"Billy will board the night train to London wearing Christopher's clothes and accompanied by his manservant. He will have all of Christopher's chests and belongings with him too." Georgina had no idea why it was called a night train when one had to cross the sea in a boat. Still, hers not to reason why. "If everything goes as it ought we should have those two out and on their way very soon."

Cook looked around before asking, "Have you received a response from BOB?"

"We are to have a visitation in two days."

"Two days." Cook continued to roll pastry for her steak-and-kidney pie. The time couldn't pass quickly enough for her.

Chapter 30

"Mrs Chambers, I want fires in the second drawing room, the dining room and my sitting room." Georgina was pacing around her sitting room as she spoke.

"I'll have Liam take care of it." Lily made a note on the pad she kept in the deep pocket of her black dress. She was very much the housekeeper this morning.

"I don't know what to expect of this visit." When Georgina had sent that letter off to her connection in the BOBs she'd never expected the response to come from a Dowager Duchess – what if the lady herself was one of the women who were about to visit – what on earth was she to do?

"You need to calm yourself, madam." Lily too was shaking at the thought of a visit from a woman who was practically royalty. "We do not know who or what to expect. We can only do the best we can." The knocker was once more on the door in anticipation of company.

"I was desperate when I sent off that letter." Georgina continued to pace. "I knew as soon as Clementine arrived at my door that I would need the help of the BOBs. I expected a note of encouragement or an offer of help. I

222

never expected someone to actually visit – and people of such distinction. *What am I to do*?"

"We have as much as possible well in hand." Lily had never seen her mistress like this. "You have set up a way for the twins to be together. What more can you expect of yourself?" She held back her opinion of someone who gave so little notice of their visit. With the reduced staff she had on hand! What would these people expect?

"The Earl of Camlough informs me that Billy looked every inch the part when he left his house." Georgina could feel her stomach turn. "I think the man was impressed by our Mr Flint. Billy will be in London as we speak, pretending to be Christopher Winstanley – he won't be able to keep up the deception – an exchange must soon be made." The change in Clementine now that her brother was with her was astounding. "I have neither the connections nor the funds to make such a thing happen. I had to ask for help if my plan was to work."

"We have coped with everything thrown at us so far," Lily demurred.

"By ignoring everything going on past our front door – that cannot continue."

"I suggest you allow Sarah to dress you. The bronze dress the girl has fashioned suits you better than anything I have ever seen you wear." She hoped to turn her mistress's mind to other things. "Sarah can tend to your hair too." Lily could not continue to stand here. She had matters to attend to. "They are arriving at eleven, right?"

"Yes, yes." Georgina was struggling to control her breathing.

"Cook has everything well in hand. She and Ruth have been baking dainties to serve with morning tea and coffee.

Bridget has been scrubbing and polishing the public rooms and Sarah is waiting to assist you." Lily consulted her notes. She needed to put the finishing touches to each room on this floor. "The maids need to change their aprons before the guests arrive." She silently thanked Billy Flint for leaving his men at her disposal. They might well be uncouth but they were willing to turn their hands to anything she asked of them – which was a great deal more than could be said of the male staff employed in this house in the past.

"Where are the twins?" Georgina looked around as if expecting the twins to appear by magic. The two seemed to be constantly underfoot.

"I banished them to the attic," Lily said. "They are pulling the place apart with much hilarity." She'd already had to ask them to keep the noise down. There was no need to advertise their presence.

"What on earth are they doing up there?" They usually lounged around – talking privately – demanding service.

"You suggested Clementine disguise herself as a young lad. They are searching through the discards of your stepsons to see if anything would suit." Lily too wanted to see the back of this pair. Christopher had only resided here for a few days but even that was more than enough.

"I shudder to think of the mess they will leave behind them." The pair had no notion of picking up after themselves. They created chaos everywhere they went.

"If it keeps them out of our way it will be worth it." Lily turned to leave. "I'll send Sarah to you. We have much to do before your guests arrive."

"The Dowager Duchess of Westbrooke – Lady Beatrice Constable – Lady Arabella Sutton!" Lily opened the door of the sitting room and stood back to allow the august personages to enter. No one would guess from her appearance that she'd been running around shouting orders until minutes before their guests knocked.

"Your Grace," Georgina felt her knees tremble, "I hadn't expected a visit from you personally. Lady Sutton, Lady Constable, please, come in and be welcome." She gestured towards the dainty chairs that decorated her sitting room. "I'll ring for refreshments."

Georgina thought the three women looked very much as she imagined the three graces, Fate, Hope and Charity, would look if they came to earth. They were each beautifully groomed, slender and somewhat tall for women. They presented an image of feminine beauty. It would be a very foolish person who failed to recognise the determination in their gaze.

"Not just yet," the Dowager Duchess, a sweet-faced woman renowned for her beauty as a debutante, said. The three women stood glancing around. "Firstly, we do not stand on ceremony while on BOB business matters." She waved one bejewelled hand at her companions. "We have no time for indulging in 'm'ladies' and 'your graces'. It becomes fatiguing, I do declare. We are Beatrice," she pointed to the blonde middle-aged lady in blue giving her name the French pronunciation. "Arabella," again the gesture, this time to the youngest of the threesome, a dark-haired lady exquisitely gowned in pink. "And I am Constance," She put one hand on her own lavender lace-covered chest.

Georgina stood as if struck dumb. She made no mention of their A, B, C of names. If they were tired of their titles then surely they had heard every trite comment on their initials.

"My carriage and that of my clerical staff," the Dowager continued, "are at this moment standing outside your front gate. It will do your reputation no harm to allow the curious to observe my heraldic shield on a carriage at these premises. My secretary will join us shortly. The carriage will be moved to the mews as soon as we send for our clerical staff."

Georgina frantically wondered what she was supposed to do with clerical staff.

"Constance," Lady Arabella smiled at Georgina as if requesting her to join in a jest, "we have much to discuss and this room simply will not do."

"We need a large table for paperwork," Lady Beatrice explained.

"If you would follow me?" Georgina had prepared for this. The need for a large table had been mentioned in the letter. "We can use the dining room."

"Perfect," the Dowager said.

"One moment, Georgina." Lady Arabella turned to the housekeeper standing waiting for instructions in the hallway. "Please have the carriages sent to the mews. The clerical staff will need someone to greet them there. Perhaps you would serve refreshments to them downstairs until we send for them? And you may tell Watson we need the papers she holds brought to the dining room."

"Yes, m'lady," Lily responded, bobbing a little curtsy.

Arabella smiled and all three followed their hostess into her dining room.

"The Winstanleys will be removed from your home this evening," the Dowager said. "Lord Sutton, Arabella's husband, has his yacht standing ready. They will travel from Kingstown to Liverpool where they will sail for America. We have arranged for Mr Flint to be met in London and directed to Liverpool. He will travel back to Dublin on the yacht."

Georgina watched the woman command her troops, almost breathless with admiration. The Dowager was seated at the head of the dining-room table, her two ladies standing close to the files of documents Watson had placed on the table.

"We were much impressed by your solving of the problem the Winstanley twins presented to you." Lady Beatrice smiled sweetly.

"You did not need a great deal of help from us," Arabella said. "Well done!"

"Now!" The Dowager slapped the table. "The matter of the twins is out of the way. We have something further to ask of you." This was the reason she had come to meet the girl personally. They had much to discuss. The problem of the twins was a minor irritation.

She passed a sheaf of papers she received from Lady Beatrice to Georgina after first checking them.

She waited while Georgina quickly perused the papers. When she snapped her head up at first view of the generous cheque that had been included with the papers, the Dowager held up her hands to stop any thanks that might be forthcoming.

"The Winstanley family are well placed financially," Arabella smiled. "We saw no reason you should be out of pocket. Christopher was pleased to write a cheque to cover your expenses."

Georgina blushed to think her financial problems were so well known. She did not return the cheque however –

the money would make her life a great deal easier for a time.

"Would you be interested in becoming involved more fully in the matters that concern the BOBs?" Constance had been impressed by the girl's quick thinking when presented with a problem not of her own making.

"I have long been an admirer of the work the BOBs do but in truth I don't know a great deal about the organisation." Georgina couldn't see how she could be of help to these women.

"My great-great-grandmother started the organisation as a way to pass time. Brides of Breeding was started on a whim – a way of amusing bored ladies." There was silence in the room while the dowager seemed lost in thought. "It was a social club to begin with – over time the need for action was made clear to all – and, to the credit of those first women, they took action."

"Through the years the BOBs have helped a great many women – not all of them of the upper class," Beatrice said.

"I would be willing to help in any way I could," Georgina had never forgotten that the organisation these women belonged to helped her friend Eugenie escape her abusive husband. "I would like to make myself available to you but I fear I am not suitable. You must all be aware of the disgrace that hangs over my head."

"The rumour of your husband divorcing you?" The Dowager waved a hand in dismissal. "The people who matter know that the situation you find yourself in is not of your making."

"Nonetheless it will put me forever in disgrace." Georgina glanced at all three women. "I confess I will be glad to be free of the man I married. I was sorely tempted to contact the BOBs on my own behalf many times. Being left without funds is my major concern at this moment."

"If you agree to join us you would be employed by the BOBs. You would receive a stipend," the Dowager said softly. "We have a not inconsiderable fund at our disposal."

"In what capacity could I possibly serve?" Georgina couldn't imagine anything she might have to offer to the organisation.

"A major problem to the organisation throughout the years," Beatrice said, "has been what to do with the women we help escape their situation. There is the matter of surviving in hiding to be considered – always. Unfortunately, where a runaway wife is concerned the family monies remain with the man – much as in your own case."

Georgina remained silent.

"Through the years we have helped not only women who need to escape a difficult situation but those who have no wish to enter the state of matrimony," the Dowager continued. "There are a great many more of those than you might imagine. Of those, the Catholics can escape into nunneries – not an ideal solution, in my opinion."

"If we are to talk at length," Georgina said as the ladies exchanged glances, "allow me to send for refreshments." She did not wait for their agreement but stood to pull the tapestry bell pull. "A pitcher of iced lemonade and some dainties, I think." The ice man had delivered that morning thankfully.

She turned back to her guests. Lady Beatrice had taken

a seat but Lady Arabella remained standing.

"Do sit," said Georgina.

"I never sit when I can stand," Arabella said. "Now I need to tell you of my involvement in the BOBs."

The door opened. Lily entered to receive her orders and left the room on silent feet.

"I originally contacted the BOBs because I was one of those women who did not wish to marry." Arabella ignored the laughter of her fellow committee members. "Obviously I did marry – it would take too long to tell you of the details – suffice it to say I married and became a member of the BOBs."

Lily was back with Ruth and Bridget. The maids entered the dining room carrying heavy trays. Lily gave soft-voiced instructions to the girls.

Lady Arabella, ignoring the servants, continued to speak.

"I presented an opportunity to the BOBs." She tapped her long fingers on her corseted waist. "There are only so many nanny and governess positions available to our runaways. We women are not equipped to seek gainful employment." She accepted the glass of iced lemonade from the tray Bridget held. "I would be tempted to accept the challenge myself if I were not happily settled."

"We were excited when Arabella told us of her findings," Constance said.

"I met two young women in Paris," Arabella continued after a sip of her drink. "I was fascinated by them. They appeared so free – so full of life – and appeared to have sufficient funds for their needs." She shrugged. "I invited them to my Paris home for tea."

"Arabella is forever seeking diversion," Beatrice put in.

She would not like anyone to think badly of her friend. It was not usual to invite chance met strangers to your home.

Lily left the room, leaving the two young maids standing against the wall in case of need.

"The women were American." Arabella smiled at Georgina's surprise. "They told me of their employer. The more we spoke the more I understood just what I had discovered. The opportunity for our runaways is outstanding."

"She brought her findings to the committee and we agreed with her." Constance held her glass aloft, seeking more lemonade. Ruth was by her side instantly to replenish the liquid.

"We sent two of the women we held in hiding out to America almost immediately." Beatrice too required more lemonade.

"It was a disaster," Constance said sadly.

"What happened?" Georgina asked when it seemed the women were lost in thought.

"Come here, child!" Arabella waggled her fingers in Bridget's direction. The girl stepped forward. "This is the uniform of the American organisation that employed the women I spoke of." Arabella, with a hand on Bridget's shoulder, turned her slowly around. The long black dress Bridget wore was covered by an elaborate lace-trimmed white apron with stiff white straps that crossed her back. "The two women in Paris thought it highly amusing that my maids wore the uniform they thought of as their own." She released Bridget and pushed her gently back to her position.

"They were maids?" Georgina was lost.

"No," Arabella said. "The young women I met in Paris

231

were employed by a company called Harvey's. They work in hotels and restaurants along a railway line. The Atchison, Topeka and Santa Fe line – doesn't that sound exciting?" She waved her hands, distressed that she'd wandered from the point. "The young women are helping to settle the American Southwest." She gulped at her drink, still thrilled at the thought.

"That sounds dangerous." Georgina hadn't touched her drink, too involved in the story Arabella was telling.

"The women are lodged in the company's own hotels," Constance said. "They have chaperones and a housekeeper. The girls are expected to keep to the highest standards of behaviour."

"They are free to travel," Arabella said, much caught up with the idea. "They may change hotels or restaurants as they wish. The girls I met made no secret of the fact that it is very hard work. But they both admitted they wouldn't change their lives for the world. They plan to make the most of the opportunities open to them."

"There is also the possibility of marriage with oilmen or cattle barons," Beatrice put in. "There are wealthy men seeking brides and a shortage of the right kind of women, we are given to understand."

"The freedom these American women enjoyed left me gasping in envy," Arabella said. "They serve as waitresses – not a well-thought of profession here, I agree. But to hear the two girls I met describe their situation – well, it is different to anything we understand."

"Why was the placement a disaster then?" Georgina would be tempted to take up one of the positions herself.

"The uniform was the first major problem," Constance said sadly. "To the well-raised girls we sent, the uniform was that of a servant."

"They were incapable of adapting to the new circumstances they found themselves in." Beatrice felt some sympathy for the girls.

"They had no clue of how to conduct themselves as free women." Arabella had been broken-hearted when the first two women failed at what she saw as a golden opportunity. The tales the women told had almost succeeded in changing the mind of the committee members. Arabella had feared the chance for such liberty for women had been lost.

"If they were anything like young Clementine Winstanley I can understand completely," Georgina said with feeling.

"Yes," Constance agreed. "The young women had not the sense God gave a goose."

"But how does any of this concern me?" Georgina asked.

"It is all very well to rescue some young girl from a perilous position," Beatrice said. "What do we do with them afterwards is the question."

"We believe," Constance looked at her companions, "that with training before they leave Ireland the women we rescue would be ideal employees for this Harvey organisation."

"The women we have helped think only of escaping their current situation," said the Dowager. "They give no thought to how they will live out the rest of their days. It is impossible to live without funds. That is simply a fact of life. These young girls have been protected by parents or guardians. We can no longer send them out to fend for themselves." There had been too many suicides within the numbers they tried to help. The loss of young life upset everyone.

"We are raised to be pretty and useless," Arabella said. "A woman of intelligence is despised – called a bluestocking – advised by her mother to hide her brain when in male company – even the clothes we wear restrict us."

"Surely you do not intend to send everyone who seeks help out to America?" Georgina asked.

"Indeed not," Constance laughed. "Fetch my maidservant," she pointed at Ruth. "I wish to use the ladies' withdrawing room."

"You see? We are unable even to tend to our bodily functions without assistance," Arabella said as Ruth rushed from the room.

"We cannot change everything overnight, Arabella." Constance agreed with her friend but she was older and well knew how slowly change came about.

Georgina was fascinated by everything they said but was growing increasingly frustrated. "What exactly do you expect from me?" she asked again while they waited for the Dowager's lady's maid.

"We want to set up a school," Beatrice said. "The women we help need somewhere we can train them to step from one way of life to another. We have done this to some small extent in the past."

"We want you to think about opening your home to these women and teaching them," said Constance just as her maid appeared. She stepped out with her. She almost sighed in relief. She really needed to relieve herself. Growing old was so tiresome.

"My house a school?" Georgina tried not to fall off her

chair. She had never thought of such a thing.

"We would give you all the help we could," Beatrice said softly.

"I gleaned all the information I could from the American women," Arabella added. "The women will need to learn to ride. I can offer them riding lessons on my family's estate in Wexford."

"Surely well-brought-up young women already know how to ride?" Georgina objected.

"Side-saddle only and not always well," Arabella's eyes gleamed. "The American women ride astride – with split skirts to preserve their modesty." A delighted peal of laughter escaped her at Georgina's shock. Arabella had tried riding astride herself. It was very liberating. She could not wait to teach others.

Constance re-entered the room. "I am feeling slightly peckish. Perhaps we could have tea now?"

Chapter 31

"What do we think?" the Dowager Duchess asked.

Their hostess had excused herself for a moment – allowing the women to speak frankly.

"The lack of servants is obvious," Arabella said. "The house itself is in a good location. The canal – if an emergency arises – would allow for a quick getaway. There appears to be room enough for the women we may send here. I would like to be given a tour some other time." She smiled. "I've never been in such a small house."

"There was no one on hand in the necessary." Constance, without her own lady's maid to hand, would have been forced to deal with her own clothing while using the necessary – a not very satisfactory state of affairs in her opinion.

"We've heard that she was struggling," Beatrice said, "But I have seen no sign of the uncouth men she is supposed to have about."

"I feel we can ask her about the rumours if that is your desire." Constance wanted the matter settled between them before their hostess returned. "Do we believe she will do?"

"Yes," Arabella said.

"We can but try," Beatrice said.

The four ladies sat to one end of the dining table while Bridget and Sarah stood to attention against the wall of the room, ready to supply anything they might need. The light lunch and delicacies Cook sent up were arranged temptingly on the mahogany sideboard. Ruth remained in the kitchen assisting Cook.

"We are – it would not be wrong to say – desperate to take advantage of this latest chance for our ladies." Beatrice, without thought, chose a sandwich from the salver Bridget held ready. "But the first two ladies we sent, as we have already said, were an unmitigated disaster."

Bridget used the silver tongs to place the sandwich on her side plate.

"I am willing to do all that I can to assist." Georgina nervously watched the two young maids performing a task usually reserved for footmen.

"The head man of this company we spoke of, is British – a Mr Fred Harvey from an undistinguished background." Constance dabbed her lips with her napkin. "In the past he employed men but that proved unsatisfactory. We hope to tempt our ladies with the opportunity to earn attractive wages and the possibility to travel and see something of the world."

Georgina watched the three ladies accept every attention from the young maids.

"The class of lady the BOBs primarily deal with would have no notion of offering service," said Constance.

"That is the problem in a nutshell," Beatrice said. "The first two ladies to be sent in reply to Mr Harvey's advertisements were totally unprepared for a life of service."

"As we should have anticipated," Constance said. "That is where you come in, my dear Georgina."

"I cannot believe that any lady would be willing to serve in a public place." Georgina was again thinking of Clementine.

"We will have to change their view of the world," Arabella said.

"So, what we are thinking of doing, my dear Georgina," Constance wanted to put the matter on the table, "is to use your house to train up the ladies before we even consider sending them all the way to America. They must learn how to care for themselves. They must be taught to handle their own funds. They must be educated to a new way of life. This is vital. You would in effect become a unique school for ladies."

"We have four ladies in need at the moment." Constance waved a hand towards the papers and files on one end of the table. "Watson, my secretary, will leave the files with you – one on the four women – names – circumstances etc. Another on this Mr Fred Harvey and the Santa Fe railway line. We feel strongly that we have discovered a way of helping our ladies that will prove a blessing to all concerned."

"We do not have hundreds of ladies applying for our help after all," Arabella said.

"Thank heavens," Constance agreed. "There are only so many old dears seeking companions or children needing stitching or art lessons. The ladies we have helped in the past have disappeared into mundane lives of genteel poverty. This Harvey company offers adventure, excitement and a chance for a better life to the women brave enough to accept the challenge."

"The women we send must keep us informed of the life they find out there in America. It is vital we are aware of the details of daily life we cannot get from newspaper articles," Beatrice said. "Such communication will be addressed to you, Georgina, if you accept our offer."

"I will need time to study your files." Georgina had to give this serious thought. It would be the answer to many of her problems, but could she do it? "I will need to involve my housekeeper and cook. I have few servants as you will have noted. I must study the matter."

"But are you interested?" Constance asked anxiously.

"I am very interested." Georgina wasn't willing to say more. "Sarah, go and ask Cook to send up a fresh pot of tea. Bridget, remove the used crockery."

She waited while her instructions were carried out.

"Ladies, you have taken me by surprise." She looked at the three women who were making no secret of their own study of her person. "The matter of schooling ladies interests me. However, after dealing with Clementine, my heart sinks at the prospect of trying to change a lady's way of thinking."

"I am positive that we offer the best chance of a new life to the ladies who seek our help. That is why we brought this proposal to your door," said Constance.

"There is another reason you are being considered for this position, Georgina," Beatrice said. "You will pardon me if I give offense." She paused to think of the best way to put her words. "The men who work on the railways – they are not gentlemen – the women will have to learn to deal with such. You have no male servants at all as far as we have observed. The men others have seen around your home are the rough and ready sort that we believe dig railway lines. The sort who would not bow and flirt with the ladies, would not pander to them. This too would be a part of their education. May I ask – do you, in fact, have such men about the place?"

Georgina blushed and wondered how to put her answer. "Well, yes. You see, I have given the use of my coach house to a certain businessman in return for his men doing some heavy work around the house for me." It sounded so questionable that she prayed they would not enquire further.

"Excellent!" Constance declared. "That suits perfectly."

"Another advantage in setting up a school," said Arabella. "We will discover who is not suitable before there is ever a question of sending them so far from home, The expense involved is not inconsiderable. We do not like to squander the BOB funds."

"The education we plan to offer them will not be wasted," Beatrice said. "The lessons will assist in every avenue of escape we offer."

Chapter 32

"Did you ever see anything as wonderful as their clothes, Ruth?" Sarah sat on one of their chairs pulled away from the table in their room.

Ruth stood behind Sarah, twisting her hair into pin curls before they slept.

"The jewels!" Sarah sighed deeply. "They sparkled so – I never thought to see anything so beautiful."

Bridget lay on her bed looking and listening to her two friends. How could they talk about clothes and jewels at a time like this?

"I don't know how they managed to eat all of those cakes and sandwiches Cook sent up." Ruth dipped her fingers into the bowl of water she'd put on their little round table. She had to wet Sarah's hair before twisting it into a curl and attaching two hairpins in an X shape to the hair. "I thought ladies were all so tightly corseted they fainted if they ate overmuch."

"I do not believe you two!" Bridget jumped from her bed and in bare feet almost stormed over to the table. She knelt on one of the chairs pulled sideways and put her bent elbows on the table. "How can you both be talking about those women and their silly ways – as if that were important?" She glared when Ruth didn't stop in her work. "Sarah, Ruth, you both heard the things they were talking about when we were in that dining room."

"We are not supposed to discuss anything we hear when in the presence of our betters." Sarah was quoting Sister Mary Margaret.

"You have eyes and ears the same as me, Sarah Black." Bridget wanted to turn the table on its side and dance in frustration. "To those women we were invisible." She waited to see if either of her friends would pay her the attention she thought the matter she wanted to discuss deserved. "They complained about the lack of servants."

"Were you listening at the door?" Ruth paused for a moment to stare.

"How else am I going to know when I can or can't go into the room?" Bridget shrugged.

"The Dowager Duchess was right to expect servants to attend her. *Ow!*" Sarah yelped when Ruth pulled her hair painfully. "Are you two not worried about the things we're learning in this house? It's nothing like I expected. I thought Reverend Mother Aloysius had come to take us away that time she visited."

"Grow up, Sarah!" Bridget snapped. She had things she wanted to discuss. "The nuns are glad to see the back of us. They have hundreds of girls to place. As long as they receive our wages every quarter why should they be concerned about us?"

"I'm worried as well." Ruth continued in her work regardless.

"What is going to happen to us when our time here is up?" said Sarah. "It will become well known in Dublin

242

society that the house we began our training in was not quite up to snuff."

"Sarah!" Bridget felt there should be smoke coming from her nose. She wanted to pull the little hair Sarah had from her head. "You will not have to worry about your hair any longer – *because I am going to scratch you bald-headed!* I want to talk about what we heard today."

"What about it?" Sarah sighed in relief when Ruth tapped her shoulder to let her know she'd finished pinning her hair.

"Did you not hear the same thing as me, Sarah Black, Ruth Brown?" Bridget's mind had been spinning with the possibilities revealed in that dining room. Ruth had been there for some of it and Sarah had surely heard enough when she'd joined her, to understand what was on offer.

"I don't know what you're talking about, Biddy." Sarah went to look for her nightcap.

"*The work in America!*" Bridget wanted to take her friend by the shoulders and shake her. "The work for women that pays well and allows for travel and adventure – Sarah, how can you not be excited by the very thought of it? Ruth," she tried to stop Ruth from tidying the table, "did your heart not beat with excitement as you listened to them women talking?"

"But that sort of thing is not for the likes of us, Biddy." Sarah covered her pin curls with the nightcap.

"You shouldn't have been listening," Ruth said as she put the chairs back under the table.

"Why isn't it for us?" Bridget's chin was up.

"I didn't hear all of it. What are you talking about?" Ruth continued to tidy up after herself.

"Biddy's just dreaming." Sarah pulled the bedclothes

back. It was late. They had to be up early in the morning.

"I am not dreaming." Bridget put both fists on her hips and glared at her friends calmly preparing for bed. "Those women spoke of jobs going for young women." She beat her chest with one closed fist. "Well, what are we?"

"Biddy, they were talking about females of class. Not throwaways like us." Sarah's voice was all-understanding.

"*How is anyone going to know what we are if we don't tell them?*" Bridget demanded with a roar.

"What is it you think we can do, Biddy?" Ruth was tired. But she knew Biddy wouldn't let them sleep until she had said what she felt.

"We can plan to go to America when our time here is up!" Bridget almost danced in place now that they were listening to her. "We can watch and listen and learn. It will be years before we are free to leave this place. I want to be ready to take any chance going of a better life."

"You are standing there wide awake – dreaming." Sarah settled down in her bed.

"I heard those women – the clerical staff – talking before they left." Biddy was so excited she couldn't stand still. "The Dowager's secretary – well, she said that she wanted to go to America."

"Why would anyone want to leave a good position with a Dowager Duchess? You must have misheard." Sarah punched her pillow and rolled over. "We need to sleep, Biddy."

"You shouldn't be trying to ape your betters, Biddy." Ruth yawned.

"My name is Bridget. I'm not going to answer to Biddy anymore." She put her chin in the air. She stood while the other two settled down to sleep. Were they really willing to settle for a life in some basement? Was it only her who longed for something different? She didn't want to scrub up after others. She wanted better out of life. This was the first time in her life she'd heard of something that might serve her purpose.

She climbed into bed, sure she would never sleep. While she'd been listening to those three fancy ladies talking about the chance to be found in America her heart had beat so fast she thought she'd faint. Why couldn't they travel to America and work for this man Harvey? If they listened and learned – they could take advantage of the opportunity just like the women those people were planning to send to this house. Why couldn't her friends see that?

Bridget tossed and turned, the words she'd heard playing over and over in her mind. She knew the mistress would accept the job those women offered. What choice did she have? She needed money to live on, just like everyone else.

Money! Bridget's sigh shook the bed. What could they do about money? Their earnings would be paid to the nuns until they turned sixteen. Five long years away in her case – how could she bear it?

Those people had mentioned teaching women to handle their own funds. She'd make sure she was in the room when that was going on. If she listened and learned everything she could, she could learn to walk and talk as if she'd been born to money. She would make a plan to learn everything she could from the women who would pass through this house. Look at that Clementine – she had been useless. She couldn't even entertain herself. Bridget didn't need constant company. She would be sorry if she couldn't make Ruth and Sarah see what she saw but she was going to America – someday. She had as much chance as the women who would be sent here to learn to look after themselves.

"I can hear you thinking, Biddy," Ruth groaned.

"*Bridget!*"

"Bridget then, will you for goodness' sake go to sleep!" Ruth yawned hugely. "Tomorrow is another day."

While Bridget was busy plotting and planning her escape into a brave new world, Georgina was explaining the proposition to her two faithful servants.

"I don't see what I can teach them," Cook said when she'd listened to the plan. "Having them here will make a great deal of work for the kitchen – they will have to be fed after all. I have only the one pair of hands. Young Ruth is a little treasure but she can't be everywhere."

"You could teach them how to boil water – I doubt they know." Georgina too was concerned about this proposal. She had to accept. She needed a source of income. "Clementine was the most useless individual I ever came across." She had felt deeply sorry for what had happened to the poor girl. No woman should be attacked like that. However, dealing with the young lady day to day had been extremely difficult.

"If the women we are sent are anything like young Clementine," Lily said, "it will be impossible. They will need to learn to look after their own clothing. They will have to be taught to pick up after themselves. If we are to consider sending someone like Clementine out into the world to fend for herself," the mere thought was horrifying, "the three orphans from the convent have more of an idea of life than that young woman"

"That knowledge was brought home forcefully to me," Georgina said. "I wonder if I should share some of my own life experience with these women." She sighed. "I really don't know what we are to do with them. The only solace is – I don't think the BOBs do either – we will all be learning together."

"We could put a bigger table in the kitchen, I suppose." Cook looked around her realm. "They will not be waited on hand and foot. They can eat down here. That should shock them." She almost laughed at the idea.

"The maids can teach them to tidy their rooms." Lily too began to plan and wonder.

"The women will be learning at the same time as we ourselves," Georgina said. "If we can keep one step ahead of them at all times we should be able to manage. We are three intelligent women after all. We each have something to offer."

"We can sit here and talk and plan until the cows come home." Cook stood. "We will know better how to go on when the women arrive. This is a new situation for all of us. You can't plan for something you know nothing about."

"Wise words." Lily pushed to her feet.

"Everything will look better in the morning." Georgina yawned. "I have a great deal of reading to do. The women left me papers to study. I'll pass on what I glean from those as soon as I have finished."

"Billy Flint will be back soon," Cook said.

"We'll have to tell him about the school for ladies we are going to be running." Lily wouldn't worry about it. Time enough for that when she knew what was what.

"The BOBs seemed to think Billy and his men would be part of the women's education." Georgina stood. "I'll have to discuss the matter with him."

The three ladies parted, each to seek out her own bed.

Chapter 33

"Richard," Georgina stepped briskly into the office, leather-gloved hands outstretched in greeting, "thank you so much for agreeing to see me at such short notice."

"My dear Georgie," Richard walked from behind his large mahogany desk to accept the outstretched hands, "it is always a pleasure, I do assure you." He led her to a chair pulled close to his desk. "The note you sent around with your lad made the matter sound urgent." He assisted her to sit before returning to his own black-leather chair.

"I need advice, Richard." Georgina was determined not to weep all over the man. She was so angry – so frustrated – if she were a different sort of female she would spit. "Business advice."

"Of course." He put his elbows on his desk and made a steeple of his hands.

"I am in receipt of a cheque," Georgina took a deep breath. "It is rather a generous cheque. I unthinkingly took it to the bank."

"Yes?" he prompted when she seemed incapable of continuing.

"Are you aware that I cannot open a bank account in

my own name – that any monies I lodge belong to my husband?"

"I have never given the matter much consideration." Richard was being careful in what he said. "Surely you know that everything you have belongs to your husband?" It was a fact of life.

"How am I supposed to survive?" Georgina jumped to her feet and began to pace. She simply could not sit still. "I must have money to live on – I have people to support." She spun around to glare down at him. "I understood the man was filing for divorce – surely that changes matters?"

"Have you been served with papers from a lawyer?" Richard asked.

"All I have received are outrageously large bills in my name from some of Dublin's most expensive lady's fashion houses." She dropped back into the chair. She cringed to remember her visits to those same fashion houses. She had presented herself and demanded an explanation of the charges. The superior ladies' assistants in the shops dismissed her out of hand as a fraud. It was demoralising.

"Georgie, you have been allowing Whitmore to blacken your good name." Richard hated to hear what people said about his friend. He would allow no slander of her in his hearing but he couldn't be everywhere. "You have accepted everything he has said or done – never opposing him. He is holding court from his hospital bed – revelling in the role of injured hero."

He had taken Simpson to one side and questioned him on the matter. In Simpson's opinion the man had run mad. It was unfortunate the doctors tending him did not agree. Simpson informed him Whitmore was fixated on forcing his wife to pay for what he deemed her part in causing his accident.

"Richard, a divorce from that man would seem a gift to me." Georgina knew she should be horrified, distraught, desperate to save her good name but why couldn't the man simply let her go?

"You and I may say that within these walls." Richard sat back in his chair. "However, you must never admit such a thing in public. You will be pilloried."

"Am I not being pilloried already in the eyes of society?"

"I have something to suggest that is perhaps outrageous." Richard had given much thought to Georgie's plight.

"The situation I find myself in is outrageous. You, my friend, have my best interests at heart. I know this." She leaned forward to touch one of the hands resting on his desk.

"Go to the newspapers!" Richard almost spat the words. To even suggest such a thing was a disgrace. But the situation was dire – Georgina needed to take action – even if such action was distasteful.

"Richard!" Georgina was shocked rigid. One simply did not wash one's dirty linen in public. The newspapers – how shocking!

"Georgie," Richard knew what he suggested was daring, "you have been a virtual recluse since your marriage."

"But to go to the newspapers, Richard – I couldn't." Georgina paled at the very thought.

"I have a friend," Richard said slowly. He hoped he was guiding her in the right direction. The situation was such that he was unsure. "He is a reporter – a good chap. I could – with your permission – discuss the matter with him." He paused for a moment, thinking of his friend Skip. "I warn you though that he is like a terrier when he thinks he might have a good story. If we open this can of worms you must be ready for whatever falls out." He had no knowledge about using the press for his own gain. Skip would have to advise them both.

"I must discuss this matter with some people." Georgina felt sick to her stomach at the thought. Was she to lose her position with the BOBs before it ever started? She did not wish to lose the chance they offered her – she was spending their money after all. She would need their understanding and permission before she could go any further.

"I will discuss the matter with Skip, my reporter friend," Richard said. "We will be guided by him. I will endeavour to mention no names when I consult him." That was the best he could offer. "In the meantime – the matter of this cheque – would you trust me to be your bank?"

"Richard, you would be prepared to do that?" Georgina was in desperate need of funds.

"I don't keep large sums of money about the place. I could advance you a sum now and lodge the cheque in my account. You simply need to sign your name to the back of the cheque. I will keep the cash in my safe here for your convenience."

"I cannot thank you enough, Richard," Georgina searched in her reticule for the cheque. "I have accounts I must settle." She intended to remove her custom from several shopkeepers who had recently treated her with a lack of respect. It would give her a great deal of pleasure to pay off her accounts and inform them she was withdrawing her custom.

"Let us take care of that matter." Richard reached across the desk to take the cheque she held out. He almost whistled when he saw the account the cheque was drawn on. Shame Georgina couldn't lodge it in her own name. It would do her reputation no harm to be associated with the Dowager Duchess of Westbrooke. The woman was a leading light in society.

"We will share a pot of tea and you can tell me how you come to know the Dowager Duchess." He would give some thought to how he could make use of this information to Georgie's advantage.

"Richard," Georgina could smile now – the lack of funds had concerned her greatly, "I do believe you are a gossip hound."

He stood to open the safe concealed behind a painting of his great-grandfather that hung on the wall behind his desk. "I will admit only that I am known for keeping my ear to the ground." He turned to look over his shoulder. "How much money do you need at the moment?" He mentioned an amount that brought a gasp to her lips. "Will that suffice?"

"Half of that will be sufficient, thank you." She wondered what he considered a large amount of money. Hadn't he said he didn't keep a lot of cash about? The amount he had offered to her seemed a fortune. He offered her the cash which she gratefully accepted. She took the paper money and stuffed it into her reticule.

"You can call on me any time you need funds." He put the cheque in the safe before locking it once more and replacing the painting.

"You should count that," Richard objected.

"There is no need between us." Georgina trusted him. If he broke that trust she would be devastated.

"Before I order tea . . ." Richard chose his words with care. "My dear, I know something of the Dowager Duchess of Westbrooke – are you involved in the BOBs?"

"You have heard of the BOBs?" She didn't know quite what to say. The society was not exactly a secret but they did not care to advertise their work. What should she say? She couldn't bear to lie to Richard.

"I donate money to the cause – privately of course – as does my father." He wondered if he should say more. Trust was earned, he thought, before saying, "My father and I offer the BOBs lessons in handling their funds."

"You are a man of surprises, Richard." Georgina felt a warmth in her heart to hear this man donated his hard-earned money to a cause that supported women.

"My father and I have never supported the opinion that women have weaker brains than men." He laughed with great good humour. "No one knowing my mother would ever dare to even think such a thing."

"How is your mother?" Georgina settled back in her chair to chat. She sighed in delight – it had been such a long time since she felt at liberty to enjoy exchanging views – she must learn to count her blessings.

"Mother is well." Richard too was delighted to share Georgina's company. He had missed her. She had been such a large part of his growing-up years. Their mothers had been friends. Why had he allowed so many years to pass without checking up on her? He wanted to give himself a kick for his neglect. That he was in England during that time getting a sound education was no excuse.

His friend had needed him and he hadn't been there for her. He would not fail her again – he would do everything in his power to help her.

"As you know mother is very involved in her charity work. It seems to me that the woman is forever looking for someone needing her help and advice. My father and I come last in the pecking order." He smiled, not meaning a word of it. He adored his mother as did his father.

"Order that tea, Richard." She slapped the desk. "We have much to talk about."

Chapter 34

Bridget saw them pass the laundry-room window. She was up to her elbows in hot water, scrubbing the household linens. The sight before her froze her in shock. She had no idea what to do – if she should do anything.

"There's some woman here says she wants to see yeh." Smith, a tiny weasel of a man, walked into the kitchen without knocking. He glared at Georgina sitting in the kitchen alcove enjoying a cup of tea. "Billy asked me to deliver yer note to that fancy address. This one came out of that house and said how she wanted to talk to yeh – thought I'd bring her in to see yeh – see what's what."

Liam sniggered before he could stop himself. Even he knew better than that. Imagine bringing a nob into the kitchen!

Arabella Sutton's delighted laughter echoed into the clear blue air before she appeared in the open kitchen doorway, her maid at her elbow. "Georgina – I adore your household – I simply adore it!" She had been visiting a member of the BOBs when a note from Georgina had been carried in to her hostess.

Sarah put her head out of the sewing room. She

disappeared back inside when she saw the company.

"Lady Sutton!" Georgina felt quite faint. Dear Lord, how could she invite a lady of means into her kitchen – well, not much choice now – the woman was here. She had sent a note around to her contact within the BOBs as soon as she returned from visiting Richard. "Do come in – may we offer you refreshments?" She was aware of Cook and Ruth standing like statues.

Lily, viewing all from her office, closed her eyes in disgust. That it should have come to this. She stepped from her office, determined to take the situation in hand.

"No, thank you." Arabella smiled while avidly looking around. She'd love to poke her nose into everything. She was never allowed downstairs in her own home. Her servants would walk out en masse at what they would consider an offence. "I've come directly from having tea with a friend."

"If you would take Lady Sutton upstairs, madam." Lily tried to act as if a lady of fashion appeared in their kitchen regularly. "I believe Cook is capable of looking after her lady's maid."

"Thank you." Georgina knew her friends were as horrified as she. "If you would follow me, Lady Sutton."

"Oh – Arabella, please!" Arabella prepared to be amused.

"You said in your note that you needed to consult the committee of the BOBs." The two women were sitting in Georgina's sitting room in the easy chairs on each side of the fireplace. A gently glowing fire warmed the room pleasantly.

"I have a decision to make." Georgina gazed into the

flames, trying to find words. She had not expected such an instantaneous response to her missive.

"Can you tell me what you want advice about?" Arabella questioned when it appeared her companion could not find words. She hoped Georgina was not going to refuse the offer they had made to her.

"You are aware my husband seeks to divorce me."

"It is common knowledge." And much whispered about and giggled over but she would not hurt Georgina by saying so aloud.

"I should first tell you that I do not care about the divorce. It is a blessing to me. I long to be free of the man – you may think me cruel since details of his accident have been released – I simply do not care what people say of me." She took a deep breath. "That has nothing to do with the matter I wished to discuss." She gave herself a mental shake. "I don't know where to start. I am in receipt of invoices in very large amounts from some of the better shops in Grafton Street – invoices in the name of Mrs Whitmore – I have no knowledge of these purchases."

"How dreadful!"

"You will have seen many domestic situations in your position with the BOBs." Georgina looked across the fire into eyes melting with sympathy. "I was – I don't know how to put it into words – I allowed my husband to make me a prisoner of my own fear – I became a recluse. That situation is being used to my disadvantage now. The woman being called the 'Second Mrs Whitmore' by the press is using my name to run up bills that I cannot pay – I would not even if I could afford to – it is a matter of principle." She took a moment to gather her thoughts. "I have been treated in a very shabby manner by shop assistants." She pushed to her feet, unable to remain seated. "I thought to accept Whitmore's decision to divorce me with dignity and silence on my part. That option is no longer open to me. I must react. I can no longer allow the man to put obstacles of his choosing in my path. That woman's actions – they have the hallmarks of Whitmore – I have no doubt that he is encouraging the woman in her schemes to discredit me." She sat back down.

"What has this to do with the BOBs?"

"I have been advised by someone I trust to approach the press." Georgina looked at Arabella as she spoke, seeking her reaction.

"For what purpose?"

"My friend – you would know him – Richard Wilson." She waited for Arabella's nod before continuing. "He has a trusted friend who is also a member of the press. Richard suggests I tell my story – my point of view – to the public at large."

"What do you think of that suggestion?"

"I want to do it. I am tired of being the butt of that man's abuse. I would prefer that the divorce go through and the man leave me alone but that will never happen. I must protect myself."

"I agree." Arabella leaned forward to put a hand on Georgina's knee. "It will not surprise you to know that we made a study of you before we approached you. We were all shocked that you had never approached us for assistance in fleeing the situation you found yourself in." At the time they hadn't known if it was stupidity that kept her in a nightmare marriage when she well knew of a way to leave it.

"But how could I have ladies here?" Georgina waved

her hand around vaguely. "Women who are running away from a bad situation – they could not stay here – not with the press sniffing around."

"It may not be quite as much of a problem as you perceive." Arabella was well known for making instant decisions. "The first group of women contains no females fleeing a husband. The four women –" She suddenly started to laugh. She laughed so hard tears came to her eyes. She pulled a lace-trimmed handkerchief from her pocket and attempted to stem her mirth. "Watson, oh dear Lord, you will not have heard! Watson, the Dowager Duchess's secretary, is to join your company!"

"Oh! That's good." Georgina couldn't understand why that was a cause of such hilarity.

"I'm sorry. That was rude of me. But my dear Georgina – the Dowager – she is beside herself." The laughter exploded again.

Georgina waited until Arabella had regained control of herself.

"I doubt the press will be interested in the ladies who will be in your home," Arabella said when she was calm once more, "and they will surely not think to photograph anyone not of interest to the public. The women will have to present the appearance of servants, will they not? So I don't see the problem. We knew of your difficulties when we approached you. If you would care for my advice?"

"Please."

"The matter of the press is your decision alone – you must do what you think best in that situation. As for the BOBs, we have the four women – and Watson – close to hand. We want to begin their training as soon as possible. Would that be a problem for you?"

"I shouldn't think so." Georgina was almost weak with relief.

"Now!" Arabella jumped to her feet. "Show me around your house and if you have plans in place – share them with me."

"I thought to make them share a room from the beginning," Georgina said as they climbed the stairs. "In the documents you left with me it clearly stated that the women share rooms in the staff hotel. I believe we must make them aware of this from the start." She opened the doors leading into her guest bedrooms.

"You did not think to put them in the servants' quarters in the attic?" Arabella asked.

"No, my attics are full of years of the family's discards. Besides, I did not get the impression that the rooms available to – the Harvey women as we are calling them – would be small and badly furnished – as those of servants would be. Do you think I am wrong?"

"I have not given the matter a great deal of thought." Arabella could not imagine putting two beds in one bedroom.

"I have studied the papers you left with me in great detail," Georgina said as she continued to lead her guest around her home. "We must be completely truthful with the women who come here. They must make their decisions from a position of knowledge. It will not do to send them off unaware of the great changes they must face."

She turned to look at her guest who remained silent, listening carefully.

"I believe this will hold true for all the women who may pass through my home. The Harvey situation is unique – those who do not wish to avail of that chance, they too will still need to understand the challenges facing them – that is important."

"Do you believe many will change their minds?" Arabella was fascinated. She had never been part of the group who followed the fate of the women they helped. She would change that.

"Not if I share my own experience of marriage with them."

"My dear!"

"They must be made aware of their options." Georgina was insistent. "We women have been kept in the dark too long. I don't intend to continue that tradition." She continued to expound her ideas to her guest.

"You have given a great deal of thought – in what to me is a short amount of time – to what we have requested of you." They were back in Georgina's sitting room. "I am impressed. I see no problem with you contacting this gentleman of the press. That is your own business. The BOBs have not purchased your freedom. You must act how you think best in your own affairs."

"I mean no insult but I must ask – have you the power to make statements on the BOBs' behalf?" Georgina was weak with relief. Something had to be done about her situation.

"I do," Arabella said. "If I might make a suggestion – and I hope you are not insulted – it concerns your household staff."

"Please."

"Employ a scrubbing woman or two and a laundry maid," Arabella said. "The young maids you have to hand will be tied up giving instruction to the women we send you. That will now form the most part of their duties, I should think."

"I thought Mrs Chambers and I would train the ladies?" Georgina was surprised.

"Your maids are young and innocent," Arabella said. "The bloom of youth is still on their cheeks." She paused for a moment. "I think their very youth will act as a whip on our ladies – they will not like the fact that servants – and such young ones at that – are more knowledgeable than they."

The women laughed together at the idea.

Chapter 35

"I believe if we place a bed at either side of the window …"

Georgina heard the conversation from across the corridor. She stood in her dressing room trying to decide on an outfit suitable for meeting a gentleman of the press. She could imagine the scene across the hallway. Lily walking back and forth while the three young maids followed in her footsteps like chicks after a duck.

"Will they be needing somewhere for their clothes?"

That was Sarah – Georgina thought with a smile – always worrying about the proper care of garments.

"In the same room?" Lily stared down at the silver-haired child in shock. The idea of ladies of quality dressing themselves without assistance was hard for Lily to imagine – but to have their clothing in the same room! Surely not!

"I don't want to speak out of turn …" Bridget didn't want to let anyone know how closely she had listened to every scrap of conversation she could hear about the goings-on of the house. "But the ladies coming to this house need to learn to take care of themselves – isn't that right?"

"Yes . . ." Lily said slowly. It would appear she would have to give more thought to her own attitude to the expected guests. They would be ladies of breeding – that was a fact – yet they were not to be treated as such – how would she manage to change the habits of a lifetime?

"I think they'll need something like the room you set up for the three of us," Ruth said in her logical fashion. "They will have a great deal more than we three, I know, but wouldn't they need to have what they need in their room?"

Across the corridor, Georgina slapped a hand across her mouth. It wouldn't do to allow the laughter she could feel tickle her ribs to escape. Lily would be mortified to think anyone was listening to this discussion.

"How on earth do the nuns put old heads on young shoulders?" Lily asked, not expecting an answer.

Bridget had been examining the large light-filled bedroom with great interest. "We would have to remove the washstand," she said, "but if we put a wardrobe and a chest of drawers at each side of the room, I think that would work." She looked at Lily for approval of this idea.

But Lily had collapsed onto the feather-stuffed mattress of the large double bed that sat in solitary splendour in the centre of the guest room.

"How will we manage?" she groaned. "Who will clean and light the fires – who will clean the room – who will keep order?" They couldn't expect ladies of gentle breeding to do such chores.

"You are worrying unnecessarily." Georgina appeared in the open doorway of the guest room. She was wearing the bronze gown Sarah had made for her. The rich colour of the gown and the style were very flattering to her colouring and slim figure. It had quickly become a favourite. Her hair hung loose around her shoulders – she had been unable to arrange it in the latest fashion. She needed Lily's assistance. "The ladies who are being sent to us are aware that they can no longer be treated like delicate flowers."

She entered the room, looking around with new eyes. She had never had to turn a room into a dormitory before. It should be a challenge – one more.

"We will all be learning together with this first batch of women." She smiled at the three wide-eyed young maids. "What we are about to do has never been done before. We have no guidelines to follow. We will learn together what is required." She sighed deeply. "But I do not believe the ladies should be placed in these rooms." She held up a hand when Lily looked like objecting. "It would be better to leave these rooms as they are for unexpected guests. The floor above this can be arranged for what I am thinking of as our students."

"But . . . but . . ." Lily was shocked. "Those rooms are smaller. How will we ever place two ladies to a room?"

"We will have to," Georgina insisted.

Bridget, Ruth and Sarah said nothing. The rooms in this house all looked roomy and beautiful to their eyes. Why was such a fuss being made?

"I have need of your assistance with my hair, please, Lily." Georgina glanced at the fob watch pinned to the bodice of her gown. "And I wish you to accompany me to my meeting."

Lily pursed her lips and followed her mistress. She did not approve of this meeting with a press reporter. No good could come of appearing in the dailies.

The three young maids were left without instructions.

"Let's have a look at those rooms with the changes needed in mind," Bridget suggested.

"When will you ever learn your place, Bridget?" Ruth sighed, shaking her head.

"In this house – no one will know their place, it seems to me." Bridget wanted to step out of the role her birth had condemned her to – was that so wrong?

"Working here we will never learn how a great house is run," Sarah almost cried. "If the people supposed to be teaching us don't know what they are doing! What are we supposed to do? We will never rise through the ranks of a great house. We will be condemned to accepting lowly positions."

"Honest to goodness," Bridget made for the open door, "the pair of you are enough to drive me out of my wits. We are being offered a great opportunity here – why can you not see that?" She walked down the long hallway and up the servants' staircase, the other two on her heels.

"Is all of this too much for you, Lily?" Georgina asked.

The two women were strolling along the Grand Canal in the direction of Mount Street Bridge. The first meeting with the newspaper reporter would take place in Richard Wilson's business chambers.

"It is a lot to take in." Lily had not realised she was so set in her ways. The changes taking place all around her were confusing to a woman who had always known her place.

"I'm sorry, Lily, but you must understand I cannot afford to refuse the monies offered."

The pair walked along, each lost in her own thoughts.

They acknowledged the greetings of passersby automatically – ignoring the screams and shouts of barefoot children running along the bridle path alongside the canal.

They were greeted with courtesy by Richard's male secretary. Lily was again seated in reception while Georgina walked into the inner office.

"Georgina, my dear!" Richard jumped to his feet. "Come in, do! I want to introduce you to my friend Mr Edwin Barrington-Bowes."

"Skip, please." A young man with a charming smile walked across the room to reach Georgina's side. He held out his hand, "I am delighted to meet you, Mrs Whitmore."

Georgina was aware of the door closing at her back. She tried not to stare at the outrageously dressed young man. The green velvet jacket and flowing cravat the man wore appeared effeminate to her eyes. Was this the eye-catching apparel of a reporter? She had no way of knowing, never having met a reporter before.

"Skip, I am at a loss," she said. "I agreed to speak with you but find myself unsure . . ."

"Come and sit down, Georgina," Richard could see that his friend's appearance had shocked Georgina. "We will speak of your problems. I hope you don't mind but I've already told Skip some of the background."

"I find myself at sea, I'm afraid." Georgina accepted a seat by the side of the fireplace. Her stomach was dancing in a most unsettling fashion.

Skip refused Richard's offer of refreshment, preferring to get down to the matter at hand. He was seated across the fire from Georgina, examining her appearance from under lowered eyelashes. She was nothing like he had imagined. He sat comfortably with legs crossed, a notebook open on his knee – a pencil to hand. He took notes in his own version of shorthand.

"Our friend Richard has filled me in on some details, my dear lady. What I need now is the situation in your own words," he said softly.

Newspapers were a great source of information and entertainment for the people of Dublin and those living in the surrounding areas. The long pages of text were studied word for word by many. There were those however who scanned the bold print headlines, seeking something that might interest them. It was these he had to attract. The common man would find this lady's plight of no interest to him.

"I would like to do a series of short stories." The challenge of turning the tide of public opinion in her favour delighted him. "I thought to use your experiences – of which Richard told me – concerning your treatment from shopkeepers when you tried to remedy the charges placed in your accounts." The public would have to be brought to understand her predicament.

"I have no accounts in my own name." Georgina could feel colour staining her cheeks. How embarrassing to find herself in such a position! "I have never been in the position of charging items for my own use."

"Why don't you tell me of the situation in your own words?"

She began to speak and Skip noted down the items of interest. He made special note of the shops that had sent invoices for goods delivered. Where had the goods been delivered if not to the address on the invoice? He felt his blood hum. He had something here. He listened and noted, not interrupting the woman. She gave details in a well-organised and clear fashion.

"I am going to order a tray of tea," Richard stood when it appeared to him the interview was drawing to a natural place to stop and consider what had been said. He had stayed silent through Georgina's painful rendering of her circumstances.

"Have you been to the hospital to visit your husband?" Skip asked when Richard had left them to order the refreshments. The office door stood open as was only right and proper.

"No." Georgina looked into the empty grate. She could not bear to put herself in that man's reach.

"I would suggest you rectify that matter," Skip said slowly.

The accident had been reported in the newspapers at great length. The public felt great sympathy for a sea captain who lost his legs crossing the street. There had been many articles devoted to the man's bravery in the face of such adversity. This woman was being vilified in the press. It was his job to change their minds about her. He delighted in the challenge.

"Your husband will eventually be moved to a private clinic," he said, "when it is decided that Doctor Steevens' Hospital has done everything it can for him. He will be forced to learn to live with his injuries."

This woman's refusal to tend to her husband in his own home had been made much of by the press. The good Captain had been very generous in granting interviews.

"I . . ." Georgina shook with fear.

"I'm afraid it is something you must do." Skip had been told by Richard Wilson of the abuse this woman suffered at her husband's hands. He could sympathise but she had to show her face at the hospital. "The Captain has been entertaining the public, through the dailies, from his hospital bed. He has the common man on his side. You can no longer afford to ignore the slurs on your good name. You must begin to fight back. Surely that is the point of this interview?"

"I would accompany you," Richard said, coming back into the room at that moment.

"I too would like to be present," Skip said.

"Would you – why?" Georgina stared at Skip.

Skip looked at Richard, seeking help. How could he tell the poor woman that he needed to see her husband for himself? Richard had told him something of the man. He would not vilify the man, sight unseen. He had the ethics of the press to consider.

"I have no objection to you visiting my husband and making your own judgement, Mr Barrington-Bowes," Georgina said when the men remained silent. "I, however, will not accompany you. I cannot. I'm sorry. I simply cannot." She closed her eyes briefly. She couldn't escape the man. No matter how she tried.

Chapter 36

Georgina gazed down at the sleeping Grand Canal from her bedroom window. The barges tied alongside it were dark but for a soft light to mark their presence on the inky-black waters. How many nights had she stood here dreading the arrival of her husband? How often had she pressed her aching head against this glass and silently cried? Times without number. She refused to continue to sorrow – she had a chance of a new life – she was going to grab it – but, dear Lord, how?

Sleep was impossible to find – the silent darkness seemed to welcome in all of the terrors she fought during the day – her mind twisted and twirled with the problems facing her. How could one sink into sleep in such a state?

"The rooms have been prepared to the best of our ability." She walked away from the window, the sound of her own voice a comfort in the darkness. "We will have a better idea of how to arrange matters when the first of our 'students' have arrived." She continued to pace back and forth, not feeling in the least tired. "I will endeavour to create a better home than that offered by Miss Austen's School for the children of the gentry – that will not be too difficult."

She had met her friend Eugenie on her first days at Miss Austen's school in Dalkey. That friendship had sustained her – the two lost young girls had clung together. It had been on a brief visit to Eugenie's home that she had first met Richard Wilson. He was a friend of Eugenie's older brothers. How was it possible so many years had passed?

"The women coming to me have so much courage." She was unaware that her steps had quickened and her hands had formed tight fists. "To be willing to risk everything for a chance at a better life – refusing the one offered by their parents – what sheer courage in the face of adversity! I am in awe of their fortitude." She beat clenched fists against her thighs which were covered by the filmy material of her night attire. "Eugenie and I never thought of disobeying our parents. We were both good girls constantly trying to win their approval. We argued the matter certainly – we feared marriage – why did we not discuss the matter between us?" She had thought over the years how much happier they would both have been if they had run away. Why had they not – others had – why not them?

"I must try to sleep," she muttered. The sheets on the bed had long since cooled from the application of the heating iron one of the maids had passed over the linen. She snuggled down trying to clear her mind. Her problems would be waiting for her when she awoke. She would do something about them then.

"Liam!" Georgina called when she stepped into the basement kitchen, frightening the life out of her young staff members. "I will want you to run across and ask Mr

Flint to call upon me." She waved her hand at the young lad and three maids who had got to their feet at her entrance. "Sit down, do, and finish your breakfast."

The three maids and Liam, seated around the table in the alcove, had been enjoying a well-deserved meal. They had been working since five that morning – five long hours with only a mug of tea and a chunk of buttered bread to sustain them. The house had been dusted from top to bottom. Windows opened to allow fresh air to circulate – fires checked. The kitchen range cleaned, polished and brought to a burning blaze with supplies laid to hand for Cook. Cook and Mrs Chambers were at this moment enjoying a meal served by Bridget in the housekeeper's room off the kitchen.

"I will have tea and toast with Cook and Mrs Chambers." She walked through the kitchen to the housekeeper's room.

"Sit down, she says," Bridget whispered, keeping an eye on the disappearing back of her mistress. "Who does she think will make the tea and serve it?"

"*Shh!*" Sarah hissed.

"Honest to God, Bridget!" Ruth carried her meal over to the range and placed it in the warm oven. It would keep warm until she could eat it. "You would cheek the Holy Ghost, you would!" She glared at an unrepentant Bridget.

"I'll take the tea and toast in," Bridget offered.

"Put my plate with yours, would you, Ruth?" Liam pushed his chair back. "I'll give the mistress's message to Billy and come right back." He left the kitchen as he spoke.

"I'll hold the bread to the fire to toast," Sarah offered. The bread had to be held on a long toasting fork over the flames in the range

"I want it golden brown, mind," Ruth ordered while filling the kettle.

"I think we should start as we mean to go on." Georgina waved permission to continue eating while taking a seat at the small round table in the housekeeper's room off the kitchen.

"It doesn't do to let good food go cold." Betty admired the rich orange yolk of the egg on her plate. She ignored Georgina's comment, knowing she'd get around to telling them what she meant. "Let us enjoy the food the Lord has provided before we get stuck into the problems facing us." It didn't do to hurry your food – problems were always better handled on a full stomach.

"We could do with a fresh pot of tea," Lily said to Bridget who had entered the room with the china and utensils needed to set a place for the mistress.

"Yes, Mrs Chambers. The mistress has ordered one – Ruth is seeing to it." Bridget laid a place setting on the table top. She examined her work, dipped her knee in a small curtsy, then left the room. If she wasn't so hungry she'd have lingered outside the door hoping to hear something of interest.

"Billy picked up the post," Liam – panting only slightly from his dash across the garden to the mews – entered the room after knocking and gaining permission. He placed several white envelopes and a small package on the table top. "Billy said he'd be over about eleven if that suits." He waited to see if he'd have to run across the garden again.

"Thank you, Liam." Georgina had given Billy a key to the post box that stood on the lawn at the front of the house after the neighbours had taken to verbally abusing her when they saw her standing outside. It was cowardly, but she felt she had enough to contend with. She stared at the envelopes with distaste. They looked like more invoices to her. She would not open the post now. Time enough when she was in her own private room upstairs – bad news could always wait.

Liam went back to the kitchen and joined the others to finish their breakfasts.

"Billy reckons we'll be getting them women any day now," he said. They each kept one ear open in case their elders needed any service from them. It wouldn't do to ignore the bell from Mrs Chambers' room.

"I wonder what they will be like?" Bridget shoved egg and bacon into her mouth, almost groaning at the wonderful explosion of flavour. They had never received food like this in the home. They were all three gaining weight, their uniforms tight-fitting now, with the improved diet.

"I wonder about their clothes." Sarah was very conscious of having to handle the knife and fork correctly. They were all learning to handle utensils. They had only eaten with spoons at the home. Well, she thought, porridge and stew didn't need anything else.

"I don't know how we are going to manage to feed them with only Cook and me," Ruth worried.

The three women in the housekeeper's room also worried about the new arrivals. The success of the venture they were entering into was important to all three for different reasons.

"I believe the mews should become the main entrance

to this house." Georgina spread golden butter on one of the four slices of toast sitting on a warmed plate. "We all saw Lady Arabella's shock when she entered by the kitchen." She paused to chew. "It will underline the changes facing our charges, don't you think?"

"It will only be the first of many." Lily Chambers had pushed her cleared plate to one side and was enjoying a fresh cup of tea. She didn't ring for the maid to clear, knowing they needed to eat too.

"Ruth and me will never manage to feed and clear after a dozen people on our own." Betty was worried about the lack of staff in her kitchen. "That's not counting those men of Billy Flint's. They like to step into my kitchen for a cup of tea and a bite to eat. I don't begrudge the men, mind – they turn their hands to anything we ask of them – a bit of food is the least of it."

"Lady Arabella suggested I employ two women to scrub and one to do the laundry. What do you think?" Georgina was reluctant to employ a great many people. They too would have to be fed and paid a wage. She needed to see how their new venture worked before she invested some of her precious funds.

"I've given this a great deal of thought," Lily said slowly. "We will have need of cleaning staff. We cannot continue to do all that needs doing. I believe the three young maids we have to hand will become teachers for the women coming to us."

"How so?" Georgina didn't mention that the BOBs had suggested the same thing.

"If these women are anything like that Clementine!" Lily sighed deeply. Why did the gentry raise their women to be completely useless? It was a crying shame in her opinion. "The maids will have to show them how to do everything. They won't know how to do the simplest chores. Wasn't that the problem with the first group of women they sent to America?"

"I see what you mean," Georgina said. "Ruth will have to demonstrate how to clear and wash dishes. They will not even know how to boil a kettle. Sarah will be on hand to teach them the care of their clothing. After all, they will not be receiving new outfits at the drop of a hat. Bridget will teach them to pick up and tidy after themselves." She smiled. "We have everything well in hand."

"Those three young maids are willing and cheerful." Cook poured a fresh cup of tea. "I worry that the work will all be too much for them. They have no one to oversee their work. We have no head maid since Violet left us. We are asking a great deal of ones so young."

"We can make no firm plans until the five ladies we are expecting are under this roof." Georgina fingered the post absentmindedly. She noticed one of the envelopes was stamped with a family seal. She cleaned her butter knife on a piece of bread before using it to slit the envelope open.

"We have run out of time, ladies," she said after quickly scanning the beautifully written words on the page. "The first of our ladies arrive tomorrow. We will see if all of our worrying and wondering has been in vain." She placed the document on the table and simply stared at her companions.

Chapter 37

"I don't know how to tie these," Sarah wailed, holding the long starched white apron straps out to the side of her body carefully.

"If you would step away from the long mirror!" Bridget gave her friend a gentle push.

Billy Flint's men had found the long wood-framed mirror hidden under a mountain of junk in the stables. It might be mottled with brown spots and spiderweb cracks but the girls loved it. One of Billy's men had kindly attached it to the wall of their room.

"Vanity, Miss Black, vanity!" Ruth was sitting on the bed tying the laces of her new shoes. She admired the shine of the black leather, almost giddy with the idea that no one before her had worn these shoes. They fit neat and snug to her narrow feet. She turned her ankle to admire the small heel of the shoe, feeling very grown up.

"Sarah Black, will you please stand still?" Bridget had her own apron to fix. "Ruth Brown, get up off that bed – you're wrinkling the blankets. Honest to goodness – the pair of you – you are enough to drive the saints mad."

"That won't be a problem for you so, Bridget

O'Brien." Ruth straightened the bedclothes. "No one has ever thought of you as a saint."

"Your brain is bright and your tongue sharp today anyway." Bridget tried to hide her smile.

"I can't help being delighted and excited." Sarah was almost dancing in place. "I've never had anything bought just for me before." She held out the long black skirt, admiring how it fell over the stiff petticoats she wore underneath. "Can you imagine – this is shop bought – *just for me*."

"Yes, yes, it's thrilling," Bridget cast a sideward glace at her own image in the mirror. The long black skirt of the uniform touched onto the tops of her shining new black shoes, hiding her new black grosgrain stockings completely. The black bodice was tight with a high neck and long sleeves. She hadn't yet attempted to put on the white wraparound apron that was giving Sarah so much trouble. "I hope I'm not the one expected to wash, starch and iron these aprons."

"Will the two of you for goodness' sake get dressed?" Ruth, wearing her own new uniform but not yet her apron, walked over to join them. She watched carefully as Bridget drew the long white straps of the apron over Sarah's shoulders and crossed them before buttoning the straps down at the waist at the back. "The first of those women will be here before we are dressed and ready to greet them."

"If we dress Sarah in all of the new paraphernalia," Bridget stood back to examine her work, "we will be able to work out what goes where." She stared at the stack of gleaming white cotton and lace placed carefully on top of their table.

"These go over our arms." Ruth passed two white

tubes of linen and lace to Bridget.

"How do you know?" Bridget held the tubes open for Sarah to slip her hands inside.

"There is a sketch here." Ruth shook the heavy brown greased paper with dark black lines etched into it in the air. "It shows you how the uniform is meant to look." She breathed a sigh of relief. It was lovely to be surprised with new uniforms but no one had shown them how to wear all of this stuff. "This goes on the top of our head over our hair." She held a circular confection of lace and ribbons in the air.

"What shall we do with our hair?" Sarah, her arms covered from wrist to elbow in the white tubes, rushed to the mirror.

The other two left her to fiddle with her hair and admire her own image while they helped each other with their own aprons and cuffs.

"Have you ever heard the like of their names?" Bridget looked over her shoulder to check Ruth had not twisted her straps. "I hope we don't have to address them by their full moniker."

"Must be nice to know who you are," Sarah said sadly. "Where you come from." She was twisting her white hair over the circular tube she had made from scraps of material to give her hair the appearance of fullness. "What your name is – your family."

"I don't know about that. I think their names make them sound like a herd of cows." Bridget too felt the tug of not knowing who she was – but there was nothing they could do about that – it was the way it was. She turned to assist Ruth.

"Those poor women are going to be shocked by

everything," Ruth turned under Bridget's fingers. "I expect them all to burst into tears as soon as they arrive. The mistress has told us what she wants us to do but I am dreading it."

"We have to start as we mean to go on." Bridget was almost sick with excitement. This was it – the start of her own escape into the big world – she wanted what these women were being given. She would listen and learn. "You look lovely, Sarah," she said as she and Ruth walked over to join their friend in front of the mirror.

"It was clever of you to make those sausage things to go in our hair." Ruth admired how the sausage of material was hidden by Sarah's hair, adding a fullness to the rolled hairstyle. They did not have enough hair – yet – to form the popular Gibson style.

"Sit down at the table, both of you," Sarah ordered while attaching the flat white disk to the top of her head. "One of you check that my ribbons are hanging straight." She shook her head to admire how the long white ribbons attached to the back of the disk fluttered in the breeze she created and down her back. "I'll fix your hair and put the cap on for you."

"Look at you three!" Lily walked across the kitchen to admire the maids in their new dress uniforms.

She was wearing her own black bombazine housekeeper's uniform, a long chain of keys hanging from her waist. She had insisted on ordering the new uniforms for the household staff. The girls in particular needed to present a good image on this first meeting with the women soon to arrive.

"Turn around." She examined the placement of the

straps while each girl slowly twirled in front of her. "Let me see your hands – have you each got a handkerchief?" She examined the spotlessly clean hands and nails of each girl. She gave a brisk nod when each produced a clean white handkerchief from her skirt pocket. "You'll do."

"We all look daft done up like the dog's dinner." Liam, wearing his own new suit, looked very uncomfortable. "I don't know why I have to wear this lot." He pushed his hands into the pockets of his knickerbockers which were fastened by a button below his knees. The long dark stockings he wore were already beginning to wrinkle. The collar of his white shirt was barely visible under the dark jacket he wore.

"I have to say," Cook appeared in the kitchen from her bedroom wearing her own dress uniform, "I'll be glad to get this lot off. I don't know how they expect anyone to do a lick of work dolled up like this." She too wore tightly tailored black but her white apron covered her only from the waist down. The fancy white lace bonnet covering her hair was in danger of falling into her eyes.

"*They are here!*" Georgina stood at the top of the stairs and shouted down. "*Mrs Chambers, upstairs if you please!*" They had discussed this first meeting. It was vital the arriving women knew from the beginning how their lives had changed. "Cook, you know what to do."

There was a brief hesitation before Lily hurried from the room. The three maids stood to attention in a row. Cook came to stand at their backs. Liam, after a glare from Cook, walked over to join them. The noise from the garden and mews was growing louder.

"*Billy!*" a loud shout carried to the waiting people in the kitchen. The sound of feminine squeals accompanied the shout. "*Billy Flint, will yeh get out here and take care of these women for Jaysus' sake! I've taken pigs to slaughter that didn't make this much noise!*"

"*Shh!*" Cook said when the maids and Liam started to giggle nervously. She was having a hard time hiding her own smile. Those poor women wouldn't be accustomed to treatment like this – how could they be? Billy's men were a law unto themselves.

"Should I open the kitchen door?" Liam turned to stare up at Cook. "I know the mistress said to let them wait a bit, but . . ." the noise from outside increased, "we'll have the whole street out with all that racket."

"We had best see what's going on." Cook gave Liam's shoulder a little pat. They would have to take each thing as it came about.

The scene that met their eyes when they stepped out of the kitchen was like something from a French farce Cook had once seen at the Gaiety. The garden was strewn with leather trunks and boxes – men tried to pull resisting women from two carriages, one of which belonged to the house – screams and curses echoed around the walled garden space.

"*What in heaven's name is going on here?*" Cook had a very loud voice when she needed it. "*Ladies, stop this at once! Is this any way to behave?*" She clapped her hands loudly.

The people in the garden fell silent and turned to her – glad of someone to take control. The sound of smothered sobbing came from the interior of the carriages. "Billy, get everyone out of that second carriage if you would." Cook looked at the luggage strewn around. That lot was not coming into her clean kitchen. "Our own carriage can

284

stand for a minute."

The three maids stood to one side of the kitchen doorway, staring in amazement at the confusion.

"Right, lads, jump to it!" Billy pulled open the door of the second carriage.

He hoped it hadn't been rented or all of this would be around Dublin in minutes. A tale like this would delight the men in the local pubs. Those silly females clucking like chickens. Were they not supposed to be in hiding for feck's sake? "Ladies," he held out a hand, not caring who took it. He wanted those women out of his hair and inside the house as quickly as possible.

"Thank you!" Verity Watson took the proffered hand and with this assistance stepped onto the wooden steps that had been placed close to the carriage door. She took a gulp of fresh air, glad to be out of that confined space. She had been perilously close to slapping the silly women bemoaning their lot – she had been forced to share the carriage with them – but dear Lord – how would she survive their company for an extended period of time? She too was terrified of this step into the unknown. She didn't need weeping females falling all over her.

"Miss Watson," Cook stepped forward, "how nice to see you again."

She stared at the bedraggled, pitiful women weeping quietly inside the carriage. What on earth were they going to do with this lot? She clapped her hands and ordered them to step down. It was several moments before she was obeyed. "And you would be?" she snapped at the first to reach the grass and pebbles of the kitchen courtyard.

"Euphemia Locke-Statton." The hand that pushed the fashionable bonnet away from mouse-brown hair shook.

"I am not accustomed to being treated in this fashion."

"Next!" Cook gently pushed the young woman out of the way.

"Octavia White-Gershwin." A pretty strawberry blonde stepped out of the carriage. "I too object to our treatment."

"Ladies, you were asked to have one piece of luggage packed to see you through several days." Cook looked at the luggage the coachmen had thrown any old how onto the ground. "Pick that up now and come into the house."

"You, girl," Octavia White-Gershwin snapped her fingers in the general direction of the three maids, "that one." She pointed to a piece of luggage and began to walk away.

"No." Bridget took a tight hold of Sarah's arm when she began to step forward to pick up the luggage. "We were told not to."

"But . . ." Ruth knew what they had been told but this went against everything the nuns had taught them, "they are gentry."

"Not any longer." Bridget crossed her arms and left it up to the other two what they would do.

"Those maids are not yours to command." Cook put a heavy hand on the young woman's shoulder. "Pick up your own bag."

There was a tense moment when it looked like the young woman would object. Cook glared until the woman hung her head and walked over to pick up the smallest bag from among her luggage.

"*Liam, take these women into my kitchen!*" Cook shouted to the fascinated young lad. "Billy, get the rest of their luggage from this carriage and let the coachman get back to his own place of business." She looked meaningfully at Billy. They needed to know where this carriage had come from. She trusted Billy to find out the details.

"I am Ermatrude Willowbee." A stout little woman stepped from the house carriage. She looked around the garden with eyes rimmed in pink. She took a handkerchief from her pocket and blew her nose vigorously. She picked up a piece of luggage and followed after Liam.

"Felicia Hyde-Richards." A tall proud blonde woman followed after 'the little mouse' as Cook thought of Ermatrude.

"If you will all make your way into my kitchen." Cook needed help. These young women were not ready to be taught the new facts of their lives. "Billy, store all of this luggage in the stables please. We will sort something out presently." She turned with a heavy sigh to follow after the still weeping women.

Chapter 38

"Have you eaten?" Cook looked at the bedraggled group of women standing like broken flowers in her kitchen. They had drawn close together as if seeking somewhere to hide.

"We have had little to eat in the last few days," Verity Watson replied when it appeared no one else was willing to answer. They were all tired and hungry – frightened – not knowing what would happen to them. She had never been on this side of the escape the BOBs offered. If they allowed it, she would be suggesting many changes.

"Right!" Cook pushed the silly bonnet out of her eyes. She was changing out of this outfit before she did anything else. Really, how were you supposed to get a lick of work done tied up like a Christmas roast? "Bridget, take this lot up to the mistress. Ruth, pull that kettle over on the range and get a pot of tea going. Sarah, you sort out the crockery we'll be needing for this lot." She turned towards her bedroom. "Liam, get changed. I'll hang your uniform up in my room." She was still giving orders as she hurried down the basement hallway towards her bedroom.

Bridget stepped forward. "If you would follow me, please." She walked past the group still standing staring.

Ruth pulled the kettle over to the hottest part of the range. Sarah began to pull dishes out of the tall kitchen cupboard.

Bridget looked over her shoulder to check that the women were following. They were still standing still. "We need to get on, ladies. Please pick up your bags and follow me."

They at last began to follow her.

"Wait here, please," Bridget said when they reached the main hallway. She rapped lightly on the door of the mistress's drawing room. At the first whisper of permission she stepped inside to find Mrs Whitmore and Mrs Chambers standing together. She closed the door behind her.

"They are a sorry bunch," Bridget said when no one spoke. "I left them standing in the hall. They are waiting for you."

"Bring them in." Georgina was shaking visibly.

"If I might make a suggestion," Lily said. "Have them taken to the dining room. It would be easier to talk and question them while seated around a table."

"Cook asked them if they had eaten," Bridget said. "I think she's going to make them something to eat."

Lily nodded at Bridget. "The dining room it should be." The girl should have waited to receive permission to speak – but really – with the way things were going all house rules seemed to be going out the window.

"Very well." Georgina had thought to welcome them into her own room. Perhaps this was better. "Bridget, take them into the dining room."

Bridget nodded and, with a little bob, left.

Georgina put a finger to her lips when it looked like Lily was about to speak. She crossed to the door of her drawing room and listened nervously to the commotion outside her door.

"Ladies." Georgina with Mrs Chambers at her shoulder walked into the dining room. She held herself stiffly erect. This first meeting would set the tone for all others. She was not pleased with what she had heard of them. These women had tried to order Bridget about – failing, they had been unnecessarily rude. She would not allow that to continue. "I am Georgina Corrigan-Whitmore." If they were going to use double-barrel family names she would do the same. She walked to the head of the table. Standing with her fists clenched on her chair back, she stared at each woman. "I am not your hostess – you are not guests in my home."

Lily said nothing. She stood behind Georgina and stared at each woman, trying to form an opinion. They were a motley lot – she had thought they would all be young – not so – some were older than her mistress.

"I have no wish to be rude or ungrateful but . . ." the pretty blonde woman began.

Georgina waved her back into her chair when she stood upright to speak. "Please go ahead," she said.

"My name is Felicia Hyde-Richards." The woman looked around at her companions. "I was wondering if you could tell me," she waved a hand around the table, "tell us – what is happening?"

"I will arrange for tea and sandwiches to be served." Lily pressed her mistress into her chair at the head of the table. She glanced at each woman before taking her leave.

Georgina looked around the group. She had expected young girls – adventuresses – girls alight with excitement. These women looked bruised by life – they had the same look in their eyes that she saw in her own mirror.

"You, all of you," she put her hands on the table-top and simply stared for a moment. "You applied to the BOBs for assistance. In the past the BOBs found employment for women such as you. They sent such women on their way to sink or swim under their own power. That proved not altogether successful." She would not speak of the suicides or those consigned to mental homes. These women were frightened already. "I have been asked to prepare you for the change in lifestyle that you are all facing." She gulped at the responsibility that had fallen to her.

"I was companion and general servant to my great-aunt." Ermatrude Willowbee put her hand in the air like a child seeking attention. "I sought a new post in a similar position. I thought the BOBs could help me. I had not expected to be herded around the countryside willy-nilly."

"How long were you with your great-aunt?" Georgina ignored the last comment. They would learn about each other over time. She knew something about all of these women. She had files on them but nothing compared with actually listening to them tell their own story. She believed they all needed to listen to each tale told. "Why have you left your position?"

"I," the poor little woman fought tears, "I was with the family for fifteen years – from the age of twelve to now. My great-aunt died. I understood she would leave me enough to survive on – this did not prove to be the case."

"I'm sorry to say your story is a familiar one." Georgina sighed deeply. This was going to be a great deal more difficult than she had first supposed.

In the kitchen – Cook once more in her familiar uniform – commanded her troops. Ruth had removed her dress apron and was covered from neck to ankle in one of cook's cast-off cover-all aprons. She stood at a work bench tearing apart hot ham shanks. Sarah and Bridget were buttering a great quantity of bread.

"We will not continue to provide this level of service." Lily stood well away from the work area. She had no wish to be splattered with grease and meat juice.

Liam, once more in his tattered clothing, was enjoying the change in the routine of the house. He'd have a lot to tell his family when he next visited.

Lily looked around and fought despair. She was too old for all of these changes. She had tried to think of ways of reducing the work involved in keeping house. "Cook – we must have an oilcloth table cover somewhere that we can use in the dining room instead of linen. It would cut down on our laundry if we didn't have to launder huge tablecloths."

"We have and I'll get it." Cook grimaced. "But I want you to know it will hurt my heart to send food out of my kitchen to be served in such a way."

"We haven't the staff to prepare, serve, and clean. It is important that we start as we mean to go on." Lily too was upset at the lowering of her standards.

Back in the dining room Georgina was walking back and forth, trying to find the words to explain the order of things to come.

"I have been asked to prepare you all for the uncertain future you are facing." She stood for a moment, wondering how much to say. "I too am struggling. I am a married woman with a husband who is doing everything in his power to drive me insane." She held up her hand to silence the questions she could see on their lips. "You will all learn more in the coming weeks, I am sure. I have been asked to educate you all in a way of life that is foreign to the upperclass female of the species."

"I beg your pardon?"

Georgina didn't know who spoke nor did she care.

"We are raised to be useless." She looked around. "We have no knowledge of taking care of ourselves. We do not know how to work for a wage. When misfortune visits us we turn to family and friends for help. In many cases," She glanced at Verity and Ermatrude, "we are taken advantage of – we work for no wage – we have nothing of our own to sustain us. The BOBs are hoping to change this."

She stopped speaking when Lily after a brief knock opened the dining-room door, Bridget and Sarah at her heels. The girls were both carrying trays of sandwiches. They held the trays well away from their white aprons.

Liam with a folded oilcloth in his arms followed after the women.

"Could one of youse women give us a hand spreading this?" he asked.

He knew he was being cheeky and might get a clip around the ear from Mrs Chambers but he couldn't spread this tablecloth with all them women sitting like statues watching his every move.

There was a shocked silence for a moment before the

women moved. Some stood away from the table. Verity and Felicia offered their assistance and the colourful oilcloth was soon spread over the table.

"Leave the dishes on the sideboard, Bridget. Put the sandwiches on the table, Sarah," Lily said.

The women looked at each other but were too hungry to object to the shabby service.

"You will each need to set a place for yourself at table. We will return with the tea presently," Lily said.

The four servants left without another word.

"We will all have to learn together how this house will function from this day forth." Georgina hid her smile. It looked as if Lily was taking control. "You are the first group of women to be treated in this fashion."

"Lucky us," someone muttered.

"Yes." Georgina turned with a smile. "You are lucky. You may not feel so at the moment but I am confident that you will all step into your new situations from a far stronger and more educated position than any that have come before you."

There was silence while each woman struggled to remember how their own servants set a table. They were each wondering what was to become of them. They were all trying desperately to come to terms with the changes that had been forced upon them.

"If I might make a suggestion –" Verity Watson paused to watch the two young maids struggle into the room under the weight of the items they carried.

Bridget had to say something. "I'll pass along the table pouring tea." She felt as if the weight of the huge teapot she carried was enough to break her arms. "There is milk and sugar on the table for those who want it."

"Verity," Georgina said, "you wished to say something?"

"I feel I am in a unique position." Verity reached for the milk and sugar. "I worked for many years as secretary to the BOBs. I have seen the organisation from the inside, you might say." She had been shocked by the treatment this group had received from people paid handsomely to assist them.

"Yes." Georgina stood and began walking the length of the table. She leaned over Octavia White-Gershwin's shoulder. "I am listening," she said when Verity stopped speaking. "Ladies, you must learn to serve your own food." She put a sandwich from the serving plate in the centre of the table onto the plate in front of Octavia. "Pray continue, Verity."

"I believe we must document our findings about this endeavour." Verity took a sandwich and watched while the others followed suit. "We are the first to be prepared for the change in our lifestyle. We will learn as each day passes. A document of our individual findings would be of great interest to the BOBs and any who come after us."

"An excellent suggestion." Georgina walked back to her own place. "At this moment, however, let us eat the food prepared for us. We have a great deal to do to get each of you settled in." She wanted to put her head on the table and scream. How would she ever manage?

"I do not wish to cause problems but . . ." Felicia Hyde-Richards felt somewhat human after drinking the tea and consuming several of the sandwiches, "I wish to request – to know – is it possible to take a bath? I have been in these clothes for what seems like weeks."

"Felicia, is it?" Georgina waited for the nod from the young beauty. She was determined to put the correct name to each face as soon as possible. "We have set up what I suppose you could call a bath house." She thanked God for Billy Flint's common sense. It was he who had suggested making a bath house out of the wash room at the back of the house. "I do not have sufficient servants to haul water for six baths." She gestured, including herself in their number. "I doubt you will have people willing to haul water for you wherever you settle. As I have stated, we must learn a new way of going on – together."

"I confess I would be willing to stand in a river to wash," Felicia said. "I feel unclean."

"I too would welcome a bath." Euphemia Locke-Statton glanced around the table. "We have all been forced to sleep and travel in the same outfit for some time."

"You were asked to have one bag to hand that held all you should require for one night – have each of you done this?" Georgina thought of the luggage she had seen thrown around her garden and wondered who had managed to carry along a mountain of luggage while they tried to escape.

She received nods from each woman.

"I would like to be shown to my room," Octavia White-Gershwin said.

"You will be sharing a bedchamber." Georgina had been dreading their reaction to this. She was glad the matter was out in the open.

"I beg your pardon?" Octavia was sure she had misheard. Was it not bad enough that she had been forced to flee her home?

"I am sorry, ladies." Georgina could not imagine sharing a bedchamber with a stranger. These women – apart from Verity Watson – had no knowledge as yet of the Harvey organisation. She wondered how many of them would be willing to take the chance on offer. "I am following the BOBs' instructions. They wish you all to learn to share bedchambers. You are no longer ladies of good families but females with no money and no prospects, depending on the charity of others."

"I am willing to work for my keep!" Ermatrude almost wailed.

"That is the very attitude we wish to change!" Georgina slapped the table top. She could not afford to feel sympathy for these women. They had to learn to stand on their own two feet. "The labourer is worthy of his hire. You will no longer work only for the food in your stomach and the roof over your head. Have you not been taught that lesson rather forcefully, Ermatrude?"

"What else can we do?" Ermatrude looked around at the others. They were all pretty. She wasn't. She needed to make herself useful.

"That is what we are here to learn." Georgina looked at each woman. "The BOBs are giving you this chance to change your own destiny. We must all work together to learn how to survive alone in the world. It is frightening – I do understand – but it is also a great opportunity. It is up to all of you to grasp this chance for an independent life."

There was silence in the room as each person avoided the eyes of the others.

"We cannot achieve everything at this moment in time. We will each have to learn as we go along. In the meantime

I will show you to your bedchambers." Georgina pushed away from the table and stood. She had thought to allow them to pick the person they would share a room with – it appeared she would have to force the choice upon them. "Just this once the servants will clear the table. In future we will eat in the kitchen and each person will clean up after themselves." She didn't allow them time to argue but began to walk from the room. "If you would follow me."

She listened to the mutters of the women behind her and ignored their comments.

Upstairs, she threw open the door to a bedchamber and stepped back. "Octavia, Euphemia, this is your room. Felicia and Verity, you are next door. Ermatrude, you will be across the corridor."

"Why does she get a bedchamber of her own?" Octavia looked willing to argue.

"Because that is what I choose," Georgina glared. "You are five – that is an uneven number. I was given to understand that I might receive more young ladies at a moment's notice. There is a second bed in the room. Ermatrude will have to share at such a time. Ladies, that is the last time I will explain my decisions. This is my house. We follow my rules. It is that simple."

She stood in the hallway and waited while they entered the rooms she had indicated.

"If you will each prepare a bag with a drying towel, soap and a change of clothing I will arrange for water to be heated for bathing."

She walked swiftly down the stairs.

"How did it go?" Lily Chambers came out of her room when she heard her mistress being greeted by cook.

298

"I pity them." Georgina saw no point in hiding anything from the people in the kitchen. They would all have to pull together to make this work.

"They looked a sorry lot," Cook said.

"The table in the dining room needs to be cleared. I have informed them that in future they will be served meals in the kitchen and must clear after themselves. I'm afraid it has been one shock after another for them." She walked towards the back door. "I must speak with Billy Flint. They requested baths – time to put his plan into effect."

"Bridget, clear the dining room," the housekeeper ordered. "Ruth and Sarah, check the servants' dining room. We all will be using it for meals from now on."

"Are we to eat with them?" Ruth was shocked into asking.

"I see no other way of going on." Lily had tried to think of the best use of the little staff she had. "Cook cannot be asked to make and serve three different meals at each sitting."

"Do you think any of them will be willing to help in the kitchen?" Cook jerked her chin towards the ceiling.

"It is my understanding that they will all be asked to help," Lily said. "How much help they will be – well – that is another matter."

"*Jimmy!*" Billy Flint shouted from where he stood in the open door of the wash house. "*Time to go to work, lad!*" He glanced around at the work his men had already done. There was a new bolt on the inside of the door and shutters on the inside of the only window. They had carried down one of the fancy roll-top baths from the house. It was sitting ready to be filled in one corner of the room. There was a standing tap and a copper boiler in the outdoor space. A hole in the centre of the room made emptying the bath a simple matter. The walls were freshly whitewashed.

"Jimmy will keep the fire going under the copper boiler. He will refill the water each time the copper is emptied. He'll keep the room set to rights and all." He turned to glance at the woman at his side. "If it is not too cheeky on my part," he stopped for a moment before almost spitting out his request, "I'd like permission for me and my men to use this as a bath house as well." He had learned the value of being clean when he travelled for the first time in his life as a gent. He'd liked the feeling and sought to find ways to improve his own appearance. He had been using the public bath houses but wanted his men to smarten up as well. The public bath houses charged for their service. He'd save a bit by using this room and it was more convenient for him, being on his doorstep so to speak.

"You may use this room when it is free." Georgina thought of the cost of coal to keep the water boiling but made no mention of it. The man at her side was worth his weight in coal to her. "I need to employ a washerwoman and two scrubbing women. Do you know of anyone seeking such work?" She had decided to ask this man as he appeared to know everyone in and around Dublin.

"Would that be daily work?" Billy knew women who would kiss his feet for the chance to earn a few bob to add to the family kitty.

"I'm not sure."

"I don't know how a house such as yours is run." Billy

thought of the house on Merrion Square. There appeared to be servants constantly underfoot in that house. This woman had only two old women and childer to help her. "Why don't we say three days a week at first and see how that works for you?"

"That would be ideal," Georgina agreed. "I'll trust your judgement." She didn't have time to interview staff. "If you would find three women for me I would be grateful."

"Easily done." He turned at the sound of shuffling. "Here comes Jimmy."

Upstairs in the house the five women were trying to settle into a new way of living.

"I have never shared a bedchamber before," Felicia said. "Do you want to pick a bed?"

"I don't suppose it matters," Verity sat on one of the beds and stared at the young beauty standing uncertainly in the room. "My name is Verity," she offered. "You, I think, are Felicia?"

"How silly, of course we have never been properly introduced." Felicia gazed around. "I don't know how to go on in this situation."

"None of us do."

"I intend to do everything I can to make a success of whatever is offered to me." Felicia had thought she would be forced to offer her body to a wealthy man. She had been prepared to be some old man's darling. If she could make a life for herself with dignity – that would be so much better.

"I too intend to apply myself to learning everything we are taught here." Verity stood. "We need to organise our bags for bathing."

"I don't have soap and a drying cloth in my bag," Felicia said. "Do you?"

"No," Verity smiled. "But I will in future."

"That's a good attitude." Felicia could almost feel the tension draining from her body. She had been so afraid. "I have so much to learn."

"We all do," Verity liked this young woman. "May I ask, if it is not too rude . . ."

"You may ask me anything. It would appear we are to be living cheek by jowl. It will be impossible to keep secrets under those circumstances."

"How . . . why . . ." Verity shrugged. "All of the luggage you brought with you. I could not help but notice. How did you ever manage to make an escape with all of that to carry with you?"

"My brothers Thomas and Peter helped me escape." Felicia's breath caught as she fought tears. She had not had time to grieve for all she had lost. "I do hope I will be able to keep in touch with them. I love them so much." She wiped the tears that fell from her eyes on the shoulder of her gown. "They have promised to write to me through the BOBs."

"You must give the BOBs permission to share information with your brothers," Verity said. "It is not unusual for males to seek information through them. We do not share information about our runaways without express permission from the lady in question."

Felicia wanted to know the story behind the other women in this group. But she could not do that without being willing to share her own story.

Chapter 39

Georgina sat at the head of the long table in the servants' dining room attached to the kitchen.

Ruth, under Cook's watchful eye, placed a large tureen of soup on the table before taking her seat.

Georgina stood to serve. She looked around at the familiar and unfamiliar faces feeling a sense of wonder – how had her life come to this? "If you would each pass me your soup bowl, please?" She held out one hand, the other holding the silver soup ladle. "Perhaps we could discuss our first day together?"

"I cannot speak for the others," Felicia said from her seat across the table from Cook and the four young servants, "but I am extremely grateful for everything done for me. I enjoyed my bath thoroughly – and the food is delicious." She smiled at the cook. "However," she paused for a moment, "I feel completely out of my depth and useless."

"But willing to learn." Georgina carefully filled a china bowl. "That is very important. I saw Ruth teaching you to peel potatoes."

Liam, wearing his new suit again, sat almost frozen in

303

place. He had never before been invited to sit down at the servants' table. The array of cutlery in front of him was confusing. He'd sit here and watch and learn. He'd promised Billy Flint he'd take careful note of every little detail.

"If we are to discuss our feelings," Euphemia dabbed her lips with her napkin, "I am frightened." She fought tears, not willing to cry in front of the servants. "I had never thought to find myself in such a situation." She longed to curse her brother's name to the sky. How could he have gambled away their home and her dowry? It was his fault she was in this predicament.

"None of us could ever have imagined such a situation," Georgina said softly. "We can make the decision to sink into melancholy," she looked at each person at the table, "or we can decide to grab life by the neck and shake. It is up to each person here to decide what they will do."

"It isn't fair!" Octavia dropped her spoon into her soup bowl. She made to push her chair from the table. She couldn't do this – dine with servants – in the kitchen – it was past bearing.

"*Stay!*" Georgina ordered. She waited until a startled Octavia had settled into her chair again. She leaned forward to stare at the bowed head of the haughty woman. "No one ever said life was fair, Octavia."

"If I may comment?" Cook was passing the bowls of soup down the table to her young helpers. "I am the oldest female here. I am also one of only two who have been earning their living for years." She gave a nod down the table to Lily Chambers sitting at its foot. "I believe this gives me some insight into the world you are about to enter." She waited to see if she had their attention. She wasn't going to waste her wisdom.

"Oh, that it should have come to this!" Euphemia wailed before putting a well-filled spoon of soup into her mouth.

"Taking advice from a servant, you mean?" Cook didn't like this one's attitude at all. "I am not the one who is homeless and penniless."

"I for one would like to hear what you have to say, Mrs Powell," Verity raised her eyes from her soup bowl to say. "Perhaps I have a different attitude as I have been in service to my relative for some years as has Miss Willowbee." She dabbed her napkin to her lips. "I am twenty-five years old." She heard the gasps but ignored them. She knew she looked much older. "When you are in service to a relative – no matter how kind – you are given to understand that you are expected to disappear into the background." She fought tears. "I have watched my true self disappear day by day and year by year. I intend to make the most of the opportunity that has been placed before me."

"I am not so brave," Ermatrude Willowbee almost whispered, not raising her eyes from her almost-empty soup bowl. "I wish only to find a position where I can employ my skills and be assured of a settled future."

There was silence while everyone concentrated on their soup. When everyone had finished, Cook pushed to her feet.

"Ruth, Sarah, clear the soup course, please." Cook stood for a moment, hands on her hips. "There will be no fish course. We will not have hours to pass chatting around the table of an evening. Tonight we will serve you but after this it will be different." These women needed to realise that everything had changed for them and the quicker the better, in her opinion.

"There are women," Lily Chambers said over the noise of the clattering china being removed, "who are fighting for freedom and votes for women. To our shame these women are not being supported by all women everywhere." She slapped the table. "As they should be!" She took a deep breath. She would not lecture these women no matter how much she wanted to. "The BOBs is a wonderful organisation – of that there is no doubt – but they are ruled by women of high social standing – these women have not a clue about the problems facing women such as yourselves." She made sure to catch the eye of each woman at the table. "You are the first being offered a chance to change your lives. It is important we make a success of this venture. It will take the good will of everyone here to make sure we put in place a scheme that will help all of the women who pass through our hands now and in the future."

"We," Octavia gestured to Euphemia sitting by her side – they had discussed the matter in the bedroom, "understood that we would be placed as governesses in wealthy households. We are both well educated. Is this not the case?"

"Is that your true desire?" Georgina watched Bridget jump to her feet to help her friends set the table and deliver the food.

"You are both too young and attractive to be given such positions of trust in a household," Verity said absently. She was watching every movement the maids made. She had much to learn. "Not all men abuse their servants but far too many do, I'm afraid."

"That is always a worry in a household with attractive servants," Lily said softly. She almost smiled at the look of horror on the faces of the young women. They would have seen such abuse and ignored it in the past – the shoe was on the other foot now.

"You speak as if we have a choice." Felicia too was watching the maids. "I wish you would share it with us. I for one am terrified of the future – it would be a great relief to know of something I can do to earn my way in life." She had not told anyone of the only choice she thought she had.

"May I be the one to speak of this?" Verity looked down the table at their hostess. "I have spent much time in study of the matter."

"Very well, "said Georgina. "But let's wait until everyone is seated."

The maids scuttled to the table to take their places.

"It is not considered polite to discuss important matters over food." Georgina smiled around the table. "It is said to lead to indigestion. But I believe everyone here will sleep easier if certain matters are made clear. Please share everything you know, Miss Watson."

"There is an organisation." Verity was almost shaking with excitement. She could not wait to step out into this new world. "It is in America." She ate some of the delicious food on her plate while shocked gasps and whispers echoed around her. She had known that would be a shock – best to get it out of the way.

"Verity – America – really?" It was Felicia who breathlessly broke the silence that had fallen over the group. Her two brothers were heading for the state of

Kentucky. Would she really have the chance to travel to America?

Verity waited until she had chewed the food in her mouth before replying. "A Mr Fred Harvey, an Englishman, has a large organisation. This man is offering an opportunity for women to earn a good salary. He is also offering opportunities for advancement within his organisation for those who do not wish to marry."

"I have never wanted to marry." Octavia was clutching her cutlery with white-knuckled hands. America – she had given it no thought.

"I have no wish for travel and excitement," Ermatrude said.

"We will force no one to accept this challenge," Georgina said.

"There is much to learn before we can even think of applying for a position with the Harvey Company." Verity had an idea of something that would suit poor Miss Willowbee but she would not mention it yet. "There is also the opportunity of making a marriage connection if that is your wish. I understand that the area Mr Harvey's organisation functions in is overrun with single wealthy men. It appears that there are fifty men to every woman in the American Southwest."

"I assumed we were all of us in the same position – no dowries – seeking positions with a good family?" Euphemia had leaned forward to listen. "My brother – it shames me to state – gambled away the family monies."

"I have made a study of the Harvey Company and what they offer." Verity had read everything she could on this matter since first hearing of the Harvey Company. "Your social background and education will be all of the dowry you will need for the type of men seeking a wife in the Southwest of America." She ignored the gasps her words brought.

"The positions on offer with the Harvey organisation will come as a shock to you all." Georgina said. "You must remember we are speaking of America – a young country with very different notions than our own."

"It would perhaps be best if you tell us what is expected of us." Ermatrude had had all of the shocks she could stand.

"Mr Harvey is seeking attractive ladies of good character to work as waitresses in his hotels and restaurants along the railway lines travelling through Southwestern America. These ladies are known as Harvey Girls and are becoming almost legend as the 'women who will settle the west'. It is not at all what you would imagine from the role of waitress as we know it."

Georgina allowed the cries and shouts of horror to echo around the room before putting a stop to it.

"Ladies! There is no need to make a decision at this moment in time," she said, wiping her mouth with her napkin. She wished she too could take advantage of the opportunity on offer to these women. "We will, I hope, together put in place a course of study that will enable women such as us to survive to a ripe old age in relative comfort."

Bridget was almost biting her tongue. She longed to shout at these women who were clearly horrified at the chance being offered them. Could none of them see the great adventure they were being offered? She longed for the day when she would be old enough to put herself forward for the same chance. She would listen and learn.

Her time would come.

Ruth and Sarah were holding hands under cover of the table. This strange household was not what they had expected when they left the convent. What was to become of them? They knew Bridget was almost humming at the very thought of such an adventure. Would she leave them behind?

Liam was thrilled the women seemed to have forgotten he was there. He'd have much to tell Billy Flint.

Cook looked at the strained faces across the table from her and almost sighed. If she were a younger woman she would be the first to grab at the chance being offered. What was wrong with these young women that they couldn't see the great freedom being put before them?

"Nothing can be decided tonight." Georgina continued to eat. She had problems of her own. It was up to each woman to consider what would serve them best. She could offer choices but they had to be willing to learn.

"There is much to think about!" Felicia wanted to dance around the table with joy. She was being given a chance to escape the fate she believed awaited her – and join her brothers in America! She would learn whatever she had to in order to avail of this chance.

"I would like to mention something." Lily had waited until silence had fallen again. "You, all of you, look delightful." That wasn't quite true – poor Misses Watson and Willowbee looked faded. "The outfits you are wearing while fashionable will not serve you well over the next little while. Do you have anything in your luggage that is not quite so," she waved a hand around seeking the word she sought, "delicate?" She'd barely bitten back the word impractical.

Chapter 40

"Ladies, I would like to introduce you to my good friend Mr Richard Wilson." Georgina stood in the dining room looking around at her charges – such a change in so short a space of time. The long woollen skirts worn with shirts and jumpers looked to her eyes like a uniform in spite of the slight differences in colour and shape. In the ten days these ladies had been with her they had showed a willingness to learn that enchanted her. There was still some grumbling in the ranks but all in all they were learning to pull together. "Mr Wilson has agreed to discuss the handling of our personal finances with us."

She had insisted the three young maids be here for this lecture. Lily and Cook preferred to take tea in the peace of the housekeeper's sitting room. Liam was with his hero Billy Flint.

The dining-room table was once more covered in a colourful oilcloth. There were paper, ink and pens close to hand for the taking of notes.

"Ladies!" Richard stood with his hands in his trouser pockets. He felt uncomfortable addressing a room full of women. He was more comfortable in the company of men. "I have given a great deal of thought to what I should say to you all." He tried to ignore the way the women were assessing him. He fought the urge to loosen his shirt collar. Time to take charge.

While he was speaking Georgina had taken her seat at the opposite end of the table from where he stood.

"With the exception of our three young maidservants," Richard had met the maids frequently while out and about with Georgina, "you have all been raised to be useless – this is no reflection on your good selves – but rather on our society as it exists now."

He waited to see if they would object to his words. When no one spoke, he continued.

"We are almost in the year 1900 – times are changing – and we must change with them." He pushed his hands through his hair. "We have all seen the faded creatures forced to live on the charity of their relatives. We all know people who have been left destitute by the action of the men charged with their welfare. You ladies have a chance to change your destiny. You are being offered a unique way of living." He looked around the room. "You will not succeed if you do not learn to handle your own finances. This matter is vital. You must learn to plan for your own old age. That may sound ridiculous when you are in the full flower of your womanhood – but flowers fade." He wondered if he sounded as pompous to their ears as he did to his own.

"We none of us," Octavia looked around quickly, "have any money to speak of."

"At this moment in time," Richard agreed. "However, it is my understanding that that is about to change." He took his hands from his pockets and leaned over the empty chair at the head of the table. "It is important you learn to put a price on your own talents and services." He held one hand up at their collective gasp. "In this room we have examples of slavery – I am not exaggerating the situation – there are slaves sitting here."

"Explain, please," Felicia looked around, unsure of what was being discussed – slavery was against the law surely?

"Take these three young maids for example." Richard gestured towards the maids who were staring at him with open mouths. "I have been given to understand that you ladies are being forced to experience just how hard they work. They are on the go from early morning to night – yet the wages from their labours are paid – not to them – but to the convent that raised them. That in my eyes is a form of slavery. They have been given no choice but sent out to toil for the profit of others."

"I have never thought of it in that way," Georgina at the other end of the table objected. "It is how things are done."

"Bridget," Richard smiled, "I can almost see you chomping at the bit – anything you say in this room will not be held against you – you have my word."

"I'm sorry." Bridget turned to the mistress. "You have been everything that is kind and good to us." She winced when Ruth and Sarah pinched her to shut her up. "I resent toiling from the time I open my eyes in the morning to the time I sleep at night for money that is paid to the convent. I know you have said life is not fair – but I do not feel the convent has earned my money. We worked hard enough for them when in their care." She waited for the ceiling to fall in on her head for daring to say so much.

"*That*, ladies," Richard hit the chair back, "is my idea of slavery and it doesn't stop there. I understand we have two at this table who have worked for years with no financial gain." He gestured towards the Misses Willowbee and Watson. "They too were enslaved simply to survive. You must change your thinking – *all* of you."

"That is a great deal easier said than done," Octavia said.

"I am aware of that," Richard sighed. "In an ideal world we would all have charge of our own destiny. We must deal with what we have to hand. I want you all to start thinking of the value of the service you offer. No matter what positions you accept when you leave here – you must learn to put a price on the services you offer. Miss Willowbee, I am given to understand, wishes to remain in a secretarial position within a household." He looked down at the woman trying to disappear into the furniture. "Well, men receive payment for such services – why should she not?"

"You are turning our thinking on its head." Verity had often expressed the same argument to herself – but only mentally – she would never dare to voice it aloud.

"I want to help you step out into the world with the tools you need to survive." He pulled out the chair and sat down. "This is our first meeting. I wanted to shock you into thinking for yourselves. You have – most of you – been trained from birth to allow men to do your thinking. That has not been a great success for you, has it?"

"We have been left destitute and floundering," Octavia said. "I was content to drift along as my brother's hostess. He is older than I and because of being born male inherited my father's estate. I did not resent this." She

314

looked around her. "I gave no thought to the fact that I had been deeded into his care like a piece of furniture." She shrugged. "It was simply the way things are done."

"What changed?" Richard had read her files – her case was typical.

"My brother – again by the virtue of being male – inherited a distant cousin's title and estate. I was overjoyed for him. I gave no thought to the woman and girl child left homeless and almost destitute by this event. The woman had been a very wealthy heiress – her money of course went to her aged husband on marriage. She and her child were left with practically nothing. I'm glad to say that my brother did the decent thing and married the widow and took her child as his own."

There were murmurs around the table at this – it was a gratifying outcome to the matter as far as they were concerned.

"And so?" Richard prompted when the woman had battled with her emotions and won.

"I behaved disgracefully." Octavia looked around at the company. "I believed the woman should be at my brother's feet slavering with gratitude. That gratitude of course should extend to me – after all, I was sister to this paragon of virtue." She made a noise between laughter and tears. "I soon got my comeuppance. My new sister, after much provocation from me, threatened to consign me to a home for the insane."

"So, you believe you are the only one at fault," Richard said when no one else commented.

"Yes, of course." Octavia had thought long and hard about her attitude.

"Anyone want to comment?" Richard looked around.

It fascinated him to see that it was young Bridget who was biting her lip to keep her words firmly locked behind her teeth. The others simply stared back at him. "The wrong done to you, Miss White-Gershwin, belongs on a great many shoulders – not least your parents for making no provisions for your future. Our society is not perfect. There are those of us seeking to change it – but change does not happen overnight."

"I mean no disrespect," Felicity said, "but how does this affect us?"

"I am hoping it will make you think and plan for your own future. Take the reins of your life in your own hands and hold tight. You have been placed in a precarious position by the action of others. You need to learn how to plan for your own future. That is where I come in." He sat back with a smile.

"There is so much for us to learn," Verity said. "I have been without funds for all of my life. I never thought of charging for the services asked of me."

"Isn't it wonderful how we are taught that asking for remuneration for services is for the lower classes only?" Felicia said bitterly.

"Everything is so different now," Euphemia agreed.

"We have so much to learn. Will we be able to do all that is being asked of us?" Octavia asked.

"You will have the time to find out." Georgina leaned back in her chair. It had been a good beginning, she thought.

"I will be on hand to teach you all how to plan your financial security," Richard promised. "I can't make you follow my advice of course but I will give you the tools necessary to make a success of your life. You may not live in great comfort but you will survive without falling on the charity of others. Ladies, it is important that we make a success of this venture. You are the first to be offered such an option. Those that follow will be walking in your footsteps. It is important that we plan carefully. We will be learning together."

"That thought is a little overwhelming," Verity Watson said.

"Not all of you ladies will take the position on offer in America, I know." Richard had been given the information about the Harvey Company. He had made some enquiries of his own into the matter. "Those of you that do will have an exciting opportunity. There will be much for you to study. The Harvey company believes in promoting from within. Each of you could well rise within the company. I believe too there are a great many wealthy men seeking brides in the American Southwest. Who knows what your future may hold? There will be investments that may pay richly. You may return to Ireland at some point as wealthy women in your own right – anything is possible – for those who dare."

"From your lips to God's ears, Richard," Georgina said with a smile.

"I had planned for this first session to be merely a getting-to-know you meeting – I wanted to give you all a little to think about," Richard went on. "In future sessions I hope we can enter into discussion on what you hope to achieve. We can discuss other employment options. I am afraid there are not many available. The female of the species is not, I am sorry to say, well paid in the work place. That too must change." He sighed deeply. He could not change the world overnight, however much he might want to.

"I would like to learn more about the chance of a new life in America," Felicia said. "It seems too good to be true that we can earn a good salary and be able to advance within a large company."

"I too would like to know more," Euphemia said.

"We have been so busy learning to live together and function in a new way that we have not entered into serious discussion about the Harvey Company and what is on offer," Georgina told Richard.

"That is something that must be discussed in great detail." Richard stood up. He pushed away from the table. "I will make further enquiries and we will learn what is on offer together. We will then be able to discuss the matter at our next meeting."

"Thank you for taking the time to come and meet with us, Richard." Georgina too stood.

There were general murmurs of thanks from the gathered women.

"Georgina, if I might have a word?" Richard had something to discuss with Georgina – in private.

"I will have Cook serve us tea in my sitting room." Georgina shivered. She was not looking forward to the coming meeting but she could no longer avoid her own problems. "Ladies, if you would restore order to this room. I am sure Ruth would be happy to give you more instructions in the making of tea and coffee."

Chapter 41

"That was far more frightening than I imagined." Richard wiped imaginary sweat from his brow with a wide smile. "I doubted I would get out of that room with my virtue intact."

"Well, I have to say, old friend, you are a visual delight – to the female eye, that is." She laughed with him. It had amused her to see the reaction of the other ladies to his male beauty.

"I wanted to ask you, have you received any papers concerning the threatened divorce?"

"No," she answered simply. "I don't imagine I will. It was an empty threat in my opinion. Why should he seek his freedom from his doormat of a wife when my very presence leaves him free to tomcat around without ever being able to promise a golden ring to his latest fancy?"

"I wondered about that." Richard had begun to take an interest in women's rights when he seen what had happened to his childhood friends. That both of them should have made nightmare marriages was beyond the bounds of chance.

At this point Ruth delivered a tea tray. Georgina

thanked her and waited until she had gone out to speak.

"Could *I* divorce *him*?" she asked. She busied herself with pouring tea, not willing to meet his eyes when she whispered the shocking thought aloud.

"It would be very difficult." He hated to admit to the prejudice of his own sex. "I know of no lawyer who would be willing to accept your case. The man would be shunned by his fellows. I'm sorry, my dear. I do not think that is an option we might follow."

Georgina passed him a cup of tea and they sat for a while in silence, each lost in their own unhappy thoughts.

He finally broke the silence. "Have you been following Skip's articles in the dailies?" His old friend had met with the Captain and not been at all impressed with the man.

"It is rather difficult to miss them." She'd been mortified to see her name in the newspapers. "I gather he is having success with them – his articles have moved from page four to front-page news."

"The latest article regarding the order of a horseless carriage is receiving a lot of comment." He sipped his tea, his blue eyes staring at her over the rim of the delicate china cup. He hated to remind her of what awaited her outside these doors but she needed to face society.

"That order at least I was able to cancel." She had been supplying Skip with the details of the bills that continued to arrive in her post box. She dreaded to see the postman approach her house. Skip was making much of her husband's mistress receiving goods while the poor wife received the bills. If the articles were about someone else she would have been much amused by them.

"Georgie, Dublin is gearing up for the holiday season. The Christmas balls are always well attended. Your friends intend to increase the whispering campaign." He dragged breath into his lungs, dreading to see the pain he was sure to bring to her. "Georgie, you need to visit your husband." He waited a moment but when she remained silent continued. "You need to be *seen* to visit. I'm afraid you cannot put it off any longer. The man will soon be moved to a private clinic. The visit should take place when you are comparatively safe in the larger institution of Doctor Steevens'." Skip had suggested the visit, insisting the staff of the hospital would provide unwitting witnesses to the Captain's reaction to Georgie's visit.

"The very thought of putting myself within that man's reach again," she took a deep breath. "terrifies me." She pressed a hand to her stomach.

"He will be unable to leave his hospital bed." Richard tried to keep his eyes away from her feminine attractions. He couldn't even begin to imagine losing the use of his legs. Surely the man would be unable to hurt Georgie in his present condition?

"He will have Lewis by his side." She knew the man was capable of obeying any and every vile order her husband might issue.

"It must be done, I'm afraid." Richard wanted her to face her nightmare. "My dear, the sooner you visit the better." He had left his day free of appointments with this in mind.

"Do you happen to know the visiting hours at Doctor Steevens' Hospital?" Georgina stared at him, her mind in a whirl.

"I do." He'd checked before he came here. "I am free this afternoon." He looked at her, sad to see the colour leach from her face. "I cannot say when I will be free again."

"So soon?"

"It is best to get it over with."

"Very well." She had been a coward long enough. Richard was offering to accompany her. She would have to endure this visit but she was determined it would be her first and last.

"I will return for you at two." Richard put his cup and saucer on the table before getting up. "I will be by your side to offer whatever assistance I may." The fear in her eyes almost crippled him. What could she fear from a man so injured? "Should I order a carriage?"

"That won't be necessary." She hadn't moved from her seat, her large whiskey-coloured eyes clouded with painful memories. "I'll have Billy Flint organise my own carriage for the journey."

That afternoon Georgina sat in her carriage, two of Billy Flint's men on the box. She had changed into the bronze dress, hoping it would give her courage. Richard sat by her side, silent. She was unable to relax. She had been unable to eat the lunch Cook put before her. She was shaking but determined.

"*We're here!*" Jones pulled the horses to a stop.

The hospital had been easy to find, being across the road from Kingsbridge railway station. The journey from her home had seemed all too short to Georgina.

Jones' companion jumped down to open the carriage door and lower the steps.

"Allow me." Richard jumped down and offered his hand. He could feel her shaking when she placed her hand in his. There was nothing he could say to ease her fears.

"Well, well, well, look who's here!" Charles Whitmore

was sitting against a mountain of white pillows.

Georgina stood in the doorway of the large white room, frozen in shock. She could not force her feet to move forward. It was only the pressure of Richard's hand on her elbow that moved her forward. She almost tripped before she remembered how her feet were supposed to work.

How was it possible for him to look so hale and hearty – it would be difficult to tell he had been so severely injured – the cage covering his lower legs was the only indication she could see of the harm he had suffered.

"Darling," he laughed and turned to the woman sitting by the side of the bed, "meet the wife!" He paid no heed to the man who accompanied the woman he had married. "Seems she made an effort to come and see me – bloody good of her, isn't it?"

"How do you do?" said the beautiful blonde woman sitting holding Charles hand in both of hers, without looking in Georgina's direction.

"Well, why are you here?" Charles barked when the bloody woman just stood there. "Lewis!" he said to the man standing almost to attention against one wall of the private room. "Get a chair for the wife – no need to get one for the weak-wrist with her – they won't be here long."

Georgina accepted a seat in the wooden chair Lewis placed far too close to the bed for her liking.

"I believe you wish to divorce me," she said, finding her spine. "To marry this charming lady no doubt." She recognised the yellow-silk gown the woman wore. She had received the bill for it. "I wish you every happiness, my dear." She smiled nicely at the blonde woman. "I have had no paperwork concerning the divorce. I thought to tell you of this oversight on your part." She looked at the blonde her husband had not had the manners to introduce her to. "The Second Mrs Whitmore, I presume?" She used the title the newspapers had given this woman. "I have received a great many bills on your behalf, I believe. I'll make sure you receive them. I have no means of paying such large sums."

Richard stood back against the wall, fascinated. He remained silent, taking everything in – wishing he could make notes to pass along to his friend Skip. Perhaps he should have waited until Skip could accompany them.

"You will not speak to her like that!" Charles yelled, pulling his hand from the blonde's. He held onto the iron head of the bed with one hand and leaned over with a clenched fist, attempting to slap the impudent woman across the face. How dare she speak to his woman like that? He would not allow it! *"She has been by my side every moment. Where have you been, you bitch?"*

He was furious that she managed to push the chair far enough away from the bed to evade his fist. He wanted to jump out of this bloody bed and beat sense into her stupid head. The frustration of his inability to walk like a man incensed him. It was all her fault. How dare she sit there and judge him!

"Get out of my sight, you stupid bitch! If you can't pay your bills it's nothing to do with me. I will enjoy thinking of you in debtor's prison." He laughed aloud, pleased with the thought. He'd have to encourage his little love to spend more money – shame the order for the horseless carriage had been stopped.

A nurse entered the room. "You must not excite

yourself, Captain." The shouting was disturbing the peace of the hospital. "There are too many people in this room – two visitors only per patient." She looked at Georgina. "I will have to ask you to leave. Our patients need peace."

"With pleasure!" Georgina jumped to her feet. She had known this visit would achieve nothing – she had visited – that had to be enough.

"*Lewis!*" Charles roared. "*Bring her here – by the hair!*"

"I think not!" Richard jumped forward when the man looked willing to obey his master to the letter. He took Georgina's elbow and began pulling her from the room.

The horrified nurse attempted to keep Lewis away from the obviously shaking woman.

"*Lewis!*" Charles roared. His clenched fists longed to feel her bones break. He had been too gentle with her in the past. Look where that had led him. Look what she had brought him to!

"*Sir!*" Lewis managed to grab Georgina by the hair.

Richard, unable to believe what was happening, turned to see Lewis dragging Georgina by the hair, dislodging her little hat which had fallen to the floor.

An orderly ran into the room but froze at the shocking sight before him. The nurse was shouting at him to do something – but what could he do?

Georgina was forcibly turned, tears of pain leaking from her eyes. She would not allow this to happen again – she would not be delivered for a beating – she used her hands to try to ease the pain of the grip in her hair. Then, with a shout she used her knee to disable Lewis. She stood free while he rolled on the floor groaning.

Richard picked the hat up from the floor and pushed it

into Georgina's hands. He threw a look of disgust towards the man on the bed. He ignored the man rolling on the floor, clutching his hands over his injury. Without a word spoken, he pulled a shaking Georgina from the room.

"I am so sorry," Richard said when he felt they were far enough away from the room of that devil. He watched his friend lean against the wall while trying to restore order to her hair. The tears falling from her eyes were allowed to drop unnoticed by her.

"I am the one who is sorry. I did not want you to witness the ugliness of my life with that man." Georgina pushed the hat over her hair any old way. She wanted only to escape.

"I want to share every moment of that visit with Skip." Richard was finding it difficult to believe what he had seen. He felt a failure as a man. He had never before been party to such a scene and had stood frozen with shock – useless – while Georgina had been mistreated by that manservant.

They walked swiftly down the echoing hospital corridors, each eager to escape. Richard didn't know what to say – how to excuse his own lack of action – she had been forced to handle her own defence.

The carriage was waiting for them. Richard helped Georgina inside. He followed closely on her heels, pulling the door closed behind them.

"I am so terribly sorry." Richard stared at the shivering figure in the corner of the carriage. "I had no idea you would be subjected to such horror." He could not bear to watch her suffer alone. Moving slowly and with great trepidation he pulled her gently into his arms. The

326

movement of the carriage pushed her deeper into his embrace.

"You have nothing to apologise for," Georgina whispered into his chest. How could such a gentle man understand the twisted mind of someone like her husband? She settled into his arms and allowed herself to wallow in a sensation she had never known before – the gentle embrace of a male. She rested her aching head in the hollow between his head and shoulder, content not to move. The clip-clop of the horses' hooves were a gentle lullaby. She dozed – escaping from her dark memories – as the carriage made its way through the Dublin streets.

"I hate to disturb you," Richard whispered as the carriage slowed, "but we are almost at your home." He watched while she pushed herself upright.

"You should have pushed me away." Georgina turned her head away from his interested blue gaze. She did not want him to see the colour racing over her face. How could she have fallen asleep atop the poor man?

"Why are we passing your door?" he leaned forward and asked when the carriage continued in the direction of the mews. He kept his eyes turned in the direction of the street, allowing her to collect herself.

"There will be no one in the main part of the house." Georgina restored order to her appearance. "We are living primarily in the basement these days. It was Billy Flint's suggestion – and a good one."

"Indeed." Richard sat in bemused silence while the carriage moved around the row of town houses.

"*Billy!*" Georgina almost exploded out of the carriage when it came to a stop in front of the double doors to the side of the carriage house. "*Billy Flint! Billy, where are you?*"

Richard stepped from the carriage onto the cobbled laneway.

"*What's all this shouting for?*" Billy, with one of his men, pulled open the heavy doors that opened onto the back garden and long cobbled walkway leading to the back of the house.

"*I did it, Billy!*" Georgina was aware of the crowd of women gathered in the back garden. She had forgotten about the lessons that would be taking place in the garden at this time. She ignored everything and threw herself at Billy as soon as the doors were open, almost running under the horses' hooves. "*I did it!*" She threw her arms around his neck and laughed madly. "*I did it!*"

Richard looked around with open-mouthed astonishment. He looked at the women dotted around the grass, two by two, facing each other – were they holding weapons? What were those rough-looking men doing with the women? Dear Lord, he wondered, had those men been teaching these women to fight? Merciful heavens, even Mrs Chambers and the cook were present. What on earth was going on?

"Did what?" Billy had been forced to close his arms around the laughing figure as she clung to him.

"I used the pain, Billy, just like you told us!" She released him to turn in a giddy circle. "*Ladies, I did it! I used the pain – I did it!*" She disappeared into the feminine crowd that gathered around her shouting questions.

The men withdrew from the group and stood against the wall of the house, watching the excitement. The women shouted and questioned. They didn't allow Georgina to answer before the next question was put to her.

"Want to tell me what that's all about?" Billy walked over to stand by Richard. They stood out of the way while the coachmen handled putting away the carriage and horses.

"I have no idea." Richard was examining this man he had heard so much about but never met.

The two men studied each other then without comment turned to watch Georgina spinning around the chattering group. Richard wondered what had happened to the sad-eyed shivering waif he'd held close to his chest.

"Richard!" Georgina returned to his side. She took his hand in hers, still glowing with excitement. "Billy, come along!" She put her other hand in Billy's and pulled the men over towards the women. She was grinning like a fool she knew but she couldn't hide her joy.

"Richard, you will not know – I have not had time to tell you – but Billy suggested he teach us women ways of defending ourselves." She laughed at the surprised face turned towards her. "He and his men are forever yelling at us to 'use the pain'!" She released their hands to stand with hers on her hips. Billie's men were teaching the females not to fear physical pain – not to fold in on themselves to avoid hurt but to use their anger at being hurt to retaliate. "So today when I was attacked – I did just that – I used the pain and got free." She was almost dancing on the spot.

"Maybe you should tell us what happened," Billy said to Richard when the crowd around them began to tighten in a circle.

"To my shame," Richard's voice carried over the heads of the people hanging on his words, "Georgina was attacked by her husband's servant." There was a shocked murmur from the crowd. "I was too slow to take action." He was mortified by this. "She was forced to defend herself – which she did in grand style – I was very impressed."

He stood back while Georgina took over supplying the details as well as actions to demonstrate her movements.

"She needed this," Billy stood beside Richard and whispered. He could see the other man's shame. He understood from Georgina's movements what had taken place. "She needed to know she could protect herself from that madman's clutches. If I had known of your visit to see him, I would have advised you to stand back and allow her to protect herself."

"How can you say that?" Richard glared. "That man's servant almost pulled the hair from her head – to the delight of her husband and his mistress, I might add. I allowed her to be injured while in my care."

"This is not about you. This is about her." He used his chin to gesture towards the laughing figure. "Look at her. She has been given back her dignity. She knows now that she will never again be a victim. She protected herself."

"She shouldn't have had to," Richard said. "I was there."

"This time," Billy agreed. "But how many times has she faced that man and his lackey on her own?" He allowed that thought to settle. "We can't always be on hand to protect the ladies. They need to learn to protect themselves – this lot more than any other, it seems to me."

They watched the women laughing and joking.

"*Someone take them sticks away from those bloody women!*" Billy shouted suddenly. The women were dancing like wild things while holding the sticks over their heads chanting '*Use the pain!*' in voices dangerously close to screams. "They'll put someone's eye out if they're not more careful." He watched the men he had chosen to teach the women as they jumped to obey his order.

"Are you really teaching women to fight?" Richard was feeling more and more bewildered.

"I am," Billy said without apology.

"What are they wearing in heaven's name?" He had only just noticed their unusual attire. Well, he'd had other things on his mind.

"Those, I am told, are called split skirts." Billy grinned. "They wanted to wear men's pants to work in." He shook his head, trying not to imagine the beautiful Felicia running around in tight men's pants. "I trust my men but I wasn't going to put that kind of temptation in their way."

"The world is run mad." Richard continued to watch the scene in front of him, unable to believe his own eyesight.

"It has for these women," Billy said soberly. He knew what had brought them to this house and to a certain degree what awaited them. "They need to learn – all of them – how to take care of themselves." He turned at the other man's snort. "I have advised them to avoid any situation that looks dangerous – run away as fast and far as possible – it's not always possible though, is it?"

"So I am learning." Richard had been standing right there when Georgina was attacked. If she had not managed to free herself from that man's grasp, what

331

would have happened? Would he have been in time to save her from her husband's cruel intentions?

"Did she really knee old Lewis in the balls?" Billy jerked his head to where Georgina was still holding court.

"With a great deal of relish, if I am to be the judge of it." Richard turned to smile at the other man. "She put a great deal of force behind it, I can tell you. We left him writhing on the floor clutching his family jewels." He could laugh now at the memory.

"Good for her!" Billy nodded.

"Richard Wilson." Richard held out his hand to the other man. It was a bit late for introductions but better late than never.

"William Armstrong." Billy took the hand. He used his formal name as he judged this man might be of some use to him in reaching his future goals. It was never too early to put a plan in place. "Or Billy Flint as I'm called around here."

"Billy at this moment then." Richard was fascinated. Georgina appeared to be running a very unusual household. He would make it his business to visit more often. He would hate to miss any of the fun.

"*All right, everyone!*" Cook clapped her hands and shouted over the noise of the people still exclaiming and questioning. "*I have the kettle on – let us all have a cup of tea – and celebrate this victory!*" She was delighted to hear that aul' Lewis had met his comeuppance. She wished she'd been there to see it. "*Wipe your feet before you come into my kitchen!*" she shouted over her shoulder. "Ruth, Sarah, I'll need you. Liam, you come along too." With her troops following at her heels, she disappeared into the house.

"Richard," a breathless Georgina suddenly appeared in front of him, "I've been extremely rude. Have you met Billy?"

The two men started to laugh. She looked from one to the other for a moment before joining in. She felt so liberated. She had broken free from a man's cruel hold. She felt as if she could conquer the world.

"Come inside and join our madhouse in a mug of tea." Georgina, without conscious thought, took Richard's hand and began to pull him along in her wake as she had done as a child. "You too, Billy."

"Do you think there might be any of Cook's fruit cake on offer?" Billy followed along. His men were already inside. They never willingly turned down a mug of tea and a bite to eat.

Richard stood against one wall of the kitchen, staring at the scene around him. It was organised chaos if such a thing existed. The kitchen table held thick slices of rich fruit cake and enamel mugs of black tea. There was a large enamel milk jug and sugar bowl for everyone to serve themselves. The men were seated on clever little stools that Georgina had informed him one of Billy's men had made. The crowd of people cluttering up the kitchen – all from such different social backgrounds – laughed and chatted as if they were long-time friends. He had never seen anything like it. What on earth had been going on in this house? He wouldn't stay away so long next time. Now that he knew where the rear entrance was, he determined to use it again.

Chapter 42

"Ladies!" Georgina, from her position at the head of the table in the servants' dining room, looked around at the faces turned towards her. The first meal of the day had quickly become a time of discussion. "I think it is time to mention something that I've been thinking of."

The women had been with her now for some weeks. The time seemed to have flown by. To her delight the three maids and the women were settling into a rather strange family group.

"You have all changed so much in the time you have been with us." She sipped at the cooling tea in her cup, nervous about broaching this subject.

"Time is getting away from us." Lily looked at the timepiece pinned to the bodice of her black dress.

She too was proud of the efforts this group had made to fit into the household. They seemed willing to turn their hands to anything which had surprised and pleased her. She had dreaded their arrival yet now she would be sorry to see them leave. Ah well, such was life and all you could do was get on with it. There was a lot to get done in the day. They couldn't sit here while Georgina sought for words.

"I have several matters I wish to discuss before we leave this room to attend to our chores." Georgina took a firm hold of her nerves. "But before I mention my ideas," get on with it for heaven's sake, she mentally ordered herself, "I wondered how you each felt about your given names." She saw the surprise on their faces. "I don't mean the three maids as their names are perfectly acceptable. I did wonder – Euphemia – are you happy with your name or would you consider abbreviating it to suit your new identity?" She held her breath. "Richard has always called me Georgie and I must say I like how it sounds."

"What name were you thinking of?" Euphemia had never been called by a diminutive. She thought she might like it.

"Mia," Georgina said immediately. "I thought Mia for Euphemia."

"Yes, I like it," said Euphemia positively.

"And for you, Octavia," Georgina said, "I thought Tavie."

Octavia White-Gershwin looked at her work-roughened hands. She turned her arms around, examining the bruises she had received from a broom-handle they used to fight. There was a constant pain in her legs from the strenuous exercise they got from riding astride.

"Yes, I like it," she said. "I think it suits the new me."

"Ermatrude would have the choice of Erma or Trudy. What do you think, Ermatrude?"

"I don't know," she said.

"I think Erma sounds nice." Bridget didn't fear speaking out in this group. She had a voice and opinions and was allowed express them. Besides, she had a soft spot for this poor woman. She seemed so lost at times. She tried to join in with all of the activities. She was willing but at times there was such a lost look to her face that Bridget worried for her.

"Erma?" Ermatrude didn't really see what difference a name made but she was willing to go along with the idea. "I suppose so."

"Good. Verity and Felicia, your names are fine." It was Bridget referring to the other women's names as those given to the cows in her books that made Georgina think of changing them.

Ermatrude – or Erma – looked so troubled. Georgina wondered if it had been a mistake to give her a bedchamber to herself. She seemed to be always outside of the group.

"Erma," she said, "I know you are worried about your future – but I have an idea which I'll discuss with you at length. I believe it will please you." The Dowager Duchess needed a secretary and Verity Watson was convinced this little dumpling of a woman would suit. She had to be convinced of her own worth before the suggestion could be put to her. There would be no more working for nothing just to keep a roof over her head – not if she had anything to say about it.

"So, now that everyone has been renamed," Cook would have to find Liam – no doubt the lad was with Billy Flint, "can we get on with our day?"

"The postman has been." Jones entered the room with a stack of post before Cook could make her escape. He walked over to Georgina and put the post on the table. He didn't wait for a response but turned to walk back out.

"Tell Liam I want him!" Cook called after him.

"Yeah, I'll send him over to you, Cook," Jones said before disappearing into the kitchen.

"Well, you don't need me for this." Cook stood up. "Ladies, get these dishes into the kitchen. They need to be washed and put away before we can do anything else." She hurried from the room. She had meals to plan. This lot took a lot of feeding.

Lily remained seated while everyone else jumped to their feet. They moved very slowly, giving more attention to Georgina's post than the dishes they picked up.

The three young maids could find no excuse to linger. They carried the first of the used dishes from the room.

"Anything interesting?" the newly named Mia asked, making no secret of her interest.

"I . . ." Georgina had used her knife to open two of the envelopes. She stared at the two pieces of stiff board in her hands as if afraid they would explode in her face. She tried to ignore the rest of the post – she recognised shop invoices when she saw them. "I don't understand." She raised confused eyes to see the five women gathered around the table waiting. "These are invitations to balls – Christmas balls – I never receive invitations to balls."

"What will you wear?" Felicia sat back down.

"You have become something of a celebrity." Verity too took a seat. "You have been in the dailies."

"Having you at their ball," Tavie said softly, "would be seen as a coup by some hostesses."

"I have never been to a ball," Erma put in.

"It has been a great many years since I last attended a ball." Georgina clapped a hand to her mouth. "One is from the Dowager Duchess of Westbrooke – I am invited to attend her annual Christmas ball!" she almost wailed. "It is the social event of the season. I have never been invited before."

The room exploded in cheerful chatter. Georgina was ignored while clothes, hair, skin care, shoes and other matters were mentioned and discussed.

Lily Chambers left the room unnoticed. They didn't need her for this.

"What is going on in there?" Cook asked when Lily stopped in the middle of the kitchen floor. "They sound like a flock of magpies."

"The mistress has received an invitation to the Dowager Duchess of Westbrooke's annual Christmas ball." That fact was only just now sinking in. Lily and Cook exchanged glances under the fascinated eyes of the three maids busily washing dishes. "That is not the only invitation she has received."

"About bloody time!" Cook snapped. "It is a shame the way that poor girl has been hidden away in this house. I hope to God she accepts the invitation and dances her feet off. You're only young once."

"Ballgowns," Sarah up to her elbows in soapy water whispered in terror. "I've never done a ballgown."

"Now's your chance," Bridget said under the noise of the conversation being carried on behind them.

"Trust you, Bridget O'Brien," Ruth felt her heart sink for poor Sarah. "You're game for anything, you are. What did Lady Sutton call your style of riding horseback – neck or nothing, wasn't it? That's how you go at everything. The rest of us are not as brave." She'd been terrified the first time she had to get onto the back of a horse – but not Bridget – she had taken to riding astride like a duck to water. She didn't see why they had to learn to ride anyway. When would they ever use that skill? It was ridiculous for them to be included in the activities planned for what the mistress called 'the students'. But nobody asked her opinion.

"Mrs Chambers?" Mia stepped into the kitchen through the open doorway of the servants' dining room. "Could we send for the wise woman?"

"What chores had you planned for today, Mrs Chambers?" Erma couldn't be seen but her voice could be heard.

"We need to strip chores back to the bare minimum today, Cook," Verity walked into the kitchen. "There is much to plan. We have very little time to prepare Georgie for the coming season."

"In the name of God," Cook groaned, "are we never to know peace in this house?"

"I don't want to go to these balls," Georgina's voice could be heard. "I have already told you. I am not going. There is no need to prepare me."

Lily Chambers ignored her mistress and took command. "Ladies, the dishes need to be cleaned and put away. The dining room tidied. Cook, if you could prepare a big pot of stew for everyone I think that might be best." The house had been cleaned down and fires cleaned and set before they sat down to eat the morning meal. "We will need to hold a council of war and plan our strategy – Cinderella *will* go to the ball."

"I have a chicken I was going to dress." Cook was willing to do anything to help her young mistress enjoy something of a social life. "I can make a pot of stew with dumplings. But I'll need help with the vegetables. I've only the one pair of hands."

"Right, ladies!" Lily clapped her hands. "Front and centre! We need to get organised. We can't sit down to plan until certain matters are taken care of – we'll work together."

"Does anyone want to know what I think?" Georgina stood in the doorway.

"*No*," Cook and Lily said together.

"Why is the wise woman needed?" Lily suddenly remembered someone asking for the woman.

"We will need lotions and potions," Mia stepped forward to say. "There are potions for giving a shine to hair – lotions for improving skin – we will need them all. I hope your wise woman is skilled."

"She is the best," Cook was giving orders to the females cluttered around her but she still had time to say her piece. "Bridget, get Liam – he can run across and get Granny Grunt."

The house seemed to tremble at the hive of activity taking place within its walls. The women were determined that Georgina would go to the ball – whatever she might think about it.

Liam was sent dashing off to summon Granny Grunt.

Felicia stood off to one side watching the reaction of the other women. Should she mention the items in her luggage? She'd brought the chests with her as a gesture of defiance. Her time spent in this house with these women was helping to heal the wounds inflicted upon her spirit by her own relations. '*Use the pain.*' If her uncle stood in front of her right now she would '*use the pain*' to punch him in his blubber-filled face.

"I have chests full of clothing fashioned for a rather large lady." Felicia's voice cut through the chatter. "There is an enormous amount of ribbon and trim on the gowns that we might use." She would never tell them that her uncle had sent them to her home. He wished her to have her seamstress make something of his first wife's finery – so she could be properly dressed when he offered her to his rich friends for their amusement.

Sarah clapped her hands. "Wonderful! And we need to see what is in the chests in the attic!" Sarah had never even seen a ballgown.

"We need to make a list," said Verity.

There was a collective groan when she said this into the noisy kitchen. The woman was a terror for making lists and plans for every little thing.

Chapter 43

"I can do it." Granny almost wept over the taste of the chicken-and-dumpling stew. It was nice to have someone else do the cooking once in a while. The joy of the company of a group of women added to the pleasure. "I will need money. I don't keep a stock of beauty aids on hand." She didn't have much call for such things.

"My mother and grandmother kept journals about beauty products." Georgina remembered listening to the women talk about personal grooming when she was a small child. "I think, although I'm not sure, that it was their lady's maids who dealt in such things."

"Someone had to teach the lady's maids." Granny had many recipes she'd tried over the years. She supplied many of the lady's maids with beauty-care products. It was a very small part of her work though. These women would need a large amount of goods. "I will have to order more lanolin. I haven't enough goose grease to hand – I suppose you could help there, Cook?"

"I use the goose grease meself." Cook didn't want to hand over some of her precious stock.

"How much goose grease would you need?" Georgina

was trying to give in gracefully. No one was listening to her constant denial of any wish to attend society balls.

"A lot." Granny waited until she had chewed the food in her mouth to reply. "You have all – if I am any judge of it – neglected to take care of yourselves. Fancy ladies spend hours every day titivating themselves." She sniffed. "They haven't much else to do with their time."

"I know my cousin spends a great deal of time and money on her appearance," Verity agreed.

"I don't have the time for a lot of fuss." Georgina knew she was protesting in vain. They were all determined that she would attend at least one of the balls she had been invited to – and she did not want to feel like a country cousin amongst the Dublin cream of society.

"You have good skin." Granny knew about the marks on this young woman's flesh. They would have to use clothes to hide those. "And you have never taken up the fashion of burning your hair." She shook her head. "A more ridiculous fashion I have never seen." She had been called in, time without number, when some silly maid burned a woman's hair clean off her head. What they expected her to do about it she'd never know.

"I would like to learn how to improve my appearance," Verity said in a soft voice. "I have spent so many years trying to fade into the background." Her voice broke. She fought for a moment to regain her poise. "I would love to learn to make the best of myself."

"I have a special soap I make for use on the hair," Granny said. "You could all use it. It softens the hair and gives a shine." She was almost deafened by the demand for details.

"We really should make a list," Verity said when the

clamour of voices died down. They rose again in objection to her suggestion.

"A list is a good idea." Granny was a firm believer in keeping notes. "I will need to know what supplies I have on hand and what I'll need to order."

"I'm glad I only made a stew for dinner." Cook looked around. "Apart from Granny Grunt, there is not one of you taking a blind bit of notice of what you're eating. That's enough to break a cook's heart."

She was shouted down with objections and compliments. The last thing they wanted to do was insult the woman who worked so hard to keep them supplied with delicious meals.

"You lot will need to start using hand creams." Granny glanced around the table and sniffed. "I've never seen such rough-looking hands in my life. I don't care where yez are all going after this – you need to start taking care of your hands – and that includes you three." She stared at the young maids. "We will make a detailed list of what's needed. I'll need someone to help me put my lotions and potions together – because, looking around at you lot, you're going to need a great deal of help."

"I would like to be the one to help you." Bridget had been listening carefully. If they needed such things as lotions and potions it would be a good idea for her to learn how to create them. She and her friends had no money to buy such things.

"I think that is an excellent suggestion," Lily Chambers said. She thought a young girl like Bridget was wasted as a maid. She sighed deeply – what else could the poor child do – at least she had a roof over her head and food in her belly. The three maids, thanks to the students, were learning a great deal more than household chores. She prayed they would be able to use what they were learning to improve their lives.

"Perhaps . . ." Georgina started to laugh aloud. The thought suddenly running through her head tickled her fancy. She was aware of the others at the table staring at her – it only made her laugh louder. She fought to regain control of her mirth.

"Something has obviously amused you," Lily said when her mistress appeared to be calming down. "Care to share it with the rest of the room?"

"Well," Georgina used her napkin to try and force the humour back, "I had a sudden thought." She looked around, amusement shining bright in her eyes. "I thought – since Cook will have to cook the geese to extract the fat – we could serve a special meal to Billy Flint's men – you ladies could serve them."

There was a stunned silence before the objections started coming fast and furious.

"You had better explain your thinking," Lily said when the group had finished exclaiming their shock aloud.

"It is my understanding," Georgina was aware all eyes were upon her, "that you ladies – that is, those of you who choose to work for the Harvey group – you will be serving uncouth men – members of the working class – you can't deny Billy Flint's men fit that description." She waited but only stunned silence greeted her remarks. "I believe it would give those of you who are thinking of travelling to America a taste of what is to come."

"That may well be an excellent idea," Verity's voice cut into the silence that had fallen over the group. "Perhaps this is the time I should mention I am in contact with a lady working for the Harvey Company."

"How? Since when? Who is she?" The voices clashed one over another.

Verity ignored the questions being shouted at her. "I took the liberty, when the first two women were sent to America." They had all heard of that first disastrous placement. "I contacted a friend working for a family in New York. My friend was very unhappy but thought she had no other options. I gave her all of the information I had on the Harvey Company. My friend applied and got one of the coveted positions."

"Verity – I think you're a bit of a dark horse." Granny was enjoying the drama taking place around her – added a bit of salt to the meal, she thought.

"I correspond with my friend Agnes." Verity couldn't continue to eat while she talked. She pushed her almost empty plate away from her. "What she tells me of the company excites me. Yes, they serve uncouth men – but these men are wealthy beyond the dreams of avarice. They have made their fortunes in the oil and gold fields. I believe there are also wealthy cattle barons. The women who work for the Harvey Company are becoming recognised for bringing class and style to the southwest." She looked around, finding her audience hanging on her every word. "We cannot begin to imagine how vast the land of America is – we will have to wait to experience it – but the possibilities to improve our lot in life – ladies, they appear to be as vast as the land."

"Does anyone know when this lot will be leaving you, Georgina?" Granny asked. She had been told all about this man Harvey – it sounded too good to be true.

"In the New Year – it will depend on sailings, I understand."

"I want to go," Felicia said softly. "The thought of setting out on this journey excites me." She looked around the company. "I don't like to think about leaving though – silly, isn't it?"

"We are being asked to leave everything we know behind. We are to become pioneers," Mia said.

"I do not want to leave Ireland," Ermatrude stated. She'd agreed to give up her name – become Erma – but she did not want to travel such a long way.

"Erma!" Georgina sighed. How many times must she say the same thing to this woman? "I have a position in mind for you. One of status here in Dublin – you already have the skills you need – but you must work on becoming more aware of your own worth. The skills you possess as a social secretary are valuable. You must begin to believe that." She wanted to bang her own head against the table. The stubborn look on Erma's face made her want to scream. The woman fought any suggestion of putting a value on her abilities.

"Before we get into all that," Cook pushed her chair back, "we need to clear the table. I have apple pie for dessert – someone needs to make tea and coffee. I've only the one pair of hands."

"Verity!" Lily called as people got up from the table. "If you would get pen and paper we can make lists while we enjoy cook's excellent pie."

"I have some news." Granny moved to take the seat Lily Chambers vacated. She leaned in to speak only to Georgina. "It's about your husband." It was all around Dublin how the man had treated this woman when she went to visit.

347

"What has that man done now?" Georgina put her elbows on the table and leaned in to hear what Granny had to say. It was hard to hear as Granny was speaking softly and the women and girls were carrying on several conversations as the table was cleared.

"He is being moved." Granny leaned in until the women were almost joining foreheads. "The hospital here can do no more for him. He has the luck of the devil that his injuries didn't turn septic." He should have died from such injuries.

"I was aware that he was going to a private clinic." Georgina couldn't bring herself to care what happened to the man. She wanted him gone from her life.

"He is going to a special place in Belfast," Granny had received this news from a woman who worked at Doctor Steevens' Hospital. She was only a cleaner but they heard more than the doctors or nurses realised. "Seems there is some man there doing something with artificial legs – I think it's because of soldiers and sailors – but nonetheless your husband is going to consult with this man."

"Do you think there is a possibility he would be able to get around again?" Georgina felt faint at the very thought.

"I don't know," Granny shrugged. "I can't see how it could be done. I know there are one-legged sailors but I've never heard of anyone walking around without at least one leg to stand on."

Chapter 44

"I am thinking of writing to Sister Mary Margaret and asking her advice." Sarah pulled the comb through her white hair while examining her own image in the mirror. She could see her two friends getting ready for bed in the glass.

"Would she know about ballgowns?" Bridget asked absentmindedly.

"Honest to God, Bridget O'Brien!" Sarah glared at her friend's image in the mirror. "Where is your head?"

"What did you mean then?" Bridget wanted to crawl into her bed. She was tired and morning came very early.

"I'm worried." Sarah continued to comb her hair – thrilled to see it growing. "We are being taught to talk back to our betters and ride horses. Now they want to teach us to dance. What good will any of these things serve us when we go to our next positions?"

"Yes." Ruth was already in bed. "I'm worried too. I never thought I'd be preparing a meal for a bunch of hairy-handed louts." She put so much energy into presenting meals. She wanted them to be appreciated. Billy Flint's men attacked food – never taking the time to enjoy it.

"Well, now!" Bridget stood by the side of her bed. She put her hands on her nightgown-covered hips and glared. "Aren't you two turning into fine snobs? Have yez forgotten that Reverend Mother always said 'anything you learn in life is never wasted'? What is wrong with yez?"

"Don't say yez," Ruth yawned. "It's vulgar."

Sarah put a nightcap over her hair. It was no good trying to curl it – it was a lot of pain and effort for very little result. "What will we do when we have to leave here? We were supposed to have four years of practical training – not horse riding and dancing." She pulled back the bedcovers.

"If you two are so worried," Bridget sat in bed with her legs drawn up to her chest, arms wrapped around her knees, "why don't you talk to the mistress and Mrs Chambers?"

"I couldn't!" they said together.

"Well, you will get nothing if you don't ask." Bridget settled down. "I am going to learn every skill on offer. I have told both of you. I am going to America. I am going to be a Harvey girl."

Her two friends ignored her. They had heard it all before.

"Right, ladies!" Bridget knocked on the closed bedroom doors. "Let's be having yez! There is a cup of tea downstairs if you're quick. Don't forget to empty the chamber pots." It amused her to hear the groaning complaints from each room. They were getting better at waking up in the dark hours of the morning.

"You are a bad-natured so-and-so, Bridget O'Brien," someone groaned. "Think we can't hear you laughing at us?"

"Well, it takes little to amuse little minds." Bridget never thought she'd be quoting Mother Consolata. "Come on now, up and at 'em!"

She ran lightly down the stairs. The women would get each other up now. She could have a cup of tea before they began the clean-down of the house.

"Ruth, your blood should be bottled." Bridget took the enamel mug of tea her friend passed to her.

"Are they up?" Sarah's face was almost buried in her mug.

"They are moving at least." Bridget put both of her cold hands around the hot mug. "Morning, Liam!"

"Yeh can go off people, yeh know, Bridget O'Brien." Liam his hair standing on end was scratching and yawning. "I don't know what you have to be so cheerful about every morning."

"Yes, sit down and shut up, Bridget." Ruth had her own tea in hand. "Let the rest of us wake up."

Bridget couldn't sit. She was up. She walked over to the kitchen window, staring out into the dark morning – not even the birds were up yet. What would it be like to lie in bed of a morning? She would never know. She listened to the students stumble into the room for the first cup of tea of the day.

"Did you make your beds?" she turned to ask as she did every morning.

"*Yes, miss!*" they chorused good-naturedly.

"We have to get the place swept out and dusted quickly this morning." Bridget walked over to join the sleepy group gathered around the teapot. "We have a lot to get done today."

"Sarah, after we get the morning work done," Felicia

yawned, "you and I need to go into the attic and start looking for a ballgown."

"You will need more than one," Verity muttered into her mug.

"What? Why?" Sarah almost dropped her mug – more than one ballgown to be assembled – it was impossible. She didn't know anything about ballgowns.

"You can tell us while we work." Bridget almost pushed everyone out of the kitchen. They would stand around talking all morning if she didn't. She pushed sweeping brushes and dusters into limp hands.

"What did you mean by more than one gown, Verity?" Sarah couldn't rest until she knew – order had quickly been restored to the three bedrooms used by the students. The women were now dusting the doorways and sweeping down the hallway. "I thought the mistress said she would only attend one ball."

"She did," Verity went up on her toes to reach the top of the door frame she was dusting, "but that's not realistic. She will have to attend several balls before she can attend the Dowager Duchess's ball. That is the social event of the season. It would be foolish to make that her first step out into society."

"I couldn't claim to know Dublin society." Mia was listening, fascinated. She had been a leading member of her own social set but very much a visitor when in Dublin.

"Why is the ball given by the Duchess such a major event?" Tavie too had been active in her own community but Dublin was the capital city. She had never been a leading light in Dublin society.

"The ball is held in the ballroom of Dublin Castle."

Verity had heard the servants talking about the event. She had never attended herself of course but the servants hung on the words of the lady's maid and other senior servants who attended the ball. "The Dowager says her Dublin house on Merrion Square is too small to hold the crowds that attend. The country seat is too far out of town – guests would have to stay overnight – so Dublin Castle it is."

"I am not sure I would know what is suitable for such an event." Felicia had thought putting a gown together for a ball would be fun but she had no experience of high society. "I think we need advice on what is being worn."

"Lady Sutton?" Erma had been paying close attention. If she was going to apply for the position of social secretary to the Dowager – it would be as well to learn all she could of the woman. "I think that one would be the woman to consult. She always looks like a fashion plate to me."

"Would you lot keep yer voices down?" Liam growled. He was dragging his supplies behind him. It was his job to clean out the fireplaces and set fires ready to be lit in the cold grates. "The mistress and Mrs Chambers are trying to sleep don't forget."

The women and Liam carried out their work diligently.

"You must have run around the place this morning," Ruth said when they appeared in her kitchen. She alone cleaned the kitchen every morning. She loved having the big room all to herself. "The servants' dining room needs a good going-over." She dried her hands on a towel. "I need someone to help make the toast. I've only the one pair of hands. I have the trays ready to go up." She pointed to the trays sitting out on the kitchen worktop.

353

"You can decide amongst yourselves who does what." She hoped the egg man would come this morning. They were getting very low on eggs.

They quickly set to work. Only after the trays had been delivered to the bedrooms would they be able to sit down to their own first meal of the day.

"This is delicious, Ruth, thank you," Verity said when all nine people were sitting around the large table in the servants' dining room.

"You say that every morning." Ruth was pleased nonetheless by the compliment.

"I think working so hard makes the food taste better," Erma said. "I was not accustomed to physical labour before I came to this house."

"None of us were." Tavie took a golden-brown piece of toast from the platter that Mia held out to her.

"Does anyone else think we all look the better for it?" Felicia asked.

"Verity certainly does." Mia took a piece of toast and put the platter in the middle of the table.

"Thank you!" Verity was delighted her efforts to improve her appearance had been noticed.

There was silence as everyone settled down to enjoy the large quantity of food presented to them every morning.

"What about a lady's maid?" Felicia's voice broke the silence when all had liberally sampled the food. The table was beginning to look bare as the food disappeared.

"I do wish you wouldn't do that," Erma said. "You have obviously been thinking about something you haven't shared with us – then you suddenly say it

354

completely out of the blue. It is very confusing."

"Sorry." Felicia watched Ruth stand and pick up the large teapot.

"I understood what you meant." Mia too had been thinking about the upcoming ball season.

"One of us will have to do it," Tavie said.

"What are you all talking about?" Ruth, with the refilled teapot in hand, entered the room to ask. She'd had the kettle on the boil. They drank a great deal of tea at this first meal.

"The mistress will need a lady's maid in attendance on her when she attends the Christmas balls," Verity explained.

"I thought she was only going to one?" Ruth had missed the conversation that took place while the housework was being done.

They all took a moment to fill her in on what had been discussed.

"I think I could do it." Felicia had never given great thought to what her own lady's maid had done for her, but she remembered the basic tasks. Surely she would be capable of performing the same chores for Georgina?

"I would not advise it," Verity put in.

"Why not?" Felicia said.

"I have heard much talk about the carry-on of the upper classes at these balls," Verity said. "There is a great deal of alcohol served at these events. To hear it told, a great number of the gentlemen take advantage of the female servants." She sighed deeply. "You are too pretty, Felicia."

"Billy Flint has taught us how to defend ourselves," Felicia objected. "He says I'm a good student. Surely I would be safe in the company of the other lady's maids?"

"The Dowager's lady's maid – an older woman – carries a hatpin to defend herself," Verity said. "The men, she informs me, are well into their cups and don't care who they drag off into the night. The castle has a great many withdrawing rooms where screams do not carry."

Chapter 45

"Mrs Whitmore!"

Georgina wanted to close her eyes and hide from the shrill voice calling her name. She stood still as a statue, allowing Tavie to remove her pelisse.

"I do declare you are becoming quite the fashion leader." A murmur of voices appeared to agree. "And your escort – the divine Richard Wilson once more?"

"I shan't be a moment, madam." Tavie, dressed all in black as befitted a lady's maid, her glorious strawberry-blonde hair covered by a black-lace bonnet, hated to leave her mistress to the tender mercies of these cats – but she had to hang the pelisse up.

Georgina looked around the crowded ladies' withdrawing room. She smiled sweetly at the women taking in every inch of her appearance. She promised herself that this would be the last social engagement of the season for her. How did other women breathe at these events? She was corseted so tightly that drawing breath was an effort – and, surrounded by groups of women and their maids, the room was airless.

"I will tend to your hair now, madam." Tavie hurried

back to guide Georgina further into the room towards a wall of mirrors. Dainty stools sat before each mirror.

Georgina on Richard's arm stood on one of the wide red-carpeted stairs leading up to the Dublin Castle ballroom. The stair was so long and wide it was possible for three couples to stand abreast.

"Richard," she said, "are you becoming the subject of gossip on my account?" She hid her words behind her fan. She was glad the gown she wore was fashioned in the narrow style. Some of the ladies wore crinolines that took up a great deal of space on the staircase. The flowing trains of the narrow gowns trailed attractively behind their wearers. She was being careful not to step on the trains that flowed from the stair above them.

"I am being subjected to a great deal of nudge, nudge, wink, wink." Richard too was conscious of minding his step. He sighed deeply. These affairs were tedious. "I am afraid there are two rules in this case. I am seen as a fine fellow while you my dear Georgie are a fast piece." He smiled down at her glowing face. The change in his friend delighted him. The gowns her young helpers had designed and made for her were astonishing. To his eyes she was the best-dressed lady here. With the cream of Dublin society in attendance that was saying something.

"Better to be thought fast than put upon." Georgina didn't care what these people thought of her. She had attended two other Christmas balls – unwittingly providing a great deal of entertainment for the bored crowds. She gathered her lilac skirts in her hands and prepared to step up as the crowd moved. Richard gathered up the white and purple overdress that trailed behind her.

"I must say that team you imported from Paris have done a fine job of dressing you, my dear." He'd been amused when Tavie informed them that she had let it be known among the lady's maids that a specialised team was responsible for Georgina's gowns over the holiday season. It had proved necessary to give the masses some information as Georgina was not seen around Dublin in attendance with the usual designers and beauticians. His friend had caused quite a stir when she'd attended her first ball.

"Haven't they just?" Georgina tried not to laugh aloud. She hid her smile behind her fan. "I am very pleased with their work."

They fell silent, making their way gradually up the long staircase. The walls around them were beautifully decorated with paintings. The low-hanging crystal chandeliers cast a golden glow over the glamorous crowd. They had no time to admire the grandeur around them as they were processed towards the major domo waiting to announce them into the ballroom. Richard had the embossed invitation in the inside pocket of his black evening suit.

"My dear Georgina!" The Dowager Duchess, looking very regal in a deep purple gown so dark as to be almost black, greeted them with a wide smile. She leaned forward to press air-kisses over Georgina's cheeks. The noise from the ballroom behind her became a frantic buzz at this familiar greeting. "Richard, how lovely to see you!" A bejewelled white hand waved towards the ballroom floor. "Do enjoy yourselves, my dears!" She turned to the next couple, well aware of the fascinated reaction of the packed crowd.

"Well," Richard stepped into the glittering ballroom, "that put the cat well and truly among the pigeons." He walked slowly with Georgina on his arm around the long walkways to the side of the dance space, towards the orchestra sitting on a dais at one end of the room. "By embracing you the Dowager has singled you out as a friend. That will be the topic of conversation around dinner tables for weeks."

"I hope you are taking in every little detail." Georgina accepted a glass of champagne Richard had taken from a passing waiter. "The ladies of my household will never forgive us if we do not have detailed descriptions of the glamour and grandeur surrounding us." She sipped from the glass and continued to stroll along at his side. She – like a lot of other women present – had attached the loupe in the train of her gown over the middle glove-covered finger of her left hand. The white train embroidered with deep purple flowers was a thing of beauty but difficult to manage in these crowded circumstances. Some women allowed the trains to flow behind them – at their own peril – an unguarded step of their own or of another guest might lead to disaster.

"I am growing accustomed to being grilled by your household." He had been amused by the demands for every little detail of the evening after their first outing together. He found the frank comments of the ladies of Georgina's household vastly entertaining.

"I had not expected so many red-coated officers to be in attendance," Georgina looked at the men chatting in groups around the outer walls of the room. "Silly of me when there is a garrison based here."

"The unmarried officers are a great deal of the appeal

of this annual event." Richard felt quite drab in his plain black and white. The officers in their red-jacketed uniforms with gold braid and medals on their chest were catching the eyes of the women.

"This ballroom is a visual feast," Georgina said. "I am fighting the temptation to lie on the floor so I may more fully appreciate the painted ceiling."

"That would certainly give the old biddies something to talk about." Richard laughed aloud at the image that came into his head. Georgina was proving to be a delight to escort. "Do you wish to admire the food laid out in the dining room?" He knew it would be impossible for her to eat anything herself – ladies' corsets were not designed to allow their wearer to indulge.

"Torture," Georgina almost groaned. The tables would be magnificently presented with towering displays of delicious foodstuffs. She would have to admire while Richard indulged. "We would never be forgiven if we did not have every detail of the food too at our fingertips."

"It will be my pleasure to escort you into the dining room when the orchestra breaks."

They continued to stroll along the walkways that bordered the dance space. They stopped occasionally to exchange greetings with other couples strolling the same pathways.

"Georgina!"

Lord and Lady Sutton stepped in front of them.

"You look delightful. Your gown is perfection!" Arabella nudged her husband. "Why have you never imported a Parisian team for my toilette?" She was aware of the people leaning in to hear every word spoken. The news of Georgina's team of French experts was the talk of the town. Everyone was green with envy.

Lord Sutton smiled down at his wife, well aware of the deception taking place. "Wilson," he greeted Richard. Lord Sutton had met this pair many times. He smiled down at his wife before turning to the other man. "Have you had enough of this affair yet? Care to join me in the smoking room? We can enjoy a cigar and a bit of sanity while the ladies gossip." He laughed aloud at the sharp nudge from his lady's elbow.

"My dear?" Richard looked down at Georgina.

"Do go!" She waved one hand. "Enjoy the chance to escape this hothouse."

"I would be delighted to take the time for a cigar, Lord Sutton." Richard stepped away to join the other man.

"Capital."

"Those diamonds you are wearing, my dear," Arabella leaned in to whisper when the gentlemen had taken their leave, "sold, they would set you up for life."

"The monies would go to my husband." Georgina placed one gloved hand on the diamond-and-platinum necklace. She wore the matching diamond bracelets over her long white satin evening gloves. The tiara and long earrings sparkled in the light thrown out by the chandeliers. "In this form he cannot touch them. They are part of the entailed estate." They continued to stroll around the long walkway, attempting to avoid the listening ears.

"I am lost in admiration of your antecedents. To have insured their treasures could not be touched by greedy gentlemen. A very clever group of women, your ancestors!" Arabella laughed while nodding at acquaintances they passed.

The two women continued to stroll around the ballroom, attracting much attention and not only from the women present. The male officers too took careful note of the two beauties strolling along without ever stopping to flirt. The older women seated around the room kept an eye out for anyone daring to step out of line. Georgina and Arabella were forced to stop often to admire a gown, a new way of fashioning hair and accept compliments and comments on their own attire.

"I wanted to be the first to tell you ..." Arabella smiled sweetly at a group of frowning black-draped women as they passed in front of them. "I have offered Octavia White-Gershwin the position of my social secretary."

"Tavie?" Georgina was shocked enough at this news to stop walking. At the pull on her elbow from Arabella she started again. "Truly?"

"Truly Tavie – sounds like a music hall number." Arabella snorted with amusement. "The woman has a fine mind. She would be an asset to anyone with a great deal of social demands on their time." She pressed a hand fleetingly to her corset-covered stomach. "I am once more with child." She shushed Georgina when she went to speak. She did not want the matter to become public knowledge yet. "I need help. I want someone who will not kowtow to me. Lord knows your Tavie will not do that."

"Is Tavie going to accept the position?" Georgina smiled and nodded at the groups they passed but made no effort to stop and chat.

"She wants time to think it over and I suppose discuss it with the rest of your household. The women have become very close, have they not?" She looked to the side for a moment – it would appear more time had passed then she had realised. "Hush now – here come our escorts – we will talk more on this matter another time." She gave her husband a dazzling smile. "Are they not the two most handsome men here?" She accepted the arm her husband offered. "Well, my dear," she could be heard to ask as they stepped away, "are you once more ready to enter the fray?"

"She is a delightful woman," Richard remarked as they turned away from the ballroom.

"Exhausting." Georgina followed his lead.

"I thought you might like to sit down." He led her into a room set aside for dining. The long white draped tables at one end of the room were covered with mouth-watering displays of culinary art. White-suited chefs stood ready to receive compliments while servants stood ready to assist. It was to one of the tables dotted around the long room that Richard led her.

Georgina took a seat, resigned to watching Richard enjoy the goods on offer. She was burning the constricting corset as soon as she returned home, she promised herself silently. It was ridiculous that she should be unable to eat a bite of the tempting morsels on display before her. She was hungry, darn it.

"The waiter will bring our food and drink," Richard said as he took a seat opposite her. "I ordered some of the tiny mouthfuls on offer for you." He laughed at her look of disgust.

Chapter 46

"I ain't seen as many spuds since me army days," Jones, sitting in front of a barrel of potatoes, complained.

"That's cos you was always on KP duty," Smith, a sacking apron covering his good suit, said.

"Less talking, more peeling!" Cook shouted. "I've a small army of people to feed."

There were groups of workers sitting around the kitchen preparing the vegetables for the following day. Cook would serve two meals tomorrow – one to the ladies of the house and another to the men staying with Billy Flint – those that had no homes to go to. Liam stood off to one side happily gutting geese. He knew he would be given any left-over food to take home to his family. He made a careful pile of the giblets to take to his ma. She made the best soup out of the necks. They would all eat well tomorrow – Christmas Day.

The sound of excited voices and laughter carried into the kitchen from the servants' dining room where the students were enjoying decorating the room for Billy Flint and his men.

"I am so excited about wearing my new outfit."

Bridget stood with her two friends, peeling and slicing carrots and parsnips under Ruth's watchful eye. "You did a marvellous job of making them, Sarah."

"We will all be able to wear our new outfits to Midnight Mass." Sarah had used material from the trunks Felicia had brought with her to make three complete outfits for herself and her two friends. Together Felicia and Sarah had made good use of the yards of exquisite material fashioned into gowns for an obviously very stout lady. The material had been made into many new gowns for the members of the household in most need. "I love the swish of our new petticoats."

"I'm looking forward to having a lie-in," Ruth put a slim slice of carrot into her mouth. "I don't think I've ever had one of those before."

"It's all so exciting!" Bridget's hands never stopped moving. "The upstairs dining room looks so beautiful with all that holly and ivy draped around it. The crystal and silver gleam so in the light." She sighed in pleasure.

"The ladies have done a marvellous job of it," Sarah agreed. "It was so much fun searching for the best shrubbery. I'm glad the park had so much of the red-berried holly left when we got there. Felicia was afraid we had left it too late."

It had been an exciting afternoon searching for the greenery to decorate the house. Felicia had been with them as the girls had never experienced Christmas decorations and had no idea what was required.

"I think Cook's salt-pastry decorations are wonderful." Ruth had been beside herself at learning a new skill. The salt-pastry wreaths, bells and crowns would be broken up after Christmas for the birds. She hoped to be allowed keep some of the delicate art for their room.

"It has been a strange year for us." Bridget swept the growing pile of green-feathered carrot-heads and skins into her sackcloth apron. She carried the pile to the buckets set outside the door for the local pig man. The buckets were set outside the mews doors three times a week for the pig man to collect. The hanging hams in the kitchen came from his small backyard farm.

She was soon back. "Have you heard? We are to get a new teacher for the riding lessons soon."

"Who cares? But have you been listening at doors again, Bridget O'Brien?" Ruth didn't know what her friend was coming to – she seemed to have forgotten all of the lessons the nuns had drummed into their heads.

"How else would I learn anything?" Bridget was totally unrepentant.

"*You will come to a bad end if you're not careful!*" Sarah hissed.

In her sitting room Georgina stared at the blonde rag doll she held in her hands with a frown. Today was Bridget's birthday. She was twelve years old. It broke her heart to think of how mature the young girl was for her age. All three of the maids were far too advanced for their years. They had not been allowed a childhood. Was that a good or a bad thing, she wondered? She had enjoyed a protected childhood. She had been far less mature than the three maids when she had entered into marriage. Perhaps it was best not to protect children too much. She sighed deeply. What did she know of anything? She felt young and unsure of herself even now.

"What should I do with you?" Georgina spoke to the green-painted eyes of the rag doll. "I can't present you to Bridget as a gift from her mother. I would be unable to explain where I got you." She touched the woollen stands of hair falling from the doll's head. Had Bridget ever had a doll of her own, she wondered. It would appear not – she had listened in horror as the girls chatted about the toys brought to the orphanage by benefactors at Christmas. The threesome wondered what happened to the toys as they were removed from the children's hands as soon as the benefactors left the orphanage.

"I promised Reverend Mother that you would be given into Bridget's hands on her eighteenth birthday," Georgina whispered to the doll. "I must insure that this is done. I will have to have you placed in a safe place." She hugged the doll close, wondering where her friend Eugenie was now. She must be thinking of the little girl she'd been forced to give up. Today would be a day of sorrow for her old friend. She wished she could contact her. "How could I tell Eugenie that her beloved child scrubs my steps?" Georgina fought back a sob. "Life is so unfair!" she wailed into the doll's hair. "I will drive myself insane." She put the doll back into the deep drawer of her desk. "It serves no purpose for me to sit here dwelling on all of life's difficulties." She stood away from her desk. "I will join everyone else in the kitchen. The worries of the world will wait until darkness falls, I'm sure." She hurried from the room, seeking the company of women. The three young maids needed to have a nap if they were going to attend Midnight Mass with the rest of the household. She'd see to that now.

"Look at us!" Bridget took hold of her friends' hands and

pulled them over to the mirror. She was beaming with sheer delight. "Look at us!" She danced in place, her black-buttoned boots gleaming from the polishing Liam had given them, the skirts of her many petticoats swishing as she moved. "We will not stand out when we walk into church. For the first time in our lives we will look like everyone else. There is nothing to make us stand out from the crowd."

"We don't look like maidservants." Ruth worried that they were reaching above their station. It never did to get your hopes up. They were servants and so they would always be.

"I know what you are thinking, Ruth Brown." Sarah admired her own image. "I made these dresses for us out of the discards of others. You know that – you and Bridget helped me unpick seams – these dresses are the result of our hard work. There is no need to feel guilty because we look well dressed for the first time in our lives. We are working girls now. We should be able to afford to dress ourselves."

"But apricot?" Ruth touched the rich apricot-coloured dress she wore. "It is not a serviceable colour. Brown or black would have been better."

"I'm glad my dress is green." Bridget too touched her dress.

"The rich don't wear brown, Ruth, so there was no brown dress to cut down." Sarah nudged her friend. "They wear black for mourning but I wasn't going to make our dresses out of mourning clothes, thank you very much."

"I love my dress." Bridget picked up the wide skirts of her dress and whirled around the room. "It is beautiful,

Sarah – thank you!" She smiled at her friend.

"Are we all ready to dine?" Sarah stuck her nose in the air but spoiled the effect by falling into a fit of the giggles.

"I don't know what you two are coming to," Ruth huffed.

Cook had made steak-and-kidney pies for this evening's meal. She said they were easy to make and she had too much work for tomorrow's celebration to bother with a fussy meal for this evening. They were dining in the servants' dining room before enjoying an evening of entertainment in the basement drawing room. The Catholics would leave the house as a group to attend Midnight Mass later.

"That meal was delicious." Lily Chambers looked around the table. "I love a good steak-and-kidney pie."

There were murmurs of agreement from the others. The days of them spending hours over a many-course meal were long behind them. They had adjusted to a new way of living. They had to.

"You stay where you are," Lily ordered the young maids as they moved to get to their feet. "I'll clear the table. I haven't changed into me finery yet. The students will clean the kitchen and wash up this evening." She almost laughed at the look of shock on the faces of the three maids. "In the olden days the masters of the house would wait on the servants on Christmas Eve."

"That must have been long ago and far away." Tavie stood to gather the dishes from the table.

"I vaguely remember my grandfather talking about such things." Mia too began clearing the table.

The three maids sat open-mouthed as the table was

cleared. They looked at each other – uncomfortable – what were they supposed to do?

"I received a letter from my brothers." Felicia, with the others at her heels, returned to the dining room. The dishes had been put to soak. They could be washed later. The meal wasn't over yet.

"I too have heard from home," Tavie said. "I wanted to let my brother know that I will be working for a titled lady."

"I had understood that once you accept the assistance of the BOBs that all contact with your family is frowned upon." Georgina had been concerned when the post had been delivered with letters for her students.

"I believe it depends on the circumstances," Verity said. "I don't think there is a hard and fast rule about keeping in touch." She looked around the table at the women she had spent the last months with. They were a surprising group. "Unfortunately, in some cases the women the BOBs help are running from their families. I do know the BOBs refuse to give any information out about the women they help."

"Yes," Georgina knew this to her cost. She had begged for news of her friend Eugenie to no effect.

"I wrote to my brothers to tell them what had become of me." Felicia had cried when she wrote the letter to the address she had for her brother's new employer in America.. The news she had to share was so much better than anything they had feared when they helped her escape. "My brothers are making new lives for themselves in America." She touched Erma's hand as the woman took her seat at her side. "Erma has agreed to act as our go-between. I do not want to lose touch with my brothers or the women here. It will be difficult to stay in touch as we all move in different directions. Erma has agreed to keep track of my address and keep all of us apprised of any developments regarding our movements. I can't thank her enough."

Erma blushed and hung her head. It was little enough and it meant she too would have correspondence of a personal nature.

"We must keep in touch!" Verity said. "I feel we have become close during this time we have spent together."

The conversation was interrupted by Cook and Lily returning to the dining room. Felicity jumped to take the heavy tray from Lily. The students then quickly set the cups and saucers on the table.

Cook put the lovingly decorated cake, beautifully displayed on a silver stand, in the middle of the table.

"*Happy Birthday, Bridget!*" Cook stood back and beamed.

"*For me!*" Bridget clapped both hands to her mouth. She had never had a birthday cake before. This one even had her name on it. She clapped her hands in delight and smiled around the room. "Thank you!"

Chapter 47

"Sarah," Liam said, "Mrs Chambers wants to see you in her room." He threw the empty hessian sack onto the floor of the second drawing room.

"Me?" Sarah almost fell off the ladder she was standing on. "Why?"

"How would I know?" Liam began to stuff the greenery the women were removing from around the room into the sack. "You better hurry. Mrs Chambers doesn't like to be kept waiting." He sucked his finger. The darn holly was full of prickles. Still, it would be grand in the fire when it dried out completely. He loved to watch the colourful sparks that flew when he put a bit of holly on the fire.

"I'll finish taking the greenery off the walls." Bridget hurried over to take Sarah's place. "You get off." She held the ladder knowing Sarah must be worried sick. None of them had ever been sent for like this before.

"Thanks." Sarah was brushing off her clothes while hurrying from the room.

"Do you know what's going on, young Liam?" Tavie, a broom in hand, was sweeping the fallen greenery into a corner.

"Haven't a clue." Liam didn't stop stuffing his sack. "I was coming in after leaving me last sack in the yard when the housekeeper saw me." He shrugged, not seeing what all the fuss was about. Mrs Chambers wasn't going to eat the maid. "I was told to send Sarah down to her room and that's all I know." He wanted that made clear. It didn't matter how much they might tickle him – he knew no more.

"Where is Sarah going in such a hurry?" Mia put her head around the drawing-room door. "She didn't say a word when she passed Erma and me." The two were clearing the hall of all festive greenery.

The women and Liam continued to clear all signs of the festive season from the house. They had said goodbye to 1898 and welcomed in 1899 in fine style. It was time now to get down to the serious business of planning the year ahead.

Tavie leaned on her broom when the room had been returned to its pristine condition. She had been aware of the two girls exchanging worried glances at their friend's failure to return quickly. The women had cleared the dining room and hallway – the stairs too were clear of decoration.

"Ruth, Bridget," she said, "I think we deserve a pot of tea. I've been eating dust for what seems like hours."

"That sounds like an excellent idea." Felicia entered the room, her cheeks flushed from her vigorous work outdoors. "Verity and I have been roundly chastised by Cook for the dust and dirt we seem to have collected on our persons while beating carpets." The two women were carrying a rolled carpet between them.

"I've asked Jones to heat the copper," Verity said. "I

thought we would all enjoy hot water to wash the grime from our skin." She laughed. "I never thought I'd be grateful for flour-sack aprons." She gestured towards the rough apron that covered her dark clothing. "We will have to brush each other down, I think."

"Ruth," a pale Sarah appeared after the group clattered down the stairs to the kitchen, "Mrs Chambers wants to see you." She was aware of the questioning glances she was receiving but ignored them. She didn't want to talk yet. She needed time to think.

"They certainly bring life to this house." Richard Wilson stood as the sound outside Georgina's sitting room faded into the distance. He used the brass tongs from the fireside companion set to add more coal to the fire that burned brightly in the grate. He had been cloistered with the mistress of the house for some time. "I hope you enjoyed the holiday season?" He wished he could have spent some part of the holiday in this house with her – but that would have caused comment.

"There were a great many female visitors to this house over the holidays." Georgina had been surprised and secretly delighted by the stream of visitors who found their way to her door. "The alcohol Charles's sons left in place came in useful. I was able to offer drinks to my visitors." She laughed to think of it. "The bottles are almost dry and so they can remain. I have no intention of ordering spirits – they are too costly. Tea will have to suffice from now on."

"The details Skip printed in the papers of your attendance at balls did you no harm." Richard settled back in his seat to one side of Georgina's roll-top desk. He was in no hurry. Dublin business had not yet returned to its usual bustling pace.

"At least I've been removed from the front page!" Georgina laughed. "The doomsayers following the total eclipse of the sun at the beginning of this year have taken over every newspaper. Long may they continue." The eclipse at the very start of the year had people expressing views almost evenly divided between doom and great good fortune.

"I have received news of Whitmore." Richard hated to introduce the man's name into what had been an enjoyable meeting. "The man has been moved by ambulance from Doctor Steevens' Hospital. He has checked into a private hospital in Belfast. His lady friend and Lewis also travelled to Belfast. They went by rail. They have rented a small residence in a desirable part of the city."

"I don't want to talk about that man. I don't want to think about him." Georgina knew she hadn't seen the last of the Captain. He would still find a way to make her life a misery. But, for this moment she was free of him.

Richard looked at his dear friend, worried that she was burying her head in the sand. Whitmore was insane – no matter what the good doctors declared. He'd keep an eye on the man's movements and enlist the help of Billy Flint to keep Georgina safe. If she wanted to pretend Whitmore was not a problem, he'd allow it – for now.

"I want to start work on these plans." Georgina trembled and rattled the papers on her desk – all of the dreams – the hours spent in planning – she felt almost sick at the thought of putting those plans into action. "The thought of entering into so much debt is keeping me awake at night."

"There is no need for you to enter into debt, my dear Georgie." Richard's smile was wide – his eyes sparkling.

"What do you mean? We've spoken of this. I don't have the necessary funds to update this house." She had spent hours studying the figures she'd received from friends of Billy Flint's. The changes must be made. They would make life so much easier for everyone and it was necessary to move with the times.

"You will agree that my father is a wily old bird?" Richard was glad he could finally share this secret with his friend. He had hated to see her so worried about funds.

"Of course." Georgina was perplexed by what seemed like a change of subject.

"Well, so was your father." He held up one hand, silently asking for a moment. "I was unaware of this matter until recently." He shook his head at his father's secretive ways. "It would appear that your parents realised the mistake they had made in entrusting your future to Whitmore."

He waited to see if she would speak but when she remained staring at him – shock clear on her lovely face – he continued.

"They were not in Switzerland for a vacation, as we were led to believe, when they lost their lives in that tragic accident. They were there to speak with bankers. They moved their funds out of the country." He pinched the bridge of his nose and avoided the hurt look in her eyes.

"That is what happened to the money!" Georgina slapped the desk. How many times had she been beaten and cursed because of the inheritance that man had been expecting upon the death of her parents?

"Yes." Richard could guess what Whitmore's reaction

had been to the relatively small inheritance Georgina had received from her wealthy parents. "The money is tied up in such a way that your husband cannot touch it." He leaned over to touch her hand gently. He had been angry with his own father when he'd shared this news with him. Georgina had suffered greatly at Whitmore's hands. "It was decided that you would not be told of the monies available to you – not while Whitmore lived." The man was a great deal older than Georgina after all.

"I need a moment." Georgina buried her face in her hands. It was such a shock to learn that she was not the penniless creature she had thought herself. She had never been able to explain the lack of an inheritance from her parents – to herself or her husband – in spite of repeated beatings. The images that burned behind her closed lids sickened her. She would have told the man anything to stop the pain.

"They were right. That was the right decision." She sighed deeply and licked dry lips. What more could she say?

"The funds are available to you and only you." Richard wanted to pull her into his arms. How much she had suffered for the mistake her parents had made choosing that man as a husband for their only child!

"That man will learn that I am spending a great deal of money," Georgina whispered. She could not imagine what form his revenge would take – she would never feel safe from him. "It will be impossible to hide the work being done on the house."

"My father has thought of this," Richard said. "It will be made known – through whispers – that a fund for home improvements had been built into the trust left for the house." He waited a moment to add, "I doubt anyone will question the matter but my father suggests that we take Billy Flint into our confidence. That man can keep an eye open for anyone displaying an unnatural interest in your affairs."

A gong sounded through the house.

"Will you join us for lunch?" Georgina was glad of the interruption. She had a slight headache – her brain reeling from this new information.

"Good Lord," Richard pulled a gold fob watch from his waistcoat pocket, "is that the time?" The time he spent with Georgina seemed to pass so quickly. He returned the watch to his pocket and stood. "I have invited William Armstrong to join me for lunch at my club." He smiled, waiting for her to process his words.

"Will–" Georgina stared for a moment. "Billy Flint's alter ego?"

Richard laughed at her surprise. "Have you seen Billy dressed in the clothing he inherited from Christopher Winstanley? He cuts quite the dashing figure – puts the rest of us to shame."

"I've heard the other men jesting about his elegant clothing." Georgina too stood. "But I haven't set eyes on Billy 'all dressed up to the nines' as his men call it."

"I've arranged to meet him here." Richard admired Billy Flint. The man had been given a rough start in life but was determined to improve his lot. If he could help him fit in with polite society – well, he would do all that he could. In his opinion no man deserved to be denied his place in life simply because of an accident of birth.

A knock sounded on the door.

"That will be him now," he said. "He is very prompt."

He offered his bent arm to Georgina, delighted when she slipped her arm into his. They walked together towards the door.

"Let me look at you," Georgina said when they had stepped into the hallway. Billy was lit by the bright winter sunlight streaming through the oval glass over the entry door. He wore a pale grey suit with a charcoal overcoat. He held his charcoal hat in his hand. She stepped away from Richard and walked slowly around the blushing figure of William Armstrong. "I must say, William," for this man was no Billy, "you clean up well." She admired the tall strong figures of both men. "The ladies of Dublin will be hard put not to faint as you gentlemen walk by."

Chapter 48

Bridget watched and waited. Sarah and Ruth were walking around as if they had the worries of the world on their shoulders. Why were they called into Mrs Chambers' office? Why wasn't she?

"What did she have to say?" Bridget stood alongside Ruth at the kitchen table, putting the final touches to the evening meal.

"*Shhh!*" Ruth hissed. "She is the cat's mother." She used an oft-repeated warning from their time spent at the orphanage.

"Is it bad?"

"Honest to God, Bridget O'Brien!" Ruth was aware of Cook keeping an eye on them.

The other women were trying to question Sarah while they set the table in the servants' dining room. The nudges and demands had been going on for hours. Both girls had been questioned ruthlessly while everyone took turns having a bath.

"Ladies!" Georgina sat at the head of the table. She leaned back to allow Ruth to pour soup into her bowl. "It would appear you are all eaten alive with curiosity." Lily had told her of the interrogation the two young maids had been subjected to. The women glanced around the table with similar guilty expressions.

"I am sorry," Mia said. "I was concerned for the two maids." She looked around at the others. "We have only been in this house a few months," she shrugged, "but I feel as if we have become close to each other."

"I think," Tavie smiled, "that we are all becoming nervous at the thought of how little time we have left here. The thought of stepping out into the world is honestly terrifying. The chance to turn our attention to the two maids gave us something other than our own problems to ponder on – it was irresistible. I too am sorry if I upset anyone."

"I wouldn't mind knowing what's going on," Cook said.

There was silence while every head turned in Georgina's direction.

"I had planned to tell you all of my plans this evening," Georgina said. "This is Nollaig na mBan after all – which, for those with no Gaelic, translates as the Women's Christmas. The day some call 'Little Christmas' when we take down our decorations and women everywhere put up their feet."

Liam as the only man of the house had been sent across to join Billy Flint and his men – much to the lad's delight.

There were snorts of derision around the room at the thought of women everywhere putting up their feet.

"Now to put your minds to rest about our two young maids," Georgina could almost see the intense interest being paid to her words, "Mrs Chambers has questioned

Sarah and Ruth about their hopes and dreams for their futures. We have been very fortunate in welcoming such skilled young women into this house. Sarah is a skilled seamstress." She smiled when the others murmured in agreement. "Ruth, according to our cook, has a natural aptitude for producing meals that delight the palate."

"She is proving to be a dab hand at making cakes too." Cook said. "Shouldn't think there was much call for cakes at the orphanage."

Bridget sat with her tongue firmly locked behind her teeth. She hadn't been asked about her hopes and dreams.

The conversation was put on hold while the main course was served.

"There is so much happening," Georgina continued when all were served and seated. "Erma and Tavie will be the first to leave us. Each has been offered and has accepted positions in prestigious households. Erma has been in talks with the Dowager Duchess's master of the household. She leaves us to take up a paying position with the Dowager Duchess of Westbrooke."

The group exclaimed aloud at this news.

"Ruth will attend the home of the Dowager two days a week and take instruction from the Dowager's French chef."

Bridget grabbed her friend's hand under cover of the table cloth – thrilled for her.

"Tavie has accepted a paying position with Lady Sutton – as a companion and social secretary. Sarah will be given into the care of Lady Sutton's French maid twice a week. She will be receiving instruction in the creation and care of a lady of high fashion's wardrobe." Georgina waited while congratulations were offered. "The departure of Verity, Felicia and Mia will be delayed."

She felt almost assaulted by the shouted demands for an explanation.

"I am not happy with the arrangements made for them when they reach America." She'd had Billy Flint talk to the sailors always to be found around the Dublin port. It would seem they needed help when they reached New York. She couldn't allow these first three of her students to arrive in America alone and uninformed.

Bridget felt her heart sink as again there was no mention of her name. Did they think she wanted to be a drudge for the rest of her life?

"I have yet to discuss Bridget's future with her." Georgina was happy to see the smile return to Bridget's face. The two maids had been offered choices. They had been unwilling to discuss any life but one of service. She didn't think Bridget would be happy to remain a servant. She needed to discuss that young woman's future with her. How to do that without revealing the secrets that surrounded the girl?

"I don't know how I feel about this delay." Verity looked at Mia and Felicity who shrugged but remained silent.

"In the meantime I am making changes to the house itself." Georgina thought she may as well share the rest of the news with the group. The workmen would be here before most of these women left. "I am installing bathrooms and a toilet on every floor of the house."

"I am sure the next group will be glad of such modern plumbing." Mia wondered about the delay in their travel plans. She was tempted to write to her brother thanking him for gambling away her future. She had been content to stay at home and marry a suitable gentleman. What would life hold for her in the New World? "It has been a great adventure bathing in the washhouse." The others laughed with her.

"Will having workmen underfoot interfere with your ability to welcome women who need shelter?" Erma asked. It would be one of her duties to send the women to this house. "They cannot be housed here if walls are to be knocked out."

Georgina hastily swallowed the mouthful of food to answer. "Indeed not." She didn't want Erma to discourage women who might need her aid. "In fact we are to have a newcomer any day now." She ignored the demands for information about the woman. "You may have noticed the extensions along some of the back walls of this row of houses?" She waited for their nods. "Those extensions house bathrooms. Each of our bathrooms will have a gas water heater." She was delighted by the exclamations of surprise. She couldn't wait to have the new feature in place. "That will also mean, Cook," she waited until her friend looked at her, "that you will have one of the new fancy gas stoves in your kitchen. No more stoking the fire every few moments to check on your cakes and bread."

"Well, I never!" Cook wasn't sure how she felt about any of this.

Chapter 49

"This day has been as long as a week," Bridget groaned and threw herself onto her bed. She watched her two friends walk into their room from under lowered eyelids. They had not had a chance to talk in private.

"Mrs Chambers gave me a fancy notepad." Ruth put the red leather-bound book onto the table. She passed her hands over the cover in a silent caress.

"Me too." Sarah put a matching book onto the table. "Will you write our names in them, Biddy? We don't want to get them mixed up." She opened the thick book of blank white pages to show an empty label inside the cover. "See, it has a place for our names." She turned to her friend lying on her bed – only a gleam of green under her lids showing she was paying attention. "You have the best handwriting of all of us."

"What are they for?" Bridget walked over to the table.

"Mrs Chambers said I should write down every recipe I want to keep with me." Ruth once more caressed the red leather. She had never owned anything so beautiful before. She played with the brass clasp that would lock the book. Imagine – it would be for her use only – she wanted to clutch it to her chest.

"I am supposed to keep note of designs and special stitching," Sarah sighed. "Mrs Chambers suggested I draw a picture to help me remember special folds and such."

"What's going on?" Bridget looked at her friends, a frown between her brows. "This isn't normal," she waved her hands at the books, "is it?"

"There is nothing normal about this house." Sarah sat at the table.

"Mrs Chambers said," Ruth sat at the table, pulling the book close and wrapping her arms around it, "that this book," she patted it like a favourite pet, "should go with me to every position I take up. It will be my bible of cooking." She sighed, deeply delighted at the very thought of it.

"You will both be working with French people." Bridget too sat and waited. She was feeling her friends out – wanting to know what else had been said between them and Mrs Chambers. They had been in her office for an awfully long time.

The other two exchanged glances. They hadn't had a chance to discuss what had been said in their meetings.

"I am going to learn to speak and read French." Ruth almost pushed the words out of her mouth. She knew how much Bridget longed to learn foreign languages and more of the world. She had always been so hungry for knowledge. It was a shame the nuns had forced her out of their school when she turned nine – they said she had learned as much as they wanted to teach her. "It seems French is the language of food."

"Cook doesn't know French, does she?" Bridget

couldn't imagine that good woman speaking a foreign language.

"No." Ruth leaned closer, not wanting her words to be overheard. She wouldn't hurt Cook for the world. "Mrs Chambers said Cook was – well – a cook." She hadn't quite understood the difference herself. "She said with the help of the Dowager's Frenchman I would be trained up to be a *chef*."

"What's the difference?" Sarah asked.

Ruth smiled. "It seems chef is a fancier cook and gets paid more money."

"Then you better be one of them." Bridget nodded.

"I am going to learn French too," Sarah hadn't wanted to mention the French and art lessons she'd been offered. She knew how hurt Bridget would be to be excluded from learning a new skill. It wasn't fair that the nuns had made her into a scrubber and laundry woman. "Mrs Chambers said as how there are people who pretend to be French just to earn more money – call themselves Henri instead of Henry if you wouldn't be minding. It seems the French are considered the masters of dressmaking – although she didn't call it that – she said something in French but I understood what she meant."

"Are you two happier now that you're going to have more training?" Bridget thought that she would soon be sick of hearing what Mrs Chambers said. "You have been moaning about the strangeness of this house since we got here."

"I've been made to see that we are going to be given the chance of a lifetime working here." Sarah was greatly relieved. She'd been worried sick about her future. "We'll be receiving more training than any other orphan has ever been offered. Can you just imagine us speaking French?" She almost squealed she was so excited.

"I thought we three would always be together," Bridget said sadly. "I suppose that was stupid."

"We will always be friends," Sarah held out both of her hands. The other two each grabbed an offered hand. "We were always going to be separated when we turned sixteen – even if we found employment in the same house – I would be in the sewing room and Ruth in the kitchen. We'd never see each other." She didn't like to mention that Bridget would be scrubbing the steps and considered lower in the house hierarchy than they – they wouldn't even sit at the same table to eat.

"We'd better go to bed." Sarah released their hands.

"I don't know if I'll sleep," Ruth said.

Bridget said nothing but stood to begin getting ready for bed.

In Georgina's sitting room the mistress of the house was staring into her fire, listening to the silence around her. "If anyone had told me of the changes that would take place in my life when the old year began I would have thought them deranged," she whispered aloud to the empty room.

She stood abruptly, unable to sit still. She walked over to a nearby table and poured a glass of sherry. She was thinking and fretting about the new arrival, her mind going around in circles. What were the BOBs thinking of? What was Eugenie thinking? It would be wonderful to see her old friend – catch up on her life – but that man Henderson was still in Dublin – did Eugenie know? How on earth was she going to keep mother and child safe and hidden in a town as small as Dublin?

She sincerely hoped her old friend knew what she was doing.

"This year is the last of the old century – who knows what the new century will bring!" She raised her glass to her lips. All she could do now was put one foot in front of the other and continue to dream impossible dreams.

THE END

Leabharlanna Poiblí Chathair Baile Átha Cliath
390
Dublin City Public Libraries

Now that you're hooked why not try
Through Streets Broad and Narrow? the first
book in the bestselling series.
also published by Poolbeg

Here's a sneak preview of
chapters one.

THROUGH
STREETS
BROAD AND
NARROW

Chapter 1

The sound of her own teeth chattering woke Ivy Murphy from her uneasy sleep. She had a crick in her neck and every bone in her body wanted to complain. Ivy didn't know if the aches she felt were the result of her uncomfortable position in her battered fireside chair or her shenanigans in the street earlier. The Lane had celebrated the brand-new year with a lively street party.

Ivy didn't drink alcohol but she'd been the first to start dancing and singing. To someone unused to celebration it had been a wonderful way to greet the year 1925. She'd been giddy with happiness until she'd returned home.

Ivy stared in the general direction of the battered clock ticking away on her mantelpiece. She had no idea how long she'd slept. She'd been waiting for her da to come home, praying he had a few coppers left in his pocket.

"Stupid woman," Ivy muttered, trying to stand.

It was pitch-black and cold, the fire in the grate having died completely. She couldn't see her hand in front of her face. By feel and familiarity she found a couple of matches and pulled the chain on one of the glass-covered lamps situated on the side of the mantel. She struck the match off the mantelpiece and held the tiny flame to the gas jet. The light flickered weakly. The gas supply coughed and sputtered. A sure sign indicating the need for more money in the gas meter.

"Da, are you home?" She kicked the black knitted shawl she'd used to cover her knees away from her. The darn thing was wrapped around her ankles. She stumbled, shivering in the cold predawn air. "Da, where are you?" She held her arms in front of her as she made her way to the second of the two rooms they called home. She pushed the heavy wood door ajar.

"Da, it's black as pitch in here." She sniffed the air like a hound. Her da smelt like the bottom of a barrel after a night on the tiles. "Da!" she shouted again even though she knew the back room was empty of life. "Where in the name of God did yeh get to, Da?"

Ivy longed to collapse on the floor and scream like a banshee.

"It's past four in the morning. Where can he be? The pubs are all closed," she sobbed.

Last night, not for the first time, Éamonn Murphy had cleaned out the jar she kept her housekeeping money in – the rent-money jar was empty too. Thanks to her da's two-finger habit, Ivy always checked her cash before she went to bed. There wasn't a penny piece to be found in the place. Her da had waited until Ivy joined the street party before stealing the money and disappearing with his drinking cronies.

The sound of footsteps coming down the entry steps had Ivy spinning around towards the window of their basement flat. It wasn't her father: the footsteps were steady. Ivy froze for a moment. Should she blow out the gas lamp and pretend she was asleep?

"Miss Murphy! It's Officer Collins, Miss Murphy." The soft words were accompanied by the rap of knuckles on the entry door. The Murphys were fortunate in that their basement rooms had a private entrance, a luxury in the tenements. "Miss Murphy!"

"Officer Collins!" Ivy opened the door, trying to make out the features of the man standing in the concrete cage that framed the iron steps leading down to the doorway. Officer Collins was a familiar face to the residents of these tenements. "What in the name of God are you doing at my door?"

"Could I come inside, Miss Murphy?"

Barney Collins wished he was anywhere but here. He'd walked the streets of this tenement block known locally as "The Lane" for years. Ivy Murphy was a well-known local figure. She'd pushed a pram around the high-class streets that existed only yards away from the squalor of The Lane from the time she was knee-high to a grasshopper.

Ivy stepped back and watched the tall police officer remove his hat and bend his head to enter the tiny hallway. "I can't offer yeh a cup of tea," she said, leading him into the front room. "It's a bit early for visitors."

"I wonder if we could have a bit more light on the subject?" Barney Collins couldn't see a thing in the flickering gaslight. With Ivy's pride in mind he held out a copper penny and offered it to her with the words: "Saves you searching in the dark." Barney well knew everyone in these tenements squeezed every penny until it screamed but right now he needed to be able to see the woman.

"Give me a minute." Ivy was glad the dim light hid her burning cheeks.

She hurried into the hallway and quickly pulled the door of the cupboard that hid the gas meter open. The strength went from her legs when she noticed the broken seal on the money-box of the meter. Her da had nicked the gas money as well. Ivy passed the penny through. Might as well be hung for a sheep as a lamb, she thought, catching the penny in her open palm and passing it through the meter again.

"Thank you, Officer," Ivy said, returning the coin to the policeman. "I had several coins on top of the meter." She lied without a blush but she was mortified at being forced to play penny tag with a police officer.

She quickly lit the second gas lamp on the mantel. With very little fuss she raked the fire and in minutes had a blaze climbing up the chimney. When you came in freezing from the winter conditions you needed to get the fire going, fast. Paper, sticks and small nuggets of coal were kept close to hand.

Ivy wiped her black-stained hands on a damp rag hanging by the grate, before turning back around to face Officer Collins. To give her father his due, he was a dab hand at finding nuggets of coal spilled around the docks. He sold some for drink money but always made sure there was enough at home for his own comfort.

"What's going on?" Ivy sank down into one of the chairs flanking the fireplace. She gestured towards the chair on the opposite side of the fireplace.

"I'm afraid I have bad news." Barney Collins perched on the edge of the chair, staring at the woman opposite.

Ivy Murphy was a good-looking young woman. In the proper clothes she would stand out in any company. Her blue-black hair pulled back into an old-fashioned bun suited her face. The starvation diet of the tenements gave her face a high-boned patrician appearance. Eyes of brilliant blue framed by thick black lashes stared across the space between them.

"Just get it out quick, please." Ivy forced the words out. Her lips felt frozen and her teeth wanted to rattle, but she sat stiffly upright. "What has me da been up to now?"

"There's no easy way to tell you this, Miss Murphy." Barney Collins swallowed audibly. "Sometime during the early hours of this morning, in what we believe was a drunken stupor, your father Éamonn Murphy fell into the cement horse trough outside Brennan's public house and drowned."

"Me da is dead?" Ivy fell back against the chair, her hand going to her incredibly narrow neck, almost as if she needed help holding up her head. "That's not possible. I'm expecting me da home any minute."

"I'm very sorry for your loss." Barney Collins wondered if he was going to have a hysterical woman on his hands.

"He's really dead?" Ivy whispered. "You're sure? It's not some kind of mistake?"

"I'm sure, Miss Murphy. I know your father well enough to make a positive identification."

"Yes, I suppose you do." Ivy wanted to float away, disappear. What on earth was she supposed to do now?

"Ivy, Miss Murphy, is there anyone I could call to be with you?" Barney Collins couldn't just leave the poor young woman here alone.

"There's only me and me da," Ivy whispered. "All the others left." Her three younger brothers had taken the mail-boat to England as soon as each turned sixteen. Ivy hadn't seen or heard from them since.

"I could knock on Father Leary's door if you like," Barney offered. "I pass his house on my way home."

"He'd only be round here with his hand out!" Ivy blurted out before slapping her hand across her mouth. It didn't do to badmouth the clergy in Holy Catholic Ireland.

"I see." Barney Collins was astonished to hear anyone dare to voice a negative comment on the clergy. The poverty-stricken families living in this slum were devoted Catholics. The people of The Lane accepted the decisions of the priest before the law of the land. Every family gave pennies they couldn't afford to the Church each Sunday and every Saint's Day. It was a wonder the local church didn't burn down with the number of candles these people lit.

"I'm sure you don't see." Ivy grinned in spite of herself. "I have a problem . . ." she paused, wondering how much to say, "with the Church. It's a well-known fact in these parts."

"I'll have to leave you to it then," Barney Collins was unsure what to make of this situation. "The death certificate and your father's body will be waiting for you at the morgue in the basement of Kevin's Hospital. Because of the time of year," he shook his head – it was a rotten start to 1925 for this woman, "it will be a few days before the body is released into your care."

"Thank you for coming in person to tell me." Ivy stood waiting for Officer Collins to push himself upright, then slowly walked the police officer to the door. She

398

wanted a cup of tea and time alone to think.

"I'll keep in touch if you don't mind," he said.

"Thank you." Ivy held out one pale, cold, shaking hand, offering a handshake as a token of her gratitude. It was all she could afford.

"Let me know if I can help in any way." Barney Collins stepped through the open door and replaced his uniform hat on his head. "It seems almost insulting to wish you a Happy New Year," he shrugged, "but I don't know what else to say." He began to climb the iron stairs leading up to the street. When he reached street level he turned with his hand on the iron railings to look down. The door was closed tight, the gas lamps extinguished.

Ivy wasn't even aware of turning off the gas lamps – the habit of saving money by any means possible was bred into her bones. She dropped back into her chair, staring without seeing into the fire.

"What in the name of all that's good and holy am I going to do now?" she croaked aloud, tears running down her cheeks unnoticed. Her da had left her without a brass farthing to her name. There was no way she could give him the send-off he would want, the kind of send-off his friends and drinking cronies would expect. Her body began to shake as she tried to grasp the situation she found herself in. What would she do? Where could she go?

Ivy finally gave in to the sobs she'd been forcing back since she heard the news. Her big, tough, rascal of a da was gone. She'd never see him again. She'd never again scream at him for the trouble he never failed to bring to her door.

"Tea, I need a river of tea." Ivy wiped her hands across

her wet cheeks, her eyes sore from the ocean of tears that had poured from her shaking heart.

She grabbed the heavy black kettle from the grate and without conscious thought picked up the galvanised water bucket. She hoped she could get down the back of the tenement building to the communal outdoor tap without anyone seeing her. She didn't want to talk to anyone. All she was capable of thinking of at this moment was her desperate need for a cup of tea. She wanted to think, plan, try and find some way out of this nightmare.

While the heavy stream of water slapped against the bucket a smoky rasp issued from the half-open door of the outside toilet.

"Jesus, would yeh have some mercy for the suffering of others!"

Ivy raised her eyes to heaven, praying she'd have all the water she needed before Nelly Kelly came storming out to see who was out and about at this hour. Nelly made no secret of her admiration for Ivy's da. She'd try to barge her way in to see him. Ivy knew enough about the mating of animals to know what the noises coming from her da's room meant whenever Nelly closed the door that separated the two rooms. Nelly was the last thing she needed this morning.

The kettle and bucket filled at last, she scurried away and back to the basement.

There she sat for hours at the table under the window of their front room, moving only occasionally to tend the fire and add hot water to the tea she sipped through pale lips. She held the chipped enamel mug to her mouth with two hands, trying to force her mind to settle into some useful train of thought. She listened to children scream in the street and barely flinched when the steel rim the boys were playing with fell down the basement steps with an unmerciful clatter. Even Nelly Kelly's screamed curses and shouted abuse failed to penetrate the daze she'd fallen into. She had to think.

She'd visit her da. That was the Christian thing to do. Her head almost wagged off her shoulders as she nodded frantically at the first solid idea that had come to her. She'd go and see her da – then she'd be able to think.

She stood and stared around the sparsely furnished room, wondering what she should do first. She banked the fire with wet newspaper, causing clouds of grey smoke to fill the chimney breast.

Without thought she picked up the threadbare old army overcoat one of her brothers left behind. She pulled the coat over her shaking body. Throwing the black knitted shawl over her head and shoulders, she wrapped the belt of the coat around her waist to hold the long ends of the shawl in place. Without a backward glance she let herself out of the only home she'd ever known.

Ivy ignored the shouts of the children playing in the square cobblestoned courtyard. She was aware of the women leaning in the open doors of the block of twelve Georgian tenements at her back but didn't respond to their shouted greetings. She stared without seeing across the courtyard at the local livery, a long barn-like building that snaked along one complete side of this hidden square. Mothers yelled at their children from the row of two-storey, double-fronted houses that marched across the furthest end of the square but Ivy didn't hear them.

She bowed her head, covered her face with her shawl and walked quickly across the cobbles towards the tunnel that was the only entry and exit point to this hidden enclave. The square sported the official name of Verschoyle Place but the inhabitants, for no apparent reason, never called it anything but The Lane.

Ivy wrinkled her finely formed nose at the stench that seemed to reach out of the tunnel and choke her. The wide tunnel was cut into a high wall that formed the fourth section of the square. The wall protected the rear entrances of the prosperous Mount Street houses from their impoverished neighbours.

One wall of the tunnel stretched along the side of the last house on Mount Street. The wall on the opposite side formed the side wall of the public house that occupied the rest of Mount Street and backed onto the livery. The drunks who fell out of the pub daily used the tunnel as a public toilet. The women of The Lane battled constantly with the odour of stale urine, but no matter how many times they scrubbed the tunnel out, it still stank.

Ivy stood for a moment with the rank-smelling tunnel at her back. She ignored the shouted comments of the drunks standing outside the public house as she gazed around at a world that had suddenly become alien to her. She knew this area like the back of her hand. How could she suddenly feel so lost?

The Georgian mansions that marched along both sides of Mount Street blazed and sparkled in the sharp icy-cold air. Snow-white steps leading up to impressive doors with polished brass fittings lined both sides of the street. One row of Mount Street mansions elegantly hid most of the poverty-stricken world mere steps from their rear gardens. Mount Street was a different world entirely from the world Ivy and her friends inhabited.

Which way should she go? If she had a ha'penny for the charabanc she could walk through Merrion Square towards Grafton Street and public transport, but it would be Shank's mare all the way for her. The biting cold of the stones under her feet ate through the paper covering the holes in the soles of her shoes.

Ivy turned towards the Grand Canal. She'd follow the canal, walking along the pathways worn bald by the constant passage of the horses that pulled the barges travelling from Dublin to Kildare daily. Following the canal would take at least twenty minutes off the hour-long walk. The bare earth should be warmer and softer than the stone pavements.

Ivy felt invisible, a lost soul no-one could see, moving along the river path without friend or family to comfort or console her. Her da was gone. The big noisy laughing rogue that broke her heart once a day and twice on Sunday was dead. What was she going to do without him?

Ivy had been looking after her da since her ninth birthday. Ever since her ma had taken the mail-boat to England leaving her da alone with four kids under nine to raise. Ivy covered her mouth with her hand, pushing back the laugh that seemed disrespectful under the circumstances. Her da raise the kids? That was a joke. Ivy had become the mother and chief earner of the family from that day to this. It was Ivy who walked the streets pushing a pram, begging clothes and unwanted items from the wealthy houses that encaged her world. It was Ivy who sat up all night cutting and stitching at the discarded clothing, turning rags into money-making serviceable items she'd sold back to the servants of the houses she frequented.

She stepped off the path to let a horse-drawn barge pass her by. She waved to the people on board, wondering what life would be like living on one of those floating homes. Was it any better than the life she led? She shrugged and turned to walk on.

A sudden thought almost brought her to her knees. The rent book – had her da changed the title-holder like he'd promised? Sweet Lord, was she about to lose her home as well as everything else? She thought back frantically to her twenty-first birthday – hadn't her da boasted to his cronies about being a modern man and changing the rent book to her name now she was a woman grown? Whose name was on the rent book? If it was still in her da's name she'd be evicted. Her ma had shouted often enough, "You can eat in the street but you can't sleep in the street!" Dear God, was she about to become homeless? She could end up in the poorhouse.

Ivy tried to think back – late last year, when she turned twenty-one, had the name on the rent book been changed? She'd check as soon as she returned home. It would be the first thing she did. Ivy shook herself like a wet dog. She couldn't think about that, not now that she was at the back end of Kevin's Hospital. Garda Collins said the morgue was in the basement. She'd visit her da and pray for a miracle, some kind of a sign.

Ivy stared at the large signs with pointing arrows in despair. How she longed to be able to read the words! She could follow the arrows with her head held high then. A sigh that seemed to start at her feet shook her slender frame. It wasn't to be. She was ignorant, stupid. The pretty squiggles meant nothing to her.

Ivy ignored the tuts of disgust she received from the

people she asked directions from. She was used to that. She just wanted to see her da. Make sure it was really him. Maybe the police had made a mistake. Her big laughing da couldn't be dead. Not her da, the larger-than-life Éamonn Murphy.

It took a lot of time and effort but finally Ivy was outside the cold grey doors that led to the morgue. She was shaking, unaware of the tears that soaked into the part of the woollen shawl she'd wrapped around her face. Her hands were blue, frozen, but she forced herself to apply pressure and push the heavy doors apart.

See Poolbeg.com for more . . .

The Ha'penny Place

Through hard work and determination, Ivy Rose Murphy has come up in the world. She still begs for discards from the homes of the wealthy which lie only a stone's throw from The Lane, the poverty-ridden tenements where she lives. These discards she repairs and sells around the Dublin markets.

But being in the ha'penny place may soon be a thing of the past for Ivy. She is fast turning herself into 'Miss Ivy Rose', successful businesswoman. With her talent for needlework and a team of neighbourhood helpers, she has begun to supply an upmarket shop in Grafton Street with beautifully dressed dolls.

Her fiancé Jem's livery business is going from strength to strength, and Emmy, the little girl Jem is raising, is thriving and happy.

Then Ivy's wealthy friend Ann Marie Gannon, with her beloved camera, spends a day at the airport photographing planes.

Little does she know that her visit can destroy all Ivy's hopes for the future.

ISBN 978-178199-9455

Ha'penny Chance

Ivy Rose Murphy dreams of a better future. For years she has set out daily from the tenements known as 'The Lane' to beg for discards from the homes of the wealthy – discards she turns into items to sell around the Dublin markets. And now she has grander schemes afoot.

But, as her fortunes take a turn for the better, there are eyes on Ivy – and she is vulnerable as she carries her earnings home through the dark winter streets. And, to add to her fears, a well-dressed stranger begins to stalk her.

Ann Marie Gannon, a wealthy young woman who has struck up an unlikely friendship with Ivy, wants to protect her. But will the stubborn woman she admires allow her to do so?

Jem Ryan, who owns the local livery, longs to make Ivy his wife, but she is reluctant to give up her fierce independence.

Then a sudden astonishing event turns Ivy's world upside down. A dazzling future beckons and she must decide where her loyalties lie.

ISBN 978-178199-9547

Ha'penny Schemes

In 1920's inner-city Dublin tenements, Ivy Rose Murphy struggles to survive and thrive in the harsh poverty-stricken environment she was born into. She is trying to adapt to her new role as a married woman. There are those jealous of the improvements she has managed to make in her life. To Ivy it seems everyone wants a piece of her. She is stretched to breaking point.

Ivy's old enemy Father Leary keeps a close watch on her comings and goings. She has attracted the attention of people willing to profit from the efforts of others. She needs help. Ivy's friends gather around to offer support – but somehow Ivy is the one who gives hope to them.

Ivy's husband, Jem Ryan, is a forward-thinking man. He is busy making a better life for the family he longs for – but can he protect Ivy when her enemies begin to close in?

ISBN 978-178199-8229